ALSO BY FREIDA MCFADDEN

THE
PERFECT
SON

FREIDA McFADDEN

Poisoned Pen
PRESS

Sourcebooks, Poisoned Pen Press, and the colophon
are registered trademarks of Sourcebooks.

Published by Poisoned Pen Press, an imprint of Sourcebooks
P.O. Box 4410, Naperville, Illinois 60567-4410
(630) 961-3900
sourcebooks.com

Originally self-published in 2022 by Freida McFadden.

Cataloging-in-Publication Data is on file with the Library of Congress.

Printed and bound in Canada.
MBP 10 9 8 7 6 5 4 3

To my family

PROLOGUE

Transcript of police interview with Erika Cass.

PD: "Can you please tell us what happened, Mrs. Cass?"

EC: "Am I under arrest?"

PD: "Why do you ask that?"

EC: "I know what you found. I know what you must be thinking."

PD: "What do you think we found, Mrs. Cass?"

EC: "A...a dead body."

PD: "And can you explain how this happened?"

EC: "I..."

PD: "Mrs. Cass?"

EC: "Am I under arrest? Please just tell me."

PD: "At this time, no, you are not under arrest. But obviously we need to know what happened."

EC: "He was...stabbed to death."

PD: "And who did it?"

EC: "..."

PD: "Mrs. Cass?"

EC: "*I* did it. I killed him, Detective. And I would do it again."

CHAPTER 1

ERIKA

You're not supposed to have a favorite child.

If you ask most mothers, they'll say something along the lines of "Sammy is really smart, but Nicole has a great heart." They refuse to choose. And some of them are sincere. Some mothers genuinely love both their children equally.

Others, like me, are lying through their teeth.

"Good morning!" I say as my fourteen-year-old daughter, Hannah, pads into the kitchen. She's in her bare feet and an old pair of gym shorts, and her reddish-brown hair is in disarray around her face. She's supposed to be dressed and ready for school, but clearly she's not. She always waits until the last possible second to get ready. She likes to keep me in suspense over whether she's going to make the school bus. But I've learned from experience that nagging her doesn't help at all—in fact, it only seems to slow her down—so I turn back to the eggs I'm scrambling in a frying pan.

"Mom!" Hannah can't seem to say that word anymore without the whiny edge to her voice that draws the word out for at least two syllables. *Mo-om.* I remember how happy I was the first time she said mama. I shake my head at my old naïve self. "Why do you have to say it like that?"

"Say it like what? I just said good morning."

"Right." Hannah groans. "Like that."

"Like what?"

"Like… Oh my God, you know what I mean."

"I really don't, Hannah."

"You say it like… I don't know. Just don't say it like that."

I'm not sure how to respond, so I focus my attention back on the eggs. I pride myself on making fantastic eggs. It's one of my superpowers. My eggs are so good that when one of Hannah's friends ate them the morning after a sleepover, she said that I should be the lunch lady at their school. It was the highest compliment.

Hannah yawns loudly and scratches at the rat's nest on her head. "What's for breakfast?"

I ignore the irony: if I asked Hannah what she was making for breakfast while she was very clearly in the middle of cooking eggs, she would have a meltdown. "I'm making eggs."

"*Eggs?* I *hate* eggs."

"What are you talking about? I thought eggs are your favorite breakfast."

"Yeah. When I was, like, eight years old."

I put down the spatula I've been using to slowly stir the eggs. That's the trick to making good eggs. Cook them low and slow. "I made them for you this weekend, and you ate them up."

"Yeah, but that doesn't mean they're my *favorite*. God, Mom."

I don't know what to say to that. It seems like lately, every conversation I have with my daughter is an exercise in trying not to say something mean back to her. I close my eyes and repeat my mantra to myself: *I am the adult. This is just a phase.*

After fourteen years, it's harder to convince myself it's all just a phase.

"What else is for breakfast?" Hannah asks, even though she is two feet away from the refrigerator and three feet away from the pantry.

"Frozen waffles?"

"Yuck." She sticks out her tongue. "What else?"

"You can make yourself some cold cereal."

"What kind of cereal do we have?"

I sigh. "I don't know, Hannah. Go look in the pantry."

She lets out a grunt as she stands up that would make you think she is ninety years old rather than a high school freshman. She limps over to the pantry and studies the boxes of cereal intently.

While Hannah contemplates the cereal selection, my son, Liam, joins us in the kitchen. Unlike his sister, Liam is fully dressed in a surprisingly nice blue button-down shirt and khaki slacks. I bought a new wardrobe for him over the summer when he shot up four inches and all his old clothes looked comically short. He recently turned sixteen, which means he went to the DMV last month with my husband to get his learner's permit to drive. I had thought that my son getting his learner's permit would fill me with terror, but I'm oddly calm about the whole thing. Liam will be a good driver. He'll be careful, he'll pay close attention to the road, and he'll never drink and drive. I'm certain of that much.

That's not why I'm worried about him driving.

"Eggs. I love eggs. Thanks, Mom!"

Liam's lips spread into an appreciative smile. He was always an attractive kid, but in the last couple of years, he's grown downright handsome. We were out at a restaurant as a family last weekend, and I caught a woman in her twenties giving him a second look. A full-grown adult was checking him out! There is something about his thick dark hair and chocolate-colored eyes that almost twinkle when he smiles. Unlike Hannah, Liam never needed braces, and his smile reveals a row of perfectly straight, white teeth.

According to my mother, Liam looks very much the way my father did when he was young. My father died when I was a child, and I barely remember him, but I've seen pictures, and I agree the resemblance is uncanny. I keep one of those photos in a drawer by my bed, and lately, every time I look at it, I get a pang in my chest. It was hard enough knowing my dad never got to see me grow up; it's another sting to know he'll never meet the grandson who looks just like him.

Hannah pulls a box of Cheerios out of the pantry and studies the label, her nose crinkling.

"What's in Cheerios?" she asks me.

"Poison."

"Mom!" That was at least four syllables right there. *M-o-o-om.* "You *know* I'm trying to lose weight and be healthy. Don't you want me to be healthy?"

Hannah has always been a little on the chubby side. I think she looks cute, but in the last year, she's been obsessed with losing ten pounds (although she has not done anything to lose them). In fact, when I brought home a bag of chips that I had been planning to pair with guacamole to bring to a moms' night out last month, Hannah demolished it before I made it out the door. I ended up bringing some sliced-up apples. They haven't invited me back.

"Of course I want you to be healthy," I say.

She rolls her eyes. Hannah has mastered the eye roll. It's her favorite facial expression. It can be used when I've asked her to do something she doesn't want to do or when I've said something so terribly uncool that she just can't bear it. Or best of all, when I express any sort of love or affection.

"Eggs in two minutes," I say to Liam.

"No rush. I'm gonna have some orange juice." Liam goes for the fridge, but he's not quick enough. Hannah shoves him aside to get to the quart of milk. He lets his sister get away with it without commenting.

"What are you all dressed up for, Liam?" I ask as I turn off the heat on the stove. Usually, my son wears jeans and a T-shirt, regardless of the weather. I'm just happy when they're clean.

"Debate." He finally gets his turn and grabs the orange juice from the fridge. He pours himself a brimming glass, so full that the juice is licking the edges, threatening to spill over. Like every other teenage boy in the world, Liam has a huge appetite, even though his build is lanky and athletic. "We're competing against Lincoln High after school."

"Can I come to watch?"

Hannah rolls her eyes. "*Seriously?* Liam's debates are mega boring."

5

Liam smiles crookedly and takes a swig from his orange juice. "She's right. It won't be fun for you."

I scrape the eggs onto a plate for him, giving him his portion in addition to the eggs I made for Hannah. I'll make more for my husband later if he wants—Jason should be back from his run before long. "It will be fun if you're up there."

"Okay, sure." Liam digs into the plate of eggs. For some reason, I get a lot of satisfaction out of watching my children eat. It dates back to when I was breastfeeding. (Hannah says it's super weird.) "These eggs are great, Mom."

"Why thank you."

"What's your secret ingredient?"

I wink at him. "Love."

Hannah lets out the longest sigh I've ever heard. It lasts for at least five full seconds—which is a long time for a sigh. "Oh my *God*, the secret ingredient is Parmesan cheese. Mom *always* puts Parmesan cheese in the eggs. You know that, Liam. God, you're such a…"

He lifts an eyebrow. "I'm such a what, Hannah?"

"You know what."

For a moment, the two of them stare at each other, and it's so quiet in the room that I can hear the coffee machine humming. But then Liam snorts loudly and goes back to his eggs. I envy his ability to ignore his sister's irritability. If eggs are my superpower, ignoring Hannah is Liam's. Nothing she says ever gets to him. And the truth is, despite their sparring, Hannah adores Liam. The minute she started walking, she was following him around. These days, he's probably her favorite person in the house. I suspect I come in fourth, after Jason and probably her phone.

"Well, I think the eggs taste especially good today," Liam says. And he smiles, blinking up at me with those eyelashes that Hannah complains are unfairly long. "Thanks, Mom. You're the best."

And Hannah rolls her eyes.

I love Hannah. I really do. I love her more than I love my own life. She's my daughter. She's my little girl.

But Liam is my favorite. I can't help it. From the moment he was born and I became a mother, I knew no matter how many other children I had, he would be my favorite. Nobody else had a chance. Even if Hannah liked my eggs better and didn't roll her eyes, it wouldn't matter. Liam would still be my favorite.

He's my favorite, even knowing what he's capable of.

And I will protect him with every fiber of my being.

CHAPTER 2

ERIKA

Just as Hannah and Liam are finishing up their breakfast, the back door slams shut. It's Jason, back from his jog.

About a year ago, I purchased a scale for our master bathroom. The first time my husband stepped on it, he was horrified. "Did I really get that fat, Erika?" he asked me about twenty times over the next several days. Followed by "How could you let me get that fat?" By the end of the week, he made a solemn oath that he was going to get back in shape. He was going to eat right and exercise and get back to the weight he was when we got married. (To be fair, he was at least ten pounds overweight when we got married.)

At the time, I laughed. But then he actually did it. He jogs every morning now. He doesn't buy giant jugs of M&Ms. He switched from regular Coca-Cola to diet (or Coke Zero, which he says tastes much better than diet, although I am skeptical). I don't know much about what the numbers should be on the scale, but it's obvious that at the age of forty-five, Jason is in the best shape of his life. I never noticed that he had been getting a gut until it vanished. And recently, when we got together with some other couples, another wife commented on my husband being "hot." I was oddly proud. Although it made me feel like I need to start taking kickboxing or Zumba or something to firm up some of those soft, saggy areas on my middle-aged body.

"Erika!" Jason limps over to the stove to join me, his T-shirt damp with sweat. His knee has been acting up for the last few weeks, but he's trying to push through it. "Are you making eggs? I'm starving."

I crack an egg into the sizzling pan. "You got it."

He leans in to kiss me on the neck, which is nice, despite how sweaty he is. "Egg-cellent."

Hannah groans. "Oh my God, Dad. Please."

"What's wrong?" Jason blinks at her. "I'm just egg-cited about your mom's cooking."

Liam laughs. We're all used to Jason's puns. The general rule is that they're always terrible, but sometimes they're so terrible that it's funny.

"Please stop, Dad." Hannah shakes her head at him. "You're being so cringey right now."

Cringey is the word Hannah frequently uses to describe basically everything that Jason or I do. I hate that it bothers me on some level, although Jason seems to find it amusing. His reasoning is that he was never cool, so why would it bother him that his teenage daughter doesn't think he's cool?

"Don't you have to get ready for school, Hannah?" Jason says. "Don't you have an egg-xam today?"

Even I laugh this time, although it's more because of the look on Hannah's face.

Hannah dashes upstairs to get dressed and hopefully brush her hair so I don't get accused of child neglect, while Liam wanders into the living room, because he has a sense of when we want privacy. I continue to stir Jason's eggs. Low and slow.

"You know I've been eating your eggs for twenty years?" Jason muses as he runs a hand along the back of my neck. "Twenty years of Erika's eggs."

"Aren't you sick of them?" I say it as a joke, but there's a tiny part of me that's serious. After all, Jason spent the last year getting in great shape. He's gotten a lot hotter. All he needs is a shiny new car and contacts to replace his wire-rimmed glasses and he'll be in full-on middle-age crisis mode.

"Hell no." He pulls me to him and presses his lips against mine, which totally interrupts the egg-cooking process, but I don't mind. He hasn't shaved yet, and his chin tickles mine. "I hope I get to eat your eggs for another twenty years."

"Gag!" Hannah, coming down the stairs, interrupts what *had* been a very nice little moment between me and Jason. She's dressed in blue jeans and an oversize T-shirt, with her hair pulled back into a messy ponytail. She's probably going for stylishly messy, but it's just messy. "You two need to get a room."

"Um, this is *our* house." Jason raises his eyebrows at her. "If you want to start paying rent, then you can tell me when I'm allowed to kiss my sexy wife."

Hannah just rolls her eyes.

"All right, Hannah," I say. "You've got to get a move on. The school bus is going to be at the corner in…" I look down at my watch. One minute ago. "Damn it."

"Oh no. I guess you have to drive us."

"Gosh, funny how that worked out."

Hannah hates the school bus with a passion. From the moment she wakes up every weekday, she's plotting a way for me to drive her to school. We've already agreed that when Liam gets his license, he can drive the two of them to school every morning. Of course, he'll be in college in less than two years. And the thought of Hannah being behind the wheel is nothing short of terrifying.

I finish cooking Jason's eggs and reluctantly pile Hannah and Liam into my green Toyota 4Runner. I never thought I'd be the sort of mom who drives an SUV, especially one so freaking big. I held on to my little Honda Civic even after we had Liam. But then Jason pointed out how hard it was going to be to strap two car seats into the back seat of the Civic, and I knew it was time to upgrade. So we got the SUV. I know this sounds melodramatic, but the first time I saw it parked in my garage, I almost burst into tears. But now I'm used to it. It makes me feel safe, which is important when you've got your kids in the car. That's why, when Jason took Liam out for a driving lesson last week, he used the 4Runner.

Hannah has called shotgun, which is unfortunate because it means that she's going to be controlling the music in the car. She's very much partial to music by young men who don't look like they're capable of growing facial hair yet.

"Can we *please* listen to something different?" Liam complains about two minutes into the drive. I have to agree. "*Anything* else?"

"You know," Hannah says, "Justin Bieber is an incredibly talented singer."

"Oh, is he?"

"Yes, he is!" She adjusts her messy ponytail. "He has a phenomenal vocal range."

Liam smirks. "Sure. That's what you like about him. His vocal range."

"So I think he's cute. So what? It's not like you're interested in *Olivia* for her intelligence."

Olivia? Who is *Olivia*? I glance in the rearview mirror just in time to see Liam's entire face turn red. He has become incredibly skilled at masking his reactions to things, but he couldn't hide it this time. But when I look away for a moment and then check the mirror again, he's regained his composure.

The car skids to a halt at a red light. "Who is Olivia?" I ask as casually as I can manage.

Liam looks out the window. "Nobody. Just a girl."

But thank God Hannah is in the car with us. "*Just a girl?*" She snorts. "Liam is totally in love with her."

He laughs. "No, I'm not."

"Oh my God, you *so* are. Don't even deny it." Hannah gives me a look like I'm her new confidante. "You should see the way he looks at her. He's *totally* into her."

"Whatever."

I glance in the rearview mirror one more time to look at my son. Liam is the most composed sixteen-year-old kid I've ever known. That's why he's so good at debate, in addition to his natural intelligence and his diligent preparation. He *never* loses his cool. He never lets anyone know what he's thinking. But I've known him long enough that I can usually tell. Usually.

I'm really glad I'm going to this debate after school. I want to see Liam perform. That was the reason I told him

I want to come. And I meant it. But now I've got a new, more important reason for going.

I've got to figure out who Olivia is.

And I've got to keep something terrible from happening to her.

CHAPTER 3

Transcript of police interview with Sharon Anderson.

PD: "Can you tell me how you know Liam Cass?"

SA: "He attended kindergarten at the school where I work as the principal."

PD: "For how long did he attend?"

SA: "About four months."

PD: "And this was eleven years ago?"

SA: "That's correct."

PD: "So you still remember a child who attended your school for four months over a decade ago?"

SA: "Yes. I remember Liam. Very well."

PD: "And what was your impression of him?"

SA: "At first? He seemed like a great kid. Real cute. Smart—certainly the smartest kid in the grade. I remember he got up during assembly and gave this long speech he memorized. I couldn't believe a kindergartner could remember all that. I was impressed."

PD: "How come he only attended the school for four months? Isn't the school year nine months long?"

SA: "Liam was...expelled."

PD: "A kindergartner was expelled?"

SA: "It's unusual. But the circumstances called for it."

PD: "I see. And why was that?"

SA: "There was an incident."

PD: "Can you describe the incident to me?"

SA: "Yes..."

PD: "Will you please describe the incident, Mrs. Anderson?"

SA: "It was...there was a girl."

PD: "Yes?"

SA: "Well, she and Liam were friends. They often played together at recess, or so his teacher told me later. And then one day during recess, the girl...disappeared."

PD: "I see. And did they find her?"

SA: "Yes. They did. And she was...fine."

PD: "Where did they find her?"

SA: "Does this have to do with that girl from the high school? The one who..."

PD: "I'm afraid we can't discuss it at this time."

SA: "Yes. Yes, of course. But do you think Liam is the one who..."

PD: "Once again, Mrs. Anderson, this is not something I can discuss."

SA: "Of course. I'm sorry."

PD: "Now can you tell me where they found this girl?"

SA: "So...the story I was told is that Liam and the little girl were playing janitor. They sneaked away

15

and went to the custodial closet during recess. It seems she was quite infatuated with Liam, and he talked her into it."

PD: "And what happened in the custodial closet?"

SA: "They found a roll of duct tape. And they were playing with it."

PD: "How were they playing with it?"

SA: "..."

PD: "Mrs. Anderson?"

SA: "I'm sorry. It was just...so shocking. I still can't get over it. That a kindergartner would..."

PD: "Would what?"

SA: "He convinced her to let him bind her wrists with the duct tape. Then he put tape over her mouth. And then..."

PD: "Yes?"

SA: "Well, we're not sure what he did next. The one thing we know for sure is he locked her in the closet and walked away. And even when she was noticed to be missing and teachers were looking for her, he didn't tell anyone where she was. It was several hours later when we finally found her—she was bound on the floor of the closet and refused to speak to anyone. For days, actually."

PD: "What do *you* think he did?"

SA: "I don't know. He was just a little boy. It's hard to imagine he could have done anything that bad. But the look in that girl's eyes when we found her..."

PD: "I see."

SA: "Of course, her parents were hysterical. And given everything that happened, we had no choice but to expel Liam from the school."

PD: "When you confronted him about what he did, how did he react?"

SA: "He apologized. Of course he did. He claimed it was all just a fun game and she had agreed to it. He even cried. But..."

PD: "But what?"

SA: "But I never believed him. Even when he was sobbing in my office, it seemed incredibly fake. I don't think he was sorry at all. Not even a little bit. The only thing I think he was sorry about was that we found her."

CHAPTER 4

ERIKA

I make it to the school about sixty seconds after the school bus arrives.

Hannah says a quick goodbye and then darts out of the car. I remember when she was in preschool, how she used to cling to my leg with both arms when I tried to drop her off in the morning. When I would try to leave, she would shriek at the top of her lungs like somebody was trying to murder her. Now if I attempt to even kiss her goodbye, she's mortified beyond all belief.

Liam is the opposite. When he was younger, he never had any trouble at all separating from me when I dropped him off. He would kiss me goodbye and then run off to play without a second thought. And now, he leans forward from the back seat and kisses me on the cheek, oblivious to anyone who might witness this show of affection.

"Bye, Mom." He opens the back door. "I love you."

I smile. Liam has an incredible knack for saying the exact right thing. "I love you too, sweetheart."

He swings his backpack onto his shoulder and hurries toward the front door before the bell rings. I watch him, looking out for any girl who might be Olivia. Anything that will make my job easier. And this isn't an easy job. It's just going to get harder as he gets older.

"Is that Erika Cass in there?"

I jerk my head up. Jessica Martinson is standing outside my car, peering through my cracked-open window. I don't know where she came from, because her car is nowhere in sight. She must have been meeting with somebody in the school, which is not unusual for Jessica, who is head of the PTA. Jessica and I used to be close, years ago, when Liam and her son Tyler were friends.

Jessica and I only became close because of Liam and Tyler's friendship, and we've grown apart since the boys stopped spending time together. I have to admit, it concerned me when they stopped being friends. I asked Liam why he didn't have Tyler Martinson over anymore, and he just shrugged. If it had been Hannah, that question would have sparked an hour-long monologue about everything Tyler had done wrong. But Liam isn't like that. He doesn't talk about things the way his sister does.

Kids grow apart. As they have grown older, they no longer share any clubs or common interests. Tyler is more popular than Liam, and they run in different circles. Tyler plays football, and Liam does track and debate. Also, Liam doesn't have any close friends—he doesn't seem interested in having the sort of tight friendships that other kids have. But I always worried about what caused their friendship to fracture. Growing apart—that's fine. But it scares me that Liam might have done something to accelerate the demise of their friendship.

It certainly wouldn't be the first time.

"Actually," Jessica says, "I'm so glad I saw you, Erika. There's something I need to speak with you about. It's urgent."

Urgent? A knot tightens in my stomach. What's Liam done this time? "Oh?"

She tucks a strand of her golden-blond hair behind one ear. She has a messy ponytail, like Hannah, but unlike Hannah's, hers is painfully stylish. "Can we grab some coffee? Do you have time?"

I have a long list of errands to take care of this morning, but I can't say no. "Sure."

"Great! How about Charlie's?"

Charlie's is a diner about five minutes away from here. Good for a quick cup of coffee in the morning. Jessica and I have met up there dozens of times over the years. "I'll drive right there."

She winks at me. "See you in five."

As Jessica hurries away to her own monster SUV, I look down at my hands gripping the steering wheel. They're shaking. What does Jessica want to talk to me about? It can't be that bad, could it? She seems friendly enough. But that's the thing with Jessica. She could tell you something horrible right to your face with a smile on her lips. I've seen her do it before.

I throw my car back into drive and make my way to Charlie's.

CHAPTER 5

OLIVIA

Thanks to Liam Cass, I'm failing math class.

No, I probably won't fail, but things aren't looking good for me. I'm good at math—I've always gotten As, if not an A+. But this semester, I'll be lucky to swing a C. And it's all because of Liam. It's because from the moment I step into the classroom at ten thirty to when the bell rings forty minutes later, all I can focus on is the boy sitting in front of me.

I've never been that into boys. I can't say the same for my best friend, Madison, who thinks about boys nonstop. Madison has *definitely* failed classes before because of a cute guy sitting in front of her. She has blown off studying for tests to hang out with the boys she liked. It's sort of her *thing*. And I always made fun of her. Like, how could you prioritize a *boy* over your education? I mean, boys my age are all pretty idiotic and not even that attractive—they mostly have greasy faces and scraggly little beards.

I want to get into a good college—that's my priority.

How could you jeopardize your entire future for a cute guy? That's *so* pathetic.

Then, on the first day of school this year, Liam sat down in front of me in math class, turned his head to flash me a smile, and I was gone. He didn't have a greasy face or patchy facial hair—he was *gorgeous*. I hate myself for it, but I can't help ogling him. Every time he smiles at me, my heart speeds up. He has a *great* smile. And *really* beautiful brown eyes. His eyes are like creamy, endless pools of milk chocolate. I could write bad poetry about this guy. In another month, I'll be etching our initials in a heart scratched into the wood of my desk—that's how bad it is.

We had a test a few days ago, and it was a bona fide disaster. I can't focus when I'm studying, because the second I crack open the textbook and see sines and cosines, my mind goes to Liam. And of course, I couldn't focus when I was actually *taking* the test—not with him sitting right in front of me. I passed by the skin of my teeth—a seventy-two. Liam, who isn't having any problem at all focusing with little old me behind him, got a ninety-eight.

I've got to stop thinking about this boy. He's just a boy. My education is much more important. I've got to focus.

Focus, Olivia.

Except when Liam comes into the classroom today, he's not wearing his usual jeans and a T-shirt. He's dressed in nice khaki slacks and a dress shirt. And a tie. Oh my God, he's wearing a *tie*. Usually he's cute, but in dress clothes, he's upped his game. It's like a sneak peek into how handsome he'll look when he's an adult. Against my will, my stomach starts doing cartwheels.

Focus, Olivia!

As Liam slides into his seat in front of me, he flashes me that grin that makes my legs weak. "Hey," he says.

"Hey," I say back. I search my brain, trying to think of something clever or funny to say. I spend most of math class trying to do that. "You're all dressed up."

Good one, Olivia.

"We have a debate today," he explains. "It's sort of a big deal. We're competing against another school."

"Wow. Are you nervous?"

"A little." He laughs, although there's a bit of a tremor in his voice that makes me think he's more nervous than he lets on. "If we win, we get to go to the state competition up in Albany. That's pretty cool."

"What do you do during a debate anyway?"

He scratches at his dark brown hair. "Argue mostly. It's sort of fun." He raises his eyebrows at me. "Do you, um… do you want to come watch?"

"Me?" I say in an embarrassingly squeaky voice.

Oh my God, that was *such* a stupid thing to say. *Obviously* he's inviting me. Who else would he be inviting?

And what does this *mean*?

"Uh…" His smile slips slightly. "I mean, if you want. It'd probably be pretty boring for you. You probably don't want to go."

Oh no, he's taking it back. "No, it sounds like it could be fun. I don't have anything else I'm doing."

That's an outright lie. I'm supposed to be at chorus practice after school today. But the truth is that I've soured on chorus since I didn't get the last two solos I tried out for. And even if I had, I can't say no to Liam. This is the first time he's ever invited me somewhere.

His eyes light up. "That would be great. I mean, if you

can come. But if something else comes up, that's cool too. No big deal."

I can't believe it. He actually seems really happy that I'm coming. Oh God, there's no *way* I'm going to be able to focus in class now. I'm going to get a terrible grade in math this semester. And the scariest part is, at this moment, I couldn't care less.

CHAPTER 6

ERIKA

As soon as I walk into Charlie's, I blink my eyes to adjust to the neon lights overhead. Those lights have been flickering for as long as I can remember, but it's part of the diner's charm. Just like the plastic tables and ripped bench covers. Charlie's has been around forever and makes no effort to hide that fact.

Jessica has already got a table and is sipping on a cup of coffee. I watch her for a moment before approaching. I know she's my age, but she looks fantastic. She's got the same laugh lines that I do, but somehow she makes them look sexy. She has mastered the casual stay-at-home-mom look, with her T-shirt that boosts the high school football team and the fitted yoga pants paired with ballet flats. I threw on the first thing my fingers touched when I got into the bedroom to hurriedly get dressed so Hannah and Liam would get to school on time. Mom jeans and a sweater, as it turns out. What can I say? Mom jeans are comfortable.

Jessica and I are both essentially stay-at-home moms, like a lot of other parents out here. You could almost say it's epidemic. When I met Jason, I was working as a journalist at a newspaper in Manhattan. I was getting paid practically nothing, but there was a lot of upward mobility at the paper, and if I had stayed on, I'd probably have a pretty good job there by now. Maybe I would've moved on to a better paper. Maybe I'd be an editor in chief. But after I got pregnant, Jason convinced me to move out to the island. I agreed because I was sick of our tiny Manhattan apartment, but once we got to the island, the commute was insane. He pointed out that I didn't earn even close to the amount we would be paying in child care and that his income could easily support us.

So I quit. Temporarily.

I had every intention of going back to work after Liam started preschool. But then Hannah came along two years later. And between the two of them, there was always some emergency popping up. Hannah got ear infections every other week, and on the weeks she didn't get ear infections, she got conjunctivitis. And then there was the whole mess with Liam.

Right now, I work for a local newspaper called the *Nassau Nutshell*. You can tell by the name that they do a lot of hard-hitting journalism—not. They put out one paper per week, and I contribute a couple of articles, mostly on local events or parenting advice. Last week, I wrote an article featuring three meals you could cook for the whole family in twenty minutes or less. What they pay me each month didn't even cover the price of the groceries I bought to cook those three meals, but it stimulates my brain, and I can write the articles from home.

Jason always makes a big fuss when the paper comes out and reads all my articles, and it's fun to see my byline in print. No, it's not the *New York Times*. But it's something. For now.

Jessica, on the other hand, has absolutely embraced the stay-at-home-mom lifestyle. She is the most visible parent at the high school, and her kids are involved in every sport and extracurricular activity you can imagine. In my more optimistic moments, I hope that's why Tyler and Liam aren't friends anymore. Because Tyler is just too damn busy.

"Erika!" Jessica flashes me a bright smile as I slide into the booth across from her. "It's so good to spend a little time with you. It's been ages, hasn't it?"

Can we dispense with the small talk and you just tell me what urgent thing you need to tell me? I force a smile. "Yes. It really has."

"We should do this more often, shouldn't we?"

I nod. "Definitely."

We won't. I used to be friends with several of the parents at the school, but I've got my reasons for keeping my distance now.

I flag down a waitress to place my order for a cup of coffee. Whatever Jessica's got to say will be easier to take after a shot of caffeine.

"How is your mother?" Jessica asks once the waitress has left.

Jessica Martinson should be a politician. She is fantastic at remembering little details about everyone she knows. Even though I know it's all an act, I feel oddly touched that she remembered to ask about my mother. And the truth is my mother has been on my mind a lot lately. She is nearly eighty and living all alone in a small house in New Jersey. But she's tough—my father died when I was very young, and she's been doing it alone ever since.

"She's hanging in there," I say. "I'd love for her to move closer, but she's stubborn. She'll never leave her house."

"I know what you mean." Jessica takes a sip of her coffee. She has poured so much cream into it, it looks like chocolate milk. "My mother is the same way. We've got a room for her in our house, but she won't budge."

"I suppose I understand. She's got all her friends out in Jersey."

Jessica crinkles her nose. "But it's *Jersey*."

We both laugh, and I remember why I used to be friends with Jessica. She's so good at talking to people, whether she likes them or not. In that sense, she's not unlike Liam.

But she's not really like him. Not at all. Nobody is.

I clear my throat. "So what did you want to talk to me about, Jessica?"

I hold my breath, waiting for her to take another sip from her coffee. "Oh, right," she says. "I need your help, Erika. Movie night is turning into a disaster. Would you take over the reins?"

I let out the breath. I should have known that's what Jessica wanted to talk to me about. Movie night takes place at the high school once a year. They put up a big screen on the football field and charge people three dollars each for entry. They sell pizza at two dollars a slice. It's a big fundraiser for the PTA, and therefore it's on Jessica's shoulders to get it organized.

"Rachel was in charge of it," Jessica says. "But her husband—you know Rob?—he had a minor heart attack.

28

He's okay, but her head isn't in the game. The thing is in two weeks, and nothing is organized yet. Is there any chance you could take over? Pretty please?"

"Of course," I agree. Unlike Jessica, I could never stomach the PTA. When she and I were close, I used to go to meetings, but they were always oppressively boring. It made me feel guilty that all I wanted to do during the meetings was take out my phone and play *Candy Crush*. But I try to volunteer for things at the school as much as I can.

"You are a star, Erika!" She reaches out to take my hand across the table, and I resist the urge to pull away. One thing I have in common with Liam is that casual physical affection makes me uncomfortable. "Thank you so much. You'll come to the PTA meeting this week to help organize then?"

I'd rather eat dirt. "Um, sure."

The waitress arrives with my coffee, which gives me an excuse to yank my hand back. I don't pour in any milk or sugar. I like it bitter and black.

"We should all get together again," Jessica says. "Your family and mine. It's sad the boys don't hang out much anymore. And Hannah and Emma never really got along."

"Yes." I absently stir my coffee with a spoon, even though I'm drinking it black. This get-together will never happen. Tyler and Liam aren't friends anymore, and Hannah actively dislikes Jessica's younger daughter.

"Of course…" Jessica shrugs, "Tyler spends most of his free time these days with girls. You must know how that is. I'll bet Liam has a million girlfriends."

My mouth feels dry. Olivia. I've got to find her. "Actually, he hasn't really been dating yet."

"No?" She tosses her carefully layered hair. "That's surprising. Liam is… Well, I've always noticed how much girls like him. I've even heard Emma and her friends talking about him. She had the biggest crush on him for a while."

"Yes." It makes me sick just to talk about it. Knowing deep down that I can't stop this. It's like a freight train barreling down a track. You could throw a few big rocks on the track to possibly slow it down, but it's going to get through eventually. I look down at my coffee, and a wave of nausea overwhelms me. "I'm sorry, Jessica, but I just realized I've got an appointment to get to."

"Oh." She blinks her pretty blue eyes. I wonder what kind of eyes Olivia has. "Well, it was good seeing you again, Erika."

"You too." But I've already gotten up from the table, and I'm hurrying out the door.

CHAPTER 7

OLIVIA

I've never had a boyfriend.

I've never even kissed a boy. Well, that's not true. During a game of truth or dare in middle school, I exchanged a few kisses on the cheek. But I don't count those. They weren't real kisses. Not like the kind Madison has had.

Madison has had two boyfriends already. Right now, she's dating a guy named Aidan, and the two of them are *always* making out. It's like I can't do anything with Madison anymore without Aidan coming out and kissing her in this gross, slobbery way. It doesn't even look like a good kiss. If that's what kissing is, I can wait.

But I have a feeling Liam Cass won't kiss like that.

I think a lot about what Liam's kisses will be like. Not just during math class but all the time.

Madison is prettier than me, but not by a lot. On a scale of one to ten, she's probably a seven and I'm probably a six. My hair is mousy brown, and people tell me I have pretty eyes, but I know I have way too many freckles. I had a lot of freckles on my face when I was a kid, and I read they're supposed to fade when you get older. But my stupid freckles won't do what they're supposed to. Yes, they're lighter than they were, but I *still* have these tiny little spots all over my face. Even though I smear sunscreen all over myself whenever I go out and I have this giant hat with a brim that my little brother makes fun of me for wearing.

That's why I don't have a boyfriend. All my stupid freckles.

Not that I haven't been asked out before. This one guy asked me out earlier in the year, and he was kind of a jerk about it when I said no, but I didn't really like him. I don't want to go out with just anyone so I can have a boyfriend. I want to go out with a guy I actually *like*.

"There he is." I nudge Madison as we sit in the audience of the giant high school auditorium. I convinced her to come with me to the debate today, and she agreed only because Aidan has football practice, so she has to wait around anyway. A smattering of students and parents have come to watch, but the audience is pretty sparse. I've never seen a debate before, so today will be my first. Maybe I'll learn something about…

Well, whatever it is they're debating.

Madison follows my gaze to the stage, where our school debate team is assembled. And *he's* up there. Liam. Oh my God, he looks *so* handsome in that nice blue button-down shirt. Once again, my heart does this weird thing in my chest. If I didn't know better, I'd think I should go see a doctor.

"He is *so* hot," I murmur as I lean back in my seat.

Madison crinkles her nose, which is totally free of freckles. Madison doesn't have one freckle, but she always complains about her double chin. "I don't know, Liv. I don't like him."

"You are so weird. What don't you like about him? He's, like, perfect and gorgeous."

"He's…" Madison's gaze travels back to the stage. "I don't know. He just seems really… Like, when he talks, he seems so fake."

"What does that even mean?"

"It's hard to explain. I feel like everyone else is real, like they're really living life. But Liam is, like, this actor who is being paid to hang out with us."

I stare at her. "What the hell are you talking about, Mad?"

"I'm just saying. I feel like I don't trust him entirely. He's a phony. You know?"

I'm not going to point out to her that between Aidan and Liam, it's clear who is more trustworthy. Liam is a straight-A student, and he's a star on both the debate team and the track team. Whereas Aidan is built like a bull, is failing two classes, and almost got expelled last year for getting into a fistfight in the hallway at school. If anyone makes me uneasy, it's Aidan.

Liam catches my eye, and maybe it's my imagination, but his whole face seems to light up when he sees me, and he waves enthusiastically. Is it possible he likes me as much as I like him? I mean, he invited me to come today. So maybe he does. The thought of it is enough to make my heart start beating faster again. Liam Cass. God, he's *so* cute.

But then he starts talking to another girl who is on

stage with them. That's Olivia Reynolds. She and I share the same first name, but that's where the similarities end. She's on the debate team, like Liam, and she's *really* gorgeous. She has silky blond hair that looks professionally styled, and she's totally stacked. *Unfairly* stacked, given how skinny she is. When she's talking to Liam, the two of them look like a really attractive couple. Between the two of us Olivias, she's clearly the superior one.

How could Liam like me when she's around?

I try not to think about it.

By the way, Liam is totally brilliant during the debate. I don't even entirely understand what they're debating. Something about transportation between different states. It's all really boring, honestly. But Liam is *such* a good speaker. He should become a politician or something. Whenever he talks, everybody pays such close attention to him. Even Madison looks up from her phone for, like, two seconds.

The judges deliberate at the end, and our home team wins the debate. I applaud as loudly as I can. Madison just rolls her eyes. She isn't into extracurricular activities, and to be honest, neither am I.

"So are you going to go talk to him now?" she asks me.

"What?" My eyes fly up to the front of the room, where Liam is now talking to Olivia Reynolds. *Again.* God, she's really pretty. It's so unfair. "*Now?*"

Madison huffs. "You made me sit through that whole stupid, boring debate, and you're not even going to go talk to him? Seriously, Olivia?"

"He's busy."

"So? Interrupt him."

"I can't just talk to him out of nowhere."

"Why not?"

"It would be weird."

"Seriously, Liv." She holds up a hand. "I can't even."

Maybe if Liam weren't talking to Olivia Reynolds, I could go up to him. But I'm not wrong. It would be weird if I went up there now. I mean, he's going to think I'm some total stalker or something.

I start to explain this to Madison, but she's not listening anymore, because Aidan has burst into the auditorium to find her. He's still wearing his outfit from football practice, and he stinks of sweat. God, couldn't he have taken a shower or something before coming here? The first thing he does is plant his lips on Madison's, and they kiss for, like, five minutes straight. It's so gross. I try not to look. They probably wouldn't even notice if I left right now.

"Hey, Aidan." Madison separates from Aidan for a split second, probably because she needs to breathe. "Tell Olivia she should go talk to Liam."

My face burns. I'm not surprised Madison told her boyfriend that I like Liam, but I still hate that she did it. Can't Madison and I have any secrets anymore? Plus, Aidan is, like, the worst person to know. He has a big mouth, and he'll tell everyone.

"Liam Cass?" Aidan makes a face. "I hate that guy. He's such an asshole."

"Why is he an asshole?" I say. "He's really nice."

Aidan snorts. "Yeah. Nice to *you*. Anyway, you could do better, Olivia."

"That's what *I* said," Madison chips in.

"Whatever," I mumble.

"Anyway." Madison grabs her backpack off her seat. "Aidan and I are heading out. Want a ride home?"

I absolutely do *not* want to sit in the back seat while Aidan drives erratically because he has to make out with Madison and touch her legs while they're driving. I'd rather walk the two miles home.

Aidan and Madison take off through the back exit while I sit back down in my seat. I really must be a stalker, because I'm still looking at Liam. He looks so good dressed up. Part of me wants to snap a picture with my phone so I can look at it later. I'm totally staring. It's awful. But I can't stop. This is why I'm failing math.

Liam goes up to talk to the debate teacher, Mrs. Randall, and then he talks to an attractive woman in her forties who has the same dark hair and eyes that he has and also a similar nose. I think it's his mother. He looks a lot like her. He seems to be really polite to her, which is good. I read online that it's a really good thing when boys are nice to their mothers. I don't know what Madison was talking about. How could she say she doesn't trust him?

It isn't until most of the people in the auditorium have filtered out that Liam looks into the audience and our eyes meet. He gets that smile on his face again, and I feel this warm tingle in my whole body. I'm sure Liam doesn't give slobbery kisses like Aidan. I bet he kisses really well.

Oh my God, he's coming over to me.

I stumble to my feet, trying to temper the dopey smile on my lips. How do normal people smile? It's like I forgot how. God, he's going to think I'm *such* a loser.

"Hey, Olivia," he says.

"Hey," I say.

That sounded good. Casual. My voice didn't squeak, and I didn't spit when I talked. Score.

Liam rubs at the back of his neck. When he was up

there on that stage, he looked so confident. I'm terrified of public speaking, but he didn't look even the slightest bit nervous. But now he keeps rubbing his neck and shuffling his feet. "So, um, you saw it?"

"Uh-huh." I squeeze my fists together. They seem abnormally clammy, like I've got a fever. "You did a really good job. I mean, I think so. I've never seen a debate before."

"Thanks." He coughs and smiles. "It went really well. We won."

"I know."

"Oh."

And now we're both just standing there. I rack my brain, trying to think of something interesting to say before he walks away. "Did you get to your math homework yet?"

That'll do.

He shakes his head. "No. I've been busy with the debate since school ended."

"Oh. Right." Duh. Obviously. God, why do I sound like such a moron? "Well, I did it, and it wasn't too bad."

Actually, that's a total lie. There was no way I could focus on math homework when I knew I'd be seeing Liam shortly.

"Okay, good." He coughs again. "Hey, listen, Olivia, me and some guys from track are going to Charlie's tomorrow after school, just to hang out and get some food. Would you...I mean, do you want to come with us?"

I stare at him. Is he *asking me out*? "I..."

The smile on his face falters. "It's no big deal. Either way."

"No, I mean...yes. I would like to come. That would be great. It sounds like...fun, you know?"

His brown eyes light up. "Yeah, it's going to be a lot of fun."

"Yeah." My mouth feels almost too dry to speak.

"So…do you want to meet in front of the school at four thirty? It's after practice, and we need time to, you know, shower and stuff."

I nod. "Okay. I'll be there."

Okay, maybe it isn't an official date, but I really think Liam might like me. I mean, he seemed really happy when I said yes. And he wants to shower beforehand so he smells good. So these are all good signs.

Oh my God, I've got a date with Liam. I'm so happy!

CHAPTER 8

ERIKA

L iam is a brilliant public speaker. He's always been good at getting in front of a crowd and doing his thing. If he were different, he would be perfect for politics. He speaks well, he's good looking, and he's incredibly smart. My son is so many good things.

Before the debate begins, Liam is deep in conversation with a beautiful girl. She seems to also be on the debate team, but she looks like she could be a model. She has blond hair that appears professionally styled. And given how skinny she is, it's amazing how large her breasts are. Do sixteen-year-old girls get implants? I'm horrified by the idea of it.

There's a woman next to me who is fiddling with her cell phone. The gray laced through her hair makes me think she's about my age—probably another parent. "Excuse me," I say.

She looks up and smiles pleasantly. "Yes?"

"Do you know the name of the blond girl on the stage? The one in the yellow blouse."

The woman nods. "That's Olivia Reynolds. She's a really strong debater. But not as good as the boy. Liam."

"Liam is my son," I say, allowing for an instant that touch of pride I often deny myself when I talk about Liam these days.

"Is he?" The woman's eyes light up. "Well, he is absolutely *wonderful*. Very talented. You must be really proud of him. I wish my son could speak half as well."

I smile, trying to enjoy the compliment, but my mind is racing. Olivia Reynolds. That's the girl Liam is interested in. And it's not surprising, because she is absolutely beautiful. Of course Liam would like her.

I've got to fix this.

I excuse myself from this woman who won't stop gushing about my son, and I step out of the auditorium. I just need to make a quick call. I'll be back in time for the debate.

I check the contacts on my phone, searching for the name Frank Marino. My heart is pounding as I click on his name. The phone rings once. Then again.

It's Frank. Leave a message.

Voicemail.

"Frank? It's Erika Cass. I need to talk to you. There's another... Please call me back. As soon as you can."

Frank is very reliable. He'll call back tonight.

I return to the auditorium where the students are assembled on the stage. Liam is behind the podium. Sometimes I look at him and I can't get over how that tiny helpless baby grew up into this handsome, intelligent young man. There were times, when Liam was an infant, when I imagined what he'd be like when he was older.

I was so naïve. I had no idea what was to come.

40

Liam gives a great performance, as usual. His team wins the debate, as if there was ever any doubt. He is an excellent performer and speaker. When he was in third grade, he had to give a presentation for class, and he insisted on wearing his nicest button-down shirt and pants. He even dug out the black clip-on tie I'd bought him for a wedding the year before. I thought he was absolutely adorable and took about a hundred photographs. It's almost a decade later, and he still takes public speaking just as seriously.

Liam is also very competitive. I don't know how much he cares about debate per se, but he definitely cares about winning. Whenever he does well in a track meet or a debate, he's in a great mood. But if he doesn't do well, he gets quiet and won't talk much that evening. Fortunately for him, he's very good at winning. And he's very good at getting what he wants.

I won't let him have what he wants this time.

Liam's eyes light up when he sees me walking over to congratulate him. "Did you see, Mom? We won! We get to go to state!"

I grin at him. "You did great."

He loosens his tie, which makes him look older than sixteen. Unlike when he was eight, he knows how to tie his own tie now—no more clip-ons. I watched him practicing it in a mirror a couple of years ago until he could do it perfectly. "Thanks."

Before I can say anything else, Mrs. Randall links her arm into mine and pulls me away from my son. Mrs. Randall is a history teacher and is also in charge of the debate team. She taught Liam American history during his freshman year and was the one who encouraged him to join the debate team. I remember Liam got an A+ in the class, and the comment on his report card was that he was the best student in the class. Hannah has her now for American history, but based on Hannah's recent comment that Mrs. Randall is a "bitch," I have a feeling my daughter won't be getting a similar grade.

"Mrs. Cass!" Mrs. Randall is almost glowing from the win, her gray hair coming loose from her sensible bun. "Liam was great out there, wasn't he?"

I nod, although I'm distracted by the fact that Liam has gone over to talk to Olivia again. "Yes. I know he's been practicing a lot."

"He is so diligent. I wish all my students had that sort of work ethic." She smiles at me. She is solidly in the Liam Cass fan club. "Next stop is Albany! And I bet we'll get to nationals this year. That will look great on his résumé when he applies to college."

Yes, in less than two years, Liam will be going away to college. I can't even think about it. The thought of him being alone and left to his own devices terrifies me.

"That's wonderful," I say.

The smile slips slightly from her lips. "By the way, I hate to bring this up now, but Hannah has missed several of her homework assignments this month."

It's the only thing she could have said to tear my attention away from Liam and Olivia. "She…she did?"

Mrs. Randall nods slowly. "Each instance of missed homework subtracts from her overall grade. And her last test score was…"

"I know." I wince thinking of the red score on Hannah's history exam that required my signature. Unlike Liam, Hannah has never been a strong student, but high school is proving to be even worse than middle school so far. "I'll talk to her about it and make sure she shows me her homework every night."

"I'm certain she can turn things around." Mrs. Randall looks back over at Liam, then back at me. "I'm sure she has it in her."

I know what she's implying, but Hannah is nothing like Liam. She doesn't look like him, and her personality is completely different. Mrs. Randall isn't the first teacher who has been disappointed by the discrepancy.

But not every teacher loves my son. He's gotten so much better at charming adults, but some of them can see right through him. There was one in particular about three years ago. That's a mess I don't want to think about ever again. When I remember what Liam did...

I've got to talk to Frank. Tonight.

CHAPTER 9

ERIKA

"Mom! Mom, are you listening to me?"

My head snaps up from the dishes in the sink. Hannah is supposed to be unloading the dishwasher while I clean the pots, but instead, she's spent the last several minutes ranting about some girl in her math class named Ashley. I've been so absorbed in the events of today that I guess I tuned her out. I have no idea what Hannah has said in the last several minutes. I close my eyes, hoping I can rewind the ribbon in my brain, but I can't. Whatever Hannah said is gone forever.

"Um," I finally say.

"I knew it!" Hannah looks triumphant. "You weren't listening to me. You *never* listen to me."

"Yes, I do."

"Fine. Then tell me something that's going on with me."

I put down the saucepan I'm rinsing off. "You're not handing in your American history homework?"

Hannah's cheeks turn pink. "I told you. Those assignments are stupid."

"It doesn't matter. You still have to do them."

"But what's the point? Why do I need to know about some stupid war that happened, like, five hundred years ago?"

"The Revolutionary War happened two hundred and fifty years ago, Hannah."

"Ugh!" She puts her hands on her hips. She's been doing that when she's upset ever since she was two years old. "What's the difference? It's still a really long time ago."

"It doesn't matter if you think it's stupid or not. It's part of your education. Liam always—"

"Right. Liam. You want me to be just like him. Because he's *so* perfect."

I turn to Hannah, staring at her pale, round face. I'm not entirely sure if she's being sarcastic or not. Most of the worst stuff with Liam happened when he was much younger—I would imagine Hannah is too young to even remember. When we sent him to Dr. Hebert, he was only seven and Hannah was five. I've tried my best to shield her from what goes on, but sometimes I wonder how much she knows.

Does Hannah know anything? *Everything?* What has Liam told her? Did she mention Olivia in the car to tease Liam or to tip me off?

"After all," Hannah adds, "he's your *favorite*, isn't he?"

My cheeks burn. I hate that it's so obvious that I favor Liam over her. I shouldn't. It's a sign of terrible parenting. I read once that most children long for their parents to be proud of them, so it makes sense that Hannah is struggling in school if she feels like she'll never do as well as her brother.

"Hannah," I say, "you know that's not true. I love both of you equally."

She snorts.

"Look. Why don't we do something together? Just the two of us. I can take you to the mall this weekend, and we can get you some new clothes. We haven't had a shopping spree in almost a year. I owe you."

My daughter narrows her eyes at me, but it doesn't take much to win her over. New clothes usually do the job. "Can we go on Saturday?"

"Sure."

"And can we go to Purple Haze after?"

Purple Haze is an ice cream shop that Hannah used to love when she was a little kid. "Of course."

Her lips widen in a smile. "Okay. That sounds good."

Of course, then I start to second-guess myself. I just discovered Hannah hasn't been handing in her history assignments. Maybe this situation doesn't call for a reward. But now that I've told her we're doing this, I can't very well take it back.

"But," I add, "we'll only go if you hand in all your history homework this week. And I want to *see* it, Hannah."

Hannah looks like she's about to start pouting, but then her shoulders drop. "Okay. Fine."

A small victory.

Before we can make a further dent in the dishes, the front door opens and the heavy footsteps of my husband and son float into the kitchen. Jason took Liam out for another driving lesson tonight. Things are going very well—Liam is a natural behind the wheel. No surprises there.

They come to find us in the kitchen, where we've barely made a dent in our chores for the evening. Jason is grinning broadly, and he slings an arm around Liam's shoulders. "What can I say, Erika? Our kid is a great driver. Just like his dad."

I shoot him a look.

"And his mom," Jason quickly adds.

Hannah snorts. "Nice save, Dad."

She has commented on more than one occasion that I've got Jason completely whipped. I don't know if it's true, but he's a good husband. I don't have to nag him to take out the garbage, he always remembers our anniversary, and he changed more than his fair share of diapers when the kids were little.

If there's one thing I would change about him, I wish he were a little less laid-back. Especially when it comes to my concerns about Liam. He's always shrugged everything off as "boys will be boys." But I know one of these days, it's going to be bad enough that he won't be able to do that anymore.

I look at Liam, and his face has no expression until he notices me watching him. Then he smiles. "I can't wait to get my license," he says.

"And then you can drive me to school in the morning," Hannah pipes up.

"Sure." Liam gives me a pointed look. "If Mom and Dad get me a car."

"We'll see," Jason says. "For now, stick with your mother's Toyota."

I brace myself, waiting for him to add, "We'll probably

get you one for your birthday." But he doesn't. Thank God. I think Liam will be a good driver, but something about him having his own car makes me a little uneasy.

"But Liam did do great today." Jason joins me at the dishwasher and starts unloading dishes on his own, even though it's Hannah's job. "He checked his mirrors when he was supposed to. He did the right thing when we got to every stop sign. I wasn't terrified even once."

Liam laughs. "Thanks, Dad."

"You've got to be careful out there," he says. He pulls out a couple of plates from the dishwasher and cocks his head thoughtfully. "Hey. Did you hear about the guy who lost his left arm and leg in a car accident? But he's all right now."

Hannah lets out a groan. Liam and I are silent.

"He's all *right* now," Jason says. "Because he has no left arm or leg. Get it?"

"No, I get it," I say.

Jason grins at me. "Well, you're not laughing, so I thought I needed to explain it."

"Nope."

Jason winks. He told his cheesy jokes even before the kids were born. But back then, a lot of the jokes involved saucy double entendres. Now they're straight-up dad jokes. But I find it endearing that he persists in making them, even though nobody laughs.

My phone starts ringing from the living room. I use the generic ringtone my iPhone came with, because I can't be bothered to change it. Truth be told, I'm not entirely sure how. My husband is a tech guy, and I can't change the ringtone on my phone.

I hurry to the phone and pick it up before it stops

ringing. I stare down at the name that pops up on the screen. Frank Marino.

Frank is calling me back.

I quietly slip outside to take the call. And I shut the door behind me.

CHAPTER 10

ERIKA

Erika Cass."

Frank's Brooklyn accent rings out on the line. It's so thick that you know he was born and raised there. I found him four years ago—in the yellow pages. I searched under private detectives and selected his name randomly. I had no idea what I was doing, and I'm lucky that Frank turned out to be as good as he is.

I don't want to think about what might have happened if not for his help.

"Hi, Frank," I say. "Thanks for calling me back so quickly."

"For you, Erika? Anything. What do you need?"

Frank is a smooth talker. That's what I thought the first and only time I met him in person, three years ago, right before the first job I hired him for. He looked just like he sounded—greasy black hair threaded with gray, yellowing teeth from years of smoking, and sharp eyes that didn't miss a thing. The man made me nervous. But he's always done everything I've asked him to. For the right price.

"The girl's name is Olivia Reynolds," I say. "She goes to Liam's school. Same arrangement as last time. Okay?"

Frank is quiet, hopefully scribbling down the information. "Olivia Reynolds. Spelled how it sounds?"

"Yes."

"Got it."

"Same thing as last time. Okay?"

"Okay, you got it." There's shuffling on the other line. "I never seen a woman so eager to cockblock her kid. Sometimes I think he's going to be discussing this in therapy someday."

My fingers tighten around the phone until my fingertips tingle. Frank has done this for me many times, and this is the first time he's felt the need to comment. "If you don't want to do it, I'll get somebody else."

"No, it's fine."

"Because if you won't do it, tell me now."

"Shit, Erika. Relax. I was just kidding around."

My shoulders relax. "Good."

"One more thing," Frank says. "My prices went up."

"How much?"

He quotes a number nearly twice what I paid last time. My chest tightens. He knows it was an empty threat when I said I would get somebody else. He knows I'm not going to get somebody else. I need him. "Fine."

"It's nice working with you, as always, Erika."

Just do your job, you piece of shit. I grit my teeth, angry I can't say the words that are going through my head. But he's going to do what I need him to do. He's going to help me save my son from himself.

CHAPTER 11

OLIVIA

Even though it might not be a real date, I could not possibly be more nervous about going to the diner with Liam tonight.

I tried on every item in my closet last night in front of the mirror. Twice. I put on a skirt that was way too short—I would have loved to have Liam see it on me, but it would've looked like I was trying too hard (also, I'm not entirely sure my mother would've let me out of the house). We're just going out for some food after track team practice, after all. In the end, I decide to go with cute casual. I tug on my cutest skinny jeans, paired with a red tank top, and then I spend another hour in front of the mirror, trying to get my hair just right.

Boys are exhausting.

Right now, I'm standing in front of the school in my cute tank top and jeans, hugging my body for warmth. My upper arms are covered in tiny little goose bumps, but my jacket isn't super sexy, and I don't want to wear it in front of Liam. I hope he appreciates how much I'm suffering for him.

Madison has decided to wait with me, but I almost wish she hadn't. She is not a source of positive energy at the moment. She's never liked Liam very much, but right now, she is downright unsupportive. It seems like she's trying to convince me to blow off Liam before this even gets started.

"And on top of everything else, he's *late*." Madison pulls her phone out of her pocket and shoves it in my face to show me the time. "Is that what you want? A guy who's going to keep you waiting all the time?"

"He told me he might be late." I start jogging in place to keep warm, but then I get freaked out about sweating. "He's at track practice. It's not his fault if he didn't get out on time."

Not to mention Aidan is *always* late. It's almost a guarantee.

Madison sticks out her lower lip in a pout. "I just think he's wrong for you."

"Based on what?"

"Based on…" She glances around to make sure we're the only people standing there. "Look, I didn't want to tell you this, but…you know, Tyler Martinson used to be close friends with Liam."

I cringe at the name Tyler Martinson. He's one of those obnoxious jock guys who plays football with Aidan. Solely because of that, I spent some time with him at the beginning of the year, and I wasn't all that surprised when he asked me out on a date. But I didn't feel even the slightest bit of attraction to him, so I flat out turned him down. He seemed astonished, like he was doing me a *favor* by asking me out and couldn't believe I said no. His obnoxious response made me even more glad I said no.

"So apparently…" Madison lowers her voice a notch. "Tyler said he had to stop being friends with Liam because Liam is legit crazy. Like, he would say and do all these crazy things, and Tyler got really freaked out."

I suppress the urge to roll my eyes. "Crazy like what?"

"I don't know exactly," Madison admits. "But apparently, it was some *really* bad stuff. Like, Tyler was actually *afraid* of him. He said Liam is really messed up, and any girl who gets involved with him will be sorry."

Now I really do roll my eyes. "Come *on*. You believe that?"

"Yes, I do! Liv, I told you I got a bad vibe about the guy. There's just something about him…"

"Well, I don't see it."

"Then you're blind."

I stare at my best friend and feel a burst of anger in my chest. Why is she doing this to me? She knows how much I like Liam. She's dated two complete jerks, and I never said one bad word about either of them. Well, that's about to change right this minute.

"Well," I say, "at least he's better than Aidan."

Madison's mouth falls open. "What are you talking about? What's wrong with Aidan?"

"Are you joking? Aidan is a total asshole. He treats you like crap, and he's practically flunking out of school. He bullies underclassmen. And he probably shoots up steroids."

Two little pink spots appear on each of Madison's cheeks. "He doesn't shoot up steroids."

"Fine. But all the other stuff is true." I look her in the

eyes, daring her to contradict me. She doesn't, because I'm totally right. "But *Liam* is the awful one. Because he gives you a bad *vibe*. Oh my God, how *awful*."

The pink spots on Madison's cheeks widen. "Fine. You want to go on a date with a psychopath? Be my guest."

With those words, Madison spins on her heels and stalks off, probably to find Aidan. Her dirty-blond ponytail swings aggressively behind her as she walks away. We've had fights before, but this feels like the biggest fight we've ever had. It makes me uneasy.

But I miraculously forget all that when Liam materializes in front of me.

He looks devastatingly handsome in his track team T-shirt, baggy jeans, and a lightweight jacket, with his hair slightly damp from the shower. He smiles at me, and my heart does a little dance in my chest. So what if Madison and I are fighting? I can't even think about that right now.

"You came," Liam says, as if he's slightly surprised and pleased.

I return his smile. "Of course I came. I said I would."

"Yeah, but…" He ducks his head down. "Anyway, I'm glad you're here."

This guy is *not* crazy. No way. I don't know what Madison was talking about. It's clear Aidan and Tyler are jealous of Liam because he does so well in school and all the girls think he's cute.

"You look cold," he observes.

I'm not going to lie. I'm pretty freaking cold right now. My teeth are actually chattering a little bit, and my lips feel like they're turning blue. But I don't want to seem like I'm complaining. "Maybe just a little."

And then Liam does something that totally melts me.

He takes off his jacket and he holds it out to me. "Here. Take it."

"But then *you'll* be cold."

"Nah. I'm okay. I'm still hot from running."

I've never kissed a boy before, but somehow it seems more significant that a boy has never made a gallant, romantic gesture for me before. I've had a crush on Liam for several months now, but at this moment, I fall head over heels.

I'm totally in love.

CHAPTER 12

*T*ranscript of police interview with Olivia Reynolds.

PD: "Olivia, can you please describe your interactions with Liam Cass?"

OR: "We're on the debate team together. We have been for the last two years."

PD: "Are you friends with him?"

OR: "Yes. I mean, we've been on the team together for a while. So we talk a lot. I mean, not just when we're debating."

PD: "Would you describe your relationship with Liam as more than friendship?"

OR: "Um. Well, no. Not exactly, but... Look, I feel weird talking about this with, like, the police. It's, like, embarrassing."

PD: "But you understand why this is important."

OR: "Yes. Of course. I mean, that's why I called you. I thought...maybe if I told you what happened to me, it would help."

PD: "And we appreciate your contacting us."

OR: "Yes."

PD: "So going back to the original question: Did you have any sort of romantic relationship with Liam Cass?"

OR: "Well, no. Not officially. But...I sort of..."

PD: "What?"

OR: "I...I liked him. A *lot*. I thought he was cute. And he's really good at debate, you know?"

PD: "Did he express romantic intentions toward you?"

OR: "Honestly? I mean, sometimes I thought he did. One time, he walked me home, but nothing happened. Obviously he liked somebody else better."

PD: "And then what happened?"

OR: "..."

PD: "Olivia, if you could tell us what you told me earlier about what happened next..."

OR: "You mean about that guy?"

PD: "Right. You said that a man approached you on the street."

OR: "Yeah. I was out walking my dog, and this old guy—he was, like, maybe fifty—he came up to me and asked me if I was Olivia Reynolds. And it totally freaked me out because, you know, you hear all these stories about some girl going out to walk her dog and she never comes home. And he looked kind of creepy too."

PD: "How did he look creepy?"

OR: "I don't know. He smelled like cigarettes and his teeth were kind of yellow. Probably because of cigarettes, right? That's why I am not going to smoke ever. Or vape. Vaping is even worse. My health teacher says you can get popcorn lung from vaping, where your lungs look like microwave popcorn."

PD: "Uh, right. So what happened next, Olivia?"

OR: "So I didn't really say anything. I just looked at the guy, but he seemed to know who I was. And then he asked me if I knew Liam, and that was *really* weird."

PD: "What did you say?"

OR: "I said yes."

PD: "And what did he say then?"

OR: "Well, he started telling me all the stuff he knew about me. Like, bad stuff. I mean, not *really* bad. I haven't done anything *that* bad. But, like, he had screenshots of all these text messages on my phone that I wouldn't want my parents or my teachers to see. And some other stuff."

PD: "What sort of stuff?"

OR: "Um, do I have to tell you that?"

PD: "We'd like to have all the information."

OR: "It wasn't illegal. I swear."

PD: "You're not in trouble, Olivia. I promise. Just tell us the truth."

OR: "Okay...well, I was dating this guy last year, and I sent him some pictures of myself that I shouldn't have. It was really stupid. And I don't know how that creepy guy ended up getting those photos. God, it's so embarrassing."

PD: "So what happened next?"

OR: "The guy said if I kept hanging around with Liam, he was going to show everyone."

PD: "So what did you say?"

OR: "What do you think? I mean, I liked Liam, but not enough to get in trouble. So I said I wouldn't hang out with him anymore."

PD: "And did you stop hanging out with him?"

OR: "Yeah. But honestly, it didn't really matter, because the next day... Well, you know."

PD: "Did you have any thoughts about why that man told you not to hang out with Liam?"

OR: "No. I was just so freaked out about the whole thing. I thought... I don't know. It was the weirdest thing ever, honestly."

PD: "Well, thank you, Olivia. This has been very helpful."

OR: "Detective?"

PD: "Yes?"

OR: "Do you really think Liam did it?"

PD: "I can't share any details of our investigation with you, unfortunately."

OR: "I just want to say...I don't think he did. I've known him for over two years, and he's a really nice guy. I'm not just saying that because he's cute. He's really serious about competing, and he's very smart and he just *wouldn't*. I don't think he *could*. I mean, what kind of person does something like that? I just can't imagine it."

PD: "Then why did you contact us?"

OR: "Because... I don't know. I don't think Liam did it. But I guess I'm not absolutely sure. You never know."

CHAPTER 13

OLIVIA

It's about a mile to the diner, and Liam and I walk together. Well, we're with half the track team and also some of their girlfriends, but Liam and I hang back behind them. His jacket is warm and smells like he does—like Dial soap. The sleeves are long enough on me that my fingertips barely poke through.

We talk about math class mostly. Liam says Mr. Gregor smells like old cheese, which is actually pretty accurate. He doesn't seem to like Mr. Gregor much, which surprises me, because a lot of kids act like smart-asses in that class, but Liam doesn't. He's really polite to Mr. Gregor—to his face. I get the feeling he's one of Mr. Gregor's favorite students, and not just because he's acing the class.

Liam stands very close to me when we walk. A few times, his hand brushes against my fingertips, and I think he's going to try to hold my hand, but he doesn't.

When we get to the diner, there are a lot of kids from our school already there. Even though it's a long walk,

Charlie's has the *best* milkshakes. They are so good, I swear. It's like the best ice cream you've ever tasted in shake form. I notice Tyler Martinson is sitting in one of the booths, and I remember what Madison said earlier. That Tyler said Liam is crazy. That Tyler is *afraid* of him.

Could that really be true? Tyler doesn't seem like a guy who would be afraid of anything. And when we walk past him, he and Liam don't make eye contact. He doesn't look at me either, and I wonder if he's still mad at me for not going out with him. I saw him with a different girl a week later though, so it looks like he got over it quick.

We all squeeze into an extra-large booth. There are six of us, and my body is pressed up tightly against Liam. I feel the warmth of his thigh against mine. And I don't mind one bit.

"Are you squished?" He looks at me with concern in his brown eyes. He has such nice eyes. I always was partial to blue eyes, but God, his are nice. And his breath smells like peppermint. I wonder if he swallowed a breath mint before coming. Because I did. I mean, I didn't want to have tuna breath.

"I'm okay," I breathe.

"Good." He grins at me. "Because if I move over one inch, I'm gonna fall out of the booth."

I return his smile. "Don't fall out."

"I'll try." He flips open the menu. "Do you know what you want to get?"

"Vanilla milkshake," I say without hesitation.

"Hey, that's my favorite too. You stole my idea."

I laugh. "Sorry."

"Do you want to split it?"

Splitting a milkshake with Liam? Yes, please. "Sure."

My doubts about this being a date are starting to fade. He walked me here, we're splitting a milkshake, and I couldn't be closer to him unless I was sitting on his lap. Also, when he orders it for us, he mumbles in my ear, "It's my treat." And even when the other people at the table are talking, he only seems interested in talking to me. His attention is completely focused on me.

Until something happens that spoils everything.

Our booth is fairly close to the bathroom, and when Tyler and his buddies get up to use it, they have to pass by us. Even though Liam and Tyler had studiously avoided looking at each other when we came in, Tyler jostles Liam's shoulder hard as he walks by. It was clearly done intentionally. I know it, and it's obvious that Liam knows it.

When Tyler comes back out of the bathroom, I'm worried he's going to do it again. But instead, as he passes by our table, he stumbles and falls to the ground with a loud thunk. For a moment, everything is quiet as Tyler gets back to his feet.

"You just tripped me, asshole!" Tyler is staring at Liam. There's a scary-looking vein bulging out on his thick football player's neck. "What the hell is wrong with you?"

Liam turns to look at Tyler, blinking his eyes in a picture of mock innocence. "Oh, I'm sorry. That was an accident."

"Like hell it was!"

"You're mistaken, Tyler."

"Say that to my face."

My heart speeds up in my chest. Tyler looks really mad. He's still got that vein in his neck, but now his face is starting to turn bright red. Liam stands up, and I notice that while the two boys are about the same height, Tyler is broader like the football player he is. Liam has more of a runner's physique. I'm scared that in a fight, Tyler would have the edge.

But Liam doesn't look the slightest bit intimidated. He looks Tyler right in the eyes. "I didn't trip you. You're just clumsy."

Tyler snorts. "What? Are you trying to show off in front of your *girl*? Not that you need to do much to impress *her*."

My cheeks burn. The last thing I want is Tyler talking smack about me in front of Liam. But Tyler's words hit home. What he said seems to upset Liam more than anything so far. "Mind your own business," Liam says in a low voice.

Tyler takes a menacing step toward Liam. Their confrontation has got the whole restaurant watching—everyone is probably hoping there will be a fight. Everybody but me. I just want Tyler to leave us alone. "Does your girlfriend know you're a psychopath?"

Liam rolls his eyes. "Is that all you've got to say?"

"It's true."

"Yeah?" Liam lifts an eyebrow. "Well, if I *am* a psychopath, maybe you should be careful. Because I know pretty much everything there is to know about your family. I know where your mom goes to yoga class. I know your dad parks his car outside the garage at night. And I know what window is your sister's bedroom."

Tyler's eyes widen.

"Also," Liam adds, "you've got a new cat, don't you?"

All the color drains out of Tyler's face. I've never seen anyone look so freaked out. I'm not even sure why. What is Liam talking about? Why is he talking about Tyler's cat? This makes no sense.

But apparently what Liam said did the trick. Tyler takes a step back.

"It wouldn't even be a challenge to kick your ass," he mutters. He moves past Liam to get back to his seat, but I notice that this time, he makes an effort to avoid touching him.

Liam drops back into the seat next to mine. There's a satisfied look on his face. A secret smile plays on his lips.

"I think you just scared the shit out of Tyler," I comment.

Liam shrugs. "Yeah, well. He's a jerk."

"Didn't you guys used to be friends?"

"No. Not really."

But that's a lie. Everyone knows that Tyler and Liam used to be tight. Still, he doesn't seem to want to talk about it anymore, and that's fine with me. I didn't come here to talk about Tyler Martinson. I came here to spend time with Liam.

The waitress brings two straws for our milkshake. I wish we only had one straw so Liam and I could have shared. But two straws are nice too. I try to time it so that I am taking a sip at the same time he is so our faces are inches apart.

"I love the milkshakes here," Liam says.

His leg is pressed against mine, and so is his upper arm. If we weren't surrounded by other kids from track team, I wonder if he'd try for a kiss. The thought of it makes my heart nearly beat out of my chest.

But before I can get too excited, my phone starts ringing in my pocket. I recognize the ringtone. It's my mother.

Great.

"Hang on." I reach into my pocket and pull out my

phone, which was a present for my birthday last year. But my mom put all these restrictions on it, so I can't play too many games or watch YouTube. Oh, and there's GPS tracking so that she can know where I am at every single moment of the day. Seriously, why doesn't she just put a microchip in my head? "Hi, Mom."

"Olivia," Mom says, "are you still at that diner? It's getting late."

Sheesh, she *knows* I'm still at the diner. She's got that GPS thing on my phone.

"It's not that late." I look down at my watch and then out the window. "It's not even dark yet."

"How are you planning to get home?"

"Um." I glance at Liam, who has his eyebrows raised. "I'll just walk."

He'll walk me home. I'm sure of it.

"Walk!" Mom says it like I suggested zip-lining home. "Out of the question! I'll drive over and pick you up."

"Mom!" I try not to sound too whiny, but I *really* don't want her to pick me up. Not now. Not when things are going *so* well. "It's still really early. Can't I stay? Please?"

"Don't you have homework to do?"

"I did it at school." (That's a lie. There was no way I could concentrate on my homework when I knew Liam and I were about to have our first almost date.)

Mom is quiet for a moment, thinking it over. I keep my fingers and my toes crossed that she says I can stay.

"No," she finally says. "I'm going to come get you now. I want you home before it gets dark."

"But Mom—"

"Not negotiable, Olivia."

"Fine," I grumble.

If Liam weren't right next to me, I probably would have fought harder to stay, but I don't want him to hear me fighting with my mother. You know—one of those fights where I explain to her that I am not a baby and she's being absolutely ridiculous. Those can go on for a while, and I've noticed they don't usually end well for me.

I hang up with my mother and shove my phone back in my pocket. "I'm really sorry," I tell him. "My mom is coming to pick me up now."

"*Now?*" His face falls. "You really have to go?"

"She's worried about me walking home alone."

He wipes his hands on his blue jeans. "I would have walked you."

I know he would have. And *his* mother isn't sitting around worrying about him walking me home and then walking home himself. Because his mother isn't crazy like mine.

"I'm sorry," I say.

"It's okay."

Then he reaches under the table with his left hand and finds mine. He gives it a squeeze, and suddenly *we're holding hands*. Oh my God, we're holding hands! He grins at me, and I grin back. The only thing ruining it a little is that my hand is getting super clammy. I sort of want to pull it away from him and wipe it on my jeans, but I'm not sure how I would explain that one.

"Hey!" One of the other guys on the team is smirking at Liam. "Cass! What are you doing under the table? Hands where we can see them, buddy!"

Liam laughs, but his ears color slightly and he pulls his hand away from mine. My heart sinks in my chest, and at that moment, my mom texts me that she's outside and I better get my butt out there ASAP.

"I gotta go," I say to Liam.

He chews on his lip. "What if I tell her I'll walk you home?"

"She's outside. I really gotta go."

"Okay." He stands up so I can get out of the booth. He rubs at the back of his neck. "I'm glad you came."

I smile up at him. "Me too."

All his friends from track are staring at us. He ducks down his head and smiles self-consciously. "Maybe another time then?"

I nod, trying not to let on how disappointed I feel right now. He's not even asking me out for another night. But it's not like we're never going to see each other again. We've got math class together tomorrow. It's my favorite class of the day now, and I don't even like math. "I'll see you tomorrow."

"See you," he says.

I wait one more beat, hoping he'll change his mind and lean in to kiss me or at least suggest going out again. But he doesn't.

CHAPTER 14

OLIVIA

I am so mad at my mom.

I was having *such* a great time with Liam. He's, like, the first boy I've ever had a big crush on. And he actually seems to like me back. And she ruined it. For no reason!

"Are you going to give me the silent treatment the whole way home?" Mom asks as she turns onto Maple Street.

I fold my arms across my chest. "You know Liam asked me specifically to come tonight."

"And he'll ask you again."

"What if he doesn't?"

"I'm sure he won't be discouraged that easily."

"You don't know that."

"Give me a little bit of credit, Olivia. Give *him* a little bit of credit."

I let out an angry huff and stare out the window. Mom knows how much I like Liam. I've been confiding in her about my crush the entire year. Especially since Madison is so anti-Liam, my mother has been my main confidante. She knows how excited I was about tonight.

"I think I saw him through the window," Mom says. She's chosen to ignore me ignoring her. I hate it when she does that, although to be fair, it usually works. "Was he the one wearing the blue T-shirt with the dark hair?"

"Yes," I admit. As much as I want to be angry at my mother, I also sort of want to talk about Liam. I'm very conflicted.

"Oh." She nods. "He's *really* cute. I can see why you like him."

"I know, right?" My palms get all clammy again at the thought of him. "And he's not *just* cute. He is, like, one of the smartest guys in the school. You should have heard him at the debate yesterday, Mom."

"Well, I'm sorry I made you come home, but I'm sure you'll have another opportunity with him."

"He held my hand." I smile at the memory. My whole body gets tingly at the thought of it. "I mean, just for a minute because one of his friends started teasing him. But…it was…"

"You should invite him over to the house."

"You mean while *you're* home?"

"Oh God. Unthinkable."

"Mom…"

Mom winks at me. "What? I'll be cool."

Oh my God, she will definitely *not* be cool. She'll probably drag out old photo albums and show him pictures of potty training.

"You can take him up to your room," she adds. "As long as you keep the door open."

"Do we have to keep it open? It's not like we're going to do anything."

Mom snorts. But I guess maybe she's right. If Liam and I were alone in a room…

God, the thought of it makes me all tingly again. I can't wait to see him again.

Mom pulls up in front of our house, and by this point, I've mostly forgiven her. Aside from Madison, my mother is my best friend, and it's hard to stay angry at her. And she's probably right. I don't think I've blown it with Liam. Aren't you supposed to play hard to get with boys?

So I'm in a pretty good mood when I get out of the car. Until I see who's sitting on the front steps to our house.

CHAPTER 15

ERIKA

The smell of the meat loaf in the oven fills the kitchen as I chop cucumbers for the salad that will be the green element of our dinner tonight. My mother raised me to always add a green element to dinner. Even though it's a guarantee that Hannah will pick it off her plate with her thumb and forefinger and look at it like it's dog poop. And Liam might also. Actually, it's fifty-fifty that Jason will too.

Still, you have to have a green element.

The front door slams shut, which means Jason is home from work. Right on time. He's removed his shoes by the door—getting him to do that was a hard-won victory. He wanders into the kitchen, looking pretty dang handsome in his shirt and tie. He offers me a crooked smile. "Smells good."

"Meat loaf."

He joins me at the counter and looks down at the cucumber I'm chopping. "Funny. It doesn't look like meat loaf."

I roll my eyes and nudge him with my shoulder. "It's in the oven. Five more minutes on the timer."

He walks over to the oven and throws it open to peer at the meat loaf inside. I hate it when he does that, because it disrupts the cooking process, but I grudgingly appreciate that he likes my cooking so much that he has to witness it in progress.

"How was traffic?" I ask. I still don't know how he can brave the commute from Manhattan to Long Island during rush hour and keep a smile on his face. Five minutes on the Long Island Expressway and I'm crabby all day.

"Not bad." He sticks his thumb into his tie to loosen it. "Can I help with chopping?"

I snort. Jason is good with computers, but cooking is not his thing. When he's chopping vegetables, he's just as likely to slice off a chunk of his finger. I'd rather not have blood all over my salad. "That's okay."

"What?" He points at the tomato on the counter. "I could chop that up for you."

"Hmm. Could you?"

"Sure. I have great knife skills or whatever." When I give him a look, he grins at me. "Come on. It's just for our dinner. It's not like we're entering the salad in a salad competition."

"How about you set the table?"

"Your wish is my command, m'lady."

I roll my eyes. "Can you yell for Hannah and Liam to come down first?"

"You got it."

Jason pulls his tie the rest of the way off as he wanders over to the staircase to yell for the kids to come down for dinner. Then he obediently comes back to the kitchen to set the table. He's being a five-star husband tonight.

"Did you have a good day at work today?" I ask as I start chopping the tomato.

He nods eagerly. "The team is making great progress. Everyone is working really hard, and we're going to have a new product soon. It's exciting."

Jason explained to me some of the software they're building, and I don't entirely understand it. He is definitely some kind of genius. It's a bit intimidating, because I'm definitely not a genius, but after twenty years of marriage, I don't feel insecure about that anymore. At least it means we can afford a nice house and nice cars. And maybe if he gets some time off, we can take a nice vacation as a family.

Hannah wanders into the kitchen in her bare feet just as the timer goes off for the meat loaf. Jason makes a big deal out of how delicious it looks, but Hannah just crinkles her nose. She glares at the gray mound, glistening with tomato sauce and its own juices. "We're not *eating* that, are we?"

"Of course not," Jason says. "That's our new TV. What would you like to watch?"

"Dad," she groans. She narrows her eyes at the dinner I just spent the last hour cooking. "It's just so…meaty. It's like this big hunk of meat."

"Yes, Hannah. That's the definition of a meat loaf."

She sinks into one of the chairs at the kitchen table. "I'd rather have chicken."

"Well, I'd rather be in the Bahamas." Jason shrugs. "We don't always get what we want. Sometimes you have to do horrible things like eating delicious meat loaf."

I smile to myself as I continue chopping the tomato. "Where is Liam? Can somebody tell him to come down?"

Hannah takes out her phone and starts thumbing through her text messages. "Liam isn't home."

What? "He isn't?" I try to keep the tremor out of my voice. "Where is he?"

"I don't know. Track practice? What's the big deal? It's not that late."

I glance out the window, where the sun has already dipped in the sky. "The sun is down."

"So?" Hannah keeps her eyes on her phone. "He probably went to eat somewhere with his friends or something. Why are you freaking out?"

"I'm not freaking out."

But she's right. I *am* freaking out. I look over at Jason, who doesn't seem even the slightest bit concerned that Liam is not home. Which makes sense, because our son is sixteen years old and practically driving. He can be responsible for himself. He's not even late yet. He's come home at this time before.

But it's not Liam I'm worried about.

My hands are shaking so badly that I slip with the knife and the blade goes right into my left index finger. Blood immediately pools all over the cutting board.

"Geez, Erika!" Jason winces and goes for the paper towels. He grabs two squares and thrusts them in my direction. "Are you okay? That looks like a bad cut."

I press the paper towels against my finger, and they immediately saturate with crimson. But the cut on my finger is the least of my concerns. Where is Liam? All I can think about is Olivia Reynolds. What if he's with her?

What is he doing to her?

I hope Frank hurries up and does his damn job.

"Erika!" Jason's voice cuts into my thoughts. "That's really bleeding a lot. Maybe we should go to the emergency room."

"No!" The word comes out too loudly, and Jason blinks at me. I clear my throat. "It's fine. Really. I just bleed a lot."

Jason tries to smile, but he looks pale. "And you were worried about *me* chopping the tomatoes…"

The front door slams, and I let out a breath. Liam is home. Thank God.

My son stomps into the kitchen, still wearing his sneakers, which have now tracked dirt all over the carpet and the kitchen floor. I've yelled at him for that many times before, but I'm not going to freak out over it right now. I'm just glad he's home.

"Mom was worried about you." Hannah speaks up before I can pretend the opposite is true.

"You were?" Liam looks surprised. "I just went out to Charlie's with some of my friends from track. You just said to be home by seven, right?" He looks down at his watch. "I'm not late."

"No, it's fine." I grab another paper towel from the counter to replace the one that's drenched in my blood. "Did you have fun?"

Liam shrugs. "Sure."

The blood seems to have slowed down, which is a good thing. I was beginning to worry I needed stitches. I've never had stitches before, except for after childbirth. "Was it just the guys from track? Or were there girls there?"

I try to say it casually, hoping he might let something

slip. But given the way Jason smirks at me, I don't think I was successful.

Liam goes to the cupboard to grab some glasses, which Jason forgot when he was setting the table. Liam has set the table many more times than Jason has. "It was just the guys."

Jason laughs. "He probably wouldn't tell us if it wasn't."

He probably wouldn't. And that's exactly what I'm afraid of.

CHAPTER 16

OLIVIA

"Tyler." I frown as I say his name. "What are you doing here?"

The last person I expected to see when I got home was Tyler Martinson. He's still got on his football jersey, and he's sitting on the front steps of my house, his elbows on his knees. When he sees me get out of the car, he scrambles back to his feet.

"Olivia," he says. "I've got to talk to you."

"Tyler!" my mother exclaims. He knows her because Tyler's mom is this intense PTA lady. She's always volunteering for this or selling tickets for that. All the other parents are always trying to suck up to her, including my mom. "How are you doing?"

"Good." Tyler shrugs. Liam is always really polite around adults, but Tyler isn't. I'm lucky he doesn't curse my mother out. "Mrs. Mercer, I need to talk to Olivia for a few minutes."

My mother hesitates. Even though she knows his

mother, Tyler doesn't look like the kind of guy you want to leave your daughter alone with. He's big, he doesn't look adults in the eye unless he's pissed off, and he resembles the date rapist in some TV movie.

"Just for a few minutes," Mom says. "Then I want you to come inside, Olivia."

I nod, disappointed my mother wouldn't give me an excuse to blow off Tyler. I don't want to talk to him. Not for a few minutes—not for a few seconds. But when my mother goes into the house, he and I are left alone together for the first time since that day he asked me out and I said no.

The thing is Tyler isn't bad looking. He's actually pretty good looking. Not as cute as Liam, but who is, right? The reason I didn't want to go out with him had nothing to do with his looks. It had to do with the fact that he's a jerk. And a bully.

For example, when we were freshmen, there was this kid in our class named Greg who was, like, the nicest kid *ever*. But he was also really scrawny, wore superthick glasses, and was definitely pretty nerdy. For some reason, Tyler made it his mission to torture Greg. I had gym with the two of them, and Tyler was always trying to find a way to throw the ball directly at Greg as hard as he could. Which, in Tyler's case, was really hard. I remember one time he threw it at Greg so hard that his glasses broke and his nose started to bleed.

He also started rumors about him online. I can't remember all the details, but it was pretty bad. I think he also photoshopped Greg's face on all these embarrassing pictures. Then he sent the pictures to the whole school.

It was stuff like that the entire year. By the time June

came along, Greg was so beaten down that he barely spoke anymore to anyone. And then he didn't come back to school in September.

Oh, and last year, there was that whole thing with Lily Macintosh. I guess they were going out and he got mad at her, and he sent everyone in the school these photos of her topless that she apparently sent him when they were going out. I felt really bad for Lily, although you have to be really stupid to send naked pictures of yourself to a guy like Tyler Martinson. Anyway, she left school too. Madison told me she tried to kill herself, but I'm not sure if that's true. I overheard Tyler laughing about it in the hallway once.

So yeah. That's Tyler. That's the kind of shit he does.

"What is it, Tyler?" I wrap my arms around my chest, because it's even colder than it was earlier. Tyler is wearing a coat, but there's no chance in hell he would offer it to me the way Liam did. He's too self-absorbed to even notice I'm cold. "What do you want?"

"I need to talk to you about Liam."

I roll my eyes. "Don't bother."

"It's important."

"Liam is a really nice guy." I raise my chin to look Tyler in the eyes. "There's nothing *you* could tell me about him that would change my mind."

"You've got to listen to me, Olivia." Tyler's voice cracks slightly, which surprises me. Is he actually upset? "I'm not joking around. Liam is… He's dangerous."

I snort. "*Liam* is dangerous?"

"I really think…" He frowns at me. "I think if you go out with him, your life could be in danger."

"Oh, come *on*! So you're saying he's a *murderer*?"

"I'm saying…of everyone I know, he's the only one who scares the shit out of me."

"Why?"

Tyler shifts between his thick legs. "It's a long story. You have to trust me."

I just shake my head.

"And anyway," he adds, "Liam has barely any experience with girls. Wouldn't you rather be with someone…" He winks at me. "Someone who knows what they're doing?"

Right. And now he's finally come to the real reason he's here. Because he's pissed off that I went out with Liam after rejecting him.

"I wouldn't, actually," I say.

I start to turn away from Tyler, but before I can, he reaches out and grabs my arm. I try to shake him off, but he holds tight.

"You've got to listen to me, Olivia," he pleads with me. "You're making a huge mistake. I promise you."

Tyler's fingers are the size of sausages. I try again to shake him off as I feel bruises blossoming on my skin. "Let me go," I say through my teeth.

"You don't understand."

"Let me go, or I'll scream."

That finally gets through to him. He opens his fist and I pull away. My arm still throbs where he was grabbing on to me.

"We'll talk about it more later," he says.

"No," I say, "we won't."

CHAPTER 17

ERIKA

Jason and I love to binge-watch TV series in bed. When we first got a television in our bedroom, it felt decadent. Up until then, we only had the TV in the living room. "What kind of TV addicts are we that we need to have a television in every room?" Jason had said. But we got the television, a flat screen that was just as big as the one in the living room. And we watch it *all the time*. I can't think of any purchase we get more mileage out of than this TV. Including our cars.

Jason has stripped down to an undershirt and boxers, and he puts his arm around me while I snuggle up against him to watch episode five of season two of *BoJack Horseman*. It's this television show about a drug-addicted horse who was on a nineties sitcom. Don't judge.

But it's hard to focus. Frank is supposed to be talking to Olivia tonight. He's supposed to text me when it's done. So until I get that text, I can't entirely relax. There's a knot in my neck that's throbbing.

"This is the best show on television," Jason says. His eyes are on the screen, and he's completely oblivious to the way I keep tapping my fingers against the bed. My nervous habit.

"Even better than *Stranger Things*?"

"Okay. Both good in different ways."

"Hmm."

My phone starts ringing on the table by our bed, and I practically jump out of my skin. But it's not Frank—he's supposed to text, not call. I pick it up and see my boss's name on the screen. The time is nine thirty. Still a respectable time to call an employee.

"It's Brian," I say. "Can we pause *BoJack*?"

"I suppose," Jason grumbles. "But make it quick. This show isn't going to binge-watch itself."

I pick up the phone, and Brian's nasal voice fills my ear. Brian is my age, but he hates technology and avoids texting or emails if he can help it. He doesn't even have a smartphone yet. He's been running the *Nassau Nutshell* for ten years, and he has a very rigid idea of how things should be done.

"Erika." He has an impatient edge to his voice, which is fairly typical. "Where is my article on the pie contest?"

As part of my incredibly exciting journalism career, I was assigned to cover a local pie-baking contest. It wasn't that bad, honestly, because I got to sample some of the pies. But it's not exactly what I dreamed about when I majored in journalism.

"I thought it wasn't due until tomorrow morning."

"So you were planning to wait until the very last second of your deadline?"

Jason reaches for my belly to tickle me, and I swipe

him away. "Brian, if you need me to have it by a certain time, why not make *that* the deadline?"

"Erika, just please get me that article."

"I'll have it first thing tomorrow morning."

"Erika…"

"First thing tomorrow morning. I promise."

Brian grumbles, but he has to accept it. There are some nights when I would get on the computer and bang out the article for him on the spot, but I'm not in the mindset right now. All I can think of is Frank. Part of me was tempted to hide in the bushes outside Olivia's house to see it all go down.

After I hang up the phone, Jason raises his eyebrows at me. "You good to go?"

"Yeah. It's fine."

"You know," he says, "now that the kids are older, you could go look for a better job. One in the city."

I snort. "How am I supposed to do that when I end up having to drive them to school every other day?"

"Liam will have his license soon. He can drive Hannah." Jason blinks his blue eyes at me. "You should think about it. I know you're not happy at the *Nutshell*."

I take a deep breath. "I'd like to. You know I would. But the kids… They just need me too much right now."

He doesn't get it. I love my husband—he's been an amazing partner for the last twenty years. But he isn't around as much as I am. He commutes into the city every day and has to travel frequently for work, and that means he misses a lot. When something bad happens, he has to hear it secondhand from me. And he's always certain I'm exaggerating.

He has no clue what our son is capable of.

My phone buzzes on the nightstand. I reach for it, noticing a text message has popped up on the screen. It's from Frank:

I spoke to her. It's taken care of.

The tension drains out of my shoulders. Thank God. Disaster has been averted once again, if only temporarily. Olivia Reynolds has been spared, and she doesn't even know it. I shudder to think of what might have happened if I were rushing into the city every day for a job. I might never have found out about this girl.

"I'll think about the job," I lie as I reach for the remote control.

CHAPTER 18

OLIVIA

It's an embarrassing fact that my bedroom isn't much different than it was when I was a little kid. I still have posters all over my walls of cute cats and dogs—there's nothing cuter than a kitten sleeping on a puppy. I still need a night-light to go to sleep. And I still have to arrange all my stuffed animals just so on my bed every night.

Tonight I cuddle with Mr. Penguin as I try to fall asleep. I push my face into his soft black and white fur, squeezing my eyes shut. Sleep, dammit!

No, this is impossible. I can't stop thinking about Liam.

I can't believe I had to leave the diner early. The more I think about it, the more I think Liam would have definitely kissed me. But instead, he didn't even ask to see me again.

The whole thing has left me feeling totally unsatisfied.

Liam is *so* cute. Everything about him makes me all tingly. Every time I close my eyes, I picture him smiling at me. Also, his teeth are nice. For some reason, I'm really into teeth. Perfect, straight teeth are really sexy to me. Is that weird? Maybe. But I just think Liam is really cute.

Liam seemed disappointed when I had to run out to meet my mother. Maybe he decided I'm not worth the effort. After all, he knows plenty of other girls at school who are prettier than I am. I'm not even the prettiest Olivia he knows.

And the worst part is I can't even talk to Madison about it. Usually she texts me, like, a million times during the night, but tonight my phone was oddly silent. It feels like a part of me is missing without Madison.

I'll have to talk to her tomorrow. Try to make this right.

I hear something tapping against my window. At first, I think maybe it's rain, but then I realize somebody is throwing pebbles against my window. I put down Mr. Penguin and get up to investigate.

Oh my God.

It's Liam.

He's standing below my window, wearing a light jacket and jeans. His dark hair is tousled by the wind, and he's craning his neck to look up at my window. He waves to me, and I open the window enough to stick my head out.

"What are you doing here?" I ask.

He tosses a pebble in the air and catches it. "Target practice."

I stare at him.

"I'm just kidding, Olivia. Could you… Can you come down?"

I glance behind me at the clock on my nightstand. It's a quarter past one. My parents are surely asleep by now, as evidenced by the lack of light coming from underneath my door. They'll never know if I slip out. And anyway, I'll be right downstairs. "Okay, I'll be right down."

I'm wearing only an oversize T-shirt to sleep in, and there's no way I'm going outside in that. Instead, I slip on a pair of jeans and a new tank top. And this time, I grab a light jacket, because the temperature has dropped precipitously overnight.

Sure enough, my parents' bedroom door is closed and the light seems to be off inside. I slip past the room, down the stairs, and into the dark kitchen. I unlock the back door and quietly slip outside, making sure not to let the door bang shut.

The light from our back porch casts a shadow on Liam's face. "Hey," he says.

I shiver despite my jacket. "Hi."

I look at the sky and see the moon is full tonight. When I was in fifth grade, we learned about all the different kinds of moons. Full moon, crescent moon, new moon. I barely remember it. But I've always loved full moons.

Liam shoves his hands into his pockets and smiles crookedly. "I'm sorry I woke you up."

"You didn't wake me up."

"No?"

"Couldn't sleep."

He nods. "Me neither." He rubs at the back of his neck. "I…uh, I couldn't stop thinking about you."

I swallow hard. "You…you couldn't?"

He lifts his eyes, which look even darker than usual right now under the moonlight. "You had to rush out. I'd been… I really wanted to walk you home."

"Oh."

"Look, Olivia, I…" He takes a deep breath. I have no idea what he's going to say. I'm not sure he does either. But then he takes a step forward, ducks his head down, and presses his lips against mine.

Oh. My. God.

It's my first kiss. My first real kiss. And it is *incredible*. Liam is a *really* good kisser. Granted, I don't have any other guys to compare him to, but I don't need to in order to know he's good. I mean, the first time I had ice cream, I knew that was good. And this is indescribable.

When he pulls away, my whole body is shaking. And when he runs a hand through his dark hair, I realize he's shaking too. He gives me a lopsided smile. "I've wanted to do that since the first day of school."

"I'm really glad you did."

"Yeah?" His eyes light up. "Me too."

And then he kisses me again.

CHAPTER 19

ERIKA

I wake up from a nightmare, feeling like I can't breathe.

I don't remember all the details from the nightmare. But I remember being in a pit in the ground. And somebody throwing dirt on me, burying me alive. And as they bury me, they laugh. A laugh that echoes throughout the shallow grave.

My heart is still pounding at the thought of it. I have to take deep breaths, trying to calm myself down.

I turn my head to look at Jason, who is sound asleep beside me. He's snoring softly like he always does when he sleeps on his back. His pale eyelashes flutter slightly, but he doesn't stir. Jason has always been a deep sleeper, and he rarely suffers from insomnia. A long time ago, before we had Liam, I could have woken him up to tell him about my nightmare. He wouldn't have been mad. He would have put his arm around me, pulled me close to him, and made me feel like everything was all right again.

But Jason can't make me feel that way anymore.

Nothing can. And he has to wake up early in the morning and commute into the city. I can't wake him up. It wouldn't be fair to him.

It was so simple back when we were young. I met Jason over twenty years ago. I was writing an article on the tech startup company he had helped found and that was quickly becoming very successful. His red-tinged brown hair, which our daughter would later inherit, was in need of a haircut, and he was also in need of a shave, but he looked adorable. As he explained what the company did, his blue eyes progressively getting wider and more excited, I blurted out, "I have to tell you, I think you're the smartest guy I've ever met."

Jason stopped midsentence and blinked at me. "Is that a good thing?"

I didn't hesitate. "Yes."

"Good. Because I think you're the prettiest girl I've ever met."

We were inseparable for a long time after that. We even spent a summer traveling through Europe in style after Jason sold his company for a bundle of money. It was on the Eiffel Tower that he got down on one knee and proposed to me. Maybe it was cliché, but it was one of the most romantic things I could imagine.

I love Jason even more than I did that day, but admittedly, the romance isn't what it used to be. I hate that he has to travel so far to get to work every day. And I hate the not infrequent business trips he has to take. And I've hated it even more since an incident that happened two years ago.

Jason told me he had a late dinner meeting at work with an investor. This is something that happens from time to time, and I didn't think much of it. But then, when he came home, he was grinning from ear to ear and reeked of unfamiliar perfume. I smelled it the second he kissed me hello. And right after that, he made a beeline for the shower.

He spent the next few weeks being particularly attentive to me. Flowers, expensive dinners out—he even bought me some diamond earrings he had caught me admiring on my computer. I couldn't help but think that Jason was filling out every checkbox for signs of a cheating husband.

I considered confronting him about it, but in my heart, I didn't believe my husband was a cheater. I imagined how hurt he would be if I even suggested it. I finally decided I must have imagined the perfume. Or maybe he'd had dinner with an investor that had particularly strong-smelling perfume and the scent clung to him. It's like when you go out to a bar and come home reeking of smoke even if you haven't had a cigarette.

And after that night, I never smelled it again. So even if it did happen, it never happened again.

But there's still that worry in the back of my head. Especially now that Jason has gotten "hot." I wish his hours weren't so long. I wish waitresses didn't flirt with him when we go to restaurants, even if he doesn't flirt back. Ultimately, I do trust him though. I don't think he would ever cheat on me—not really.

After all, it's not worrying about my husband that keeps me up at night.

"Jason," I whisper. I don't want to wake him up, but if he happens to be awake, then I wouldn't be at fault.

He snores.

Fine. He isn't waking up. And I'm not going to fall

asleep again so fast. I may as well get up and make myself some tea.

I slide my feet into my slippers and grab my fluffy blue housecoat from the dresser where I throw it every morning. I yawn and pad out into the hallway. I start for the staircase, but something stops me.

The door to Liam's bedroom is ajar.

Liam never leaves the door to his bedroom open at night. Ever. Not even when he was five years old. He always wants the door closed tight. The sight of that door slightly open is as terrifying to me as my nightmare. When it comes to Liam, the unexpected is always bad.

I walk over to the bedroom door and push it the rest of the way open. I squint into the darkness of my son's room.

It's empty.

I race down to the living room, my heart pounding. Maybe I'll find Liam on the couch, watching television. Like me, he often has difficulty sleeping. Even though I make him go to bed at ten, I know he's up far later. He told me once that he only needs five hours of sleep.

But Liam isn't in the living room. And he's not in the kitchen. Or either of the bathrooms—downstairs or upstairs. I comb the entire house and even look out on the porch and in the backyard before I race back up the stairs to my bedroom.

"Jason!"

So much for not waking him up. But our son is *missing*. I can't *not* say anything to him. What am I supposed to do now? Go back to sleep after Liam has vanished from his room in the middle of the night?

Jason's eyes crack open. He rubs at them with the back of his fists like he's two years old. "Erika?"

"Liam's gone!" I wring my hands together. "He's not in the house. He went somewhere."

I stare at Jason, waiting for him to get as upset as I am. He rubs his eyes again. Yawns. Honestly, I'm not feeling his fear right now.

"Jason," I try again, "I can't find Liam, and it's two in the morning."

"Okay, relax. He's not a baby." He yawns again. "Did you try calling his phone?"

I can't believe that somehow I did not think to do that. I'm amazed by my husband's ability to think rationally in any situation.

I snatch my phone off the nightstand, where it is charging. I select Liam's number from my list of favorites. I press his name, holding my breath, praying he'll pick up.

"Hello?"

I feel a rush of relief at the sound of Liam's voice.

Jason mouths: *Told you so*. "Liam! Where are you?"

"Oh." He's quiet for a moment. "I couldn't sleep, so I went out and took a walk."

"At two in the morning? I was worried sick!"

"Dad said I could walk around the block if I couldn't sleep."

I look at Jason accusingly. "Did you tell him he could go outside and walk around the block in the middle of the night?"

Jason taps his chin. "Uh…"

I'll deal with him later. I turn my attention back to the phone. "Liam, I want you to come home right now."

"Now?"

"Yes. *Now*."

He's quiet again. "Okay. I'll come right home."

We hang up, and now I'm free to yell at my husband. Apparently, he has absolutely no common sense. "You told him it was okay to wander the neighborhood in the middle of the night? Seriously?"

Jason sits up straighter in bed. "Okay, look, I know you're mad. But this neighborhood is safe. It's not like he's a little kid. He's as tall as I am. He's an athlete. He can defend himself."

"Not against a knife. Or a gun."

"You really think somebody is prowling our neighborhood with a knife or a gun?"

"It's just not a good idea."

"Come on, Erika. He's almost an adult. You really think something is going to happen to him?"

No. If I'm being honest with myself, I don't think anything is going to happen to Liam. I don't think he's going to get mugged or attacked. Liam can take care of himself. I'm not at all worried about that.

What I'm worried about is Liam happening to somebody else. Because my first thought when his bedroom was empty was what does he want to do that he can only do at two in the morning?

What if he's with Olivia Reynolds?

My breaths are coming in quick gasps. I'm hyperventilating. Jason springs into action as he realizes what's happening to me. He sprints into the bathroom, and I hear him fumbling around the medicine cabinet. When he returns, he's holding a bottle of pills. He fiddles with the childproof cap and finally shakes one out.

"Take it," he says.

I haven't had to swallow one of my Xanax in two months. I had been so proud of myself. But that progress is down the drain. I scoop the pill from his open palm and pop it in my mouth. I swallow it without water. Jason watches me, his brows knitted together. He used to only get a crease there when he was frowning, but now there's a crease there all the time.

"Are you okay?" he asks in a soft voice like I'm some kind of mental patient.

I'm already feeling calmer from the Xanax, even though it's probably a placebo effect. It couldn't work that quickly.

"Listen," Jason says in that same overly calm voice, "why don't you lie down?"

"Not until Liam is back," I manage.

"What if I go downstairs to wait for Liam? I'll talk to him about not going out in the middle of the night anymore, okay?"

I try to protest, but I feel dizzy and weak. That's what hyperventilating always does to me. And the Xanax probably isn't doing me any favors. "Okay. Thank you."

I lie down in the bed, and even though Jason said he was going downstairs, he lies down next to me and strokes my hair. "You need to relax more, Erika. Everything is fine. The kids are doing fine. You worry much too much."

I wish I lived in Jason's universe. Where the kids are doing fine and my biggest problem is our substantial mortgage. But unfortunately, nothing in my life is that simple.

It's my last thought as I drift off to sleep. I have no idea that my entire world is about to fall apart.

CHAPTER 20

ERIKA

Liam claims shotgun during the drive to school the next morning. He's in an unusually good mood, even though Jason read him the riot act when he got home, and I repeated the entire performance this morning. But I don't think Jason gave him that hard of a time, and I know I didn't give it my all, considering I was still out of it from lack of sleep mixed with a Xanax hangover.

On top of that, I couldn't get that angry when I knew that Jason had given him permission to leave the house during the night. Really, Jason should've been the object of my wrath. But he had already gone running, showered, and hit the road before I was fully awake. I don't think that was an accident.

Liam has commandeered the radio, and he's got a Maroon 5 song playing. He's humming along, which is very unusual for Liam. Hannah is the one who usually belts out radio lyrics in a painfully off-key voice. Despite his lack of sleep, Liam is very peppy this morning. I guess he's right—he doesn't need that much sleep. He's still humming when we pull onto the block leading to the high school.

"What's going on at the school?" Hannah pipes up.

It's a very good question. The front of the school is packed with police officers and reporters in equal numbers. It's a bad combination. I try to pull up in front of the school, but a police officer waves me to the side entrance. My stomach sinks. The last thing you want to see around your kids' school is a bunch of cops.

"Is the school even open?" I say. "What's going on?"

Of course, Hannah and Liam immediately whip out their phones to try to figure it out. I pull alongside the side entrance, where a teacher is manning the door. It seems like they are letting kids inside, although I'm hesitant to let mine out of the car.

"A student disappeared from her bedroom last night!" Hannah exclaims. "Nobody has any idea where she is."

I throw the car into park and look back at Hannah. "Who's the student?"

Not Olivia Reynolds. Not Olivia Reynolds.

"Hang on…" She's still scrolling with her thumb. "It's…" The color drains from her face.

"Hannah?"

Hannah chews on her lip. She glances at Liam, then back down at her phone. "Olivia Mercer."

"Olivia…" I frown at my daughter. "Olivia…Mercer? What year is she?"

She keeps her eyes pinned on the screen of her phone, her hair falling in front of her face. "She's, um, a junior."

I lift my eyes to look at Liam. He is staring at the screen of his own phone, his lips slightly parted. "Liam, do you know this girl?"

"A little," he says. "I've met her. But I don't know her very well."

I narrow my eyes at him. Is he lying? I can't tell anymore. I used to be able to see through him, but he's gotten too good at deceiving me. He sounds like he's telling the truth at least. Maybe he really is.

So instead, I look back at Hannah, who is an open book. Sure enough, she is looking at the screen of her phone, biting her lip hard enough that it's turned white. I get a horrible sinking feeling in my stomach. Oh my God, *did I get the wrong Olivia?* How many Olivias are there in this goddamn school?

"Maybe you two shouldn't go to school today," I say.

Hannah shakes her head. "I've got a math test today. And anyway, why would we stay home? We'll be safe at school."

"If you're sure…"

Hannah manages a smile, but it's strained. "Don't worry so much, Mom."

With those words, she grabs her backpack and gets out of the car. Liam reaches for the bag at his feet and starts to do the same, but I seize his arm. I still remember when his arm was so small and skinny I could wrap my fingers around it. A lot has changed since then.

"Liam," I say.

He shifts his backpack onto his lap. Hannah has about a million little ornaments hanging off her bag, but Liam has nothing. "I'm going to be late for school."

"Liam." I choke out the next sentence. "Where did you go last night?"

He lifts his dark eyes and looks straight into mine. "I just walked around the block."

"You swear?"

"Mom, stop it. I swear."

When he was younger, Liam had difficulty maintaining eye contact when he was lying—that's how I knew. But his eye contact is strong right now. If he's lying, he's lying right to my face and doing it very well. The truth is that I don't know what to believe. But I keep seeing the way Hannah lost her composure when she read that girl's name off the screen.

"Mom, I've got to go."

"Okay." I release his arm. "Go. But tell Hannah I'll pick you both up at school today."

"I've got track team practice."

"Skip it."

Liam looks like he's going to protest, but he keeps his mouth shut. He puts his hand on the handle of the door, poised to turn it. "Bye, Mom. I love you."

"I love you too."

The hardest thing about Liam is that when he says, "I love you," I can't tell whether that's a lie too.

CHAPTER 21

Transcript of police interview with Eleanor Williams.

PD: "How do you know Liam Cass, Ms. Williams?"

EW: "I was his second-grade teacher."

PD: "You were his teacher for the entire year?"

EW: "That's right."

PD: "And what did you think of Liam?"

EW: "Well, at the beginning of the year, he was one of my favorite students. Maybe my *favorite*. Second graders...they don't have a great attention span. They get easily distracted or silly, and I have to redirect them. But Liam wasn't like that. He was always well behaved, even when the other kids were messing around. And he always finished his assignments first. He understood *everything*. His homework was immaculate. And on top of that, he was very polite. He was also just a really cute kid. Like the kind you'd see in a commercial."

PD: "How did the other children interact with him?"

EW: "For the most part, they all liked him a lot. He was only seven years old, but he was very charming. Almost too charming, if you know what I mean. Like he was putting on an act. That's unusual for a seven-year-old. Usually with kids that age, what you see is what you get."

PD: "So what happened during the year to change your opinion of him?"

EW: "Well, like I said, Liam was an exceptionally well-behaved child. But sometimes he would say the most disturbing things. He had this sweet face, and when he said something like that..."

PD: "Like what?"

EW: "Um, well, it's hard to remember so long ago, but there was one thing he said that stood out to me. And that's why I called you."

PD: "What's that?"

EW: "We were doing a unit about families and marriage and all that. And Liam raised his hand and said that he couldn't wait to get married."

PD: "That doesn't sound so bad."

EW: "He said he couldn't wait to get married so he could stuff his wife deep in a hole and never let her out."

PD: "..."

EW: "Exactly."

PD: "Did you do anything about all those statements he was making?"

EW: "I contacted his parents, of course. I didn't take it to the level of the principal, because it didn't seem frequent enough, and he wasn't disrupting the class in any way."

PD: "So you spoke to his parents?"

EW: "Just his mother. His father was away on business and couldn't make it for the meeting."

PD: "And what did Mrs. Cass say when you talked to her?"

EW: "She was horrified, of course. I told her I thought Liam would benefit from some sort of psychological therapy, and she agreed. She said she was going to find a child therapist as quickly as she could. But the weird thing was..."

PD: "Yes?"

EW: "She was horrified, but she didn't seem *surprised*. Not really. Not the way you'd think she should've been."

PD: "And why do you think that is?"

EW: "I think she already knew Liam was having these thoughts. I mean, he must have said things to her over the years."

PD: "Do you know if she ever got him into therapy?"

EW: "She told me she did."

PD: "And did his behavior improve?"

EW: "If you're asking if he kept making those disturbing statements, the answer is no. He didn't. He never said anything like that again. But I always got the feeling..."

PD: "What?"

EW: "Well, like I said, Liam was a smart kid. I got the sense that the only reason he stopped saying those things was because he realized he shouldn't say them out loud anymore. I don't think he stopped having those thoughts though. But of course, it's impossible to know."

PD: "Yes, that's true."

EW: "I hope I did the right thing calling you. I wasn't sure if I should, but after I read what happened to that Mercer girl and remembered Liam was in the same grade...well, I just thought I should say something."

PD: "No, it's good you did."

EW: "I really hope you find her."

PD: "We do too."

CHAPTER 22

ERIKA

I'm jumping to conclusions.

Just because a girl went missing and Liam happened to be out last night doesn't mean my son had anything to do with it. Just because her name is Olivia doesn't mean she was the girl Liam was interested in. Olivia Reynolds was the girl Liam was talking to at the debate. I confirmed it was her based on her Facebook profile. This is another, completely unrelated Olivia.

I'm panicking over nothing. This is going to be okay.

I pull over on a side street shortly after the kids get out of the car and take out my phone. I do a search for "missing high school student" in our town, and the name Olivia and an article instantly pop up. Olivia Mercer, sixteen years old, disappeared from her bedroom during the night. Her mother went to wake her up for school and she wasn't there.

The police are considering the possibility that the girl has run away but think it's unlikely. All her clothes and luggage seemed to be present, and she also left behind her wallet and her cell phone. On the other hand, there were no signs of struggle or forced entry. Maybe she hadn't run away, but she had left the house of her own accord. With somebody she knew.

There is a color photograph of Olivia Mercer in one of the articles. She's not quite beautiful, but she's undeniably cute. Round face, lots of freckles, a little dimple on each cheek when she smiles. She looks like a sweet girl. The kind of girl you can't help but like.

I read about ten articles on Olivia Mercer's disappearance, but after the first three, they all repeat the same information. I refresh, hoping to discover a new article about how she was miraculously found.

But no. Olivia Mercer is still missing.

I want to go home and hide under the covers, but we need groceries. Unfortunately, the grocery store near the school will be teeming with parents wanting nothing more than to gossip about poor Olivia's disappearance. I don't want to talk about it. I don't even want to *think* about it.

There's another grocery store that recently opened up about twenty minutes away. I won't run into any parents there. It's worth burning the extra gas. Maybe driving will clear my head.

I bring up the GPS in the car to lead me to the grocery store. But as I start to type in the name of the store, the GPS brings up a list of recent searches, including one address that is unfamiliar to me. The last search on the list is 41 Green Street.

When was I searching for *that* address? Who lives there?

On a whim, I click on it. The British-accented voice of my GPS instructs me to drive straight and then make a right at the next light. I follow the directions, making a right at the light, followed by a left, and another right onto Green Street. I drive down the street, watching the numbers on the right side, which are the odd-numbered houses. I'm looking out for number 41.

It's not hard to find. It's the house that has all the police officers and reporters in front. This house is clearly of interest today.

I don't even need to check the mailbox, but I look anyway, just to torture myself. The black letters written on the gray box are like a punch in the gut:

MERCER

I turn the corner and pull over onto an empty street. I sit in my parked car for fifteen minutes, my hands shaking too badly to drive. Liam went out last night. He took my car. And he drove here. To the home of the girl who is now missing. Possibly dead.

I reach into my purse and pull out my phone, but my hands are shaking so much that I nearly drop it. I barely manage to press the button for Jason's phone number. Thank God, he picks up. Jason gets very involved with his work, and we have an agreement that I'll only bother him for level-two or worse emergencies. I think this counts.

"Erika?"

"Hey." My voice cracks, and I clear my throat. "Jason, we need to talk."

"Jesus, what's wrong? Are you okay?"

"There's a girl from the high school that's missing."

I suppress a sob. "She wasn't in her bed this morning when her parents came into the room. And Liam... I think when he went out last night, he took my car and went to see her. Her address is in the car GPS. And now she's missing. She's *gone*, Jason. Vanished!"

"Wait..." Jason is quiet for a moment. "You're saying he took the car out himself—without me?" His voice rises a notch. "That's not okay! He only has a learner's permit."

"*That* is what you're getting out of this? Jason, do you understand what I'm saying?"

"I...I guess not?"

I take a deep breath. "This girl is missing. Somebody took her, and Liam might be the last person to see her alive."

"So he should call the police and tell them what he knows so they can find out who did this."

My hands are still shaking, but now it's with anger. How could Jason be this dense? Maybe he's not around much, but he knows the stories about Liam as well as I do. And no, he doesn't believe there's anything wrong with our son. But he has to realize how this looks.

"Wait." Jason's voice breaks into my thoughts. "Are you saying you think Liam has something to do with her disappearance?"

"Yes, that's obviously what I'm saying!"

"Jesus Christ, Erika. Are you serious? You really think Liam would..."

"You know what I think."

"He wouldn't. This is our kid we're talking about."

"Right."

I hear shuffling on the other line. "Do you want me to come home?"

I let out a sigh. "No. There's nothing for you to do. Not yet anyway."

"Liam did not do this," Jason says with more conviction than I feel. "She probably just ran away and will turn up in a day or two."

God, I hope he's right. Because the alternative is too horrible to imagine.

CHAPTER 23

ERIKA

When I get home, there's a white Lincoln Continental in our driveway. I recognize it immediately as my mother's car. She's the last person I feel like talking to right now, but it looks like she's already used her key to get inside and is likely brewing herself a nice hot cup of coffee.

Even though my mother lives all the way in New Jersey, she's currently retired and single, so she doesn't think much of driving out to see us on a whim, without checking if it's okay. Amazingly, Jason doesn't seem bothered by it. His own mother died from breast cancer when he was in college, and his father passed away only a year later from a heart attack. ("He died of a broken heart," Jason told me.) So he likes having the kids' only grandparent around. I like having her here, but I wish she'd call.

Still, I have nowhere else to go. So it looks like I have to deal with whatever she wants.

As soon as I enter the house, I hear her clanging around in the kitchen. My mother loves the kitchen. She's always buying us some new gadget to use in there. The last thing she got me was an instant pot last month. She spent twenty minutes raving about all the great stuff she could cook with it. Since then, it's been collecting dust in the corner of my kitchen. I know that thing makes great soup, but I don't *like* soup.

"Erika!" Sure enough, my mother is fiddling with our coffee machine. She's the one who bought it for us, along with a year's supply of coffee pods. Her gray hair is gathered into a bun, and she has her tortoiseshell glasses perched on her nose. "I've been waiting for you for half an hour! Is everything okay?"

I don't even know how to begin to answer that question. My mother and I are close—she's the first person I told when Jason popped the question—but I never shared my fears about Liam with her. What can I say? He was her first grandchild—her only grandson. I couldn't bring myself to tell her he was anything less than the perfect little angel she believed him to be. Liam is always oozing with charm around my mother. She can't see through him the way I do.

"Everything is fine," I choke out.

Mom picks up her cup of coffee. She has selected one of the mugs with four-year-old Liam's face on it. He looks so cute in that picture—there are freckles across his nose, and he's missing one of his front teeth. But all I can think about is how that was the year I first started to realize what he was really like.

"I heard about that girl who disappeared," she says. "How terrifying. I'm surprised you let Hannah out of the house."

I clear my throat. "I'm sure she'll turn up."

"That's the worst thing about having daughters," she

says. "You're always worried about stuff like that. With Liam, you don't need to worry."

I think about the map that popped up in my car. The gap of time when he was gone last night. It's got to be a coincidence.

Please, God, let this girl have run away. Or anything that doesn't involve my son...

I plop down on the sofa, too upset to attempt to do anything else. My mother joins me with her coffee cup. The sofa shifts as she sits beside me.

"Listen, Erika," she says quietly, "I have to tell you, this isn't a social call. There's something I need to tell you. And...it's...it's not going to be easy."

I sit up straight. What does she want to tell me? Does my mother have cancer? Is that how the rest of this horrible day is going to unfold? I feel like I'm going to throw up. "What's wrong?"

She lowers her eyes. "You're going to hate me."

I look at my mother's face. Even though the wrinkles weren't there when I was a child, she still looks the same to me somehow. She's the same brave woman who raised me all by herself after my father was hit by a car and killed. She didn't date at all during my childhood because she said she wanted to focus on me. It's only in the last ten years that she's started to have occasional flings and travel. I can't imagine what sort of thing she could possibly say that would make me hate her.

"What's wrong, Mom?"

"I haven't..." She heaves a sigh and looks out the window. "I haven't been entirely honest with you, Erika. There are things you don't know. Things I have to tell you now, before you find out on your own."

She's really beginning to scare me. "Well, what is it?"

"It's…it's about your father."

"My father?" I conjure up the image of a handsome man with dark hair and dark eyes in the one photograph I keep in my bedside drawer. My memories of him are patchy at best. I remember the scratchiness of his face and the smell of cigarette smoke that used to cling to him. He died when I was not quite four years old, so he never lived to see me grow up. He never lived to see the grandson who looks more like him every single day. "What about my father?"

"The truth is…" My mother's hand trembles slightly on the handle of the coffee mug. She puts it down on the coffee table, ignoring the coaster a mere inch away from where she put the cup. On any other day, this would grind on my nerves. But today, I couldn't care less. "The truth is that your father isn't… He's actually…"

"What?"

"He's alive."

"*What?*"

Two minutes earlier, I had thought there was nothing that could ever make me hate my mother. But now I'm beginning to think maybe there is. My father is *alive*? How could that be? And how could she make me think he was dead for all those years? Daddy was in a car accident. I had accepted her word blindly for over forty years.

"I'm so sorry, honey," she breathes. "I wanted to tell you earlier, but there's no easy way to say something like that."

"How about not lying in the first place?" I grit my teeth. "Why would you tell me he was dead? What happened? Did he run off with another woman?"

I suppose that could make some sort of sense. Maybe my father ran off with some tramp, and in her anger, Mom pretended he was dead instead of a deadbeat. I still don't know if I could forgive her for lying about it for forty years, but maybe I could try.

"No," she says. "He didn't."

I fold my arms across my chest. Am I going to have to pull the story out of her? "Then what happened exactly? Where has he been for the last forty-two years?"

Mom looks down at her wrinkled hands in her lap. "He's been in prison. For first-degree murder."

CHAPTER 24

ERIKA

Everything my mother says is another punch in the gut.

My father is alive.

Punch.

My father has been in prison for over forty years.

Punch.

My father is a murderer.

Punch. Punch.

I don't even know what to say. I stare ahead at the wall, my heart jumping around in my chest. This has been the most stressful morning of my entire life. At this point, my day is going to end with me in the hospital with a stroke.

"You can see why I didn't want to tell you," Mom says, her words coming out quickly. "I thought it would be traumatic for you. And if it got out, the other kids might tease you."

"What…" I start my sentence, but my voice sounds strangled. Ugh, poor choice of words. "What did he do?"

"Well, he killed someone."

"Yes, I gathered that. Who did he kill?" And *why*?

My mother frowns. I can tell she doesn't want to tell the story, but that's too bad. She's kept this secret from me long enough. I deserve to know. "It was a woman," she says. "A woman he was having an affair with."

"Why did he kill her?"

"He claimed it was an accident. He didn't mean to kill her—that's what he said." The lines on her face deepen. "But his story didn't make sense. And obviously the jury didn't believe it. They thought he planned the whole thing."

Maybe he just wanted to see her suffer. Maybe he just wanted to see her scream.

"Do you think he planned it?" I manage.

Mom is quiet for a moment. "Yes, I believe he did. She was threatening to expose the affair, so he killed her."

"How…" I close my eyes for a moment, imagining my father throwing this mystery woman into a dark hole so she couldn't escape. "How did he do it?"

"He poisoned her."

I feel that tightness in my chest, the same as I did last night when I discovered Liam was gone. I'm on the verge of another panic attack—my second in two days. I take a deep breath, trying to calm myself down.

"Why are you telling me this now?" I ask. "After all these years, why tell me now?" And why *today*?

"Because…" She bites down hard on her lower lip. "I just found out. Your father got parole. He's out of prison."

"He's…"

"And I thought he might come looking for you," she says. "So…I wanted you to be prepared for that. If you want to see him. Or not."

116

"Right."

Today of all days, this is too much for me to take in. My father is alive and he's a murderer. He poisoned a woman. And, oh yeah, he's out of jail and might come looking for me.

"I think…" I take a deep breath. "I think I need to be alone right now."

"Of course." My mother squeezes the fabric of her skirt in her fists. "Do you hate me?"

"No. I don't hate you."

You just have the worst timing in the world.

Mom leans forward and throws her arms around my shoulders. There was a time in my life when a hug from my mother made everything right. But that time has long since passed.

I walk her to the door and stand by the window to make sure she drives away. But even after she's gone, I don't budge from the window. I stare out into my neighborhood, thinking about everything that's happened today. A girl has disappeared, and Liam may be somehow responsible. My father is alive and has been in prison for murder.

There's nothing I can do about the former, but there's something I can do about the latter. For all these years, I thought about what it might be like if my father had lived. I thought about the conversations we would have had, him standing proudly at my graduation, shaking his head when he didn't approve of one of my boyfriends, going fishing together out on the lake. And all along, he's been alive—albeit in no position to take me fishing.

And he might look for me.

Of course, I don't have to wait for him to look for me.

I could look for him. I bet Frank could track him down in five minutes flat. After all these years, I could lay eyes on my father. The man I believed to be long dead.

Then my eyes settle on my Toyota 4Runner in the driveway. The car Liam took last night to Olivia Mercer's house and then lied about.

My father is going to have to wait. I have much worse problems.

CHAPTER 25

OLIVIA

I wake up, and everything is black.

Where am I? What's going on?

I clutch my face, pushing away a throbbing sensation in my forehead, right between my eyes. How did I get here? The last thing I remember is…

Hop in the car. Just for a few minutes.

No. No, he didn't. He wouldn't.

Oh my God. I think I'm going to be sick.

I retch, but my stomach is empty and nothing comes out. I swallow, doubled over on the ground. I blink a few times, trying to adjust to the blackness, hoping the world will jump into some sort of focus, but it doesn't happen.

I can't even see my hand in front of my face. I can't see where I am or one foot in front of me.

Why can't I see?

Oh my God, have I gone blind?

But no. When I look up, there's a tiny slice of light in

the distance. There is nothing wrong with my eyes. There is simply no light wherever I am.

My head is swimming, which makes it that much harder to get my bearings. The ground is moist and grainy. Dirt? It's so hard to tell. I sit up and reach out into the distance, feeling for something—anything. My fingers finally touch something solid. It's the same consistency as the ground. Also dirt.

I think I'm in a hole.

Oh God. Oh God. I'm in a hole. I'm in a hole in the ground.

My fingers start to tingle as my panic mounts. I'm not claustrophobic, but it feels like...like I've been buried alive. One minute, I was kissing Liam, one of the best moments of my life, and now I wake up here.

Why?

I've got to get out of here. There must be a way out. There's *got* to be.

There is that slice of light above me—a way out. If I could reach it, maybe I could climb out. I get to my feet, but that's when I become aware of another sensation. *Pain*. Agonizing, brutal pain in my left ankle. So severe that I immediately collapse back down into the dirt.

What is *wrong* with me?

I pull up the leg of my jeans to feel my left ankle. It's swollen. *Really* swollen. And warm. And even touching it gently sets off a wave of unbearable pain. My guess is that when I was thrown into this hole, the fall broke my ankle. Or at least hurt it really badly.

So I can't put weight on my ankle. But I can still try to stand. This time, I put my weight against the dirt wall, which collapses slightly under the pressure. It still hurts like hell, but I manage to get to my feet, or at least my foot. I stretch out my arm, feeling for something above that I can grab on to.

My fingers fall short. I can't reach it.

Oh my God, I'm trapped here.

When he put me down here, he knew what he was doing. He knew it would be hard to escape. My only chance is if somebody comes to rescue me.

"Help!" I scream at the top of my lungs. "Help! Help me! I'm trapped!" Nothing.

I scream until my voice is hoarse and my throat is raw. But I hear nothing. No footsteps. No sound. God knows where I am. Out in the wilderness? Below his soundproof basement?

But it's clear nobody is coming for me anytime soon. Not here.

I collapse against the dirt wall. My throat is parched. I don't remember when I last had anything to drink or eat. A day? If he's planning on trapping me here, will he at least give me something to drink? He will, won't he? Otherwise, I'll die, and I'll be no good to him for whatever he wants.

I hope he brings me food. What will I do if he doesn't?

He hasn't raped me. Even though there's a gap in my memory, somehow I feel certain of this. If he had, I would know it. Right? I'm still a virgin, so I'm sure I'd feel sore if he had done that to me. That's what Madison said anyway. My jeans are still buttoned and zipped, and nothing is ripped or torn. I'm intact, except for my damn ankle.

God, why didn't I listen to Madison when she warned me about Liam?

Maybe he left me some water. Maybe there's a whole

thermos of it somewhere. I need to feel around this space and get my bearings. If there's any chance of trying to escape from here, I've got to figure out what I'm dealing with. After all, women escape from being kidnapped all the time. I've read articles about it. They use their moxie or intelligence or whatever, and they find a way out.

Or else they don't. And years later, their body is discovered half-buried in the woods by some hikers.

Oh my God, I'm going to be sick again.

I double over, retching on the dirt ground. Once again, nothing comes up. I retch hard enough that tears fill my eyes. And then, before I know it, the tears are streaming down my cheeks.

I'm trapped here. He trapped me.

I want to go home. I want my mom.

Please...

CHAPTER 26

ERIKA

Dinner is a very subdued affair.

Jason managed to make it home early tonight, which is something he doesn't get to do very often. Usually when he gets home early, I make a big deal of it and cook something special, but not tonight. Tonight, we're eating Kraft macaroni and cheese. And anybody who says a damn word about it will have their plate yanked away from them and hurled into the garbage.

Not that anyone will care. Both Hannah and Liam have barely eaten anything. Both of them are just pushing the little pieces of macaroni around their plates. Liam has barely said a word since he got home hours ago.

"I'm sorry about dinner," I feel compelled to say.

"What are you talking about?" Jason says. "I love macaroni and cheese. It tastes really *Gouda*."

Hannah comes alive long enough to groan. She can't resist complaining about Jason's puns. "It's not *Gouda*, Dad. It's that powder stuff that comes out of a package."

"Yes, I realize that, Hannah. Geez, I'm just trying to lighten the mood."

"Well, it's not helping," she says.

Jason gives me a look, then he reaches out and grabs her wrist. "Hey. No phones at the dinner table. You know that."

Wow, Hannah is sneakier than I thought. I didn't even realize she had her phone under the table. She obligingly places it in Jason's outstretched hand. She leans back in her chair, pouting. "I just wanted to see if they found Olivia."

My heart leaps. "Did they?"

Hannah hesitates. "I don't think so."

I look over at Liam, who is staring down at his dinner plate. I haven't asked him about what I found in the GPS yet. I'm afraid to. Because it's hard to think of any explanation that won't make him look really bad. All I know is that he lied to my face this morning and I couldn't even tell.

"She was in your year, right, Liam?" Jason asks.

"I guess. I didn't really know her."

Then why were you going to her house last night? At two in the morning?

The doorbell rings, which is a relief, because I wasn't doing much better at eating my macaroni and cheese than the kids were. That relief lasts only until I look through the peephole and see the two uniformed police officers standing at our door.

Oh God. I think I'm going to have another panic attack.

I take two deep breaths before I unlock the door. I plaster a smile on my face that I feel looks very genuine. Maybe Liam is rubbing off on me.

One of the police officers is a man in his late thirties with ruddy cheeks and a gut that's straining against his uniform. The other officer is a thin woman. She looks of Hispanic descent, with sharp black eyes, high cheekbones, and hair pulled back into a severe bun.

"Hello there," the male officer says in a thick Long Island accent. "Does Liam Cass live here?"

Oh no. No no no no…

"Yes," I manage. "He's my son."

The female officer flashes a smile that doesn't touch her eyes. "My name is Detective Rivera, and this is Detective Murphy. We were hoping to ask Liam a few questions. Is he home?"

"Yes?" I say, although I'm not sure why it comes out like a question. I clear my throat. "He's just eating dinner."

"Would you please interrupt him?" Rivera says.

The phony smile has disappeared from her face.

"Um…" I glance in the direction of the dining room. Jason has come out to see what's going on, and his eyes fly open at the sight of the police officers. "Does he need a lawyer?"

Maybe I shouldn't have asked that. That sounds super guilty. And we don't know for sure Liam did anything. After all, he's a sixteen-year-old kid.

"No, that shouldn't be necessary," Rivera says. She seems to be the spokesperson. "We just have a few quick questions."

"What's this about?" Jason speaks up.

"We're just trying to get some information about the girl who disappeared this morning," Rivera says. "We're speaking with some of her classmates who might be able to help us. We just want to find Olivia."

"Well, Liam says he doesn't know her." Jason folds his arms across his chest. "So I think you might be wasting your time here."

Detective Murphy flashes Jason a disarming smile. "Then this will be real quick. We just want to make sure. A girl's life is at stake, Mr. Cass. We need to do everything we can to find her."

"I'll go get him," I say. I hurry out to the dining room, where Liam and Hannah haven't moved, but Hannah is straining to see what's going on. I put my hand on Liam's shoulder, and he flinches at my touch. "There are a couple of officers out there who want to ask you some questions."

Hannah's eyes darken. "Shouldn't he have a lawyer? Aren't you supposed to have a lawyer present if you're being questioned by the police?"

It disturbs me how quickly Hannah—Liam's sole confidante—came to that conclusion. I shake my head. "They say they have a few quick questions. Just tell them the truth, Liam."

"All right." Liam gets to his feet. "I'll talk to them."

Hannah's eyes widen, but she doesn't say a word.

When I return to the living room, the two officers are sitting on our love seat, while Jason is on the couch. He's talking to the officers, but he doesn't look nervous or anything. He doesn't look like he's going to throw up any second, which is the way I feel. He truly believes Liam has nothing to hide.

Liam sits down beside Jason on the couch, sitting up straight as he always does. He doesn't look nervous either. He doesn't fiddle with the hem of his shirt or the hole in his jeans. His hands are completely steady, and he flashes the officers a brief, disarming smile. It almost makes me wonder if I'm worried over nothing. If Liam can look that calm around two cops, he must have nothing to hide.

"Liam?" Detective Rivera says.

Liam nods. "Yes."

"Would you mind answering a few questions for us about Olivia Mercer?" she asks.

"I already talked to a police officer at school," he says. "I told him everything I know."

"Yes, but we have a few more questions. Just routine stuff."

"Of course." Liam looks her straight in the eyes. "I'll do anything to help find Olivia. Please go ahead."

Rivera crosses her legs as she leans forward slightly. "Do you know Olivia Mercer?"

"Yes. She goes to my school."

"And are you friendly with her?"

He doesn't hesitate. "She's in my math class. I've spoken to her before."

His answers sound rehearsed. As if he knew what they were going to be asking him and had mentally prepared for it the same way he prepares for his debates. I wonder if they notice.

"Is Olivia your girlfriend?"

"No."

Rivera raises an eyebrow. "No?"

"I don't have a girlfriend."

Rivera lets out a laugh. "A good-looking boy like you? That's hard to believe."

"He's only sixteen, Detective," I say.

"When I was sixteen, I had two girlfriends!" Murphy says. His ruddy cheeks grow pinker.

Liam doesn't react to any of this. He flashes a brief smile but says nothing.

The smile vanishes from Rivera's face again. Her eyes are so sharp it scares me. I want to tell Liam to be careful, that she isn't going to be taken in by his charm. "So, Liam, when was the last time you saw Olivia?"

"Some of the people from track team were hanging out at Charlie's. She was there too."

"Was it a date?"

"No."

"I see." Rivera nods. "And that's the last time you saw Olivia?"

"Yes."

"Do you have any idea at all where she could be right now?"

"No," he says without hesitation. "I'm really sorry. I wish I did." And then, in an incredibly sincere voice, "I'm worried about her. I really hope she's okay."

"We do too," Rivera says.

And then it looks like they're about to get up and maybe this is over. Maybe they have absolutely nothing on Liam and he was telling the truth when he said he barely knew Olivia. Maybe they're just going around and questioning everyone in the school. Maybe this is nothing but routine.

But then, just as she's about to get up, Rivera sits back down again like she thought of something she had forgotten. "One more thing, Liam," she says.

"Yes?"

"One of Olivia Mercer's neighbors saw her in her backyard at around two in the morning, talking to a teenage boy."

My stomach sinks. This isn't over after all.

"Do you know who that boy was, Liam?" Rivera asks.

He doesn't answer, but his body stiffens almost imperceptibly.

Rivera smiles grimly. "After some of your friends told us you had brought Olivia to that diner yesterday, we showed the neighbor a few of your school photographs. And guess what? She was able to correctly identify you. She was also able to identify the Toyota that is now out in your driveway."

Liam's fists grab handfuls of the fabric of his jeans, but he quickly regains his composure.

Rivera leans in and looks him straight in the eyes. "Would you like to revise your answer about when the last time you saw Olivia Mercer was?"

Liam opens his mouth like he's about to answer, but before he does, Jason jumps up from the sofa. "No! No more questions. Not without a lawyer."

"We're just trying to find the whereabouts of a sixteen-year-old girl, Mr. Cass," Rivera says flatly. She looks at Liam. "Liam, if you can tell us where she is—"

"Liam, don't answer them." Jason glares at Rivera, a vein standing out in his neck. "This is a sixteen-year-old boy. He's a great student and a great kid. He did *not* do this."

"With all due respect, Mr. Cass—"

"No, you listen to me." Jason points a finger at them. I'm not sure I've ever seen him this upset. Even during the times I was most freaked out about Liam, he always seemed so calm. If I wasn't so panicked myself, I would think it was a little bit sexy the way he's protecting Liam. "My son has told you everything he knows. If you want to speak to him again, it will be with our attorney present."

Rivera rises from the love seat, and Murphy follows. "As you wish, Mr. Cass."

It isn't until the officers are gone that I feel like I can breathe normally again. Of course, this whole thing was a disaster. It is now confirmed: Liam was visiting Olivia Mercer last night. He was probably the last person to see her alive. And he lied about it to the police.

"What the hell, Liam?" Jason snaps at him.

Liam had been maintaining excellent eye contact while the officers were here, but he finally drops his eyes. The mask of affability he usually wears is gone, and he looks miserable. I almost feel sorry for him.

"Liam," I say quietly as I sit down beside my son, "do you know where Olivia is?"

He shakes his head. Lying again. I wish Jason hadn't stopped the officers from questioning him. I wish they had done their police thing and wormed the answer out of him.

"But you were at her house last night?" Jason prompts him.

Liam's Adam's apple bobs as he swallows. "Yes. I was there. Okay?"

"You took my car?" I ask.

"Yes. I'm sorry."

Jason runs a hand through his graying hair. I think he got ten new gray strands in the last twenty minutes. Of course, if not for my hairdresser, I'd be all gray now, thanks to my son. "What were you doing there?" he asks.

"I just…" Liam squirms on the sofa. "I like her, okay? I wanted to see her. And she came down and…you know…"

Jason frowns at him. "No, I *don't* know."

Liam's ears turn pink. "We made out a little. That's all."

"And then?"

"And then Mom called, so I came home. And that's it."

Jason narrows his eyes at Liam, but I can tell he believes the story. He was genuine in what he told the police officers. He does not believe his teenage son could possibly be responsible for the disappearance of a young girl. He knows Liam is capable of lying, but he doesn't know what else our son is capable of. Only I know the truth.

"Go to your room," Jason says to Liam.

Liam doesn't need to be told twice. He jumps off the sofa and scrambles up the stairs. I wish we could keep questioning him, but it won't make a difference. Whatever else he knows, he's told us all he's going to.

Jason drops his head back against the sofa and lets out a long sigh. "We have to get him a lawyer, Erika. This doesn't look good for him."

"Yes." I chew on my lip. "It's kind of a big coincidence though, don't you think?"

"What do you mean?"

"I mean, he just *happened* to be around this girl's house on the night she disappeared? Do you really believe that?"

He frowns. "What are you saying?"

"You know what I'm saying."

"What? You're saying you think our son murdered this girl? Really, Erika?"

"Maybe not murdered…"

I wish I had a wife so I could keep her deep in a hole. I can still hear Miss Williams's words in my ear. Liam said a lot of disturbing things, but that one was way up there. That was one of the ones I won't forget. Or his answer when I asked him about it later that night:

I'd just like to see what would happen to her, Mommy. If I put her in a hole and didn't feed her, what would happen? And if she were my wife, I could do what I wanted and no one would even look for her.

That was the day I made our first appointment with Dr. Hebert.

"You know the kind of comments Liam has made in the past," I remind Jason.

"You've always made too much of that. He's precocious. It's just words."

"It's not *just* words."

Jason blinks at me. "I can't...I can't have this conversation with you, Erika. This is our *child* we're talking about. He didn't do it. And I'm not going to let them pin it on him."

"Fine," I say. "Get him a lawyer."

Jason spends the rest of the night looking up criminal attorneys. He's convinced that a good lawyer can make this problem go away. But I know he's wrong. The only one who can make this go away is Liam.

CHAPTER 27

OLIVIA

I don't know how long I stay crouched in a little ball on the ground, sobbing my eyes out.

When I'm done, my eyes are raw and my face feels puffy. There's dried snot on my cheeks and hands. But that's the least of my problems.

I can't sit here feeling sorry for myself. If I don't want to die here, I've got to do something. I've got to figure out a way to escape. Or at least figure out a way to survive until I'm rescued.

I've got to be smart. It's the only way.

I feel along the ground, hoping to locate something that might give me a clue as to where I am or how to get free. I have to crawl, because my ankle hurts far too much to put any weight on it. It's definitely got to be broken. Even when I'm not putting weight on it, it throbs intensely.

I discover another wall across from me. I would guess this hole is about four feet by four feet. Maybe six or seven feet deep. Not very big. I wonder if he dug it himself. It would've taken him a long time if he did. I remember reading that book *Holes* when I was in ninth grade. It was about some kid who had to dig holes as part of a punishment. It was pretty good, as I remember. I think they made it into a movie.

In the third corner I check, my heart leaps when my fingers close around a tiny thermos. I pick it up, and it makes a noise when I shake it. There's liquid inside! I fumble with the cover, desperately trying to open it, even though I can't see a thing. If I spill this thermos, I'm toast. It's not much water, but I want it more than anything I've ever wanted in my life. Even more than I wanted Liam to kiss me when we were at the diner.

I hear a pop, and my fingers make contact with a straw sticking out of the container. I put my lips on the straw and take a sip. Oh my God, it's heavenly. Even though it has a slight metallic aftertaste, it's the best thing I've ever tasted. The water is cold in my mouth and my parched throat and my empty stomach. I want to guzzle the whole thing, but at the same time, I'm not sure when I'll get more. I should save it. Ration it. That's what a survivor would do.

I reluctantly close the top and gingerly put it back in the corner, now half empty. I'm not going to drink more until I feel really desperate. I need to know what the situation is. Will he come back? Will he give me more water? Food?

With the water tucked away, I explore the final corner of the hole. This corner isn't empty either. I feel something there, something long and smooth. My fingers close around it. I squint as hard as I can, desperate to see something. Anything. But it's too dark.

I keep feeling around, and I realize there are more objects in this corner. They have a similar feel and consistency. Sharp or round edges. Mostly long and thin.

Then I come across something that feels a little different. It's round, roughly the size of a melon. But it's not a sphere. As my fingers round the curve, I feel two large holes. My chest tightens as I realize what I'm touching.

It's a skull.

I can't stop screaming, even though nobody can hear me.

CHAPTER 28

Transcript of police interview with Dr. Alice Hebert.

PD: "Thank you so much for speaking with us today, Dr. Hebert."

AH: "I thought it was my obligation to do so."

PD: "Can you state for the record your profession?"

AH: "I am a child psychologist. I've been in private practice for the past twenty-three years."

PD: "So I guess you've seen it all then?"

AH: "Just about, yes."

PD: "And what made you come forward?"

AH: "When I found out a young girl's life was in danger, I felt it was my moral obligation to say something. To save her life. Even if it meant breaking patient confidentiality."

PD: "That's the reason we were so eager to speak with you today. We don't know how much time Olivia has left. We're desperate to find her."

AH: "I understand. I'll do what I can."

PD: "Based on the fact that you're willing to speak with us about confidential issues, I assume you believe Liam Cass is responsible?"

AH: "Obviously I can't say for sure. It's been many years since I treated Liam. But...yes, I believe he's capable of this."

PD: "When did you start treating Liam?"

AH: "When he was seven years old. His mother brought him to me because of several disturbing statements he made in class and at home."

PD: "What kind of statements?"

AH: "More than once, he mentioned the idea of wanting to trap a girl and watch her starve to death. He actually did play this out once when he was in kindergarten. He duct-taped a girl in a closet."

PD: "I spoke to the principal at the school, and she told me about that incident in the closet."

AH: "It was very disturbing, obviously, and his mother was quite upset over everything."

PD: "What about the father?"

AH: "I only met him once. He had a very busy job in the city, and he seemed to think we were making a big deal out of nothing. He didn't get it. But the mother was almost hysterical. We had a session without Liam, and she ran down a list of things he had done that had scared her."

PD: "Such as?"

AH: "Liam was, in many ways, mature for his age. He was very responsible. For that reason, Mrs. Cass was persuaded by him to purchase a pet hamster.

Unfortunately, the first hamster allegedly escaped, and she had to buy him another. Liam told her the second hamster escaped as well, but then she caught him burying it in the backyard."

PD: "Was the hamster dead?"

AH: "Yes, but Liam finally admitted that he was the one who killed the hamster. He let it slowly starve to death."

PD: "Jesus."

AH: "Yes. It was quite upsetting. After a few months, it was very clear Liam was suffering from antisocial personality disorder. Do you know what a sociopath is, Detective?"

PD: "That's the personality disorder when you don't feel emotions. Weren't Jeffrey Dahmer and Ted Bundy sociopaths?"

AH: "Most likely. As early as the 1800s, doctors who worked with mental health patients noticed some patients demonstrated outwardly normal behavior but had no sense of ethics or empathy. These patients were called 'psychopaths,' but then it was later changed to 'sociopaths' because of the effect these people had on society. Now both terms are used, but 'sociopath' generally refers to a milder form of the disorder. Psychopaths are much rarer."

PD: "So what does that all mean?"

AH: "Well, for starters, sociopaths don't have normal human emotions like empathy. They have no concern for the feelings of others. They also have a very high threshold for disgust, which has been measured by a lack of reaction in these patients to photos of mutilated faces. But sociopaths don't care about faking emotions. Psychopaths, on the other hand, are excellent actors. They're intelligent, charming, and fantastic at manipulating emotions. They can make you believe they care, when in fact they feel nothing."

PD: "So they're good liars."

AH: "They are pathological liars. They can tell the most outlandish stories without blinking an eye. And the other salient characteristic of sociopaths is a weak conscience. They feel very little guilt or shame or remorse. Psychopaths, on the other hand, have *no* conscience. Can you imagine what that's like? To feel no remorse whatsoever for your terrible actions?"

PD: "..."

AH: "On top of that, sociopaths have a very low tolerance for frustration or for discharge of aggression."

PD: "Meaning?"

AH: "It takes very little for them to become violent."

PD: "I see."

AH: "And they're fearless. When a normal person is put in a situation where they anticipate a painful stimulus, such as an electric shock, their sweat glands will increase in activity. But in psychopathic subjects, no skin conductance responses are emitted. They don't feel fear the way we do."

PD: "Right."

AH: "So if you put it together, Detective, you've got an individual who feels no empathy, no remorse, no fear, and who is prone to violence. It's not surprising so many serial killers are diagnosed as psychopaths."

PD: "So are you saying Liam Cass is a psychopath?"

AH: "It's hard to say. He was only nine years old the last time I saw him, and most of these personality disorders technically can't be diagnosed until eighteen. But..."

PD: "Yes?"

AH: "He was definitely a sociopath, but my gut feeling was that he was also a psychopath. Even at such a young age, he was an amazing liar and manipulator. But at the same time, when I first met him, my instinct was to like him. It took several sessions before I could see through him. And I am a professional."

PD: "So he's a serial killer?"

AH: "Be careful making that jump. Nearly all serial killers are likely psychopaths, but not all psychopaths become killers."

PD: "But you believe Liam is capable of murder?"

CHAPTER 29

ERIKA

Right after Jason and I finish loading the dishwasher, an alarm goes off on my iPhone. I pull it out of my pocket and look at the alert:

> PTA meeting at 7:30. Traffic is light. You should
> arrive in ten minutes.

Damn. That stupid PTA meeting is tonight. And I told Jessica I would go because I'm the one in charge of movie night, the most important event of the year.

"What's wrong?" Jason asks me.

"I was supposed to go to this PTA meeting tonight."

"The PTA?" He frowns. "Is this really a good time to get more involved in the PTA?"

"Jason…"

"Can't you skip it? Didn't you say you hate those things?"

"Yes, I did say that. And I *do*. But Jessica is counting on me to do movie night. And I feel like…maybe I shouldn't be antagonizing anyone now."

Jason gives me a look. "You really think you need to worry about what Jessica Martinson thinks of you?"

No. I shouldn't. But I still do. I've always longed for that woman's approval. "I won't stay for long. Okay?"

He shrugs. "Whatever you want, Erika. I'm going to go look up lawyers for Liam while you're organizing movie night or whatever it is you feel is more important than our son."

He's right. I shouldn't be organizing movie nights right now. If I'm in a position where I'm looking up attorneys for my sixteen-year-old son, my life is too complicated to be doing movie night. Maybe I'll talk to Jessica when I get there. I'll explain to her that I can't do movie night and that I'm sorry.

But then again, I don't want her to think I'm backing out because Liam is guilty of something.

I drive over to the school, and sure enough, traffic is light and it takes only ten minutes. I see the cars of all the other moms parked outside the school. Jessica's minivan is right by the entrance in the primo parking spot that she always seems to nab.

PTA meetings are held in the library on the second floor. I charge up the stairs, glancing down at my watch to find that I am now five minutes late somehow. The stupid iPhone didn't alert me soon enough. Oh well. I'll slip in the back, and it won't be a big deal. Jessica usually spends the first twenty minutes going over minutes from the last meeting anyway. These things are torture.

The door to the library creaks loudly when I push it open. I'm clearly the only latecomer, and everyone is already gathered around the conference table set up in the center of the room. Jessica is standing at the front, wearing a blue-and-white dress that looks fantastic on her. She always looks fantastic. Under any other circumstance, I might feel a twinge of jealousy, but that's the last thing I'm feeling right now.

I remember the first time I saw Jessica Martinson, back when the boys were in first grade. We had just moved to the town and were starting over after that awful incident in kindergarten. Jason thought I was being silly when I said we should move, but too many people knew what had happened. I could feel them whispering about me when I went to the supermarket. We had become pariahs there and needed a fresh start.

I showed up at a quarter to three that day to pick Liam up from first grade. Jessica was waiting as well and looked hopelessly glamorous, even in her T-shirt and yoga pants. She was surrounded by a group of women who were hanging on her every word. She loves being the center of attention—that hasn't changed. I watched them laughing at a joke Jessica had made, but I was too intimidated to try to approach them. I was never one of the popular kids back when I was in school, and I didn't expect that would change in adulthood.

It wasn't until Tyler and Liam came out of the school together that Jessica took a sudden interest in me. She walked over to me purposefully, a charming smile on her red lips. She was looking at me, but her eyes were on my son. "You must be Liam's mother. I'm Jessica—Tyler's mom."

"Erika," I said.

"Tyler talks about Liam nonstop," Jessica said, as if she was impressed.

"That's wonderful," I said, although in the back of my mind, I was hoping Liam didn't end up duct-taping him in a closet.

"Seems like the boys have gotten to be good friends." She looked down at Liam, who was standing patiently beside me with his SpongeBob SquarePants backpack on his shoulders while the other boys were running around everywhere. "Hi there, Liam. I'm Tyler's mother."

Liam held out his right hand, which Jessica accepted. "It's very nice to meet you," he recited.

Jessica laughed, utterly charmed by my son. "What fantastic manners. You trained him well, Erika!"

Amazingly, I hadn't trained him at all. Liam learned all on his own what to say to adults to make them love him.

After that day, Jessica was my best friend. Liam and Tyler had playdates once or twice a week, and we learned to count on each other if we had an emergency and needed someone to pick up our son from school. It wasn't until the end of grade school that this abruptly changed. The boys barely spoke to each other anymore. Jessica and I were still friendly but no longer friends. I never quite understood why.

And I have a feeling things are just going to get worse.

I try to slip into the library quietly, but as the door swings shut behind me, Jessica abruptly stops speaking. Everyone in the room turns to look at me.

"Oh, um, hi," I stammer.

"Erika!" she exclaims in a flat voice. "I didn't expect to see *you* here."

"Yes, I…I'm sorry I'm late."

Jessica's ice-blue eyes remain on my face. "No worries."

I slip around a few of the other mothers (and one lone

dad) to get to the only empty seat. Everyone in the room is staring at me. I thought nobody would be aware of Liam's connection to Olivia, but it's painfully obvious that's not the case. *Everybody* knows. Maybe they don't know the police were at our house tonight. Maybe they don't know Liam was at Olivia's house at two in the morning. But they know *something*.

Jessica clears her throat. "All right. Let's go back to reviewing the minutes."

I've always found PTA meetings to be a form of torture. Even though I love my kids, I just can't bear going through the planning of events for them for the entire year. I'm fine with planning one event, like movie night, although I'd rather just be a minion handing out movie tickets or pizza on the night in question. But Jessica and I go way back. If she needs my help, I have no choice but to offer it.

"We still need more volunteers for the book fair," Regina Knowles complains. "Nobody wants to do the cleanup. And that's when we need the most help."

Yes, the eternal problem. Everybody wants to help out at the events, but nobody wants to be on the cleanup crew.

"I'm sure we can find somebody to help with cleanup," Jessica says. Her eyes scan the room as several women try to look in other directions. "Rachel? Maria? Will you help out?"

Rachel Richter and Maria Sheldon look absolutely unenthused at the idea of cleaning up after the book fair. I've done it before, and it's an exhausting job to pack up all those books. We all know it. But Jessica stares them down, and they both nod an affirmative.

"Wonderful." Jessica claps her hands together. "Now

that we have book fair settled, let's talk about movie night." *Finally*. She looks over at Alicia Levine. "Alicia, I want to thank you so much for stepping up as chair of movie night."

What?

"Happy to help, Jess," Alicia says.

Is she joking with me? What's going on here?

I clear my throat and say as delicately as possible, "I'm sorry, Jessica, but didn't you ask me if I could be in charge of movie night?"

Jessica tucks an errant strand of blond hair behind her ear. "Yes, but I *know* how busy you are, Erika. And Alicia was *so* nice to step up. So...I'm letting you off the hook."

The room has gone silent again as everyone stares at me and Jessica. What she said was a bald-faced lie. She asked *me* to be in charge of movie night. And she changed her mind about it when she found out about Olivia.

She could have at least given me the courtesy of telling me in advance so I didn't waste my time driving out here when my son needs me at home.

And now the silence is broken by the sound of people whispering. I don't know what the hell they're saying, but I can only imagine. I want to yell at them that if they've got something to say about my kid, they can say it to my face. But I don't actually want that. I just want to go home.

I rise unsteadily to my feet. "I think maybe I'll just take off then."

"Feel free," Jessica says. "I *do* appreciate you offering to pitch in though, Erika. Honestly."

There have been times during my friendship with Jessica that I have wanted to slap her, but never so much as at this moment. But I'm capable of controlling my impulses. So I grab my purse and run out of the room before these women can see me cry.

CHAPTER 30

Transcript of police interview with Madison Hartman.

PD: "How long have you been friends with Olivia Mercer?"

MH: "Practically my whole life. We became friends on the first day of kindergarten. We were wearing the same dress, and we bonded over it."

PD: "So you're very close with her?"

MH: "Uh, yeah! We're best friends."

PD: "Did Olivia ever give you any indication she might run away?"

MH: "No. Never. Olivia would never run away. She wouldn't do that to her parents."

PD: "Did she do drugs or alcohol?"

MH: "Are you kidding me? Olivia was a good girl. One time, me and Aidan—that's my boyfriend— offered her a drink of some beer Aidan swiped from his dad's stash, and she wouldn't touch it."

PD: "If she were planning to run away, would she tell anyone about it?"

MH: "Yes! She would tell me. But she didn't run away. I'm telling you. There's no way. It was Liam. That bastard, Liam Cass."

PD: "You think Liam is the one responsible for her disappearance?"

MH: "I don't think he is. I *know* he is."

PD: "Why do you say that?"

MH: "Um, because Liam is a crazy person?"

PD: "Why do you think he's crazy?"

MH: "Okay, well, I wasn't totally sure before. I mean, there were rumors about him. Like, I went to a different middle school than he did, but people sometimes talked about that English teacher and what they thought he did to him. Some kids believe he did it, although I honestly didn't believe it until now. Do you guys know about that?"

PD: "Yes. We know."

MH: "I mean, mostly it was just a vibe I got from him. Obviously he's pretty cute, but he just seemed so phony. Like, a lot of girls thought he was really charming, but I just thought he was a fake."

PD: "How so?"

MH: "So here's an example. One day, I saw him messing around with some of his friends before first period, and then he was late for class. I had first period with him, and the teacher asked him why he was late. He told her his mom was driving him and she had a flat tire and that's why he was late."

PD: "A lot of kids tell lies."

MH: "Yeah, I know. I mean, I lie to teachers or my parents all the time. But they always seem like they sort of know that I'm lying. It's hard to tell a really good lie to an adult in a believable way. But Liam was so good at it. He looked right into the teacher's eyes and said it with a straight face, and the teacher didn't even suspect for a second. I would have believed it too if I didn't see him outside messing around, you know? And there was other stuff too."

PD: "Like what?"

MH: "Like I was at the athletic field after school because I was waiting for Aidan to finish football practice, and the track team guys had a meet. Liam was racing and he lost, and I could tell he was really pissed off about losing. He walked right up to this fence and kicked it so hard it broke. I was kind of shocked at how angry he seemed."

PD: "Did you tell that to Olivia?"

MH: "No."

PD: "Why not?"

MH: "Well, because last year, Aidan punched a wall and broke his hand, so I thought if I told her that story, she'd bring up the story about Aidan and act like it was no big deal or tell me I should break up with Aidan."

PD: "Olivia told you to break up with Aidan?"

MH: "Yes. I mean, not in a serious way. But she didn't like him."

PD: "Why not?"

MH: "I don't know. She thought he was a football player thug, but... What does this have to do with Liam?"

PD: "Has Aidan ever been violent toward you?"

MH: "No! Never! Aidan isn't perfect, but he's a good guy. Not like Liam."

PD: "Was Liam ever violent toward Olivia?"

MH: "No. He could be really nice when he wanted to be. That's what I'm saying—he was such a fake. And she was totally taken in by it. She was so into him...and she's not even like that. She doesn't get that into boys. He totally did a number on her."

PD: "Do you think he had any reason to hurt her?"

MH: "No. I mean, she already wanted to go out with him, and I bet she would've done just about anything for him."

PD: "So why are you so certain Liam is responsible for her disappearance?"

MH: "Because he's crazy! Crazy people don't need a reason to do something crazy, right?"

CHAPTER 31

ERIKA

When I get back home, Jason says Liam hasn't come out of his room since the cops left, so I decide to check on him. It's a relief when I knock on the door and he tells me to come in.

Strangely enough, I find him at his desk, hunched over one of his textbooks. He's reading and outlining the book, as if this was any other day. As if the police hadn't been here, only hours earlier, essentially accusing him of murder.

"Liam?"

He doesn't look up from his textbook. "Yes?"

"What are you doing?"

"Studying. I have a history test tomorrow."

"Could you stop for a few minutes? I'd like to speak with you."

If it were Hannah, she would have moaned about how I shouldn't interrupt her when she's trying to study, even though she gets distracted every five minutes by her phone when she's studying anyway. But Liam obediently turns away from his history book and looks up at me, blinking his brown eyes innocently.

"What is it, Mom?"

I take a deep breath. My hands are shaking, and I feel like I'm about to burst into tears. I remember back when Liam was younger and he used to see that psychotherapist. She used a term that I had contemplated but was afraid to ever say out loud: sociopath.

He doesn't feel empathy like you do. He doesn't feel love. He's just faking it.

As a mother, it was one of the worst things anybody has ever said to me. *Your son doesn't love you. He's not capable of it.* At the time, I refused to believe it. But as the years passed, I realized how true everything Dr. Hebert told me was.

"Where is she, Liam?" I ask. "Where is Olivia?"

He looks me straight in the eyes, the same way he did to the officers as he lied to their faces. "I don't know."

"Liam…" A tear escapes from my right eye, and I wipe it away before he can see it. Being vulnerable in front of a person who has no empathy is always a mistake. "The police know what they're doing. Whatever you've done… they're going to find out. If you tell me where she is, I can help you. I'll let her go. I can pretend I just stumbled onto her…" I take a shaky breath. "But if you kill her…"

"Mom." His lip juts out, which makes him look younger. "I swear to you. I didn't do anything to Olivia."

"I don't believe you, Liam."

His eyes darken. There are moments when I feel frightened of my son. Such as when I found him with that hamster when he was only six. He let it starve to death right in front of his eyes. The poor hamster was so withered, you could see all its little bones sticking out. You could tell it had suffered. And Liam didn't care. No, worse—he enjoyed it.

"I didn't do it, Mom." His voice is firm, almost angry. "I don't know where she is. Now can I go back to studying?"

I nod without speaking, and Liam swivels on his chair to turn back to his history book. He starts outlining again, like his mother wasn't just in the room, accusing him of kidnapping and murder. That's how Liam is. He doesn't let anything bother him.

After Dr. Hebert came up with a diagnosis, I asked her how this could have happened. Liam grew up in an upper-middle-class, happy household. We provided firm but very fair discipline. He had a wonderful childhood. How could he have turned out this way?

"There's often a genetic component," she had said.

But that didn't explain it any better. Jason and I were about as boring and normal as you could get. It didn't make any sense. How could a nice, normal couple like us produce a child like Liam? I never got it.

Not until this morning, when I found out my father had been in jail for murder for over forty years.

CHAPTER 32

OLIVIA

I have no idea how long I've been down here.

I finally stopped screaming. It went on for a long time. And even after I stopped, I was still shaking. I sat down in the corner of the hole, across from the skeleton, and just hugged myself. For hours maybe. I don't know who this skeleton belongs to, but I can't kid myself it's a good sign that it's here. Somebody else was down in this hole. And that person died here.

Or more likely, they were murdered.

The memories of how I got down here start to return more vividly. The handkerchief shoved in my face that smelled funny. Not being able to breathe. And then... nothing.

He's going to kill me. That's why I'm here. And I can only imagine the reason he put me here instead of killing me outright is that he has other plans for me before he kills me.

But everyone has got to be looking for me. My mom...

I want her so badly, it hurts. I can't imagine how scared she must have been when she came into my bedroom and found me missing. She would have called the police immediately. She'll never stop looking for me. She'll have every policeman in the whole state out searching.

And then, when the police find me, they'll throw his ass in jail. And I'll get to go home to my warm, comfortable bed. And Mom will make me chocolate-chip pancakes. And I'm not leaving my bed for a week. Well, maybe I'll go to the doctor to have them take a look at my ankle, which is still throbbing.

I'm going to get out of here. I know it. My parents will find me.

My stomach lets out a low growl. I'm starving. And thirsty. *So* thirsty. I finished the water an hour ago. I knew I should ration it more, but I couldn't help myself. I picked up the thermos and emptied it down my throat without a second thought. And now it's gone.

I wonder how long it takes for a person to die from dehydration.

Maybe that's how Phoebe died. That's what I have named the skeleton in the corner. Mom and I used to watch the TV show *Friends* in reruns, and Phoebe was my favorite character. So that's what I have called her. Phoebe. She deserves a name. I wonder if her parents are still looking for her. When I get out of here, I'll tell people she's down here. Maybe her parents can have some closure.

I'm going to get out of here. I will.

I'm going to find a way. I won't give up.

I hear a noise coming from above. Are those footsteps? Is it the police? I start to scream, but my throat is so parched I have one false start before anything comes out.

"*Help! Help me, please!*"

It's footsteps. Definitely footsteps. There is a sound of metal clanking just above my head, and then the creaking of hinges. Finally, a bright flash of light fills my vision.

After sitting in the dark for so long, the light is agonizing. I clasp my hands over my eyes to shut it out. It's a flashlight. Someone is shining a flashlight on me.

"Olivia?"

It's *him*. It's not the police. He's come back.

"Help!" I shriek, hoping a neighbor or passerby might hear. "Somebody! Help me! Let me out!"

He cocks his head to the side. "I'm afraid you're wasting your breath, Olivia. We're in a cabin in the middle of nowhere. Nobody's going to hear if you scream."

I stop screaming and stare up at him as I catch my breath. I'm not entirely sure I believe him, but he doesn't seem at all concerned that I'm yelling. So it's probably true.

"I'm sorry it took me so long to get back to you," he says. Although he doesn't sound sorry. Actually, there's no expression at all in his voice, like he's a robot. He sounds so different from usual. It's freaky. "The police are everywhere. I had to wait until night."

"Please let me out," I croak.

I peek through my fingers up at his face, squinting through the bright light. I can't believe I ever thought he was handsome. I must have been out of my mind.

"I'm afraid I can't do that," he says.

Tears spring to my eyes, but I try to keep them from falling. I have a feeling my crying won't make him feel any sympathy. "Why not? I won't tell anyone. I *swear*. I'll just say that I ran away. I promise."

"Yes. I'm sure."

"I swear!"

He smiles in a way that makes my skin crawl. "I'm sorry, Olivia. I can't let you out."

I take a deep breath. "Please… If you let me out, I'll…I'll do anything you want. *Anything*."

He lets out a laugh, loud enough that I know he must be telling the truth about us being the only people out here. "You'll do whatever I want anyway. It's not like you have a choice."

That's probably true. He's not a big guy, but he's much bigger than me. He could overpower me easily, even if I wasn't weak from lack of food and water and with an injured ankle.

"What do you want then?" I ask in a tiny voice.

He doesn't answer me.

I glare up at his face. "You better let me out right now. If you don't, when the police find me here, I'll tell them everything."

He flashes that smile again. "Oh, will you?"

"You bet I will!" A muscle twitches in my jaw as I shout up at him. "I'll tell them what you did! You'll go to jail for the rest of your life!"

I watch his expression, waiting for him to react. But his face doesn't show even a flicker of fear.

"Are you threatening me, Olivia?" he says. "I really hope you're not threatening me."

There's something in his eyes that's even more terrifying than the rotting corpse in the corner of the hole. My mouth is so dry, I'm not sure I can even manage a response. But I clear my throat. "I'm not threatening you. I'm just telling you what's going to happen."

"Well," he says, "I better make sure they never find you then."

I clutch my knees, my heart pounding in my chest. He means it. He's never going to let me out of here. Ever.

Oh God...

He lifts a large brown paper shopping bag into the air and drops it into the hole. It falls beside me, making a loud enough impact that I flinch and let out a yelp.

"That's food and drink," he says. "I don't know when I'll be able to get back here, so you better make it last."

And then the light goes out.

"Wait!" I cry. "Wait!"

His voice again, cutting through the blackness: "What?"

I swallow, hoping I can appeal to his sympathy one last time, because threats obviously don't do the trick. "Can you leave me the flashlight? Please?"

He's quiet for a moment, as if considering it. Dare I hope he might say yes? I would give anything for that flashlight.

"It's so dark down here," I say softly, "and it's so hard to tell what everything is. It's driving me nuts. If you could leave me the flashlight—"

"No," he says.

And then the trapdoor above my head creaks shut. And I hear the sound of the lock being turned, trapping me down here once again. I bury my face in my knees and let out a sob.

I don't want to die down here. There's got to be a way out.

CHAPTER 33

ERIKA

I considered keeping the kids home from school, but both of them wanted to go, and Jason said we should try to keep things as normal as we can. But Jason did stay home from work. He locked himself in the spare bedroom to work from home, even though I know he's in the middle of an important project and has a ton of meetings. He's trying to do all his meetings on the phone.

"You can go to work," I tried to tell him. "Liam will be okay."

"I think it's better I stay home," he insisted.

I didn't want to admit how grateful I was that he stayed. Nothing else happened after the police stopped by last night, but the whole night, I kept jerking awake after having nightmares. I couldn't remember any of them when I woke up in the morning, but my body was covered in sweat.

I try to get my own work done, but it's difficult. In addition to the pie contest article, I'm supposed to be writing an article about the best local playgrounds, but my head isn't in the game. Besides, Hannah and Liam have been too old to go to the playground for years. I'd like to be nostalgic about the simpler times, but I can't. Ever since Liam was four years old, he was a ticking time bomb.

I hope they find Olivia. That's all I can think about. I hope she ran away. I hope they find her in some motel, tearful and wanting to come home.

What little concentration I have is broken by the doorbell ringing. When I see Jason coming down the stairs, I realize it's has been ringing for several minutes. I don't know what's wrong with me that I don't notice a doorbell ringing ten feet away from me.

Jason reaches the door before me. He squints through the peephole, and his face turns pale. "Shit. It's the police."

Jason squares his shoulders and cracks open the door. It's Rivera and Murphy again. But there are more people behind them. This doesn't seem like a good sign. When the police come with a squad of people behind them, you know you're in trouble.

"Hello, Mr. Cass." Rivera doesn't bother smiling this time. "We have a warrant to search your home and your wife's Toyota."

I step forward. "Liam is at school."

"We don't need Liam right now," she says. "But we do have a warrant for his phone."

God only knows what's on his phone. I don't want to think about it. "Can you come by later for the phone?"

Jason is busy inspecting the warrant, but I'm not sure why he's bothering. These are police officers. If they need to inspect our house, we're not going to stop them. I only hope Liam was smart enough not to leave something behind.

My own phone starts ringing in my pocket. I pull it out and see the name of the high school. My stomach sinks. "Detective, can I take this call? It's the school."

She nods curtly, and I swipe to answer. "Hello?"

"Mrs. Cass? It's Principal McMillan. I'm afraid we have a situation."

She has a situation? She should see what's going on in my house. "What's wrong?"

"I need you to come here as soon as possible. Liam and another student were involved in a fistfight in the hallway. They're both in my office."

Oh God.

"Is Liam okay?" I ask.

"He's fine." Her voice softens slightly. "But we don't tolerate fighting on school property. I'm going to need you to come here right away."

I don't know how I'm going to manage that, but I can't say no to Mrs. McMillan. "I'll be right there."

Jason has lowered the search warrant and is staring at me. So are the two detectives. I wish I didn't have to have this conversation in front of the detectives. The timing couldn't be worse.

"Liam got into a fight at school," I say, trying to ignore the way Rivera is looking at me. "I need to go there to pick him up."

"Jesus." Jason frowns. "Okay. I…I'll stay here, and you go get Liam."

I look past the detectives at the team of people who are going to rip apart my home. I wish I could stay. I can't deal with Liam fighting at school on top of everything. I've gotten a lot of calls about Liam over the years, but nothing like this. He's never done anything to get his hands dirty before.

I grab my purse, but Detective Rivera stops me. "You can't take the Toyota. We need to search it."

"But I'll just… I'll be right back."

"Take my Prius, Erika." Jason grabs his keys off the hook on the wall where he keeps them and tosses them to me. "Send me a text after you talk to the principal, okay?"

I nod, dreading what awaits me at the principal's office. I have a feeling this is not a conversation that will be quick.

CHAPTER 34

ERIKA

When I get inside the school, my daughter is waiting for me by the entrance. I'm sure she's supposed to be in class, so I assume she's skipping. But that's the least of my problems right now. Hannah has red-rimmed eyes, and her auburn hair is in disarray—even more than usual. She looks like somebody just died.

"Mom!" she cries. And she throws her arms around me, which is something she hasn't done in public in a very long time. Although to be fair, I don't think there's anyone else in the hallway. "I saw the whole thing. It wasn't Liam's fault."

I pull away from her. It's hard for me to believe that anything that's happening right now isn't Liam's fault. "Are you sure?"

"Yes!" She swipes at her eyes with the back of her hand. "Tyler jumped him out of nowhere. What was Liam supposed to do? Just stand there while Tyler beat him up?"

"Why did Tyler do it?"

"Isn't it obvious?" Hannah blinks at me. "Everyone thinks Liam is responsible for what happened to Olivia. But he *isn't*. I *know* it."

I'm not sure how Hannah knows it. I sure don't.

"Tyler is telling *everyone* that Liam is some kind of psychopath," Hannah says. "*Tyler* should be suspended. It wasn't Liam's fault."

I have a bad feeling Mrs. McMillan won't see it that way. In any case, Liam can't go to school right now. That's very obvious. Not until this whole thing blows over.

"I'll see what I can do, Hannah," I promise her. I don't tell her about the police officers at our house who are currently searching through her brother's belongings. And my car. There's no point in making her even more upset. "I'm going to go talk to the principal now. But you need to go back to class."

But Hannah clearly has no intention of going back to her class. She follows me to the principal's office, and I don't stop her. This is hard on her too.

When I get into the administration office, Jessica Martinson is already there. The last thing I want right now is to have a conversation with Jessica, but the principal's door is shut, so I have no choice but to sit down next to her to wait. I still feel the burn of how she shunned me at the PTA meeting. After all those years, how could she do that to me?

"Hi, Erika," Jessica says in an unreadable tone. "Our boys had quite a scuffle, didn't they?"

"Yes," I say vaguely. I don't mention the fact that my daughter told me that her football player thug of a son jumped my kid. Somehow I suspect Liam will get the blame for all of this. "Boys fight, I guess."

Jessica smiles tightly. "Yes. I'm sure they're making too much of this. Hopefully they'll just get a warning and that will be the end of it."

That's impossible. They were fighting in school. There's no way they won't be punished severely. But I appreciate Jessica's optimism.

The door to the principal's office cracks open, and Mrs. Kristen McMillan stands in the entrance. She's around my age but much taller, with a strong jaw, and her hair is styled into an immobile shoulder-length helmet. The last time she and I spoke was during parent-teacher night, when she ran into me in the hallway and told me how brilliant Liam was at his last debate and how he's on his way to becoming valedictorian. She's not smiling this time as she waves us both into her office.

The two boys are sitting in chairs in front of her desk. Tyler is slumped down, holding an ice pack to his face, but Liam is sitting up straight, staring at the wall. He doesn't look great though. Tyler got in a good punch to his cheekbone, which is dark red, on its way to black and blue. His shirt is ripped, and his usually neat dark hair is in disarray. He looks like a kid who just got beaten up. Despite everything, I want to throw my arms around him.

He's my son after all. No matter what.

"They had to be pulled apart by two teachers," Mrs. McMillan says. "It's one of the worst fights I've seen during my time as principal."

"It was his fault." Tyler pulls the ice pack away from his face, revealing a split lip. "He started it."

"No, I didn't," Liam says calmly. "I didn't do anything."

"The hell you didn't!"

"Boys, calm down!" Mrs. McMillan snaps at them.

But Tyler isn't about to be subdued. "You started it when you murdered Olivia Mercer, you psychopath. Everyone knows you did it!"

Liam doesn't respond to that. He just stares straight ahead.

"That's enough," Mrs. McMillan says sharply. "Tyler, I don't care who started it. Both of you were involved in this fight."

"He deserved it." Tyler nearly spits the words. "That and more."

Mrs. McMillan looks between the two boys, her eyes narrowing. "Tyler, Liam, I'd like both of you to step outside while I speak with your mothers."

Liam immediately obeys, while Tyler tries to protest. But Mrs. McMillan has her secretary escort them outside and babysit them while she talks to the two of us. Once the door closes, her lips form a straight line, and she peers at us over the edge of her spectacles.

"Obviously there's no excuse for this behavior," Mrs. McMillan says. "Fighting is not tolerated. We can't have a repeat performance of this."

"Of course not," Jessica says. "I'm so sorry about Tyler's behavior. He just got…emotional."

I keep my mouth shut, just as my son did.

"Tyler will be suspended for a week," Mrs. McMillan says. She looks at me and hesitates. "Liam will receive one day's suspension."

A week ago, I would've been worried about how this would affect Liam's college admissions. Now I couldn't care less. She may as well have suspended him for a week. I can't send him back to school after this.

But Jessica is absolutely furious. A pink spot forms

on either of her cheeks. "A *week*? How come Tyler gets a week and Liam only gets one day?"

"For one thing," Mrs. McMillan says, "this is Tyler's second offense. I told you after he was in that fight last year that it couldn't happen again. Also, several witnesses confirmed that your son initiated the fight. Liam has an impeccable record. He's a straight-A student—"

"But he's a psychopath," Jessica bursts out. She glances at me, then quickly looks away. "I'm sorry, but that's the elephant in the room. Liam is psycho. He kidnapped that girl, and he probably killed her. Tyler was just upset about it."

I stare at my former friend, shocked she would say such a thing. Even when Tyler and Liam stopped being friends, she never said a negative word about Liam.

"I'm sorry, Erika," she says, "but you know it's true. Liam has serious mental health issues. The reason he and Tyler stopped being friends was that Tyler was afraid to have him in the house. *I* was afraid to have him in the house." She grits her teeth. "He needs to be in therapy. Or better yet, locked up."

"Mrs. Martinson!" Mrs. McMillan exclaims. "I know you're upset, but please. This is uncalled for."

I stare down at my hands. I don't know what to say. I want to defend my son, but the truth is that I agree with her. Before she can say another word, we hear shouting outside the office. Mrs. McMillan rises to her feet, and we follow her. What is it *now*?

Liam and Tyler are still sitting right outside the office, but a girl has joined them. She has dirty-blond hair that's loose around her chubby face, and she has tears streaming down her cheeks. She's pointing at them, her hand trembling.

"Where is she, you asshole?" she shouts at Liam. "Tell me what you did with Olivia!"

"Madison!" Mrs. McMillan snaps. "Please settle down right this instant!"

The girl's hands curl into fists, and I'm scared she's going to come at Liam. But instead, she stomps her foot against the ground. "He did this! The bastard did something to my best friend. And look at him! He doesn't even *care*!"

I look at Liam, who is watching Madison's temper tantrum without any expression on his face. He hasn't said a word in protest. He just stares at her like she's an insect crawling on the wall. Like he really doesn't care.

They end up having to call the school security guard to take Madison away, because she won't stop shouting at Liam. Mrs. McMillan takes me aside, a concerned look in her eyes. "It may be best for Liam to stay home until this blows over."

"Yes," I murmur. "I was thinking the same thing."

She frowns. "Liam is a good boy. It's terrible that he got caught up in this tragedy."

As it turns out, Mrs. McMillan has been successfully charmed by my son. During his two years and change in high school, he has been very well behaved. There have been no incidents during this time. The last incident he had, in fact, involved that English teacher in eighth grade. I don't like to think about that. But Mrs. McMillan clearly doesn't know about Mr. Young. She only sees what Liam allows her to see.

"Good luck," she tells me.

CHAPTER 35

*T*ranscript of police interview with *Tyler Martinson.*

PD: "Tyler, how long have you known Liam Cass?"

TM: "Forever. Like, first grade."

PD: "And you used to be friends?"

TM: "Best friends, actually. I was always going to his house, or he'd go to my house. We used to be really tight."

PD: "And what was your opinion of him at that time?"

TM: "Well, he was my best friend. So obviously I liked him. He was cool. But he had a dark side, if you know what I mean."

PD: "What do you mean?"

TM: "Like, he was really good at manipulating people to get what he wanted. Especially teachers. He could blow off his homework, and he would never get in trouble. I couldn't get away with *anything*."

PD: "And what did the other students think of him?"

TM: "They liked him too. Especially the girls. They were all, like, in *love* with him. It was really annoying. But Liam just thought it was funny."

PD: "Were you jealous of him?"

TM: "Me? No. I mean, I wasn't interested in girls back then. Now it's more annoying. They all still love him. He's like Ted Bundy. Wasn't he that serial killer women liked so much?"

PD: "You mentioned he would manipulate other people. How did he do that?"

TM: "So here's an example. In fourth grade, we had this roly-poly farm in our classroom. Liam got this idea to dump the farm on the floor and smash all the worms. That was his idea of a fun thing to do. And I went along with it because... I don't know. I thought it was fun too, I guess. Anyway, there was this other kid in the class named Michael. Nobody liked Michael because he was gross and fat and picked his nose. But Liam invited him to come with us, and Michael was so happy. But it was all a trick, you know? Because the only reason Liam wanted him to come was so Michael would get blamed for what we did. And it worked. Liam told the teacher Michael did it alone, and she believed him. And Michael didn't even rat us out, probably because he was hoping we'd still be friends with him after. But we weren't."

PD: "Did you feel bad about it?"

TM: "No. I mean, not at the time. But looking back, yeah, it was a shitty thing to do to Michael. But it was Liam's idea."

PD: "At what point did you stop being friends with Liam?"

TM: "Um, that would probably be sixth grade."

PD: "Was there a particular reason?"

TM: "Hell yeah. So Liam came to my house, and he had this little chipmunk trapped in a piece of Tupperware. He poked a couple of holes in it so the animal could breathe. And he told me he wanted to cut off the air and watch the chipmunk through the glass as it suffocated."

PD: "..."

TM: "Yeah, exactly. I was freaked out, and I told him I didn't want to do it. He tried to convince me, but I refused and told him he was a weirdo. Finally, he got angry and left."

PD: "Did you tell anyone about it?"

TM: "I told my mom because I wanted to make sure he didn't come over again."

PD: "What did she say?"

TM: "She didn't look that surprised. She just told me to stay away from him."

PD: "You mentioned before that you had another interaction with Liam that was very unsettling for you."

TM: "Yeah. That was last year."

PD: "What happened?"

TM: "Okay, so Liam's sister—you know, Hannah— she's a huge pain in the ass. She got all pissed off at me for some reason, and I guess she told him about it. So he felt like he had to avenge her or something. Even though I didn't even do anything wrong."

PD: "What did he do?"

TM: "So there was this stray cat that used to hang out by our house. My sister used to feed him, so he kept coming back. I didn't really care either way. I never fed the cat—I mean, that's not my responsibility, to feed a damn stray cat. And sometimes he'd be right in front of the door, so I had to kick him out of the way. Anyway, I got home from school one day, and the stupid cat is in my bed. Can you imagine? I thought Emma let him inside. But then, when I tried to shoo him away, he didn't move. So then I tried to pick him up to move him, and..."

PD: "Yes?"

TM: "His insides fell out."

PD: "..."

TM: "Shit, I feel sick thinking about it. Somebody sliced him through the belly, and then, when I picked him up...BAM, cat guts all over my bed!"

PD: "That must have been very upsetting."

TM: "Damn right. Oh, sorry. Am I allowed to say that?"

PD: "Say what?"

TM: "Damn. Because it's, like, a curse word."

PD: "It's okay. So what did you do next?"

TM: "I told my parents. And I told them I thought Liam did it. But they asked if I had any proof, and I didn't. So we didn't do anything. My mom just kept saying to stay away from him and his family."

PD: "And that was your last serious interaction with Liam?"

TM: "Yeah. Well, if you don't count me kicking his ass the other day."

PD: "Tyler, how do you know Olivia Mercer?"

TM: "Oh, just from around. She was in my year. And she was friends with Madison Hartman, who's dating my buddy Aidan."

PD: "Are you friendly with her?"

TM: "I don't know. A little."

PD: "Did you ever ask her out on a date?"

TM: "No."

PD: "Some of your friends from the football team said that you did ask her out and that she told you no."

TM: "That's not...that's not what happened at all. Some of us were going out for burgers, and I just invited her along. No big deal. And she was busy."

PD: "Did it bother you when you saw her out with Liam?"

TM: "Hell no. She's not even that hot. She can go out with whoever the hell she wants. Liam...half the football team for all I care."

PD: "So you weren't jealous?"

TM: "What the... I thought we were talking about *Liam*. Liam is the psychopath."

PD: "Tyler, how many times have you been suspended for fighting?"

TM: "Jesus Christ, just twice. Is that a lot?"

PD: "It's more than any of your peers."

TM: "Yeah, but... The first time wasn't my fault. The guy stole my girlfriend. You don't do that to someone."

PD: "But you threw the first punch."

TM: "Yeah. I did. But—"

PD: "And you were the one who punched Liam in the hallway first. Weren't you?"

TM: "Fine. Yes. Look, I was mad at Liam because I thought he killed Olivia. That's the reason. I'm not psycho like he is. Yeah, we used to be friends. But after I realized what he was like, we stopped being friends. I'm not like him. And I sure as hell didn't do anything to Olivia."

CHAPTER 36

ERIKA

Jason texts me that the police are still searching the house, so I take the kids to McDonald's for lunch. I want to warn Liam about what's happening, but I'm not quite sure how to tell him.

Hannah agonizes over the menu, complaining about how it's going to ruin her diet. Then she goes ahead and orders a bacon double cheeseburger with large French fries. Liam says he's not hungry, but he reluctantly orders a Big Mac and Coke. I don't have much appetite either, but I pick something randomly from the menu. We've got to eat.

Hannah is the only one who manages to eat anything. She stuffs French fries into her mouth absently, almost automatically. Liam stares at his burger. His right cheek looks worse than it did in Mrs. McMillan's office. I can only imagine how bad it will look by tomorrow.

"Do you want me to get you some ice for your cheek?" I ask him.

"No."

"It's going to get more bruised if you don't ice it."

"I don't care." He regards his burger with a look of disgust. "Mom, I'm not hungry. Can I go sit in the car?"

Somehow I get the feeling I shouldn't let Liam out of my sight right now. "No. We're all going to stay right here."

"But, Mom—"

"You don't have to eat, but you have to stay here."

"Fine." Liam slumps down in his seat and pouts. Wow, the kid's acting like a real teenager now. Hannah has always been the expert at moping when we tell her what to do, but Liam always accepted everything without argument.

"Also," I add, "there's something you should know."

Liam lifts his eyes.

"The police are at our house right now. They're searching the house and my car."

Hannah puts down her burger, eyes flashing. "*What?* Don't they need a warrant or something to do that?"

I nod. "They do. And they came with one." I look at Liam again. "They also want your phone. And just so you know, they'll be able to read anything you've deleted."

He's quiet for a moment, playing with the wrapper on his sandwich. "Fine."

"How bad is that, Liam?"

Before Liam can say a word, Hannah speaks up. "Liam didn't do anything. So they're not going to find anything incriminating."

I'm not so sure about that. But Liam doesn't give anything away with his expression. I get the feeling that my kids have been discussing this together. Sometimes I wonder what sorts of things Liam says to Hannah. He trusts her in a way that he doesn't trust me or Jason. If only I could be a fly on the wall.

"We'll go see the attorney Dad hired this afternoon," I say. "He'll tell us the next step."

I force myself to chomp down my salad. I don't have any appetite, but I need to eat if I'm going to get through what's going to happen next.

CHAPTER 37

OLIVIA

I have cataloged the inventory of the bag.

He has left me two plastic water bottles, four slices of bread, two apples, and a granola bar. If he's coming back within a day, I'll be fine. But he made a comment about how he wasn't sure when he could get back here. So how long is this food going to have to last me? Two days? Three? *A week?*

He could have brought me more food. He did this purposely. Maybe to make sure I'm weak enough that I won't be able to fight him off or escape. As if being plunged into darkness twenty-four hours a day isn't bad enough.

I have divided the corners of my small space into their various purposes. One corner is for Phoebe. You can bet I'm not touching *her*. A second corner is for me to do my business. I was able to hold off for several hours, but you can't stop bodily functions. Of course, it's not making this dank hole smell any better. A third corner is for the food.

And the fourth corner is for me to sit or sleep. I amazingly managed to get some sleep last night, although it was broken up and interspersed with nightmares.

I woke up sobbing. All I can think about is my home. How much I want to be back there. How much I want my mom.

I've got to find a way out of here.

In the meantime, I have divided the food into rations. I'm allowing myself one slice of bread total per day, half an apple, and half a bottle of water. I've already eaten the granola bar—I couldn't help myself. But the rest needs to last me for several days. It's not going to be nearly enough, but it will be enough to live on until I can get out of here.

I've been devising a plan.

If he dug this hole, he did it when the soil was warmer and more pliable. And presumably he had a shovel. But I can make a dent in the soil with my fingers. If I scrape at it hard enough, it comes free. My plan is to dig out enough to form a mound for me to stand on to reach the trap door above me. And once I can reach that, maybe I can find a way to break the lock.

He's never going to let me go. I saw the look in his eyes last night. He's out of his mind. He wants to keep me here, for whatever reason. So that means if I'm going to get out, I'm going to have to do it on my own. I can't count on the police to save me.

I'm getting out of here if it's the last thing I do.

CHAPTER 38

ERIKA

Jason texts me that the police are almost done, but they still need Liam's phone, so I herd the kids back into the car and head home. The kids both look startled by the number of police cars around our house. I can't even imagine what the neighbors are thinking. But if they've been reading the local papers, they can probably take an educated guess.

Detective Rivera is talking to Jason when I unlock the door. She regards Liam's bruised face. "What happened?"

"Just a little scuffle at school," I say. I hate that she has to see him like this. Liam has never been in a fistfight before in his life. He's not a violent kid. At least not in the way that Tyler is.

"Liam," Rivera says, "I'm going to need your phone."

Liam reaches into his pocket and hands it over to her without argument.

"It goes without saying," Rivera says, "you don't leave town without letting us know. We'll be in touch about anything we find."

With those words, she takes off, leaving my family alone again. I survey the living room, which doesn't look like much has been disturbed. I wonder what they've been doing here all this time.

"They were mostly in Liam's room," Jason says as if reading my thoughts. "And the car. They spent forever going through your car."

"Are we going to see the lawyer?" I ask.

He nods. "Yeah, he fit us in for an hour from now." He looks Liam up and down, taking in his ripped shirt and bruised face. "You better change clothes."

Liam nods and goes upstairs. Hannah goes up to her room too, leaving Jason and me alone in the living room.

Jason glances at the stairs and lowers his voice. "The attorney has a connection in the police department," he murmurs. "He said they're close to an arrest. They're hoping to find something here today that will make it a slam dunk."

I push away a sick feeling in my stomach. I can't believe this is happening. I can't believe there's a good possibility Liam is about to get arrested.

"But they won't," he says.

I wish I believed in Liam's innocence the way Jason does.

———————

Our attorney is named John Landon. He looks tall and capable, with a full head of gray hair and a suit that looks very expensive. I didn't even ask Jason what this guy is going to be costing us. I don't want to know. But I know what attorneys charge, and if this guy is any good, he's probably charging us a fortune.

Liam sits down between us in front of Landon's mahogany desk. Unsurprisingly, his cheekbone looks even worse than it did earlier in the day. He's going to have one hell of a shiner. It will be his first. He's never even needed stitches or had a broken bone before.

"What happened to your eye?" Landon asks him.

"I ran into this kid's fist," Liam says.

Jason shakes his head. "Some of the kids are giving him a hard time at school. They think he's guilty."

"Who does?" Landon asks.

Liam drops his eyes. "Everyone."

Landon nods, unsurprised. "I'm afraid it's going to get worse before it gets better. I just spoke to my contact at the police department, and it sounds like they found something during their search."

All the hairs on my arms stand at attention. "What did they find?"

Landon spreads his arms apart. "I don't know yet. But it's something big, apparently. They said to expect an arrest in the next twenty-four hours."

Liam's face pales. "You mean they're going to take me to *jail*?"

I always thought of Liam as a kid who could deal with anything. For the most part, everything seems to always roll off his back. Even when he got expelled from kindergarten all those years ago, he didn't seem all that bothered by it. But at this moment, he looks absolutely terrified. I don't blame him. I would be terrified too in his shoes. I'm terrified *for* him.

"I'm afraid so," Landon says. "But I'm hoping, based on your age and lack of priors, that you'll be able to make bail. They're trying to make a big deal out of some

183

complaint from a guy named Richard Young—a teacher Liam had."

Liam looks like he's going to be sick. Of course, we all remember Richard Young. That was the first time the police ever showed up at our door, and I thought there was a reasonable chance Liam could end up in jail. But nothing ever came of it. What Young had claimed Liam did was horrible beyond words, but the man had no proof.

As for me, I was never sure.

"Do you know what Mr. Young accused him of doing?" Jason asks.

"Yes, I do."

"So you recognize that was completely blown out of proportion." Jason folds his arms across his chest. "That guy was really paranoid. I mean, Liam was only thirteen at the time. Can you imagine? There's no way he could have…"

Landon looks at Liam for several seconds. We made him put on a dress shirt and nice pants before this visit, and aside from the bruise on his face, he looks like his usual handsome, clean-cut self. "No, I agree. It seems unlikely."

I let out a breath.

Landon folds his hands in front of him and focuses his gaze on my son. "Liam, I'm only going to ask you this one time. Do you know what happened to Olivia Mercer?"

Liam glances at me and then at Jason. "No," he says.

Landon lifts an eyebrow. "You should know that anything you tell me stays in this room. Knowing the whole truth will help me to defend you. I don't like surprises."

"I don't know what happened to her," he insists.

I watch my son proclaim his innocence. As the words leave his mouth, I get this strong sense that he's lying. But then again, he's always lying. Nothing he says anymore has any basis in reality. It makes me want to grab his shoulders and shake him.

Landon considers his words. I wonder if he's thinking the same thing I am. "Mr. and Mrs. Cass, may I speak with Liam alone?"

Jason frowns. "Why?"

"Because *Liam* is my client. The two of you are not. And the attorney-client privilege doesn't apply to you. If he gets charged, they'll almost certainly try him as an adult. So I think we should treat him as an adult."

"Is that all right with you, Liam?" I ask him gently.

I place my hand on his shoulder, even though I know he doesn't like being touched. Not that he ever complains about it when I'm affectionate, but he never came to me for hugs the way Hannah used to. He just didn't care. He never needed physical affection like other children.

"It's all right," Liam says.

Even though it almost kills me, we leave Liam in the room with Landon. Jason is just as unhappy about it as I am. As we sit in the waiting room, he keeps sneaking looks back at the closed office door. "What do you think they're talking about in there?"

"I don't know."

I glance around Landon's small waiting room—at his attractive, blond receptionist and the few people occupying seats across from us. Landon is a criminal attorney, so presumably everyone here has been accused of committing some sort of crime. The woman across from me is about my age, with schoolmarm glasses and her hair gathered into a bun. I watch her flick through a copy of *Good Housekeeping*.

What crime could this woman possibly have committed? She looks like someone I'd run into during a PTA event.

Then again, if there's one thing I've learned in the last sixteen years, it's that looks can be deceiving.

Jason bounces his right foot against the carpeting, casting a look back at the closed door to Landon's office. "I can't believe they're bringing up that garbage with the English teacher," he mutters. "If that's all they've got, they're grasping at straws."

"That was really bad, Jason. Liam is really lucky he didn't get charged."

"Charged? He didn't do anything!"

I don't know what to say. I should probably agree, but I can't bring myself to say the words.

"If he really did that…" He pushes his glasses up his nose. "Erika, our kid isn't a monster."

I can see in my husband's eyes that he means it. I wonder what it is they found in our house that's so significant and if it will be enough to change Jason's mind.

CHAPTER 39

*T*ranscript of police interview with Richard Young.

PD: "You say you were Liam Cass's English teacher?"

RY: "That's right."

PD: "And when was that?"

RY: "It was about three years ago. He was in eighth grade."

PD: "And what was your opinion of him?"

RY: "Honestly?"

PD: "Of course."

RY: "I hated him. I feel terrible saying that, because what kind of teacher hates one of his students? But there was something about Liam that I instantly disliked. And I have to say, I was alone in my opinion. Universally, all the teachers adored him. Middle school kids aren't easy, but Liam seemed like a good kid—the kind teachers hope for in our classes. He was obviously very bright and well behaved in class, and he always handed in assignments on time."

PD: "But you didn't like him?"

RY: "He just rubbed me the wrong way—I can't even say why. There was something very fake about him. And also..."

PD: "Yes?"

RY: "I have a daughter. She's Liam's age, and she had some classes with him. And a few times, I saw them talking in the hallway, and it drove me out of my mind. My wife told me I was overreacting, but given current circumstances, it sounds like I was reacting very appropriately."

PD: "So did you do anything?"

RY: "..."

PD: "Mr. Young?"

RY: "I'm not proud of this."

PD: "It's important to be honest right now. A girl's life could be at stake."

RY: "Fine. I took Liam aside after class one day and told him to stay the hell away from my daughter."

PD: "Did he?"

RY: "No. He did not. In fact, he started showing more interest in her after I said that to him. Right when he knew I was paying attention. Like he was taunting me."

PD: "Well, that's not an unusual response to authority for a teenage boy."

RY: "I'm also not proud to say that I took my frustration out on his grades. English is very subjective, and I started grading his essays very harshly. He went from an A to a C."

PD: "Did he do anything about it?"

RY: "He complained. But I refused to change his grades. I also told Lily, my daughter, that I would ground her if she spoke with him again."

PD: "And how did that go?"

RY: "Initially, I thought it was successful. Lily stopped talking to Liam, and he just ate the bad grades. I thought it was over and done with."

PD: "But it wasn't?"

RY: "Obviously I can't prove Liam did anything to me."

PD: "What do you *believe* he did?"

RY: "It was a Saturday night, around two in the morning. My wife and I were fast asleep until our dog came into our bed. She vomited all over the bed and woke us up. But once I was awake, I found it very hard to think straight, and my wife and I both noticed we had splitting headaches. I called 911 and went to Lily's room to check on her. I couldn't wake her up at all. And then I passed out in her room."

PD: "What happened?"

RY: "Carbon monoxide poisoning."

PD: "But you recovered?"

RY: "Yes. Thank God for my dog. We spent several days in the hospital, but we were okay. But if Daisy hadn't woken us up, we would've been dead by the morning. All three of us."

PD: "Did they find out how it happened?"

RY: "There was a crack in our radiator. Supposedly, this sort of thing can happen, but we have a relatively new house. It was suspicious, to say the least."

PD: "Didn't you have a carbon monoxide detector?"

RY: "Yes. That's the other thing. Our detector was disconnected."

PD: "That's a little suspicious."

RY: "Exactly."

PD: "Did you suspect Liam Cass?"

RY: "No. Not at first. I mean, I didn't like the kid, but he was only thirteen years old. I didn't even think he knew what carbon monoxide was."

PD: "So what made you suspect him?"

RY: "One of my neighbors told me and the police that they saw a kid skulking around my house shortly before it happened. I found a photo of Liam from his school records, and they confirmed it was him."

PD: "Did the police investigate further?"

RY: "They questioned Liam, but apparently he had a friend living in my neighborhood, so that was his excuse for being there. There was no other evidence he did anything. If he was ever inside my house, he left no trace."

PD: "But you believe it was him?"

RY: "I absolutely do."

PD: "So he got away with it?"

RY: "He sure did."

PD: "Did you do anything further?"

RY: "I'll tell you, Detective, there is one thing I did."

PD: "What's that?"

RY: "I gave the kid an A in English. Some things are not worth dying over."

CHAPTER 40

ERIKA

Liam barely said a word during the drive home. I made a few attempts to get him to talk, but he only answered in monosyllables. I wanted to know what Landon said to him when they were alone. Or more importantly, what he said to Landon. Did he tell the attorney the truth?

It's a relief to find Hannah is in her bedroom where we left her when we get home. After the way Olivia Mercer disappeared, I was almost scared Hannah might be gone too. Of course, why would she be? The monster was in our car.

As soon as I get into the bedroom, I dig around in the medicine cabinet for my Xanax. If there was ever a time I've needed it, it's right now. This is too much for me to deal with. My son getting arrested? You don't see that in many parenting books.

Damn it, where's my Xanax?

It's not in the medicine cabinet. I fumble through bottles of Tylenol, Motrin, Benadryl, triple antibiotic cream, antifungal cream, face lotion, hand lotion, expired antibiotics—God, why do we have so much crap in the medicine cabinet? But no Xanax.

Then it hits me. I shoved the bottle back in the drawer of my nightstand last time I took them. I wanted them next to my bed for easy access the next time I woke up in a cold sweat.

I make a beeline for the nightstand and open the drawer. The pill bottle rolls to the front, and I feel a jab of relief. I grab the bottle, wrench it open, and pop one in my mouth. I swallow it dry.

There's something else that catches my eye from within the drawer in my nightstand. At first, I think it's a photo of Liam. But then I realize it's the photo of my father. The one I always keep in my nightstand so I don't ever forget him.

Of course, I put it there before I realized who he really is. What he did.

I pull out the photograph to get a better look at it. My father looks like he's in his late twenties, about ten years older than Liam, but God, they look so much alike. The photograph is like looking into a time machine showing my son in the future. Same hair, same eyes, same crooked smile, same build. It's uncanny.

I can only imagine what else Liam inherited from this man.

I don't remember much about my father. I have a vague memory of holding his large hand as he walked down the street with me. I also remember when there was a mouse in our home and my father put out a trap to catch it. He showed me the trap, the mouse's tail captured by the metal bar, as the tiny animal squealed in distress.

He laughed when I cowered behind my mother's legs. It's one of my first memories.

I always looked at that memory as an example of my father taking care of our family by getting rid of our rodent problem. But now I wonder if there was more to it than that. Did he enjoy torturing that little mouse the same way Liam enjoyed starving those hamsters to death?

In the past, when I looked at this photograph, I experienced a rush of affection for this man who never got to see his daughter grow up. But right now, I feel something very different. Jason and I tried to do everything right as parents, but we couldn't change our son. There was something innately wrong with him. Something in his genes.

Liam is, after all, the grandson of a murderer.

I pick up my phone and punch in my mother's number. She answers after the second ring. "Oh, Erika, thank God. I was scared you were never going to speak to me again."

She has no clue what we've been through with Liam in the last twenty-four hours. Any resentment I might have felt toward her for keeping a secret from me takes a back seat to everything else. "You did what you felt was right. I can't be angry at you for that."

"I only did it to protect you. Because I love you."

She was protecting me because she loves me. The same way I want to protect Liam, even if he doesn't deserve it. Even if he doesn't love me. Even if he can't. "Mom, can I ask you a question?"

"Of course, darling. What is it?"

"What was my father like?"

"What...what do you mean?"

"His personality. What was he like?"

"Oh." She hesitates. "Well, he was...very charming.

As you can imagine. All the women loved him. Liam, I think, takes after him in looks. Don't you think?"

I think he takes after him in more than looks. That's what I'm afraid of anyway.

"Would you say he was…manipulative?"

My mother's laugh sounds hollow. "He manipulated me into marrying him, that's for sure. It was…well, I don't want to say it was a mistake, because I got you. But he wasn't a good husband, even before."

"Why not?"

"He was just very self-absorbed. He wasn't really ready to settle down. He wasn't the sort of man who wanted to stay in on a Saturday night and watch television. He always wanted to be out doing something. And when we had a child, that only made it worse."

I take a breath. "Was he cruel to you?"

She's quiet for a moment. "Yes, he certainly could be. Very cruel." She sighs. "He just wasn't a good person, Erika. Probably the best thing that ever happened was him exiting our lives. He wouldn't have been a good father."

I look down at the photograph in my hand. My mother has answered some of my questions, but I have more. I have a feeling that the only way I can possibly understand my son is to understand my father.

And there's only one way to do that.

"Thanks, Mom," I say. "I better go now."

"Are you okay, Erika? You sound funny."

"I'm fine."

"Have they found that girl yet who went missing? Such a tragedy."

"I've got to go, Mom," I choke out.

I hang up the phone before my mother can ask again

if I'm okay. I'm not okay. I don't know if things will ever be okay again.

I stare at my phone for a moment. I feel slightly calmer. It must be the Xanax.

I look back at my list of calls from the last several days. I select Frank Marino's number from the list before I can chicken out. I've got a new job for Frank.

After five rings, when I'm about to give up, he picks up the phone. "Erika! What's going on? Your little town is all over the news."

"Yeah." I swallow hard. Frank hasn't mentioned Liam, which means his name isn't in the news. Of course, since he's underage, the media can't mention him by name. But I have a feeling if he gets arrested, it will all come out somehow. The media can't mention Liam's name, but it can trend on Twitter or be shared on Facebook or whatever it is people do on Instagram. "Frank, I need you to find somebody for me."

"Find somebody?"

"Yes, like where he lives. An address." I take a deep breath. "His name is Marvin Holick."

"Okay…"

"Just so you know," I say, "he's my father."

CHAPTER 41

OLIVIA

I don't think he's coming back tonight.

Part of me is scared maybe he'll never come back. Not that I want to see him—the thought of seeing him again makes me physically ill—but I've only got three slices of bread left, one apple, and one bottle of water. I'm doing my best to hold off on eating or drinking, but my throat is painfully parched. All I want is to guzzle the entire bottle, but I know that would be stupid.

What if he doesn't come back for two or three more days? Then what?

If he doesn't come back soon, I'll die.

I can't let that happen.

I'm making some progress with the mound I'm building. It's hard to tell how big I need to make it, because I can't actually see where the trap door is aside from that tiny dim slice of light that disappears entirely at night. It's very hard to tell how high up it is.

Also, I am essentially doing this blind. The hole is

pitch-black. It makes no difference if my eyes are open or closed.

And I'm so weak. All I want to do is lie on the ground and sleep. It would be easy to do. To let starvation and dehydration take me.

Every time I start to give up, I think about my parents. My friends. My bedroom.

But I can't think about it too hard or else I'll start crying.

I've been doing all the digging with my fingers, and now they've become painful and raw. I can't see what they look like, because I have no light, but I imagine they're very red. I imagine pinpoints of blood.

I pat the mound with my palms. It's not big enough—I can tell that much. It needs to be at least a few inches higher. I scrape at the ground with my fingers and wince. God, my fingers hurt. I don't know what's worse—my fingers or my ankle.

If only I had a tool to help me dig.

I've got the empty water bottle. That's better than nothing, but it's hard to grip. And other than that, the only thing down here even resembling a tool is...

Oh no, I'm not going to do *that*.

Yes, one of those bones lying in the corner would be ideal for digging. Not as good as a shovel, but much better than a water bottle and light-years better than my poor fingers. But I can't do that.

Can I?

I reach into Phoebe's corner until my fingers touch the smooth surface of one of her bones. A shudder runs through me. I lean forward a little more until my fingers close around the bone.

It would be so perfect.

But I can't. It's bad enough I'm stuck down here. It's bad enough I'm starving to death. But I won't do *that*.

Of course, it might be the only way I'll ever get out of here. The only way I'll ever see my family again.

I pick up the bone, feeling the weight in my hand.

I have no choice.

I'm going to get out of here for both of us, Phoebe.

I'm going to let your family know you're down here. Give them closure. Give you a real burial.

And I'm going to make sure that asshole goes to prison for the rest of his life.

CHAPTER 42

ERIKA

It's at five o'clock in the afternoon the next day that I hear a crash coming from the kitchen.

I'm in the living room, trying desperately to focus on getting an article written for the next edition of the *Nassau Nutshell*, when the sound of broken glass steals what little is left of my concentration. I slide my laptop off my legs and get up to investigate.

There's a rock lying on the floor in the center of our kitchen. The window above the sink is shattered, and there's glass everywhere. I take a step and feel a sliver slice into my foot. I wince at the pain and crouch down to pick up the rock. There's a piece of paper taped to it with a word scribbled in red Magic Marker:

MURDERER

It's starting.

"What was that, Erika?" Jason is standing at the entrance

to the kitchen, still in his boxers and a T-shirt. He insisted on staying home again today, and I am intensely grateful. If Liam gets arrested today, I don't want to be alone here. Of course, if the police show up, I feel like maybe Jason doesn't want to be in his underwear. But I don't want to give him a hard time. Jason's underwear is the least of my problems.

I hold up the rock. "Somebody had a message for us."

"Shit," he breathes. "Should we call the police?"

"What's the point?" I say. The truth is Liam probably deserves it. And the last thing I want is to invite the police into our home. "Just be careful where you step until I can clean up. There's glass everywhere."

Jason glances down at his watch. "It's getting late. No police yet. Maybe they're not going to arrest him after all."

I snort. "You're joking."

"Look, I know they think he did it. I'm not an idiot. But they have to have evidence to arrest him. They can't do it on a gut feeling."

I close my eyes. I wonder where Olivia Mercer is right now. I hope to God she's okay.

The doorbell rings, and my eyes fly open. Every time I hear that ring, I feel like I'm going to have a heart attack. Jason and I exchange looks.

"Maybe it's the person who threw the rock, coming to apologize?" he suggests.

I won't dignify that with a response.

I reach the door first. I peer through the peephole and see Detective Rivera's face. Oh no.

My hands are shaking too badly to open the door. Jason has to work the lock for me. When he gets it open, I immediately see the handcuffs in Rivera's hands. I think I'm going to faint.

"Is Liam home, Mrs. Cass?" she asks me.

"You're arresting him," I say numbly.

She nods slowly. "I'm sorry."

Jason looks down at the handcuffs, his face growing pale, but he doesn't protest this time. He walks to the foot of the stairs and calls out, "Liam? Get dressed right now and come down here."

I watch as my son emerges from his bedroom wearing a plain T-shirt and a pair of clean blue jeans. Despite the bruise on his cheekbone, he looks so young and handsome now. When he catches sight of the detective at the door, he stops walking. I watch as he takes a deep breath, then forces himself to move forward.

I get seized by the desperate urge to throw my arms around him and tell him it's all going to be okay. But it would be a lie.

When Liam gets to the bottom of the stairs, Rivera steps forward. She holds out the handcuffs, and Liam takes a step back.

"Liam Cass, you are under arrest for the kidnapping and murder of Olivia Mercer."

She reads him his rights as he listens silently with a dazed expression on his face that likely mirrors my own. I can't believe this is happening. My legs are Jell-O—they feel like they're going to collapse under me.

I wonder what they found in their search. It must be something really big.

When Rivera finishes reading his rights, she holds out the handcuffs. Now Liam looks really panicked. He looks like he's about to burst into tears, but he's holding it back. I haven't seen Liam cry since he was three years old. He very rarely cried as a baby. He was such a good baby. I remember thinking to myself that it was unfair any woman should be so lucky.

"Do you have to put those on me?" he asks, unable to hide the note of desperation in his voice.

"I'm afraid so," she says without any sympathy in her voice.

At least she cuffs him in front rather than behind his back. I flinch as the cuffs snap into place. This is it. They're really arresting him. They're really taking him away to jail. My baby. In *jail*. How could this be happening?

"Liam, please just tell them where she is!" I blurt out.

For a moment, everyone goes silent.

Jason stares at me, open-mouthed. "Erika…"

The officers are staring at me too. Liam's face is bright pink. "Mom," he says, "I didn't—"

But before he can finish saying whatever it was he was going to say, Rivera puts an arm on his back and leads him out the front door. The sun is still up, and it's obvious several of our neighbors are watching him get led to the police car in handcuffs. Everyone knows what's going on. I expect more rocks through our window tonight.

And then they drive away. I follow them outside and watch the police car until it becomes a speck of dust in the distance. Jason comes out to join me. I expect him to yell at me for my little outburst in the house, but he doesn't say a word.

When we get back in the house, Hannah is standing in the middle of the living room. Her eyes are bloodshot, and she looks like she hasn't showered today. I'm fairly sure those are the jeans and shirt she was wearing yesterday. "Did they take him? They arrested him?"

Jason sighs heavily. "Yes."

A tear escapes from her left eye. "Dad! How could you let them?"

He frowns. "I didn't have much of a choice. They had a warrant for his arrest."

She stomps her foot on the ground. "This is bullshit! He didn't do it. You know he didn't!"

"Hannah…" I say.

"Don't even, Mom!" she snaps at me. "I know what *you* think of him. I see the way you look at him. At least Dad thinks he's innocent."

They both look at me, waiting for a response. I don't know what to say. Hannah is absolutely right.

"Even if he's guilty, I still love him," I finally say.

And that is the truth. Hannah and Jason might think Liam is innocent, but they're wrong. I'm the only one who can see through him. All I can hope for now is that Olivia Mercer is still alive. Maybe if he tells them where she is, they'll go easy on him.

"You have no idea, Mom," Hannah says. "Liam would never have done this. He really liked Olivia."

I wish I had a wife so I could keep her deep in a hole.

Unfortunately, Hannah is the one who has no idea what she's talking about. I know my son. And I know this won't end well.

When I first saw those two blue lines on the pregnancy test seventeen years ago, I never would have believed the baby growing inside me would end up behind bars.

Everything about Liam's early life was easy, starting with my pregnancy. I got knocked up on our first try, and in contrast to my pregnancy with Hannah, during which

I was sick for the entire time, I felt great when I was carrying Liam. People used to tell me I was glowing. And the labor was similarly easy. Five good pushes and he was out. Screaming and pink and perfect.

Liam was a really mild-mannered baby. He rarely fussed or cried. He ate whenever I offered him my breast, and he slept nearly through the night as soon as we brought him home. He was a beautiful baby too. He looked like one of the children in the magazines with his chubby cheeks and sweet smile. Other women were always stopping me in the street to admire him.

And Liam was fantastic at playing the part. When people asked him how old he was, he would hold up one finger and cry, "One!" He loved to perform. Sometimes I would look down in his crib at night at his sleeping face and wonder how I got so lucky.

It was when he was barely four years old that I first noticed something different about him.

We were at the park. I had Hannah in her carriage, and she was sobbing as usual. I was lucky that Liam could be trusted to play independently, because Hannah required all my attention. So I didn't notice what he was doing until I found him crouched in the corner of the park. I wheeled Hannah's carriage over to see what was going on.

Liam was playing with a large carpenter ant. He had built some sort of enclosure, and he would allow the ant to leave, then trap it again. I watched him do this for a minute, trying to figure out the rules of his game. Finally I asked, "What are you doing, Liam?"

He lifted his big brown eyes and smiled at me—that smile that made all the women fall in love with him. "The ant thinks he's gonna get away, but he can't! He doesn't know I'm gonna smoosh him."

Those words, said in Liam's four-year-old baby voice, made me feel really uneasy. "Liam," I said in a choked voice, "you're being mean to the ant."

He scrunched up his little face. "But it's just an ant, Mommy. Who cares?"

"It's a living creature, Liam."

But he just looked at me blankly until I told him to go play at the monkey bars again. He obligingly went back to the jungle gym, but I couldn't get the incident out of my head. That night, I told Jason about what he said, but Jason wasn't at all concerned. "Boys like to play with bugs," he said.

But he wasn't playing with the bug. He was *torturing* it.

It only got worse after that. He made more disturbing statements that got harder and harder to shrug off. And then that girl was found duct-taped in the closet when he was in kindergarten. He got kicked out of school for that one. I told him he could never do anything like that ever again, and technically, he didn't. I finally took him to that child psychologist, Dr. Hebert, but I don't believe she did anything to help him. He just got smarter about keeping his mouth shut.

And not knowing what he was thinking was the hardest part of all.

After the police take Liam away, Jason immediately calls John Landon. We sit on the sofa, and he puts our lawyer on speakerphone so we can both listen in. We have to order Hannah to go upstairs, because she shouldn't be listening to this, and also, she's almost hysterical.

"John," Jason says, "they just took him. The police.

They cuffed him and put him in the car. They're taking him to jail."

"Yes." Landon's voice jumps out of Jason's phone. "I had a feeling that was going to happen today."

"What are they going to do now?" I ask.

"They're going to bring him to the police station and book him," Landon says. "They'll photograph him and fingerprint him and then put him in one of their holding cells."

My son behind bars. Tears spring to my eyes. I can't bear it.

"We'll get him a bail hearing tomorrow morning," Landon says. "Hopefully they'll set bail, and he can go home until the arraignment."

Jason sucks in a breath. "You think they won't set bail?"

"It's possible. They're charging him with murder."

"But they don't even know if Olivia Mercer is dead!" Jason says.

"Right. They have to prove that a crime was even committed, so that's in his favor." Landon pauses. "Also, he's only sixteen. I'll argue all that at the bail hearing."

"So there's a chance they might not even be able to charge him?" I ask hopefully.

Landon is silent for several seconds. "I'm not going to lie to you, Erika. They may not have a body, but they've got a strong case against him."

My stomach drops. "What have they got?"

"Well, for starters, it's known that they were at least dating, if not boyfriend and girlfriend. We have the neighbor who is testifying not only that Olivia and Liam were together that night but that she got into his car." He clears his throat. "But it was what they found in your car that was the nail in the coffin. They found traces of blood that matched Olivia's blood type and three of her hairs. In your *trunk*."

"In my trunk?" I say numbly.

"Yes," Landon says. "If they were just on the seat, we could argue she was in the car, but the trunk is a bit more damning."

"But it's a hatchback," Jason points out. "If she was in the back seat, her hair could've gotten into the trunk. It's not like the trunk is an enclosed space."

"I can argue that. But it doesn't explain the blood, does it?"

Jason leans back against the sofa, shaking his head. I think he has just checked out of this conversation.

"Are you still there?" Landon asks.

"I'm here," I say.

"I'm going to go over to see Liam now. He's probably very scared, so I'll tell him what's going to happen next. Also…"

"What?" I ask.

Landon sighs. "I'm going to try to convince him to tell me where Olivia Mercer is. Whether she's alive. We can use that as a bargaining chip."

I swallow a lump in my throat. This is the last thing I wanted to hear. "Did Liam tell you he did it?"

"You know I can't tell you that, Erika. Confidentiality."

"Please, John! He's only sixteen years old, and he's in jail and—"

I'm sobbing now into the phone. I'm two seconds away from completely losing it, if I haven't already. I don't know how this could be happening. I was so careful. How did I get the wrong Olivia?

"Erika, Erika…" Landon's voice cuts through my

sobs. "Look, calm down. He…he didn't tell me anything. Okay?"

I gulp, trying to catch my breath. "But you think he did it."

It's not a question.

Our attorney is silent for a moment. "Yes, I do. Come on, Erika. He obviously did it. The evidence is over-whelming." He gives me a second to absorb this. "But look, even if she's dead and he buried her, he can offer to lead the police to her body in exchange for leniency in sentencing."

"Do you think she's dead?" I ask in a voice that is barely a whisper.

Landon is silent for what seems like an eternity. "Honestly? Yes. I think she's already dead. If she wasn't at first, he probably realized he had to get rid of her to destroy the evidence."

"God," I whisper. I wipe my eyes with the backs of my fingers.

"But I'll do my best for him," Landon says. "Whatever he did, I'll fight for him. That's my job."

Why? That's the question I want to ask. Because if Liam really killed that girl, he *should* be locked away in prison. He should be in a place where he can't hurt anyone ever again.

I spent his entire childhood trying to protect him from himself. I have failed.

CHAPTER 43

ERIKA

When I come downstairs later in the evening to force myself to eat some dinner, I find Hannah sitting on the sofa in the living room, slouched down as she watches television. I get close enough that I can see what's on the screen. It's *The Princess Bride*.

The Princess Bride used to be my favorite movie when I was a kid. When Hannah was four years old, I showed it to her and Liam for the first time. Liam didn't think much of it, but Hannah loved it. It became her favorite movie, and I think it still is. It's a comfort movie. It's her bowl of chicken soup.

I stand there for a moment, watching Hannah watch the movie. Her eyes are pinned on the screen, and she mouths the words along with the characters. She could probably recite every line in this movie from memory. Actually, so could I.

"Can I join you?" I ask.

Hannah looks up at me with her blue eyes rimmed

with red. The last time I saw her, she was screaming at me. But now she lifts one shoulder. "As you wish."

It's a line from the movie. An olive branch?

I sit down on the sofa next to Hannah but leave a respectable distance between us. If I sit too close, she'll complain I'm stifling her. But sitting too far away will make her unhappy too. I can't figure out how to make Hannah happy—I never could. Even when she was an infant, she would howl her lungs out while I would beg her to tell me what was wrong. Even two-year-old Liam commented once, "My baby sister is always sad."

Fourteen years later, nothing has changed.

"I'm sorry you had to see that happen earlier," I say to Hannah.

She doesn't take her eyes off the screen. "It wasn't your fault."

"I know, but…"

She turns to look at me. "You really think he did it, don't you?"

I clear my throat. "Well, I don't know for sure. I mean—"

"That's why you hired that guy to scare off all the girls Liam likes."

My mouth falls open. Hannah knew about that? It hadn't even occurred to me she might know. I thought that was my deep, dark secret.

"One of them told me." Her eyes flick back at the television screen. "I assumed you were behind it. Considering you were the one who sent him to the shrink."

"You know about that?"

"Liam told me."

I suck in a breath. "I'm really sorry, Hannah. I'm sorry

you got caught up in all this. I promise I'll do my best to keep you out of it from now on."

Hannah picks up the remote control and shuts off the television. She faces me now, her eyes filling with tears. "I don't *want* to be kept out of it. I just want my brother back home."

Hannah's loyalty to Liam is understandable. Whatever else anyone can say about Liam, he's a good big brother. People warned me when I got pregnant that bringing a newborn home when you've already got a two-year-old is a recipe for jealousy. One of my girlfriends told me she constantly had to protect her infant from her toddler.

But it was never like that with Liam and Hannah. The first time I brought Hannah home, he couldn't stop staring at her. When we finally let him hold her, under careful supervision, he was so gentle. He kept stroking her little face with open-mouthed awe.

When she was about four months old, we took her to the park, and a big dog rushed to the stroller, barking loudly enough to make Hannah burst into tears. Liam jumped in front of the dog, bravely holding up his hand. "Doggy, no!" he cried. "No hurt my sister! *No!*"

I don't know what Liam did or didn't do to Olivia, but he has always protected his sister.

"It's going to be okay," I tell Hannah. "We're going to get him home."

Hannah wipes her eyes with the back of her hand. "Do you really believe that, Mom?"

I wish I could say I did. I wish I could tell my daughter that the truth will come out and Liam will go free. But the real truth is, whether or not the truth comes out, I believe Liam will spend the rest of his life in prison.

CHAPTER 44

ERIKA

Jason and I get ready for bed in absolute silence.

The only thing we could possibly talk about at this point is the fact that our son is in jail, and it's all we've spoken about for the last several days. It's the last thing I want to talk about now. I know Jason is still peeved at me for what I said when the police showed up to arrest Liam. But it's not like I meant to make my son seem guilty. If I could take it back, I would.

I join my husband in the bathroom while he's brushing his teeth. He's got the electric toothbrush whirring in his mouth. Five years ago, Jason had a root canal, and after swearing he would never go through something like that again, he purchased an electric toothbrush and about a crate full of dental floss. He's used them both religiously, and he's had such good dental visits since then that I switched over to the electric toothbrush last year. I do feel like it gets my teeth cleaner, but the annoying part is that we can't both brush at once anymore. I have to wait for him to be done, then swap out the toothbrush heads.

As I wait, I rinse off my face, although there's not much to rinse since I didn't bother with makeup this morning. I let the hot water wash over my skin, trying not to think about what's going to happen tomorrow. Liam's bail hearing. Every time I imagine it, I get a sick sensation in the pit of my stomach.

What if he doesn't make bail? I can't conceive of not getting to take him home tomorrow. But Landon says I have to accept the possibility that Liam might be in jail for the duration.

Liam in jail. My little boy in jail. Surrounded by murderers and thieves.

"Done," Jason says as he hands me the handle of the electric toothbrush.

"Thanks," I say. We are so polite.

My hands are shaking as I try to get the electric toothbrush head in place. Jason watches me for a moment until he takes it from me and secures the brush.

"It's going to be okay." His voice is maddeningly calm. "It's just a misunderstanding. In a week, this will all have blown over."

I snort. "Do you genuinely believe that?"

He stares at me, a sad look in his blue eyes. "Erika, do you genuinely believe our son killed that girl?"

The bathroom feels stiflingly small. I've got to get out of here. I put down the toothbrush, even though I haven't brushed yet, and scurry back into our bedroom. Jason follows me, apparently still waiting for an answer to his question. I wish I had his faith in Liam. But I know things he doesn't know. As much as he wants and needs to hear it, I can't tell him I believe Liam is innocent.

"I know it doesn't look great for him." His tone is almost pleading. "But Liam wouldn't do this. He's a good kid. He comes from a good family."

Arguably, Jason and I are good parents—both of us are so normal we're boring. But Jason doesn't know my history. He doesn't know the secret about me that I only recently found out myself. And maybe I owe it to him to tell him the truth. Maybe that's the only way to make him understand. Even if it makes him look at me differently.

"Jason," I say, "there's something I need to tell you."

He inhales sharply. After the number of revelations he's had to deal with in the last few days, I feel bad dropping this one on him. But I owe it to him to be honest.

"You're scaring me, Erika," he says. "Should I…should I be sitting down?"

I reach out and take his hand, which is unsurprisingly clammy. I lead him over to the bed, and we sit side by side. Jason is staring at me intently, tapping his right foot against the carpeting.

"I recently found out something…kind of surprising."

"More surprising than the police arresting our kid?"

I take a deep breath. "It's about my father. He's…he's alive."

His mouth falls open. His face looks about how mine probably did when my mother dropped the bombshell on me. "Are you serious? How?"

It's harder than I thought to tell him the truth. Because I know what it means. I have always believed that while Liam had his issues, it wasn't my fault. But now I know the truth. Liam is the grandson of a murderer. This is in his genes. And it doesn't help matters that he looks exactly like my father. The spitting image.

I explain it to Jason as best I can considering all I know is from my mother. He listens, his face growing paler by the second. When I finish telling him everything, he mutters, "Jesus."

"I know."

"How could your mother have kept this from you?"

"I guess she thought it was easier to think he was dead. That knowing he was in jail might traumatize me."

He frowns. "Are you going to go see him?

"Do you think I should?"

"It's your decision, Erika."

"Yes, but what do you think?"

He hesitates for only a second. "If I were you, I wouldn't."

"But he's my father."

"So what? The man is a murderer. Do you really want to have anything to do with him after that?"

The conviction in his voice unsettles me. After all, there might be a time in the near future when we have to visit our own son in jail. If it comes out that Liam really did kill Olivia, will Jason disown him?

The truth is I know deep down, whether Liam did it or not, I'm going to support him. I'll visit him every week in jail if it comes down to it. I hope it's not true, and I pray to God that Olivia is okay, but no matter what, Liam is my son. No matter what he does, that isn't going to change.

I'm not sure Jason feels the same way.

"I haven't decided yet." I chew on my lip. "Obviously, this isn't the best timing. But…I'm curious. What if Liam is the way he is because…"

Jason cocks his head to the side. "Because of what?"

"Because of me. Because he's inherited it from me?"

He blinks a few times. "You're not a murderer, Erika."

"But my father is."

My husband stares down at his hands for a moment. My stomach fills with butterflies as I try to figure out what he's thinking. When I can't stand it another second, he looks back up at me. "Liam didn't kill that girl."

"But what if he did?"

"No." He squares his shoulders. "I'm sorry, Erika, but just because your father was a murderer, it doesn't mean Liam is too."

But I can see in his eyes the shred of uncertainty. For the first time, he doesn't look so sure that our son is innocent. He had no idea when he married me that I was the daughter of a convicted murderer. A *psychopath*. Now that he knows what's running through my blood and what I might have passed down, he's finally starting to believe that our son isn't the perfect child he thought him to be.

And it's all my fault.

CHAPTER 45

OLIVIA

It's night now. I know that because the slice of light has vanished, plunging me back into the worst kind of pitch-blackness.

I have almost no food or drink left. One slice of bread. Some part of the last bottle of water. I'm so thirsty I could drink my own pee. I never understood how people did that during those survival stories. But I totally get it now. I'm dizzy with hunger and thirst.

With the strength I have left, I've been working on building up the mound using Phoebe's bone. My little tower is about a foot high based on feel. Possibly high enough to reach the trap door.

I've got to give it a try. Before he comes back.

I step up on the mound with my right foot. I try to lift myself to the top, leaning against the side of the hole, but I accidentally put weight on my left ankle.

Oh my *God*.

I howl and double over in pain. My left ankle feels

worse every day. It's definitely broken. It's very swollen and warm, and I'm having trouble wiggling my toes. But then again, it's just pain. People get shot and keep moving. I have to get past it. That's my only chance of survival.

Think of happy things, Olivia.

My parents. My mom.

My room.

Madison.

I can only imagine what Madison must be thinking right now. She warned me. She warned me, and I didn't listen.

I've got to get out of here. I've got to see my family again.

I take a deep breath and get back up on the mound. My left ankle touches the ground, and it's agony, but I don't allow myself to collapse again. I stand up straight, lifting a long bone over my head. It scrapes against the roof of my enclosure.

I did it! I can reach the top!

I bang on it with the bone, and I hear metal. The trap door is locked.

Of course.

I shouldn't be surprised, because I heard the lock turning the last time he came, but my whole body sags with disappointment. I thought I was going to get out of here. I thought this was it. I'd escape and be home within the hour.

This is just a setback. Don't give up.

I take a deep breath, pushing away a wave of dizziness. This isn't hopeless. After all, it's just wood above me. If I can break through the wood, I can get out of here. I've got all the time in the world to pound against the wood until it breaks.

Here goes nothing.

CHAPTER 46

ERIKA

By the morning, the papers are all reporting that an arrest has been made in the disappearance of Olivia Mercer. It's not just local news; the national papers have picked up the story as well. They can't print Liam's name because he's only sixteen, but it doesn't matter. They can't keep people from saying his name in the online comments.

I sit in bed, reluctant to get up and face the world, reading through the comments until I can't bear it any-more. Overwhelmingly, the general public thinks Liam is guilty.

> I don't care if this kid is sixteen. He deserves the electric chair. Some people are too sick to live.

> I heard he has a long history of mental problems. Parents deserve to go to jail too for not making sure he got the help he deserves.

Lock this kid up and throw away the key!

Tragic and horrible! This is what lethal injections
are for!

But the worst are the comments from people who
obviously know Liam in real life. It looks like the majority
of the town has decided he's guilty. Or at least the ones
who are posting online.

I've known Liam Cass since grade school. He's nuts!
I could totally see him murdering someone. He's
definitely guilty!

Liam used to play with my son, but I told him Liam
wasn't welcome anymore. I knew that kid was
trouble.

Olivia was a beautiful girl. She was stupid to go out
with Liam Cass just because she thought he was
good looking. Now she's paying the price.

The family has been hiding Liam's mental problems
for years. He's a psychopath but they'll do
anything to protect him!

The kid was kicked out of kindergarten for raping a
girl. That says it all!

Great. Now the internet has convicted him of rape
when he was five years old. It's hard to read all these
comments, but somehow I can't look away. There are a

few positive ones at least, intermingled with the awful
ones.

> OMG, Liam is in my Spanish class and he is sooooo
> nice. He would never do this! I don't believe it's
> true!

> Liam is one of the best students I've ever had in
> all my years as a teacher. I may not know all the
> evidence, but it's hard to imagine such a fine
> young man could be capable of this.

> Liam is a great teammate and a great guy! This is
> bullshit! Someone must be framing him!

I finally put down my phone and stop reading when
Jason appears at the doorway to the bedroom. We haven't
spoken since our conversation last night, and I wonder if
he's still angry with me. He doesn't look angry though.
He looks pale. "I don't want you to freak out, Erika..."

"Then don't start a sentence with those words." I sit up
straight in bed, clutching the covers in my fingers. "What's
going on? What happened?"

"Somebody spray-painted something on our front
door."

I can only imagine what somebody's written on our
house. Right in front of all our neighbors, who I'm sure
saw nothing. I have been doing my best to keep the tears
back, but now they threaten to spill over.

"Erika..." He sits down next to me at the edge of the
bed. "It's okay. Don't cry. I'm taking care of it. Just stay
inside the house."

But this is about a hell of a lot more than some words spray-painted on our door. That can be painted over. The bigger problem isn't as easily fixed. I wipe my eyes, trying to get control of my tears, but I can't.

Jason's eyes soften. He puts his arms around me while I sob for our son. It's hard to stop. I just keep thinking of my little baby. The tiny, helpless bundle I brought home from the hospital sixteen years ago. In jail. He must be terrified. I'm his mother, and I'm supposed to be there to look out for him, and I failed.

"It's all my fault," I murmur into Jason's damp shirt.

His warm hand strokes the back of my head. "No, it's not. Stop saying that. You're a great mother. It's not your fault."

How could he say that though? Especially now that he knows about my father.

He squeezes me tighter. "Liam's going to be fine. This is all a mistake. He'll be home before you know it." He kisses me on the top of my head. "Look, why don't you take a shower so we'll be ready for the hearing? I'll take care of the graffiti."

Right—Liam's bail hearing is at eleven. I've got to get out of bed and shower before that happens. I don't know if I can muster up the energy though. I just keep thinking about Liam spending the night in jail. Or worse, spending the next thirty years' worth of nights in jail.

"Okay," I mumble.

Jason pulls away from me. "Are you going to be okay?"

I nod wordlessly.

"You sure?"

I swallow a lump in my throat. "Go do what you need to do."

Jason almost looks like he's going to insist on staying, but then my phone rings on my nightstand, so he takes the opportunity to go downstairs. I look over at the screen and see my boss's name flashing.

Oh God—I've got an article due today. It's been the last thing on my mind lately, but Brian is going to go nuts that I don't have it ready. I don't want to lose my job on top of everything. Especially since it's clear Liam's legal bills will be substantial.

"Hi, Brian," I say. I try not to sound as terrible as I feel. If Liam can be charming when he doesn't mean it, so can I. "I'm so sorry about the article being late. If you could just give me until tomorrow…"

Brian is silent for a moment before he says anything. "That's the thing, Erika. I need to talk to you about your article."

"I could probably have it by tonight if you really need it. Things have just been challenging here."

"Yeah," he breathes. "I heard."

Oh no.

"Oh. I didn't realize you knew."

"I'm a reporter, Erika. It's all over the news."

"Not his name," I squeak. As if it matters.

"I think…" Brian's voice lowers a notch. "I think it would be for the best if you took a hiatus from the paper. Until this blows over. You need to be there for your family right now."

"It's okay. I can still do my job."

"This isn't optional."

Oh, I get it. Nobody wants to read parenting tips from the mother of a murderer. I guess that makes sense. "For how long?"

223

"Let's play it by ear."

So…forever. Basically, I'm fired. There's probably some law against this, but I don't have the energy to fight this battle. I'm sure Brian knows it. "Fine."

"I'll be in touch," he promises.

No, he won't.

I put down the phone. I hadn't imagined it was possible, but I feel even worse now than I did five minutes ago. On top of everything, I've lost my job. At least Jason can't get fired, since he's his own boss. It's a small comfort.

I finally drag myself out of bed and into the shower. I let the hot water wash over me, not wanting to ever get out again. I want to live in the shower. What would Jason say if I refused to get out of the shower? But no. I have to be there for my family. It would be selfish to have a mental breakdown right now.

As I'm toweling myself dry, my cell phone starts ringing in the bedroom. I run out of the bathroom, dripping wet, and reach for it just before it goes to voicemail.

A voice hisses at me from the other line: "It would be a shame if somebody murdered your pretty little daughter like your son murdered that girl."

My heart nearly stops in my chest. I stare at the phone. "Who is this?"

Unsurprisingly, they hang up.

I close my eyes, wishing I could go to sleep and that this would all be a horrible dream. But no. I've got to get dressed and go to this hearing. I've got to be there for Liam, no matter what horrible thing he's done.

CHAPTER 47

ERIKA

There are reporters outside the courthouse, so we follow Landon's instructions and go around to the back. Thank God they can't use Liam's name, but I'm not sure where the restrictions end. Certainly, if the entire internet knows who he is, the reporters do too. They're not by our house, but maybe soon they will be. And if Liam gets tried as an adult, which Landon says is a strong possibility, I'm worried all those protections will vanish.

The last time I was in a courtroom was when I served on a jury nearly a decade ago. There are rows of benches in the back for people to sit, a wooden table for the defense and one for the prosecution, and then a bench at the front where the judge presides. As Jason, Hannah, and I slide into the bench in the back, I'm reminded vaguely of going to church. It's been longer since I've been in a church than in a courthouse.

Maybe we should have been more religious. Maybe that would have saved Liam.

The judge is already seated at the front of the room. The Honorable George Maycomb. He's old—old enough to be my father, with a full head of white hair and a neatly trimmed beard to match. Landon said that Judge Maycomb tends to be lenient, although when it comes to the murder of a young girl, all bets are off.

After about ten minutes, a bailiff leads Liam into the courtroom, and I get my first look at my son since the police took him away. He's wearing a wrinkled orange jumpsuit that's a size too big on him, and he looks *awful*. His cheekbone is still purple from where Tyler hit him, and there are dark circles under his eyes. He looks like he didn't sleep at all last night. He looks so bad Hannah lets out a gasp when she sees him.

For a moment, he doesn't look like a sixteen-year-old on the verge of adulthood—he looks like a scared little boy. *My* little boy. The same boy who sported a gap-toothed grin for a whole year and would hold up fingers to tell his age. I want more than anything to run up to him and throw my arms around him. I want to protect him from this.

But I can't. I did my best, and I failed.

We don't even get a chance to talk to him. Liam is led straight to his seat, but he sees us. He doesn't wave, but he nods his head—I suppose an enthusiastic hello would be unbecoming from an accused murderer. I cringe as I recall that the last thing I said to him was to beg him to tell us where Olivia is. How could I have said that in front of the police? Yes, I meant it, but it was the wrong thing to say. I wonder if he hates me.

Landon explained to us what would happen today. There will be no jury, but the charges will be listed, Liam

226

will enter his plea of not guilty, then Judge Maycomb will set bail. *If* there's bail. Given he's accused of murder, there's no guarantee.

The prosecutor is a woman named Cynthia Feinstein. She is around forty, with black eyes and an angry frown permanently etched on her lips. She looks like she wants to strap my son into the electric chair personally. When she stands up to speak, her voice is deep for a woman—intimidating.

"Your Honor." She addresses the judge, her black eyes darkening further. "There is ample evidence that Liam Cass is responsible for Olivia Mercer's disappearance. He was confirmed by multiple other students to be dating her. He was seen at her house at two in the morning, and she was witnessed entering his vehicle. Her hair and her blood were both found in the trunk of the vehicle when it was searched later. There are no other suspects in the case or persons of interest. Olivia Mercer has been missing for three days now, and given the blood in his vehicle, there are multiple compelling reasons to believe that he has killed her and hidden the body." Feinstein pauses. "Given the seriousness of these charges and the overwhelming evidence, the defendant has ample reason to leave town to avoid conviction."

When the prosecutor says it like that, it sounds very convincing. If I were the judge, I wouldn't give Liam bail. I look at my son, who is sitting quietly at the defense table, his shoulders rigid, staring straight ahead.

I wish I knew what he was thinking.

Landon gets to his feet. "Your Honor, every piece of evidence that the prosecution has is circumstantial. We don't even know at this point if Olivia has run away. Yes, they were together that night, and there is evidence she was in his car. But is that so surprising if she was his girl-friend? Moreover, the defendant is a sixteen-year-old *child*. He's just a boy."

At Landon's words, every eye in the courtroom goes to Liam. I'm glad he's in the rumpled jail jumpsuit and not in a suit. In a suit, he would have looked older.

"He has never been away from his parents for more than one night," Landon continues in a gentler voice. "Not even for a school trip. His mother works from home, and she can be with him at all times. We'd be happy to hand over his passport or whatever else you need. But this is a bail hearing to determine flight risk, and I think it's clear my client is at no risk for elopement."

Judge Maycomb strokes his white beard. He looks Liam over and sets the bail at two hundred thousand dollars.

This is cause for celebration—the judge could have easily denied bail entirely, and Liam would have been locked up again until the trial. Instead, after we put down ten percent of the two hundred thousand with the bail bond company, we can have Liam home by this afternoon. It also means that Maycomb doesn't think much of the prosecutor's evidence against Liam.

But none of us are in a celebratory mood during the drive home. The car is so silent it feels like we're coming home from a funeral. Jason drives and I sit shotgun, staring out the window. Hannah and Liam sit in the back, so quiet that I could forget they're there.

"How was last night?" Jason asks Liam in a pathetic attempt to break the silence.

Liam tugs at his collar as he squirms in his seat. He's

back in the same T-shirt and jeans he'd been wearing when he got arrested. "Fine."

"Were you able to sleep at all?"

"A little."

"Did they feed you?"

"Yeah. It was fine."

"What was the dinner?"

"I don't know. I don't remember."

I nudge Jason to try to get him to stop. Liam doesn't want to talk about his night in jail. I can only imagine it must've been horrible for him. But isn't it what he deserves?

When we get to our front door, I sense something just as Jason is turning the lock. I don't know what it is exactly, but I have a feeling like we shouldn't go inside. It's like a hand against my chest, pushing me backward. Instinctively, I step in front of Liam. Even after everything that's happened, my instinct is to put my own life in front of his.

Especially when we step inside and see the glint of a knife.

CHAPTER 48

ERIKA

She appears out of the shadows, her hair wild, her face streaked with tears. She's holding a carving knife—one of ours. I recognize the handle. It's a knife that somebody gave us as a housewarming present when Jason and I first moved in here. Jason carves the turkey with that same knife every Thanksgiving. I've used it enough times to know the blade has dulled over the years, but it's far from harmless.

She rushes at us with the knife. I take a step back, my arms outstretched to protect Liam and Hannah. Although I have a feeling Liam is the real target here. She goes right up to him, not caring that I am between them, and shakes the knife in his face.

"Where is she?" the woman shrieks at him. "Where is my daughter?"

Liam's mouth falls open, and he manages to say, "I…I don't know."

"You're a liar!" The woman, apparently Olivia's

mother, Mrs. Mercer, shakes the knife at him. "I know all about you, *Liam Cass*. My daughter used to talk about you all the time. But Madison told me what you're really like."

There's only one of her and four of us, but she's the one who has the knife. On the other hand, her right hand is shaking like a leaf. I don't think she could stab him if she tried. But I'd rather she didn't try.

"Mrs. Mercer," Jason says with his best attempt at a smile. "Please put down the knife, and we'll talk."

She doesn't make any attempt to lower the knife. "I'll put down the knife when *he* tells me where she is."

Jason pulls his phone out of his pocket. "If you don't put down the knife, I'm calling the police right now."

Fresh tears sprout in Mrs. Mercer's eyes. "Call them. I don't care. He's already taken the only thing that's important to me in the whole world."

I look at Liam's face, searching for a trace of emotion. As much as I don't want this woman threatening my son with a knife, there's part of me that's hoping this might work.

Tell us where she is, Liam! Please!

But he doesn't say a word, and Mrs. Mercer collapses into tears. She drops the knife on the ground and buries her face in her hands, sobbing. "I wish she never met you. I wish…"

I don't know what else to do, so I try to put my hand on Mrs. Mercer's shoulder, but she shakes me off roughly. She lifts her tear-streaked face and looks at Liam one more time. "Please tell me where she is. If you have any ounce of humanity left inside you, please…"

Liam's eyes meet mine. And he just shakes his head.

Jason is the one who gently leads Mrs. Mercer out of

our house. He calls a taxi for her and gets her safely inside. She seems to have calmed down, but she's still crying.

Liam watches the whole thing, his face devoid of any emotion. And when the taxi pulls away, he goes upstairs to his room and shuts the door behind him without another word.

CHAPTER 49

*T*ranscript of police interview with Hannah Cass.

PD: "How close are you with your brother, Hannah?"

HC: "I'd say we're very close. He's my best friend."

PD: "Your best friend?"

HC: "Well, yeah. He's my big brother. He looks out for me."

PD: "You understand the charges against him?"

HC: "Yes, I understand. But you guys are totally wrong. Liam didn't do anything."

PD: "You're aware of his history of antisocial behavior?"

HC: "You mean that hamster he killed? Yeah, I know about that. Mom makes such a big deal out of it. Out of everything. She's such a drama queen."

PD: "There were other incidents."

HC: "Nothing big."

PD: "Did he talk to you about his former English teacher, Mr. Young?"

HC: "I heard about it. But that was ridiculous. Liam didn't do that. He was thirteen! How would he possibly know how to give someone carbon monoxide poisoning? I barely even know what that is."

PD: "But you knew he disliked that teacher?"

HC: "Yeah, but... Listen, Liam didn't do this to Olivia. He didn't kidnap her and didn't kill her. He *liked* her. He was so excited she agreed to go out with him."

PD: "Why was he excited?"

HC: "Um, because he's sixteen and a girl he liked agreed to go out with him? Is that a serious question?"

PD: "Several of his classmates warned Olivia to stay away from him."

HC: "Like who? Tyler Martinson? He is, like, the worst person alive."

PD: "Why do you say that?"

HC: "Because he is? He liked Olivia first, and he was mad that she wanted to go out with Liam and not him. Because Liam is handsome and charming and Tyler is butt-ugly and a jerk."

PD: "It sounds like you don't like Tyler very much."

HC: "Let me tell you something about Tyler. One of my friends went out with him one time, and he was a jerk and she wouldn't go out with him again. But he kept bugging her, so I told him to stay away. And then he started giving *me* a hard time."

PD: "What did he do?"

HC: "Mostly stupid stuff. Yelling obscenities at me. Like I care. But one time when I was coming out of school, he grabbed me and wouldn't let me go. That one kind of scared me, because he's a big guy. A football player, you know? He could have... Well, I don't want to think about it."

PD: "So what happened?"

HC: "Liam found out about it, and he was really mad. I mean, *really* mad. He told me he was going to make sure Tyler never bothered me again."

PD: "What did he do?"

HC: "I don't know. But after he said that, Tyler left me alone. So..."

PD: "You never asked him what he did?"

HC: "I'm sure it was less than what Tyler deserved. Honestly, I bet Tyler is the one who killed Olivia. I wouldn't be at all surprised. Liam was there, but Tyler was the one with the motive. He would have killed someone just to get Liam in trouble. I swear to God."

PD: "Olivia was in your brother's car. There was a witness."

HC: "Right. Exactly. Liam goes on a date with Olivia, then he shows up at her house at night and isn't at all subtle about it. After doing all that, don't you think he'd realize that if she disappeared, he'd be the first one blamed?"

PD: "Sixteen-year-old boys are stupid."

HC: "My brother isn't stupid. Whatever else you can say about him, he's really smart. If you really believe that stupid story about Mr. Young, he got away without a trace. Do you really think he would do something like that when it was so obvious he'd get caught?"

PD: "Maybe Olivia wouldn't do what he wanted her to do when he came to see her."

HC: "No way. Olivia was *totally* infatuated with him. She would have done anything for him. He didn't *need* to kidnap her. I'm telling you, Liam didn't do this. You'll see. The truth will come out."

CHAPTER 50

ERIKA

My phone hasn't stopped ringing all day. I wish I could turn it off entirely, but I'm too scared of missing an important call. That said, I don't answer any numbers I don't recognize. At least eighty percent of the phone calls are threatening. People likely in my own town—my neighbors—telling me my son should be locked up, that my family should be murdered.

Even the nicer calls leave me with a bad taste in my mouth. A mother I used to be friendly with, Nancy Jeffers, called me an hour ago. She told me she didn't think Liam was guilty and that I had her "full support," but I imagined after the call, she went back to her friends to report how tired and stressed out I sounded. *Erika sounds like she's falling apart. I wouldn't want to be in her shoes.*

As I'm settling into bed for the night, my phone rings again. I pick it up and see Jessica Martinson's name on the screen.

I shouldn't answer. Nothing good can come of this call.

Then again, if anyone knows the gossip, it's Jessica.

Before I can stop myself, I press the green button to take the call. "Hello?"

"Erika!" Jessica's voice is syrupy sweet. "It's Jessica. Jessica Martinson."

As if I might not know who she was. As if I haven't had her number programmed into my phone for the last decade.

"Hi." I swallow hard. "What is it, Jessica?"

"I just wanted to see how you're doing."

"Fine." I'm not even remotely fine, but she's the last person I want to unburden myself to. "Thank you for asking."

"Of course."

I wait for her to say some pleasantry and end the call. *If you need anything, let me know.* But she doesn't say it. She just waits on the other line, as if she's got something to say but isn't sure how to say it.

"Is there anything I can help you with, Jessica?" I finally say.

She's quiet for a moment. "I wasn't going to say anything, but I feel like I need to. Erika, I think you did the wrong thing by bailing Liam out of jail."

I suck in a breath, my head spinning. "Jessica…"

"I know you're going to say it's none of my business," she says, "but we used to be friends, and I need to say my piece. We all know Liam did this. He deserves to be in jail."

"We don't know that."

"Come on!" she bursts out. "Don't insult my intelligence. I know Liam very well. He murdered a cat in my

238

home, Erika. I know you took him to see that psychologist. Clearly, it didn't work."

My throat feels dry, and when I open my mouth, nothing comes out.

"Erika, you need to let the police lock him away, and then you should *walk away*. If you support that monster, then you—"

I press the red button to end the phone call. I can't listen to another word of this. Especially because I know she's right. My son is a monster, but how can I walk away?

I sink onto the bed and bury my face in my hands. I don't know what to do anymore. My instinct is to protect Liam, but I'm not sure if it's the right thing to do. I don't know what's right anymore.

The phone rings again, and I want to throw it across the room. I crack my eyes open to look at the screen. Frank Marino. He's calling me back. This is a call I need to take. But my hands are shaking so much, I have trouble hitting the green button.

"Hello? Frank?"

He chuckles darkly. "Having yourself an interesting day, aren't you, Erika?"

He knows. Of course he knows. He's a detective. "Yes, I am."

"Well, I finally understand why you were trying to scare off all those girls."

My jaw twitches. This is not a time for jokes. "Did you get that address for me for Marvin Holick?"

"Yeah. I got it. Nice guy." There's an edge of sarcasm in his voice. "Like grandfather, like grandson."

I want to slam the phone down and never call Frank Marino ever again. But more than that, I want to find my father. He could be the answer to everything. "What's the address?"

He recites it for me, and I scribble it down on a piece of paper on my nightstand. He lives in Queens, probably less than an hour's drive from here. Right around the corner, really. I could pop over to see him tonight if I wanted.

Maybe I should.

I wonder what Marvin Holick will say when I show up at his door.

CHAPTER 51

OLIVIA

I am absolutely *exhausted*. I have spent the better part of the day hammering away at the trapdoor. My arms are aching, and I'm not even sure I've made any progress. At one point, I was sure the wood was splintering, but then, when I felt it with my fingers, it was intact. Of course, it's hard to know for sure, because I can't see a damn thing.

I also finished the last of my food and drink today. I was trying to hold out, but I was so desperately hungry and thirsty after all the work I did. Before I knew it, everything was gone.

I have no food. No drink. Nothing.

The worst part is I have devoured every morsel there is to eat, but my stomach still feels completely empty. There's a dull ache in the center of my chest. I feel like I don't have the energy to move, much less go back to hammering at the trapdoor.

But it's my only hope.

Well, that's not true. The police might find me. As I

lie in one corner of my cell, trying to ignore the ache of emptiness in my belly, I imagine what it will be like when the police storm in here. They'll find me and bring me back to my family. And best of all, they'll punish *him*. My parents will never give up on me. They'll keep looking until they find me. I *know* it.

I don't know what time it is when I hear the footsteps. I've lost all track of time, but that slice of light is gone, which means it must be dark out. I know in my heart that it's probably him, but just in case it's not, I scream out, "*Help! Help me, please! I'm down here!*"

It happens just the way it did last time. I hear the locks turning, and then the flashlight blinds me. It occurs to me that if I had spent my time building the mound higher instead of pounding on the lock, I might have been able to be ready to jump at him when he opened the trapdoor.

Damn. It's too late now.

"Olivia," he says, "how are you doing?"

"Awful," I spit at him. "I'm starving. I need food. And water."

"Yes," he says patiently. "People need water to live. Did you know that a person can survive only three to five days without water? Without water, your organs will eventually start to fail and your brain will swell up. But people can survive longer without food. Weeks. Your body will break down excess fat, and when that's gone, it will break down muscle. Your body will effectively consume itself."

I blink up at him, trying to ignore the shooting headache from the flashlight in my eyes. There's a look of fascination on his face as he recites these facts. Like I'm some sort of rat in a science experiment.

"How does it feel, Olivia?"

My hunger and thirst evolve into anger. I am not a science experiment. I am a human being. And I'm not going to play his perverted game. "Fuck you."

My anger only seems to amuse him though, just as my threats did. "Just tell me. How does it feel to be starving to death?"

"Go to hell."

He reaches into a paper bag next to him. I hear the crackling of paper, and then his hand emerges. At first, I think he's going to point a gun at me. But it's not a gun. It's a piece of bread.

He grins at me. "Tell me how you feel, and I'll give you this bread."

I want that bread so badly. Like it's a decadent piece of chocolate cake. I stare at it, wanting to tell him to go to hell again but wanting that bread even more. After all, the bread means survival. If I die, nobody can tell the police what he's done.

"I feel like something is clawing away at my insides," I say. "And I feel dizzy. A little nauseous."

Is that enough? Is that enough for you, you bastard?

I suppose it is, because he tosses the bread into the hole. I make a half-hearted attempt to catch it, but it falls past my fingers into the dirt. I don't care. I'm close to literally eating dirt. He also tosses in another plastic water bottle, but this one is only half the size of the others. And there's only one.

"If you cooperate, you'll live longer," he says. He nods at the bones in the corner. Under the light of his flashlight, I can see them clearly for the first time. The outline of ribs and a pelvis. What used to be arms and legs. "*She* didn't cooperate."

243

I wonder what's happening on the outside. I've been gone for days. People must be starting to assume I'm dead. How long will he let me live down here? It feels like an eternity, but I know it can't go on forever. If he keeps feeding me so little, I'll die in a month or two. But I have a feeling he won't drag it out that long. As he said, people can only survive three to five days without water.

And if he does somehow get arrested but doesn't tell the police where I am, that will be it. I'll die of dehydration in days.

"I'll try to come back in a few days," he says.

"A few days?" My panic escalates at the realization that all I have is one piece of bread and barely a pint of water. "But…"

"And don't waste your energy trying to escape," he says. "The wood is sturdy, and so is the lock. You won't get out of here."

With those words, he shuts the trapdoor again, plunging me back into blackness. I wrap my arms around my knees and let out a sob, but the tears don't come. I'm too dehydrated to even cry.

He's killing me.

CHAPTER 52

ERIKA

After everything that happened yesterday, I couldn't summon up the energy to go visit my father. I spent half the night tossing and turning, but then, around two in the morning when I kicked him awake, Jason sleepily suggested I take another Xanax. I have rules about how much I can take in one day, and I was over my limit, but I didn't want to spend the entire night awake. So I took one, and it did the trick.

I don't even attempt to make breakfast for the family. When I get into the kitchen, Liam is sitting at the kitchen table with a bowl of cereal. But he's not eating. He's just sifting it around with a spoon.

"Do you want frozen waffles?" I ask him.

"No."

"You've hardly eaten anything in the last few days."

"I'm not hungry."

"You've got to eat. You'll be sick if you don't."

Liam lifts his brown eyes with those long eyelashes that

make his sister jealous. "What do you care? You think I'm a murderer."

I open my mouth, but nothing comes out. What am I supposed to say to that? He's right. Ever since I found Olivia's address in our car GPS, there hasn't been one moment when I didn't think Liam was guilty.

"I still love you" is all I can say.

Liam snorts. "Why?"

"Because you're my son."

His eyes drop, and he crumples up a napkin in his fist. I don't expect him to understand. That was one thing Dr. Hebert told me repeatedly. *Liam is not capable of love.* He tells me he loves me, but he's only saying it because he knows it's expected of him. He knows it makes me happy. And it's in his best interest to make me happy.

I wonder if my father ever loved me.

I've got to see him. Somehow I feel like reconnecting with him will be the answer to everything.

I leave Liam in the kitchen and head upstairs to shower. Jason is coming out of the bathroom, his hair damp, a towel wrapped around his waist. After all the running he's done, he looks so fit. He's still very sexy, maybe even more than when he was younger. Under different circumstances, I might have been tempted to initiate some morning fun. But under these circumstances, it seems inconceivable.

"Hey," I say.

He rubs his eyes. He looks tired, and I feel bad for having kept him awake half the night with my restless sleep. "Hey."

"I was wondering if you could stick around the house with Liam. I...I need to go out."

"Where?"

"I need to take care of some things at the newspaper." The lie rolls off my tongue easily. I never told Jason that Brian fired me. "It shouldn't take too long."

"Okay." Jason slips a shirt over his head. "Take your time. I'll take care of things here."

He accepts my lie so easily that I feel guilty. Jason is so trusting. He believes me, and he believes Liam. Why am I the cynical one?

I go past him into the bathroom to use the shower. Before I jump in, I stare at myself in the mirror. A week ago, I would have said that I had aged gracefully, but now I look ten years older than my age. These have been the worst few days of my life. When Liam got kicked out of kindergarten, it felt like the worst tragedy ever. What I wouldn't give to go back to that time.

I squint in the mirror at my brown eyes, which now have purple circles underneath. They are the same brown eyes that Liam has. I say that Liam looks like my father, but really, he looks like me. *I* look like my father.

Sometimes I wonder what else the three of us have in common.

What am I capable of?

CHAPTER 53

ERIKA

I get in my car by nine in the morning and am on my way to pay a visit to Marvin Holick. Given I haven't called him, I recognize there's a reasonable chance he might not be home. But I go anyway. I need some time alone, and the drive will clear my head.

You think I'm a murderer.

I can't stop picturing Liam's face as he said those words. He looked hurt. I always believed nothing ever got to my son, but maybe I'm wrong. Then again, I have this feeling that his hurt expression is yet another act. After all, Hannah and Jason believe he is innocent, and I'm the only one who can still see through him. He needs to win me over.

While I'm driving, my phone rings. I see my mother's name pop up on the screen, and I almost let it go to voicemail. But at the last moment, I send the call to the car speakers.

"Hi, Mom," I say.

"Erika!" Mom is talking much too loud, which is what she usually does on the phone. She doesn't seem capable of controlling the volume of her voice when she's on a cell phone. "Why didn't you call me? I just found out from Jeanne during our bridge game that my grandson was arrested!"

"It's okay. He's home now."

"Okay? You know what they're saying he did, right?"

"Nope. I have no idea what crime my son has been charged with."

"Erika…"

"We're dealing with it, Mom. He's got a good lawyer."

"But… God, they're saying that he…"

"It will be okay," I say with confidence that I don't feel. But at least I can keep my mother from worrying. "It's all blown out of proportion. Our lawyer says it will be fine."

"He does?"

"Yes." If by "fine" I mean that the lawyer thinks he's guilty and should show the police where the body is. But I already lied to my husband today. Might as well lie to my mother too. "Anyway, I've got to go."

"Will you call me if anything else happens?"

"Yes."

Wow, another lie. I'm on a roll.

The address Frank gave me is an apartment building. It looks more like a tenement, with graffiti scribbled all over the brick walls and a small awning covered in holes. Just looking at it makes me want to clutch my purse tighter to my chest. Then again, it's understandable that my father couldn't afford a nicer place to live coming right out of jail. I shouldn't judge him. Not for where he lives anyway.

According to the scribble on the paper lying on the

seat next to me, my father lives on the second floor. I pull into a parking spot right in front of the building and sit there, trying to work up the courage to go see him.

I have to do this. I have to do this today.

I take a deep breath and get out of the car. I walk unsteadily to the building, glad I wore my ballet flats for the trip, because I'd probably face-plant in heels. There's an intercom at the entrance, but I happen to arrive just as a man is leaving, and he holds the door for me to go inside. And just like that, I'm in.

I walk up the two flights to get to the second floor. When I emerge into the hallway, there's an odor of urine, the paint on the walls is peeling, and the light above is flickering. My father's apartment is 203. I walk down the hallway until I reach the doorway. The numbers are etched into the paint. Before I can lose my nerve, I reach out and ring the doorbell.

Then I wait.

I wait a minute. Two minutes. By the third minute, the butterflies in my stomach are settling down. Obviously, Marvin Holick is not here right now. I'll return to meet my father another day.

But then the door is yanked open.

CHAPTER 54

ERIKA

W hatever you're selling, I'm not interested."

An old man glares at me from behind a chain. I can barely see him, but I can make out his eyes. My eyes. Liam's eyes. This is him. My father.

"I'm not selling anything," I say.

He narrows his eyes at me. "Then what do you want?"

"I…" I clear my throat. "Could I come in and explain?"

"No. You tell me what you want, and then I'll decide if you can come in."

This isn't how I wanted to have this conversation—through a door chain. But he's not leaving me much choice. "I…I'm your daughter. I'm Erika."

The suspicion in his eyes deepens for a moment, but then something changes. He shuts the door, and I hear him fumbling with the chain. When he opens the door again, the chain is gone.

He just looks like an old man now. The dark hair that was thick in the photo in my drawer is now almost gone, and what's left is white and wispy. His teeth are yellow, and he has big jowls. He's wearing a checkered shirt and suspenders. He's a shadow of the handsome man he used to be.

"Erika." His voice quakes. "I can't believe you're here. Come in."

I step into his tiny apartment, which is sparsely furnished with an old ratty couch that looks like it came from the curb, an empty bookcase, and a coffee table with one short leg. Also, the living room is beyond messy. There is laundry strewn all about the room, and food cartons all over the coffee table. I suppress the urge to tidy it all up myself. He probably hasn't lived here long enough to be a hoarder, but he's moving in that direction.

"Sit down!" he says anxiously, gesturing at his ratty sofa that looks like it's crawling with worms or bedbugs. "Can I get you something to drink?"

"No." I'd be terrified to drink out of one of the glasses in this place. "Thank you."

My father, Marvin Holick, sits down beside me on the couch. He has a nervous smile on his lips that makes him look younger—he looks a little bit like Liam when he smiles like that. He's not what I expected at all. I was expecting a Sean Connery type who would be smoking a cigarette and explaining casually in a possibly Scottish accent about the murder he committed. But this man is far from Sean Connery. He's more like Mr. Magoo.

He blinks his watery eyes at me. "I'm so glad you're here, Erika."

I smile tightly.

"I wanted so badly to contact you after I got out of prison," he goes on. "But I knew what your mother told you about me. And I thought…well, I thought you'd be better off without me in your life. But I'm really glad you're here."

I nod.

"I want to hear everything about your life." He starts to reach for my hand, but I pull away before he can make contact. "Are you married? Do you have children?"

"I'm married," I say stiffly, "and I have two teenage children."

"I have grandchildren?" His face lights up. "Do you have photographs?"

I study his wrinkled face. Is this all an act just to get on my good side? Is he actually excited to see photos of my children? Because the truth is Marvin Holick does not seem like a sociopath. At *all*. But he committed a murder. And the description my mother gave of him sounded just like Liam.

I slowly pull out my phone from my purse and bring up some recent photos of the children. My father gets out a pair of glasses and looks at the photos for far too long for it to be an act. When he gets to the one of Liam right after his debate, he lets out a gasp.

"My God!" he says. "The boy looks just like me!"

"Yes," I say vaguely.

That's not all he got from you.

"What's he doing there?" my father asks. "He's all dressed up."

"He's on the debate team."

"Debate team! What a smart kid. Wow. Your husband must be smart. He sure don't get that from me."

"Mom is pretty smart."

The smile fades from his lips. "You're right. She is."

He hands me back my phone, a troubled expression on his face. "I'm so sorry, Erika. About…well, about everything. I really screwed up."

"Yeah," I mumble.

He lowers his eyes. "You probably want to know what happened."

I don't want to know. But I *have to* know. I need to know what made him kill a woman and what I can do to keep his grandson from suffering the same fate as him—if it isn't too late. "Yes" is all I say.

He nods and sighs, sinking deeper into his ratty sofa. He runs a hand through what's left of his hair. It's hard to imagine it was ever as dark and thick as Liam's.

"I was young and stupid," he finally says. "It's a really bad combination. I met this girl. Nancy. Christ, I wish I could take it all back. I loved your mother, but…I was too young and too good looking for my own good. And then the girl told me she was knocked up. She threatened to go tell your mother. I thought your mother would leave me and I'd lose the both of you."

"So you killed her."

"No!" His watery brown eyes fly open. Those eyes used to be the same color as Liam's, but now they've lost their vividness, like a shirt that's been washed too many times. "I didn't want to kill Nancy. I swear. I just… This buddy of mine gave me some pills I could slip her that would make her lose the baby. And after that, I was going to end it with her and be faithful to your mother. I never wanted to kill her. I *swear* it."

I stare at him.

"You don't believe me." He shakes his head. "I don't blame you. The police didn't believe it either. Maybe they

254

would have if she'd really been pregnant, but she lied about that. There was never any baby." He takes a shaky breath. "And then I lost you both anyway."

I look away, unable to meet his eyes. Do I believe him?

"It was a terrible mistake," he says. "I wish I could take it back. I would have faced up to the music—whatever it took. But Christ, I paid for it. I missed your whole life. I missed out on having a grandson who looks just like me. I missed holding my grandkids when they were babies. And Angela… She never came to visit me. She wanted to forget I existed. Raise you herself."

"She did a good job."

"Yes. She sure did." He pulls off his glasses and rubs his eyes. "I don't deserve it, Erika, but I was hoping maybe I could meet your family sometime. Do you think there's a chance of that? Someday?"

"Maybe." I know it would make him the happiest man in the world to tell him yes, but I can't do that right now. He obviously has no idea about the mess Liam is in. I can't forge a relationship with my father with that going on. And I still don't know how to feel about his confession. "I'll be in touch."

"Okay." He gives me a nervous smile. "You don't by any chance have a photograph of you and the kids that I could…have?"

I have wallet-size versions of Hannah and Liam's school photos. I slip my father copies of both of them. He spends an extra few seconds looking at Liam's, his lips parted. He really did miss out. He would've loved being a grandfather to those kids.

And what would my life have been like if he had been in it? If he hadn't done such a stupid thing and gotten himself locked away? Everything could've been different.

I glance at my watch and realize I've been here for an hour. I've got to get back home before Jason starts wondering where I really am. The last thing I need is for him to talk to Brian. So I tell my father goodbye and hurry back to my car. He insists on walking me downstairs, and he waves at me until I drive away.

I don't know what I expected when I went to visit my father. I wasn't expecting a lonely old man, that's for sure. I have no idea if Marvin Holick really wanted to kill that woman or if he was telling the truth and it was all just a horrible accident. I want to believe he isn't a murderer. I want to believe that more than anything.

But I know one thing: if he is a sociopath, he's the best actor in the history of the world.

CHAPTER 55

ERIKA

I've stopped answering my phone entirely. I don't know where people are getting my number, but I've been getting death threats all day. They keep getting worse and worse. People are calling me up, telling me that they're going to kill me, my daughter, and especially my son. If I don't answer, they leave messages. It's awful.

To some extent though, I know how they feel. They blame me for what Liam did. I blame myself. It feels like there's something I could've done. Maybe when Dr. Hebert didn't work out, I could've found somebody else. Somebody better. Somebody who could have fixed him.

Or I could've done what Jessica Martinson suggested. I could have had him locked up and then walked away.

But that wouldn't have solved the problem. You can't lock somebody up for their thoughts. I could have sent him away to school, but when he turned eighteen, there would be nothing I could do.

At half past six, my phone rings, and I flinch

automatically. I'm lying on the bed, watching the clock until Jason gets home—he was supposed to be home ten minutes ago. I had been unwilling to move from my safe cocoon on the bed until I heard him come in downstairs. But then I glance at the screen and see Jason's name.

"Erika?" He sounds tired on the other line. "Hey. Listen…"

"Please don't tell me you're running late."

"I'm really sorry." He lets out a long sigh. "I've been putting out fires all day. Everybody knows about Liam. I've had two investors back out today."

My stomach sinks. I didn't think this could get any worse, but here it is. We can't afford to lose Jason's income. We've got a huge mortgage and now Liam's legal bills.

I grip the phone tighter. "How long till you can come home?"

"I've got a dinner meeting now, then I need to sit down with my staff to discuss the situation. I'm not going to be able to head home for at least two hours."

"Two *hours*?" I'm going to burst into tears. I was barely holding it together even knowing Jason would be home soon. Two hours till he gets on the road means at least three till he's home. And that's if traffic has died down by then.

"I'm really sorry, Erika," he says again.

I don't want to be alone right now. I'm scared somebody else will throw a rock through our window. Or set the whole place on fire. Now that the sun has gone down, I feel especially uneasy.

"If you want," he finally says, "I'll cancel the meetings. If you really need me…"

I'm tempted to say yes. I do need him. But we also

can't afford to lose his income. I've got to suck it up. After all, it's just three hours. What could happen in three hours? "It's fine. I'll be fine."

"If you're sure…"

"I'm sure."

He lets out a breath. "Okay, thanks, Erika. I'll be home as soon as I can."

I swallow hard. "I love you."

"Love you too."

Three hours. He'll be home in three hours. It's not that long.

I try to take my mind off it by watching television. Anything but the news. I stream a movie on Netflix just so there's no chance of hearing any news reports. The only news report I want to hear is that Olivia Mercer was found and somehow my son had nothing to do with it. Fat chance.

It's around eight thirty when I hear the knock on my bedroom door.

"Come in!" I call out.

The door swings open, and Liam is standing there. He's wearing the same T-shirt and jeans he had on yesterday—I wonder if he slept in them. He looks up at me, and his eyes are red rimmed. It's something I've never seen before.

"Liam?"

"Mom," he says, and his voice breaks.

And then he's sobbing. My sixteen-year-old son—almost a man—is crying his heart out. His shoulders are shaking, and he buries his bruised face in his hands. I leap off the bed and throw my arms around him, and he clings to me. I've never seen him like this. Even as a child.

"Liam," I say. "Honey, what's wrong?"

It's a stupid question. What *isn't* wrong? But specifically, something is bothering him. Maybe he's frightened by the prospect of spending the rest of his life in prison. I couldn't blame him for that one.

"There's something…" He gulps, trying to catch his breath. "There's something I have to tell you."

I suck in a breath. "About Olivia?"

He nods and wipes his eyes.

"Do you…do you know where she is?"

He nods again.

It's true. Everything that I feared is true. "Is she alive?"

He's quiet for a moment. "I…I don't know."

You better hope she's alive. It's the difference between life in prison and a chance at maybe getting out someday. But I don't say all that. He's already crying. No need to make him feel worse.

"We should call the police," I say. "Right now. We'll tell them where she is."

He shakes his head vigorously. "No. It's…it's not a good idea."

"Liam…"

"I'll show you how to get there," he says. "We'll go together."

"We need to call the police."

"Please, Mom." His voice breaks again. "We'll call the police when we get there, okay? We need to go. *Now*."

The urgency in his voice surprises me. After all, wherever Olivia is, she's been there for days. What is so important about going right now? But he's looking at me with his swollen eyes, and it's hard to say no. As soon as we get there though, I'm dialing 911.

"Okay," I say. "Let's go."

Liam doesn't say much during the car ride. He keeps his eyes pinned on the road ahead of us, only speaking to give me directions. When I ask him for an address, he says he doesn't have one. But he knows how to get there.

I focus on the road. Wherever he's taking me, I have to pray that Olivia is still alive. If she's alive, then we can make this right. He has a chance.

If she's dead, then he'll spend the rest of his life in prison.

When we come to a stop at a red light, I reach for my phone. "Let me just text your father to tell him where we're going."

"No," he says sharply. "Don't do that."

He says it so harshly that it gives me an uneasy feeling. It occurs to me that Liam is leading me into the woods all alone and won't tell me where we're going or let me tell anyone else. My son may have done some bad things in his life, but he's never laid a finger on me. Ever.

But now, for the first time in my life, I'm scared for my own safety. What if he isn't leading me to Olivia? What if he's bringing me out into the woods to kill me?

No. He wouldn't. Not my son. My baby. My favorite.

"Turn right here," Liam says.

I squint at where he's pointing. I see only trees, with a narrow clearing between them. "That's not even a road."

"Turn right," he says stubbornly.

I'm about to protest when I see a wheel spinning against a tree. I squint into the black woods. "Is that Hannah's bicycle?"

I look at Liam. He's staring at the bicycle too, an unreadable expression on his face. "Let's go."

261

"Maybe we should call the police," I say for the millionth time.

"Mom…"

But I take out my phone. I'm done with these games. I'm not driving my car down this tiny road to God knows where. And the fact that Hannah is here too is incredibly unsettling. It's time for the police to take over. I know when I'm out of my depth. And frankly, Liam is beginning to scare me.

He keeps staring straight ahead, squinting into the woods.

I'm calling the police. I'm telling them everything. As soon as I…

Oh God. No signal.

"Let's go, Mom." Liam puts one hand on the steering wheel, and I can only barely make out his face in the shadows. "If you won't drive, I will."

CHAPTER 56

OLIVIA

The piece of bread and bottle of water are long gone.

The lack of water is much harder to bear than the lack of food. My mouth feels so dry, I can barely get it open. It feels like my lips are sealed together with glue. And whenever I try to stand up, I feel dizzy. My head is spinning. When I doze off, I dream about water. I dream about finding a puddle and lapping it up like a dog. I'm not picky. I would drink out of the toilet bowl if I could.

Speaking of toilet bowls, I can't remember the last time I peed. I don't think I'm making pee anymore.

He's killing me. He's going to let me die a terrible death of dehydration. He's not even going to let it get to the point where I starve to death, although that would be awful too.

The only positive thing I can say is that my left ankle doesn't throb the way it used to. I hardly even notice it, except when I run my fingers along my calf. The skin is tight and swollen. I can't wiggle my toes anymore or move my ankle. I'm sure if I tried to put weight on it, it would hurt, but I don't have the strength to stand.

It's nighttime now. That tiny slice of light is gone. I have gotten used to the pitch-blackness of this hole. Whether I open or close my eyes, it's the same. This must be what it's like to be blind. It just shows that you can get used to anything. It seems normal now to feel my way around.

The footsteps over my head startle me out of my daze. Is he back? Already? It hasn't been long enough yet, has it?

Maybe he brought food or water for me. I'm willing to do anything he wants if he'll give it to me. *Anything*. I have no pride left. I just want a drink.

"Hello?"

My head jerks up. That's not his voice. That's a female voice. A young female voice.

Is it someone here to find me?

I muster up all my strength, take a deep breath, and try to yell out for help. But when I open my mouth, no words come out. My throat is too dry. I clear my throat best I can. "Help! Help me! I'm down here!"

There's a long pause and the scuffling of feet. "Hello? Are you in there?"

"Yes!" My chest fills with relief. "I'm down here! My name is Olivia Mercer! People are looking for me!"

"Hang on," the female voice says. "There's a key on the wall."

I try to get to my feet, but it's very hard. My left leg can't bear any weight, and my right leg feels like Jell-O. I've got to stand up though. I don't know how else I'll get out of here.

I hear the sound of a key turning in a lock. Metal

clangs against metal, and something drops to the floor. Before I know it, that flashlight turns on me, so bright that it feels like a knife is jabbing me in my eyes. I squeeze them shut, but it's still too bright.

"Turn the light away!" I gasp.

"I'm sorry," the girl says.

Now that the light isn't blinding me, I can see that she really is a girl—even younger than me. I take in her reddish-brown hair and round face. She looks familiar. In my confused state, it takes me a minute to place who she is.

Hannah Cass.

"Hannah," I gasp. "Your—"

"I know." Her voice is sad. "I followed him here last night. I didn't…I really didn't want to believe it." She looks like she's going to cry, and I can't blame her. As horrible as this has been for me, it will be really bad for her too. Her life will never be the same after this.

"I think he's going to find a way to come tonight," she says. "We've got to get out of here."

"Did you call the police?"

Hannah hugs her arms to her chest. "I didn't want to call until I was sure that… Anyway, there's no reception out here. We'll have to make a run for it. I've got my bike."

Run for it? That isn't going to be possible given the state of my ankle. But first things first. I need to get out of this goddamn hole.

"I don't suppose you can climb out," Hannah says.

"My ankle is injured," I admit. "That's going to make it difficult."

She scrunches her eyebrows together. "If I give you my hand, do you think you could…"

I try to stand up again. My right leg is really rubbery.

I make it almost to standing, then I accidentally put a tiny bit of weight on my left ankle. The pain is like white-hot coals. I scream and collapse on the floor.

"Olivia?"

"I can't stand up," I gasp. "I can't do it. You'll have to…go get help…"

The thought of sending Hannah away is nothing short of horrifying. It was an eternity waiting for somebody to come here, and I don't want her to leave. But there's no way I can climb out of this hole, even with her help. We need somebody bigger and stronger and possibly a ladder.

I look up at Hannah, who is frowning. "What's wrong?" I ask her.

"I think I hear something."

We're both quiet. I hear my heart pounding in my ears, but nothing else. At first. But then I hear it.

Rustling of leaves. Followed by footsteps. The sound of hinges creaking.

"He's here," Hannah whispers.

Oh my God. He's here. And he'll kill us both. Well, maybe not Hannah. Maybe he'll let her live—she's family. But I'm gone. At this point, I've clearly become a liability. It's probably not worth it to him to watch me starve to death.

"Hello, Hannah." His voice fills the room above me. I cringe at the familiar sound of it. "I thought I might find you here."

She's silent for a moment. When she speaks again, her voice is shaking. "Hi, Daddy."

CHAPTER 57

JASON

Is it finally my turn? Has Erika finished talking? Or will it go on for another hour or two?

That's Erika. Never shuts up. Always worried about every little thing. Obsessed. Especially about Liam. Anytime he opens his mouth, she has to analyze it to death. Half the time, I'm just staring at her, waiting for her to stop talking. Hannah is the same way. The two of them might not look alike, but they are two peas in a pod. Like mother, like daughter.

Liam, on the other hand. Well, you can guess who *he* takes after.

You're probably wondering why I married Erika, considering she's certainly far from my favorite person. There is no simple answer to that, but I suppose that some part of me wanted a normal life. When I first met Erika, she was beautiful. That long black hair and dark eyes. She was wearing a fitted white blouse and a skirt that left just enough to the imagination. I wanted her. And not just for that one night before disposing of the body. I wanted her a second night, which turned into a third, and then a year.

And for the first time, I could imagine a normal life for myself. Well, as normal as I was capable of. A wife—a family. It didn't seem like a bad idea, and before I really thought it through, Erika and I were getting married. In retrospect, it was a mistake. But by the time I realized that, it was too late. We already had a baby on the way.

The easiest thing to do was stash the family away on Long Island. I work long hours. No, not really. I don't work much at all. I come up with ideas that are great ideas and make me money without having to do much. The truth is I have a lot of free time on my hands, which I do manage to fill with various activities.

And the best part is Erika never suspected a thing. Not even a little bit. It just goes to show how brilliant I am at acting the part. Liam, on the other hand, leaves a lot to be desired. I suppose I can't blame him. I was equally careless when I was his age. My parents were not as understanding as Erika and I have been either. My mother was a deeply religious Catholic, and she believed I was punishment for one of her past sins.

My mother was terrified of me. It probably had something to do with me murdering her cat when I was five. She loved that cat, for reasons I could never understand. It was a cat after all. It didn't have real emotions, although it did struggle quite a bit when I held that pillow over its head until it stopped moving. That was part of the fun.

Erika took Liam to a shrink, but my parents had different ways of dealing with me. After I killed that cat, my mother locked me in the closet under the staircase. She left me there for six hours and ignored me when I banged my fists on the doors and screamed until my voice was hoarse. It didn't "cure" me. After the next incident, my father beat me with his belt until I cried. Back in those days, nobody at school cared about the welts all over my back. Beating your kids used to be more acceptable. He did it frequently.

And then, when I was fourteen, there was that girl. Michelle. My first. I don't remember all their names, but you always remember your first.

I didn't get caught by the police. I was too smart for that. But my parents knew. They had no information that could have stood up in a court of law, but it was enough for them. And I was too big to be locked in the closet anymore—as tall as my father by then. And stronger.

That was when my mother hired the exorcist.

He was a priest—or at least he had the collar. A middle-aged man with a round, red face. They surprised me when I came home from school one day, and my father, the priest, and his assistant worked together to hold me down and tie me to my bed while they drew the shades. For hours, they shouted prayers in my face and threw holy water at me. The priest demanded I repeat the prayers, and for the first hour, I refused.

By the second hour, I was willing to say whatever he wanted if he'd let me go free.

When they finally untied me from that bed, I was the angriest I had ever been in my entire life. There were bruises on my wrists where I had been bound to the bed, and I was soaked in a combination of holy water and my own sweat. I wanted to lunge at that priest and scratch his eyes out, but I was outnumbered. I had to wait.

I removed the batteries from the smoke detectors in the house. I turned on the gas stove. That night, my parents unfortunately died in a tragic fire that their only son managed to survive. I told Erika my mother died of cancer and my father had a heart attack, but there was really no way for her to know that was a lie.

And that priest—well, he was mugged a few days later in a dark alley. Poor guy—the police report indicated he suffered quite a bit in the hour before his throat was finally slashed.

After I buried my parents, I went to live with my grandmother. Nana was eighty years old, demented, and half blind. She couldn't care less what I did with myself. We got along very well.

Everybody says Liam is a smart kid, but he's not as smart as me. I made two million dollars selling my first startup company when I was only twenty-five. No college diploma. Just brains. I made a lot more on the second one. So I've got plenty of money. Money that Erika has no idea about. She worries about the income from her stupid little newspaper job, and it's hard not to laugh.

Yes, I could do without the family. But it's not so bad. I take a lot of business trips, during which I get to have some fun, then I go back home before the police arrive. I'm much more careful when I'm near home. That girl sharing the hole with Olivia was named Hallie Barton— that's what her driver's license said. She ran away from home because her mother was a drunk and her stepfather beat her up, and she was hitchhiking when I picked her up. Don't these young girls know how dangerous it is to hitchhike? I mean, look what happened to Hallie.

In any case, nobody is looking for Hallie.

I could have been happy this way my whole life. I could've continued doing my own activities on the side, and nobody would have been the wiser. But then there was Liam.

He did stupid things to attract attention. What was he thinking, duct-taping that girl in the closet? I know he was only five, but it made me sick when I heard about it. They threw him out of the school. And Erika later ended up taking him to a shrink. As many times as I told her that it wasn't a big deal, she knew it was.

Liam was a reflection on me. And I knew it was just a matter of time before people figured it out. Before Erika realized Liam didn't get his personality from her loser, jailbird father.

Years ago, I saw Liam skulking around the house of that English teacher of his. I had gone to parent-teacher night that year, and I could tell the guy hated Liam. Saw right through him the way my parents saw through me. And now Liam was going to do something stupid and obvious and probably get himself in just enough trouble that Erika would want to take him back to a shrink.

So I gave Liam a hand. Broke the radiator to cause the carbon monoxide leak. I shorted out the detector. Liam never would have been clever enough to do it himself. They were supposed to be dead by morning. A neighbor would have noticed Liam sneaking around the house, and he would've taken the fall. But the teacher didn't even die, and the police were too incompetent to arrest my son. So that was a bust.

And then this opportunity came up.

Sometimes I do listen to Hannah when she babbles on. She mentioned this girl that Liam liked, Olivia Mercer. I wonder if he really likes women or if he's like me. I am attracted to women, but only in the most superficial way—as a sexual release, nothing more. I wonder if Liam is the same. I would have said he was, but on the night he came back from seeing Olivia, he was grinning to himself like any lovestruck teenager. He's like me in many ways, but he's also different. The way he's close with Hannah, for example. The way he's protective of her. I was never close to anyone that way. Even Erika.

Although there was a time when I liked Erika quite a bit. Maybe even loved her. I don't know.

On the night Liam sneaked out to see Olivia, I knew this was my chance. Especially when I saw him pull back into the driveway in Erika's Toyota. I sent him to bed, then went out myself, following the directions in the GPS. I had been wondering how I would get Olivia to come back downstairs, but it turned out she was already on her porch. Looking up at the stars. Probably fantasizing about my son.

She recognized me when I waved to her and came over to the car. She flashed me a big smile. I should have lost that extra weight years ago, because it makes a big difference with women. Women trust you more if you're good looking. Of course, Liam takes after his mother and is more attractive than I could ever be. And that makes him more dangerous.

But to be fair, I'm extremely dangerous.

"Liam told us he was heading home," I explained to Olivia. I pasted that worried expression on my face that I've noticed parents get when their children don't come home when they're supposed to. "But he isn't back yet. I'm worried."

She frowned like she was worried too. "Oh my God, I hope he's okay."

"Do you think you could get in the car and help me look for a few minutes? It's hard to keep an eye out when I'm driving."

"Of course!"

Olivia got into the car without a second thought. I had the chloroform ready. She was out like a light. And before any nosy neighbors could realize it was me driving this time and not my son, I took off.

Liam's relationship with Olivia. The neighbor who saw him with her at two in the morning. The hair and blood I planted in the trunk. And then, after Olivia died, I was going to make her body resurface, because it's harder to get a conviction when there's no body. I had been trying to think of what else I could plant on her that would be the final nail in my son's coffin.

And now here is Hannah, messing everything up.

Well, that's what she's *trying* to do. And yes, she's messing up the original plan. The original plan was to have a little fun with Olivia and get Liam locked away for good. I didn't have any other ambitions besides that. But now that Hannah is here, I realize this plan could be even better than I originally thought.

Here's what the police will discover:

Liam kidnapped Olivia, and when Hannah discovered her brother's plan, Liam sadly had to kill both of them. And then Erika was so distressed, she took an overdose of the Xanax she keeps in her nightstand. Except they're not Xanax but something much stronger that I swapped for the Xanax several months ago.

Or maybe Liam kills Erika as well. I haven't decided on that part yet.

And I, of course, will play the part of the grieving

widower, who no longer has to deal with a nagging wife, a whiny daughter, and a sociopath son. It will be even easier than when I was fourteen and played the grieving son.

It's an excellent plan. I can't wait to see how it all plays out.

That's the fun part.

CHAPTER 58

OLIVIA

I still can't wrap my head around it entirely. Mr. Cass. Liam's dad. I had seen him once before when he was picking Liam up early from school, and he seemed really nice. And for a dad…well, he's pretty hot. *Really* hot. He looks so athletic and muscular and has a nice smile, whereas my dad is balding and has a potbelly.

So when he told me to get into the car, of course I did it. I was worried about Liam. And there was no reason to suspect Mr. Cass wanted to harm me. He's Liam's dad after all.

If people are wondering what happened to me, they must be blaming Liam. He's the one I had a date with that night. I'd bet anything that my nosy neighbor Mrs. Levy saw us kissing that night. If I never reappear, he's the one who will get blamed. If anyone goes to jail for this, it will be Liam.

"Dad," Hannah says in a choked voice, "please don't do this."

Do what? Does he have a gun? A knife? I wish I could see what's going on out there.

"Hannah." He speaks in that bland, calm voice that he used when he was asking me what it was like to starve to death. "Do you know what you're doing? You're ripping apart our family."

"I swear to God, don't come any closer."

"Hannah, come on. I'm your father. She's nobody."

"Dad…" Hannah is sobbing now. "Please…"

"I'm going to make this so simple for you, Hannah. She's not getting out of here alive. There's no chance. The only one who has a chance is you."

My heart is beating so quickly my chest is starting to hurt. "Hannah," I say, "don't listen to him. He's evil."

"Would you like to finish her off, Hannah? I'll pull her up and let you do it."

"Please, Daddy, don't…"

He laughs. It's a sound I've come to despise over the last several days. "I'm just kidding. I know you can't do it. You're not like me. You're so much like your mother, it's disgusting."

I can barely make out Hannah's face in the shadows. Her cheeks are streaked with tears.

"I'm afraid this all has to end tonight," Mr. Cass says. "For both of you."

And Hannah screams.

CHAPTER 59

ERIKA

om." Liam shakes my arm, growing urgency in his voice. "Please. Just drive."

I have no reception out here. Every bone in my body is screaming that I should call the police. But then what? My son is here. My daughter is apparently here. Something terrible is going on, and I can't imagine sitting here in this car and twiddling my thumbs until the cops show up.

Liam is not going to kill me. Sometimes I'm not sure what he's thinking, but I know that much. He would never hurt me. And the only thing I can hear in his voice right now is fear. He's scared of something.

But what?

And why on earth is Hannah's bicycle out here? I can't figure it out.

So I push on, into the woods, following his directions. I drive another five minutes on this dirt path, and finally a cabin comes into view. The cabin is dilapidated—the wood is splintered and dirty, falling apart in places. The front door is hanging by only one of its hinges. It looks like it's been abandoned for years. Except for two things:

The dim light coming from inside.

And the Prius parked right outside.

I don't know why Hannah's bicycle is out here. But I can't even *begin* to imagine why my husband's car is parked here when he's supposed to be at work.

"Liam," I say slowly, "what is going on? No more games. Tell me right now."

He takes a deep breath. "Dad went out last night, and Hannah followed him. She said he came here—she showed me directions she wrote down. She told me she was going back tonight, and I wanted to come, but she was worried I'd get in trouble if…well, if she found something really bad. But I was sitting in my room and thinking about Hannah and…I thought Dad might…"

I stare at him. "Might what?"

He frowns at me. "You know Dad is a psycho, right?"

I get a horrible sinking feeling in my chest, like my whole world is collapsing on itself. "What are you talking about? Your father is the most normal man I've ever met."

He snorts. "You don't see it, I guess. I do. I always have. That's why it scares him so much when I…well, you know. He sees himself in me. But I'm not like him. Not as much as he thinks anyway."

"This is ridiculous," I whisper. "Why are you telling me this?"

"I thought you knew." Liam blinks at me. "All those years. You didn't even… I mean, I don't know what he's doing all day, but he's *not* at work. I called his company once when I needed to reach him, and they told me he's never there. You never suspected?"

No, I never suspected anything. *Ever.*

But there were all those late nights. All those "business trips" he always had to take. I always accepted it blindly. There was that time I worried he was having an affair, but maybe it was something much worse than that.

What if I was smelling the perfume of a dead woman?

No, that's not possible. Why am I thinking this way? Jason is my husband of twenty years. He's not a murderer. I don't know what his car is doing out here, but there's got to be a reasonable explanation.

"I think Olivia is in there," Liam says. "Mom, I'm really scared he might kill them both."

"He wouldn't do that," I say. Although it's pretty clear I'm no expert on what Jason would or would not do.

Liam hesitates for only a split second before he darts out of my car. I call to him, not wanting him to go inside and face whatever is in there. What if it really is Jason? Could he have done something like this? He couldn't have. Never. I don't care what Liam says. I know my husband. A guy who can make that many puns about eggs is *not* going around murdering people. He just isn't.

I pick my way through a dirt path, littered with leaves and branches, until I reach the cabin, ten paces behind Liam. He's taller than me, so his strides are longer, and he's more surefooted on the uneven ground. We get there just in time to see Jason stumble through the broken door.

Liam stops short, staring at his father. "Where is Hannah? Where is Olivia?"

Jason's face darkens in a way I've never seen before. At that moment, it seems entirely possible that everything Liam just told me is true. That Jason is somebody I don't know at all. Someone who could've done horrible things.

But then he catches sight of me, and the dark look fades from his face like it was never there. "Erika! Thank God you're here. You've got to call the police right now!"

"Where are they?" Liam shouts at him.

Jason gazes at him with venom in his eyes. "They're both in there—dead. You should know since you're the one who killed them, you monster."

I feel like somebody punched me in the gut. "Dead?"

"I'm so sorry, Erika." Jason's eyes fill with tears as he rushes to my side. His hand is on my back. "I tried to save Hannah…"

"You liar!" Liam's face is purple. "You hate Hannah! You hate all of us!"

My legs feel like they're going to collapse under me. No, not Hannah. She can't be… No…

Jason's arms encircle me, barely catching me before I collapse. "We're going to call the police," he says in a soft, soothing voice. "They're going to punish Liam for what he did to our baby." He glares at Liam. "Don't even try to run. They're going to catch you."

Liam stares at us, his face still scarlet. But then something changes in his eyes. They grow wide, like he's seen something terrible. "Mom," he gasps.

And then, instead of running, he lunges at Jason. I see the glint of a knife in Jason's hand. He hadn't been holding it when he came out of the cabin. He took it out as he was comforting me.

Oh my God. Was he going to stab me?

Jason is still heavier than Liam, but Liam is younger and quicker. The knife clatters out of Jason's hands, and Liam grapples him to the ground. For a moment, it looks like Jason might manage to get free, but then Liam takes a swing at him, and I hear a sickening crunch. When I look at Jason's face, there's blood pouring out of his nose.

"You little asshole!" Jason howls. "I'm going to kill you."

"Mom, the knife," Liam manages.

The knife is lying in the grass. It doesn't look familiar to me—it's not one of the dull blades from our kitchen. I snatch it off the ground so Jason can't get it. My fingers close around the handle, but I'm not sure what to do with the sharp end. I point it in Jason's direction, but who am I kidding? I'd never be able to stab him.

He knows it too.

"Mom." Liam's voice is breathless. "Give me the knife."

Jason struggles against our son, who has him pinned down tightly. I'm impressed with how easily Liam is restraining him. Liam has become stronger than his father. "Erika, don't give it to him," Jason manages.

I stare at my husband. "Why shouldn't I?"

Jason's face is ashen. "You know what Liam is like. You've always known. He's a *psychopath*, Erika."

Well, that's not untrue.

Jason sees my hesitation, and he pushes on. "Erika," he says urgently, "you do *not* want him to have that knife. You know that. He'll kill us both."

Will he?

Liam looks at me with his brown eyes that are so much like what I see when I stare into the mirror. I'm not sure what to believe anymore, but between Jason and Liam, I know which one I want to have the knife.

I turn the blade around and offer Liam the handle.

My son smiles at me with those perfect, straight teeth—a smile I know is one hundred percent genuine.

"Thanks, Mom." His fingers close around the handle. "And you were half right, Dad."

I watch as Liam plunges the knife into his father's chest.

CHAPTER 60

ERIKA

Liam knew exactly where to put the knife. With that one stab wound, all the blood drains out of my husband's face, and seconds later, he's coughing it out. He's dying. He's dying quickly. So quickly that even if we called for an ambulance now, if that were possible, it would be too late.

"Erika," Jason manages, choking on his own blood. "You…"

I stare down at him, waiting for his final words to me. Is he going to tell me he loves me one last time? I don't think I could handle it if he did. I already feel like I can barely stand up.

"You *bitch*," he finishes. "After all I did for you…"

I flinch as if he hit me. Liam was right. Jason is not the man I thought he was. He's sick. He's a psychopath. And he's done something horrible. He was planning to kill me, and the only reason I'm alive right now is because my son saved me.

Jason deserves this death.

I take a step forward, standing over him. I draw back my foot, and with all my strength, I kick him right in the ribs. It's the last thing he feels before he loses consciousness.

I bury my face in my hands, wanting to cry, but I'm too stunned. Jason. Hannah. Gone. Is this really happening? I think I'm going to be sick.

"Mom." That urgency is back in Liam's voice, bursting into my haze. "Let's go into the cabin. Maybe we can still save them."

He tugs at my arm, and I follow him without thinking. My legs move automatically, but my head won't stop spinning. I'm terrified to see what's inside there. If my daughter is lying dead on the ground in that cabin, I'm not sure I could go on after seeing that. It would destroy me.

Inside the cabin is dark except for the beam from a flashlight lying on the ground. The flashlight provides just enough illumination to show there's no one in here. But I hear voices. Muffled female voices.

"Hannah!" Liam yells. He drops to his knees and plants his palms on the ground. "Where are you?"

This time, I hear the words more distinctly in my daughter's voice: "Down here!"

There's a trapdoor and a ring of keys lying on the ground, and Liam tries each one until the lock pops open. His hands are so steady—I'm amazed. How could he be so calm after what just happened? I don't think I could hold a key, much less fit one into the lock. He swings the trapdoor open and shines the flashlight inside.

There they are. Hannah. Her face is tear streaked, but she's alive. And Olivia. Also alive.

The relief I feel almost knocks me off my feet. Hannah is okay. My daughter is alive.

Thank God.

CHAPTER 61

OLIVIA

Hannah! Where are you?"

Hannah's disembodied voice floats through the air: "Down here!"

I reach into the darkness until my hand makes contact with Hannah's arm. "Shush! What are you *doing*?"

"It's okay. That's Liam. He'll help us out."

"Are you sure about that?"

"Of course I'm sure. He's my brother."

I don't point out the fact that her father is the one who trapped me here for four days with plans to let me starve to death, so somebody being in her family doesn't exactly make me feel good about them. But at this point, there's nothing more I can do.

The trapdoor swings open, and there he is. Liam Cass. The boy I'd been crushing on for nearly three months, who I used to think was the cutest guy in the whole dang school. He's holding a flashlight, but he's not pointing it at our eyes like his father did. I can just barely make out the contours of his face. "Can you get out?" he asks.

Hannah shakes her head. "No," she says. "I hurt my wrist when Dad pushed me down here. And Olivia's ankle is really bad."

Liam listens to this, nodding thoughtfully. "I can come down there. I'll help you get out."

Before I can suggest this might not be a great idea, Liam has climbed down into the hole. He's very nimble, and he gets in easily without hurting himself. Now that I can see him up close, I realize there's blood all over him. It's everywhere. It's staining his T-shirt and splattered all over his face. Hannah clasps her hand over her mouth.

"Liam!" she exclaims. "Are you... I mean, did he..."

"I'm fine." Liam makes a face. "It's *his* blood."

Hannah's mouth falls open. "Is he...dead?"

Liam nods slowly. He doesn't give any other details, and I'm glad.

"I told you not to come," she whispers, her eyes filling up with tears again. "You're going to get in trouble now."

"You've got to be kidding me, Hannah. He would've killed you. How could I let that happen?"

Then she throws her arms around him, and she hugs him so tightly that when she pulls away, her father's blood is all over her shirt too. She wipes her eyes as he crouches down next to me on the floor, where I'm clutching my ankle. In the light of the flashlight, his eyes look black.

"What's hurting?" he asks.

I show him my ankle. He shines the flashlight on it, and we both gasp simultaneously. It looks *terrible*. It's swollen to twice the size it should be, the skin is shiny and red,

287

and yellow pus is coming out of a break in the skin. I had no idea it was that bad.

"Don't worry," Liam says. "We're going to get you out of here. I promise."

One corner of his lips moves up in a crooked smile, and I remember how much I used to like him. How he used to make my heart speed up in my chest when I watched him race around the track after school. It seems like an eternity ago.

Liam is tall enough to see over the trapdoor when he stands on the mound of dirt I made. He calls to someone else to come help him. For a moment, I'm paralyzed with fear that his father is there, but then I hear his mother's shaky voice.

"I'm going to lift them out through the trapdoor," he tells his mother. "You have to help them out."

Liam is very gentle with me. He takes his time putting his left arm under my knees so he won't hurt me when he lifts me. I cling to his neck as he steps up on the mound and carefully raises me up to his mother. She is shaking like a leaf as she helps me up onto the wood floor of the cabin. My ankle gets twisted in the process, because she's not as careful as Liam was, and it hurts so bad my eyes water.

After Liam lifts Hannah out of the hole, Mrs. Cass won't stop hugging her. She throws her arms around Hannah's shoulders, sobbing that she thought she was dead. Hannah clings to her just as hard. Watching them makes me want my mother so much it's painful. At least now I know I'm going to see her soon. It wasn't like when I was trapped in the hole. This is almost over.

"He told us he was going to come back and kill us as

soon as he was done with the two of you," Hannah sobs. "He meant it. You could see it in his eyes."

I still can't manage to stand up. My ankle hurts more than I would have thought possible. It's not just broken—there's something really wrong with it. Liam looks at me writhing on the ground and bends down beside me. "I'm going to pick you up, okay?"

I flinch, not wanting anyone to get within two feet of my ankle. "It hurts a lot."

"I'll be really careful. I promise."

What choice do I have? "Okay."

He does what he did before, gently scooping me up in his arms. He doesn't even grunt when he lifts me. I had no idea he was that strong. Despite everything that's happened, a sense of calm comes over me as he holds me, and I rest my head against his chest. I feel safe here.

Liam carries me out of the cabin with his mother and Hannah leading the way. After about ten paces, he stops short and looks at something on the ground.

It takes me a moment to realize he's looking down at his father.

Mr. Cass is lying face up on the dirt. His shirt is soaked with blood, far more than what's on Liam's shirt. There's blood on his chin too, his eyes are staring up at the sky, and his mouth is hanging open.

He's dead. He's definitely dead.

It's over.

CHAPTER 62

Transcript of police interview with Erika Cass.

PD: "Mrs. Cass, can you repeat for me one more time exactly what happened when you reached the cabin?"

EC: "After we parked, I saw Jason coming out of the cabin. He had a knife, and he told me that Hannah and Olivia were both dead. He admitted he was the one who killed them, although I didn't realize at the time he was lying."

PD: "Did you believe him?"

EC: "I didn't know what to believe, Detective. Jason and I were married for twenty years. I never imagined he could do something like that. But you didn't see the look in his eyes."

PD: "And then what happened?"

EC: "He lunged at me with the knife. Thank God Liam was there with me. Otherwise, I'd be dead.

Liam ran at him and tackled him, and he dropped the knife. That's when I picked it up and..."

PD: "Mrs. Cass?"

EC: "I'm sorry. This is so hard."

PD: "Please take your time."

EC: "He got away from Liam. He's bigger than Liam. And then he came at me again and..."

PD: "And?"

EC: "I still had the knife. So I did the only thing I could do: I stabbed him with it when he came at me."

PD: "So you were the one who stabbed him?"

EC: "That's right."

PD: "It wasn't Liam?"

EC: "No."

PD: "So here's the thing, Mrs. Cass. The blood spatter pattern on Liam's clothes makes it look like he was the one in front of Jason when he was stabbed. You have almost no blood on your clothes at all."

EC: "I don't know what to tell you. Liam was right next to me. And he bent over Jason after I stabbed him, which I guess is how all that blood ended up on him. He tried to resuscitate him, but it didn't work. Obviously."

PD: "I see."

EC: "Am I...am I under arrest?"

PD: "Given the circumstances and Olivia's corroboration of your story, we are not planning to pursue charges at this time."

EC: "..."

PD: "But our investigation is not complete. There will be an autopsy."

EC: "Yes. Yes, of course."

PD: "I have one other question, Mrs. Cass."

EC: "Yes?"

PD: "Why are you protecting Liam?"

EC: "I have no idea what you're talking about.
Detective, my husband just tried to kill me."

PD: "But Liam is the one who stabbed him, isn't he?"

EC: "Detective, my husband of twenty years is dead.
This has been a really hard day. I don't... I can't
even think straight. I told you what happened. I
have nothing else to say."

CHAPTER 63

ERIKA

Detective Rivera doesn't believe my story.

She thinks Liam is the one who stabbed Jason. To be fair, he *is* covered in blood. But I couldn't take the risk that he'd go to jail for this. If anyone should take the fall for it, it should be me. I'm the idiot who married the guy. I am the fool who believed his lies for twenty years of marriage.

Detective Rivera met us at the emergency room and was plainly surprised to find that Olivia was not only alive but clinging to Liam as he carried her into the emergency room. He mostly kept his mouth shut as I told the detective my story about how I stabbed Jason in self-defense. He and I are the only ones who know the truth.

With Hannah's help, I gave Rivera directions to the cabin, where they found my husband's body.

"I can't believe it," Rivera kept saying. "I really thought…"

I couldn't blame her. I thought the same thing.

While Hannah is off getting X-rays, I'm left with Liam in Hannah's room in the ER. It's the first moment we've had alone since we rescued Hannah and Olivia. Well, I should say since *he* rescued them. I helped. A little.

There's so much I feel I need to say to him. I thought the worst of him, and he knew it. That's not the way a mother should behave. I'm ashamed of myself. I'm ashamed of the fact that I had no idea what Jason was up to.

My own husband. I can't believe it.

"You didn't have to tell the detective you killed him," Liam says quietly. "We could have told her the truth."

"It's better this way."

"Why?"

"You know why." I look down at my hands, which have finally stopped shaking. "I'm not letting them put you in jail again. Not for that."

"It was self-defense."

"No, it wasn't. And you know it."

Liam stares down at his sneakers, which are caked in a combination of mud and blood. He doesn't contradict me, and I'm glad, because we both know it would be a lie. I'm sick of the lies.

I squeeze my knees with my fingers. "But I'm sorry I accused you of… Well, you know. I was wrong. Obviously."

He doesn't look up. "Well, it's not like you were the only one who thought so. The whole town thought I killed her."

"Yes, but I'm your mother. I should have believed you."

He chews on his lip, his eyes still downcast. "Yeah,

but…let's face it. Over the years, I gave you plenty of reasons to believe I'd do something like this."

It's true, but it's a shock to hear him admit it. We always pretended like Liam was the perfect son, and he played the role to a T. "But you didn't do it."

"No. I didn't."

"Also," I add, "I want to thank you."

Liam finally looks up at me. The bruise on his cheek has faded slightly, but it's still there. "For what?"

"You saved my life. You saved Hannah's life. Even though…"

He frowns. "Even though what?"

"Even though…" I clear my throat. "Nothing. Never mind."

He cocks his head to the side. "What?"

I bite my lip, afraid to say the words that have been circling my brain for the last decade. *Your son doesn't love you. He's not capable of it.* "I know you don't feel…you know…"

Liam is quiet for a moment. "Feel *what*?"

"Dr. Hebert explained it to me," I say quickly. "I know you have trouble with…you know, emotions."

"Emotions?"

"You know, like…love."

"*What?*" Liam blinks at me. "Um, that's bullshit. You really don't think that I love you and Hannah?"

I don't know what to say to that. "It's okay if you don't. It's just who you are."

"Jesus, Mom." He rakes a hand through his dark hair. "I can't believe you're saying that. Of course I love you. You're my mom."

"But Dr. Hebert said—"

"Oh, well, if the quack psychiatrist said it, then it

must be true, right?" He snorts. "I just risked my *life* for you. I love you, Mom. If anything happened to you or Hannah…" He's quiet then, looking down at his hands. "It would be awful," he finally says.

I don't always know if Liam is telling the truth, but at this moment, I know for sure that he is. My son loves me. I always thought he was incapable of it. But I was wrong.

CHAPTER 64

OLIVIA

I've been in the hospital for five days now, and my parents have barely left my side. My mother has been sleeping in my room in a recliner because she's scared to leave me. I would complain, but the truth is I'm glad she's here. The last thing I want is to be alone in this hospital room.

I had to have surgery on my ankle. It was broken in two places, and then it got infected on top of that. I needed antibiotics through an IV, and I was also really dehydrated when I came in. My ankle is in a cast now, and the doctor told me it's going to be a while before I can put weight on it again. So I guess I better get used to crutches.

As of yesterday, I finally started feeling up to having visitors besides my parents. The first person who came to see me was Madison, of course. She gave me a huge hug, and we both cried, and it was like our fight never happened. She told me she never gave up hope that I was okay.

She's back again today. She's sitting at my bedside while my mother is downstairs in the cafeteria, and she's drawing a doodle on my cast. I've never had a cast before, and I'm actually excited for people to sign it. I remember being so jealous of the kids in my class who had casts and got to have people sign them.

Other than that, it sucks having a cast. The damn thing gets so itchy. I stuck a pencil in there this morning to try to reach an itch on the side of my calf, and the next thing I knew, the pencil was gone! When I take this cast off, half the contents of my desk drawer are going to fall out.

"Leave some room for other people," I say to Madison, whose drawing is getting a little out of control. She's going to be like the John Hancock of my cast.

"Hey, I'm giving your cast an artistic flair." She's not joking around. She actually brought different color markers for just this reason. "You'll thank me later."

As she gets back to work on her design, my nurse comes into the room. "Olivia," she says in a singsong voice, "you've got another visitor."

I must be feeling a lot better, because the thought of having two people with me in this room doesn't fill me with dread. "Who is it?"

"It's a boy. And he's *very* cute." The nurse winks at me. "He says his name is Liam. Is he your boyfriend?"

Madison freezes mid-doodle. "You're not going to see him, are you?"

"Mad, he saved my life," I murmur.

"Yeah, but if it wasn't for his dad, he wouldn't have had to."

I don't want to admit that I share her hesitation. Liam came to see me yesterday too, and my mother quickly turned him away. I was upset at her but also a little relieved.

But at the same time, Liam did save my life. When he

saw I was trapped, he jumped into that hole without hesitation and picked me up. He carried me into the hospital. He was my hero.

"Send him in," I say.

Madison gives me a look. "Are you sure this is a good idea?"

"It will be fine, but…can you give us a minute alone?"

She holds up one finger. "*One* minute. That's all you're getting, girlie."

Liam steps into my hospital room tentatively, holding a small bouquet of multicolored flowers. Madison shoots him a dirty look, but she steps aside to let him in. He steps toward my bed, holding out the flowers. "Hey. These are for you. The florist said it was, um, a summer assortment."

"Thank you," I say stiffly. "You can put them on the windowsill."

As he places the assortment next to all the others, I flash back to the last time I saw him. He was crouched in front of his mother's car, his shirt caked in drying blood, and he was coaxing me out of the car to take me into the hospital. He was so gentle with me. It was exactly what I needed.

He drops his eyes. "I'm really glad you're okay," he says.

I study Liam's features. I noticed five days ago that he had a black eye, and it's mostly faded by now, but I can still see slight bruising. "What happened to your face?"

He laughs and touches his cheekbone. "That? Oh, it's nothing."

"So tell me."

"Um, Tyler punched me when he thought I was the one who…"

"Oh."

I only heard a little bit about what happened while I was missing. It sounds like the whole town believed Liam was the one who kidnapped me. The police actually arrested him and took him to jail. While I was locked up, so was he.

"How is your family doing?" I ask.

The smile disappears from Liam's face. "Shitty. My mother cries a lot."

"Do you miss him?"

I hold my breath, waiting for an answer. During the days Jason Cass had me trapped in that hole, I grew to despise him. But I can't forget he's Liam's dad. If I found out my dad was a murderer, would I hate him? It's hard to imagine.

"I don't know, Olivia," he says. "He lied to all of us. There were other women, you know. A lot of others. The police aren't even sure how many… Honestly, it makes me sick to think about it."

I suck in a breath, realizing that if Hannah hadn't followed her father that night, I would have joined his long list of victims. And Jason Cass probably would've gotten away with it. Liam may very well have taken the fall.

"I didn't even know him," Liam says. "How can I miss him if I didn't know who he was? None of us knew."

I nod. "I know what you mean."

One corner of his lip quirks up. "Anyway, I'm sure Madison will burst in here any minute to throw me out. And I know for a fact your mom will kill me if she finds me here. So… I just wanted to make sure you're okay. And now I'd better go."

I look up at him. I keep remembering that moment

when he jumped into the hole to save me. Nobody has ever done anything like that for me before. I don't care what kind of person his father was, Liam is very different. He's a good person. He's a hero.

And also, that nurse was right. He *is* very cute. And I still get a little tingle in my lips remembering how it felt when he kissed me.

"Hey," I say.

He lifts an eyebrow at me. "Yes?"

"When I get out of here, maybe you'll let me take you out for vanilla milkshakes."

His eyes widen. "Really?"

"Well," I say, "I want to thank you for saving my life."

A slow grin spreads across his face. "I'd be okay with that."

I shrug, but I'm grinning too. "So it's a date?"

"Okay." He nods vigorously. "It's a date."

And we can't stop smiling at each other.

EPILOGUE

ONE YEAR LATER

ERIKA

I've got two eggs in the frying pan that I'm cooking up for breakfast. Low and slow. That's the trick.

I set up a radio on the counter in the kitchen. Liam and Hannah both listen to music on their phones using some crazy app, but I'm old school and like listening to the radio. I like hearing the new pop songs, the insipid DJ banter, and even the commercials. Right now, there's a Bruno Mars song on the radio, and I'm singing along to myself.

"Mo-om," Hannah groans as she looks up from her bowl of Cheerios. "You're getting all the words wrong. If you're going to sing along, don't say all the wrong words."

"I'm getting some of them right."

"You think you are, but you're not."

"Yes, I am."

"You're not. It's *really* cringey."

"Well, I don't care." And just to make a point, I belt out the wrong lyrics on purpose: "I'll slap a grenade in ya!"

"Oh my *God*, Mom."

Hannah stands up with her bowl of cereal, unable to tolerate another moment of my singing. She plunks the bowl down on the counter and lets out one more monstrous sigh before she heads upstairs.

I smile to myself as I stir the eggs. One year ago, I never would have imagined we'd be in this same kitchen, making eggs like everything was normal again. Hannah has improved her grades in school, and Liam just got back last night from the statewide debate competition in Albany, which his team won. Things are back to normal and going as well as they could be, given all the revelations that have come out in the last year.

For example, that my husband was a serial killer.

Yes, that one came as a huge shock. It was bad enough finding out he was responsible for taking Olivia. But Detective Rivera has kept me in the loop, and Jason Cass has now been linked by DNA evidence to twelve murders over the last twenty-five years. And those are only the ones where he left evidence behind. God only knows how many others there were. Because he's dead, we'll never know for sure.

The animosity we experienced when the truth first emerged was overwhelming. I thought we were going to have to leave town and change our names to escape the death threats. But then I was offered a spot on a national news show to tell my story. When I shared the tale of how I discovered my husband's secret, killed him in self-defense, and rescued the girl he kidnapped, I became a national hero. Brian offered me back my spot at the *Nassau Nutshell*, but I turned it down because I got a book deal for quite a lot of money.

Wife of a Serial Killer. Has a ring to it, doesn't it?

As I stir the eggs, Liam sprints through the back door wearing a damp T-shirt and gym shorts. He was out running early this morning. I don't know how he has the energy after getting back from Albany with the rest of the team late last night. His face is pink, and he's grinning ear to ear. "Eggs!" he exclaims when he sees what I've got in the frying pan. "You're making me some, right?"

"Of course."

"They smell amazing," he says. "I'm starving."

He's still smiling as he takes his phone out of his pocket. He's in a *really* good mood this morning, but he's been in a good mood a lot lately. He types a message into his phone with his thumbs, then grins wider when his phone buzzes in response. He's probably texting Olivia.

Amazingly, Liam and Olivia are still together. He adores her. They go out several nights a week and talk on the phone every night. She's at his track team practice cheering him on every time he runs. They're coordinating which colleges they're applying to so they can stay together after graduation in June. I'm not sure if it's a great idea—they're only seventeen and have so many new experiences ahead of them. And to be completely frank, Liam is a much more competitive college applicant than Olivia. I don't want him to give up an opportunity on her behalf.

But I can't deny she's good for him. And I certainly can't deny that he loves her. I can tell by the way he looks at her and wants to spend every minute with her.

As for me, I doubt I'll ever date again.

"I'm going to go take a shower now." Liam wipes sweat from his forehead with the back of his arm. "But when I get out, you're going to have eggs for me, right,

Mom? Five eggs." He holds up one hand and wiggles his fingers. "*Five*. I'm hungry."

"You got it, kid."

"You're the best, Mom." He kisses me quickly on the cheek and dashes up the stairs to his bedroom, whistling in the hallway. He's in an exceptionally good mood. He must be happy about winning the debate yesterday.

The Bruno Mars song has ended, and the DJ is reading off news stories. I listen idly while I cook the eggs. J.Lo is dating somebody new. New York City is determined to be the most expensive city in the country to live in. And a girl was reported missing in a town called Troy in upstate New York.

Troy in upstate New York…

I wonder if that's anywhere near Albany.

I lay down my spatula and turn up the volume on the radio. The DJ's voice fills the room: "Eighteen-year-old Kayla Rogers went out with her friends on Saturday night. Her friends stayed at a bar, but Kayla left alone. Police say she never returned to the apartment she shared with two other girls."

My hands won't stop shaking as I pick up my phone from the kitchen counter. I type "Troy, NY" into the map app. Then I calculate the time it would take for someone to get from Albany to Troy by car.

Sixteen minutes.

My eyes raise upward to the ceiling. I hear the shower running, and even over the droplets of water, I can hear Liam singing to himself.

It couldn't be.

He wouldn't. He's not like that. He's not like Jason. Not really.

It's a coincidence. It's got to be a coincidence.

I lean against the counter, my knees weak. I can still hear Liam singing in the bathroom above us as the stench of burning eggs fills the kitchen.

READING GROUP GUIDE

1. Walk through the reasons why Erika suspects her son is "different."

2. Erika has a clear preference between her two children. Despite knowing that Liam can't love her, why do you think he is her favorite?

3. Explain what happened to Liam and Tyler's friendship.

4. Hannah is the only character who remains staunchly convinced of Liam's innocence. Why is this?

5. Describe the lengths Erika goes to protect Liam, despite thinking he is guilty. What would you do in her situation?

6. Erika fears Liam inherited violent tendencies from her father. Though Erika and Jason are good parents, do

you think nature outweighs nurture in these kinds of situations? Is it possible to change someone's nature?

7. Once Olivia goes missing, the whole community turns on Erika's family. List the ways in which the Cass family is alienated. Do you think this is fair?

8. Consider the epilogue. What does Erika suspect? Do you agree with her?

ACKNOWLEDGMENTS

Those who know me know that I write my books quick but I edit slowly. I'm very grateful for all the supportive people in my life who help me through the painful editing process. It is incredible how much help I get from the point I finish my first draft to the final version. There are times when things happen in my life to make me realize how lucky I am to have the support I have—friends and family who are always there to give me an opinion or more.

Thank you to Kate for the positive support as well as the awesome and thorough editing job. Thank you to my mother for the advice on the beginning of the book. Thanks again to Rhona for cover and blurb advice—how many times did I text you??

Thank you to new friends. Thanks to Rebecca for your great advice. Thanks to Jen for the thorough critique. Thanks to my new writing group. It's incredible to have that support in my life.

And thank you to the rest of my family. Without your encouragement, none of this would be possible.

ABOUT THE AUTHOR

#1 *New York Times*, *USA Today*, *Publishers Weekly*, and *Sunday Times* internationally bestselling author Freida McFadden is a practicing physician specializing in brain injury. Freida is the winner of both the International Thriller Writer Award for Best Paperback Original and the Goodreads Choice Award for Best Thriller. Her novels have been translated into more than thirty languages. Freida lives with her family and black cat in a centuries-old three-story home overlooking the ocean.

Taking the
HELL
out of
HEALTHCARE

A patient's guide to getting the best care

Taking the
HELL
out of
HEALTHCARE

A patient's guide to getting the best care

by Nicholas Jacobs

Published by
Real House Press, San Diego, California

Published by Real House Press, San Diego, California.

Book design: Leah Cooper

ISBN: 978-0-9799394-1-9

Library of Congress Cataloging-in-Publication Data

Jacobs Nick, 1947-
Taking the Hell Out of Healthcare: A Patient's Guide to Getting the Best Care/ Nicholas Jacobs

Printed in the United States of America
First edition

2008932638
CIP

DEDICATION

This book is dedicated to everyone who believes in creating a better future, in not being a victim, and in moving heaven and earth to reach positive goals. The spirit, love, and wisdom of my family, my dear friends, and my co-workers is represented in this book. Every success that has ever been part of my life has come from them. Special thanks to Reut Schwartz-Hebron and Lois Wyse, the angels who helped this book finally come to life.

TABLE OF CONTENTS

FORWARD

Why Did I Write This Book?

 What is the ideal healthcare environment?

A healthcare environment dedicated to the creation of a healing philosophy leading to reduced mortality rates. This ideal is not only achievable, but a necessity as the baby boomers and everyone else grow older.

This book is dedicated to every man, woman, or child who has experienced the challenge of navigating the often treacherous white water of hospital care. Each year thousands of people are almost harmed, seriously harmed, or even killed due to normal *human mistakes* that occur in our nation's hospitals. Sometimes these mistakes are related to medication errors, physician or nursing misjudgments, or fatigue. Sometimes they are caused by a combination of all of these elements.

The majority of the time, however, these situations can be avoided through close observance of your own care, education, and active participation in your treatment by yourself and your selected team of care partners.

During my more than twenty plus years in healthcare senior management, hundreds of these mistakes have crossed my desk for my input and acknowledgement. Each time I pen my name to the forms describing these mishaps, it brings home the reality of those near misses or nonfatal interventions.

This book is intended to arm its reader with the proper knowledge, skills, and insider insights to, ironically, allow you to survive the world's most incredible, most effective, and most advanced healthcare system.

Let me be perfectly clear; this is not about flying in an airplane that was put on the secondary market 20 years ago following 30 previous years of service. This is about being able to enjoy and relax in a brand spanking new Boeing 757. Referring to United States healthcare, we are *not* talking about a group of misguided, under-trained, or unskilled individuals. We are talking about the most highly trained, highly educated, gifted human beings on the planet who have been equipped with the finest tools available.

The key is that these people are just that, people. They are human beings and, as human beings, as they do their work each day mistakes happen. Unlike a widget factory, six-sigma perfection is more challenging when the human body and human biology are involved, both as a caregiver and a patient. This book is not about placing blame or pointing fingers. This book is about the realities of healthcare.

The laws of probability and statistics will demonstrate time after time that one in 1000 carpal tunnel surgeries will go poorly, that one in 100,000 people will be totally paralyzed for a short amount of time by certain types of anesthesia, that during one percent of heart catheterizations the catheter may puncture and perhaps penetrate the right descending coronary artery causing damage that will later lead to another blockage or that may even require an immediate trip to the open heart surgery suite.

In the spirit of the bumper sticker made famous by the movie *Forrest Gump*, **S- - - Happens.**

This book is about how to help ensure that it does not happen to you. One of my favorite lines from one of our top surgeons has always been, "Major surgery is anything that happens to me!" Hospitalization is major when it happens to *you*. We live in a society that spends more on healthcare than any other in the world. We live in a society with the finest and fastest care available. But, it's not perfect, and this book will help you navigate your own hospital stay with insights and suggestions from some of America's finest and best providers.

We have been fortunate to have a wonderful staff of people who have contributed to this work through their wonderful compassionate care. Their combined years of experience would take us well into the 22nd century. None of this would have been possible without them and their daily care of patients. Having spent over $14 million for liability insurance coverage for

results was both normal and acceptable. Placing patients on cold gurneys and leaving them exposed in the hallways while the staff went to lunch or the specialist negotiated with his tax consultant was all part of the environment.

 WHAT CAN YOU DO?

Take control of your hospital stay. You have the right to request humane care. You are the customer and client. You pay the bills that keep the facility open, and you and your advocates are not only permitted to question you should be encouraged to question every aspect of the care that's being rendered. You have access to nursing managers, nursing supervisors, and nursing administrators. This is generally the same model that exists in every area of the hospital; i.e., radiology, laboratory, physical therapy. There is mid-management and senior management at every level. Don't be shy about asking to see whomever you need to get your questions answered. Truthfully, most senior leaders won't have the details relating to your case, but will certainly bring attention to the situation if called into the query.

Then There Were Three

It was September of 1974 when my 57-year-old father's cough was diagnosed as a lung cancer. He had stopped smoking 14 years earlier, and none of us were totally cognizant of the ramifications of his environment. All we knew was that a great person and a great father had been given a death sentence.

Ironically, our 74-year-old neighbor was diagnosed with lung cancer on the same day. The healthcare paths that these two very different men, from opposite ends of the socioeconomic spectrum, pursued on their way to death are notable and ironic.

My father did everything available to mankind in 1974-75 to arrest this disease and regain his life. This meant surgical removal of the lung, radiation, chemo and lots of morphine. He spent 18 months in hell with metastases to his spine, kidney and finally the other lung. It meant unbearable pain and total disruption to life as we knew it.

It was during the 18-month journey from his good health to horrible death that we had our first real experience with the healthcare system. It was a world that was cold, sterile, insensitive and parochial. Each journey into the hospital required leaving dignity at the door. It was like entering a negative control pressure chamber wherein questions remained unanswered, rudeness was acceptable, and no one knew or was willing to find out what was going on at any given moment. A total lack of control quickly became the norm for us. Unfortunately, near the end, it only grew worse as death, the ultimate failure in modern medicine, grew closer.

As my father's health deteriorated, we were all stunned by the lack of care that he received. We were crushed by the lack of sensitivity demonstrated toward both him and the family. Once it was clear that his death was imminent, the healthcare providers began to avoid the room. They began to avoid bathing him and avoided speaking with us. It was a horrible journey into a system that, 30 years ago, was well funded, well staffed, and even then was on its way to becoming one of America's largest employers. Unfortunately, nearly 30 years later, many of these realities still exist.

Our 74-year-old neighbor, on the other hand, had no health insurance and decided to have no treatment for his lung cancer. After living comfortably at home with his entire extended family surrounding him through 18 months of nurturing, loving care, he died. The two men, Charlie and Murph, died on the same day.

My father went through the torturous treatment provided by the healthcare system. He was cut, poked, prodded, poisoned, radiated, drugged and ignored.

We nearly depleted our family savings trying to be near him, attempting to stay by him at the tertiary care center two hours from our home.

Charlie and Murph died on the same day. For Charlie, no clergy was available. No counselors were available. No social workers were available. Murph had it all. He died ensconced in the love of his children and grandchildren, and unhampered by the negative attitudes of unhappy caregivers, and overworked physicians trained in the white coat world of high-tension, high-stakes medicine.

CHAPTER 1

Getting There

In an ambulance?

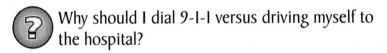

Why should I dial 9-1-1 versus driving myself to the hospital?

Dialing 9-1-1 gets you immediate medical attention. When you drive yourself to the hospital, you put yourself and others in danger. In most situations, the faster you receive medical attention the better the outcome.

There are two ways to get admitted into the hospital: through the emergency department or through a physician's office. How you get there is just as important as getting there. If you are not in immediate danger, and your physician recommends it, a family member or friend can simply drive you to the hospital for admission. If, on the other hand, you don't have a ride or there are imminent health concerns, you can request the use of an ambulance service to transfer you safely to the emergency department. The following are some important things to remember and, perhaps, some things you didn't even know about getting there.

Typically there are two basic types of ambulance services: basic life support (BLS) which usually has one or two trained emergency medical technicians (EMT) on board, and the other is the advanced life support (ALS) ambulance which travels with one EMT and one paramedic.

The primary difference between an EMT and a paramedic is that a paramedic can perform advanced life support functions such as starting IVs, giving medications, and placing breathing tubes.

The level of service dispatched is up to the individual dispatcher responsible for taking the call. There are sets of guidelines for the dispatchers to follow based upon the details obtained during the emergency call. The dispatcher then serves as a triage agent as he or she decides into which group the call falls and then, hopefully, dispatches the proper level of service.

In certain areas there are computerized systems where dispatchers ask a pre-determined group of questions, enters the responses into the computer and the computer determines the grouping. But, traditional workers feel this service is very faulty since it eliminates the human ability to judge the situation. Obviously, both systems have documented situations in which mistakes have been made in determining which level of service to send. Consequently, the initial call, no matter how desperate the situation, requires the caller to be as detailed and thorough as possible in their description of the situation.

One of the often-asked questions revolves around granting permission for a loved one to travel with the victim. This decision is determined by the individual ambulance service. Passengers may be permitted to travel in the ambulance with the victim in some jurisdictions. This appears to happen most often when the victim is a child.

General guidelines in most states are that if the patient is not in critical condition, the loved one or friend is permitted to ride along. As noted above, it is usually allowed when children are involved to try to keep the child calm. Family and friends do NOT have the right to demand to ride along, however, and many unnecessarily tense confrontations erupt over this supposed right.

If a passenger is accepted for the trip to the medical facility, it is common for the ambulance crew to inform them that a return trip home is not included. This is due to several issues, the primary of which is that the ambulance may be dispatched for additional patients directly from the hospital. Consequently, it is important for the passenger to be sure that they will have a way to return either to the accident scene or to their home.

Everyone should check if their insurance coverage includes ambulance services. Many people assume coverage is automatic. Many times, it is not covered. It is also important to check to see if it covers transfers from hospitals to other locations, i.e., nursing homes, rehabilitation hospitals, dialysis units, or MRI facilities.

It is usually a very wise decision for individuals to purchase ambulance service coverage from local ambulance companies to supplement their insurance coverage. This service is typically very inexpensive and, in the event services are needed and insurance is insufficient, these membership fees can save the patient and their family a significant amount of money.

In non-emergency situations, if possible, it is a good idea to look for local services for wheelchair vans. This form of transportation is significantly less expensive than ambulance services staffed by EMTs and paramedics. The service is also typically timely, efficient, and staffed with at least one medically knowledgeable individual. Although this service is not available everywhere, it pays to check and see if it is available where you live.

There is a common misconception that ambulance services are completely staffed by volunteers and are a "free taxi" service to take you wherever you may need or want to go to meet your healthcare needs. Unfortunately, this is almost never the case, and the resulting bills can be astounding.

CASES I HAVE SEEN

This is an area that continues to create chaos and concern on an almost daily basis in most areas of the country. Many ambulance companies were encouraged, and later forced, to become independent of their local fire departments because of restructuring of Medicare funding for this service. However, the public, which still refers to hospital employees as *orderlies* and medical units as *wards*, has never really made the transition to the *new world order*. Except in urban areas, where the tax base subsidizes much of the cost, ambulance services are a business, albeit it a nonprofit one. They are obligated and required to be self-sustaining and that typically can't occur through candy or submarine sandwich sales.

Because of this, they need to charge appropriate fees to maintain rolling stock; i.e., ambulances, special response vehicles and other transport vehicles. They must also maintain large payrolls for the numerous healthcare professionals required for this work.

The result has often been outraged, indignant, emotional family members receiving large bills for work performed during patient transportation. They usually are completely flabbergasted that, just because they did not pay their $50 family membership, they are now faced with thousands of dollars in bills incurred by transporting their dying family member to the hospital.

The other issue erupting from time to time is that of underestimating the degree of medical severity presented by the victim or their family member and, consequently, responding with BLS rather than ALS equipped ambulances. Now, in some areas, this is not an option; only BLS crews are available. This happens primarily due to economic pressures, mismanagement, or lack of population base to support an ALS system. When it does occur, however, it can mean the difference between life and death for the patient. This is primarily due to the fact that, as you've read in so many other sections of this treatise, state licensure bureaus clearly define the role of each medical professional. Right or wrong, to go beyond the scope of your licensure standards results in the loss of that license and, in many cases, the loss of that professional's living.

The bright side is that ALS paramedics are trained to do miraculous, life saving things in very perilous situations. Not unlike what we see on television, they are competent at placing breathing tubes into lungs in upside down burning vehicles. They can place an IV in an arm with rolling veins while the person is trapped in a mangled vehicle. They know what to do in the absolute worst emergency situations, and they do it well.

As an editorial comment, it is unfortunate that many states limit the paramedic's practice to the streets. Strong nursing unions have time after time blocked the progress of the paramedic in the hospital scenario due to RN training cross-over issues. The paramedic can give medication, place IVs, intubate patients, and provide phenomenal care for that individual until the gurney crosses the threshold into the hospital emergency department. There, their life saving work, unless it is contributing to a situation that otherwise could have resulted in the death of the patient, will lead to licensure suspension, fines and possibly worse sanctions for the hospital, and other incomprehensible acts of discipline.

My only experience with a pre-hospital situation that was troublesome was when my mother had a massive stroke. The paramedic crew arrived and became *nervous* because the situation was serious, and the individual involved was related to someone who might have some knowledge of his or her skills. Unfortunately, that was not the case. All I cared about was saving my mom, and I was not a critic. The result was a missed intubation and a call for a second crew to help. When the second ambulance arrived the intubation process was completed, but, upon arrival at the hospital, we were informed that they had, in fact, missed the lung. What might have lead to this series of events? My mom believed in predestination and was ready to die. Or, possibly, the dispatcher did not clearly hear the severity of the situation and dispatched a BLS or a rookie crew, or perhaps it was just the human factor. Regardless, my mom did die, but no one attributed the death to her poor treatment. The death came due to her advanced age and a massive stroke. The intervention was a noble effort to save her; the prudent person rule definitely applied in this situation. Would it have been any different for the medical commander's mother? Definitely not.

 WHAT CAN YOU DO?

Join your local ambulance organization. Support their efforts. Donate to their fund raising events and activities. Make sure that your insurance covers ambulance service to an extent, and if it doesn't, don't be caught without some type of supplemental coverage.

If you find yourself speaking to a dispatcher, be calm, thorough, and as complete as possible. It could mean the difference between life and death for the individual in question.

Finally, if you or your loved one just needs to get to the doctor or to an x-ray facility, check with the patient transport program in your area. Wheelchair vans are tens of times less expensive than ambulances and, for most situations, are adequate forms of transportation to private appointments.

CHAPTER 2

The Emergency Room
Look before you leap

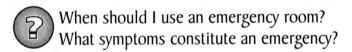 When should I use an emergency room?
What symptoms constitute an emergency?

Your son or daughter is traveling with the school hockey team or band or cheerleaders, and they are injured. They are taken to an emergency room and need treatment. The child is a minor and neither a parent nor guardian is available to approve treatment.

Except for life-threatening situations when the Good Samaritan rules always override all else, your child cannot be treated. End of story. Are there any exceptions? Generally, pregnancy tests are permitted from age 14.

You have some discomfort. You're pretty sure that it's nothing, but you think it might be a good idea to have it checked out. You go to the emergency room for tests and triage. No immediate diagnosis is possible. The physician suggests that you stay for observation. Depending upon the nature of your projected problem, i.e., heart, gall bladder, blockage or obstruction, you may be placed in a regular hospital room, or you may stay in the emergency room or, in some situations, you may be placed in an actual area designed exclusively for observation.

The good news is that everything turns out just great. You're fine. You are sent home with a clean bill of health. The bad news is that you still receive bills for your stay that require you to pay some money out of your own pocket. Co-pay and/or deductible payments are assessed.

How can that be, you ask? Why should I have to pay anything for observation? It takes either a very mature or very generous person to step up to the proverbial plate and reflect upon what expenses were incurred by that hospital. All of the equipment needed to monitor you, all of the personnel to check on you for observation are present, and all of the costs associated with this process are ongoing. So, when you ask yourself why you stayed imagine being sent home for observation during what may be the beginning stages of a heart attack.

Another common expectation is that you will see the doctor much more than you actually do. During the typical doctor's office visit a nurse or technical assistant sees the patient first. They take your blood pressure, measure your height and weight, and ask several routine questions. Then the physician comes in and takes care of you. In the emergency room (ER), especially when it is busy, nurses are trained to do much more than simply take a few notes. Nurses will often do much more clinical work. They will follow protocols without having to have the doctor even look at you. It is important to realize that this is a normal part of the ER.

Families are typically the ones that seem to be most bothered by this situation and, unless they are insistent, they are also typically kept out of the mix during serious situations. Interestingly, it is commonly the people who are truly sick who don't seem to mind the nurses working on them more. It is only those people who have average or not serious problems who tend to find this process disturbing.

It is also important to understand that the ER is a very different and complex place and misunderstandings can occur regarding room availability. For example, if rooms one and two have the most effective lights and the most equipment, and rooms three and four are scaled down, and room number five is the least equipped, conflict can abound. Whenever a patient fighting for his life comes in, due to the severity of the emergency, patients sometime need to be shuffled to other appropriate rooms. Whenever doctors make these arrangements with their staff, patients sometime get the impression that the physicians don't care about them. That, in fact, because they have been sent to the worst room, they sometimes feel that the physician doesn't believe that their problem is serious enough. It's all about managing perceptions and expectations.

? Why can't I use the emergency room as a doctor's office?

Understanding the differences between expectations and protocols during an ER visit versus a regular physician's office visit can mean a world of difference in terms of patient satisfaction and comfort. In addition, most insurance companies do not cover emergency room visits for things that could be handled by your primary care physician.

What should a patient know or try to provide for the staff? It is very important for the patient and/or family member to be aware of all medical allergies. It is also critical to know which medications have been prescribed to the patient. A lack of this type of information can slow down the patient's treatment tremendously.

It is also important for the patient to understand that normally a nurse will check them out and triage them first before any other services are performed. During this step the emergency status is determined.

It is also important to understand that, unless there is an immediate crisis situation, the patient's history will be documented prior to treatment.

One of the unknown insider challenges that takes place in the emergency room is when the patient demands that their personal physician be contacted. This can be a great cause of stress for the physician and/or the patient. This can be especially problematic if the call needs to be placed in the middle of the night and the emergency room doctor and patient have differing views.

For example, when a patient feels that he/she is experiencing a true emergency and wants their family doctor notified it may, in reality, be non-emergent. The patient might just have a stable, but very painful condition. A call to the family doctor from the emergency room physician could be harmful to the doc-to-doc relationship. This is because it can produce a *boy who cried wolf* impression leading to a future scenario where the family physician would not take calls from that ER physician.

It's important for patients to realize that family physicians do NOT need to know about your condition right away unless it's a life-threatening emergency. While it is logical to assume the attending doctor would always call back no matter what, many times it doesn't work that way in the hospital world.

Are there any tricks to getting better attention or quicker service in the emergency room?

Managing expectations is the single biggest problem that the staff and patients experience at the emergency room. If you have been a patient, you may understand. If you haven't, you will discover the total frustration and lack of empowerment that the ER can bring to you or your loved ones in a non-emergent situation. Simple fracture? Wait. Nose bleed? Tilt your head back, and wait. Stomach ache? Wait and wait and wait.

The ER is NOT intended to work like the lines at Disney World where your entry into that line determines the order in which you will be seen. It is absolutely wrong to think that the ER is and should be run on a first-come, first-served basis.

So, how does it work? Well, true emergencies come first, and it's not up to you to determine what is the definition of a true emergency. These emergencies are defined by the department and are usually prioritized by how life-threatening the condition or situation is to the patient.

People often assume first-come, first-service and become frustrated because they may be forced to wait longer if other patients with more life-threatening conditions come into the ER after them. Even more frustrating still is when the patient does not know who or what is ahead. You don't know if you arrived minutes after a heart attack or a gunshot wound victim. Are you directly behind the child who accidentally swallowed poison? The sometimes ironic and absolute worst part of this scenario is that you may also have arrived just after the pizza delivery boy from Papa Johns, and that too can slow down your visit to the ER.

The department must decide what is the emergency, not the patient. If a person is in very serious pain, but stable, they may be forced to wait behind someone else who may have a more life-threatening condition. This creates a perception for that patient that may make them upset. They may believe that their condition is very serious and deserves attention, but when they see others going ahead, become frustrated. What the patient perceives may be very different from how the department runs; it's all about expectations and understanding this difference between an ER and an optometrist's office.

CASES I HAVE SEEN

The most distressing cases I have ever observed have not been the aggressive or overly assertive patient or family member, but the quiet, self-deprecating type of patient or family member who doesn't want to bother anyone while they are actually having a stroke or a heart attack.

Time after time, we have seen patients quietly take their place in line, downplay their feelings and then proceed to get progressively worse. What has happened? We have had patients who might have been helped earlier, and in very important ways, if they had just let the registration clerk, triage nurse, or anyone know that their condition was worsening.

Other cases indelibly etched in my mind contain outraged family members yelling and screaming because grandma didn't get her enema while the four year old next door is bleeding to death or the two year old is choking on a piece of a balloon. It's a very delicate place both to work and to be treated.

 ## WHAT CAN YOU DO?

Try to be as prepared as possible. I carry a card in my wallet with my prescription drugs and vitamins listed. My history is available to all of my family members. I call ahead for non-emergent but necessary visits to gauge what the wait may be. For example, at 2 p.m. on a typical Saturday, the wait may be 30 minutes or less, but 2 p.m. on Easter Sunday every gallbladder in the area may become active from the heavy meals being consumed, and I might have a four hour wait ahead.

Understand that laboratory tests, x-rays, CT scans, and visits by sub-specialists might all automatically result in a four or five hour visit. No matter if the tests are negative or positive; the time involved may be exactly the same.

So, ask questions. While only the doctor can provide a diagnosis, all other staff members can at least answer questions about what is going on and what the tests or pills will do.

In most hospitals the attending physician will be called on an emergency-only basis. If the patient's condition can wait, it would be timelier for the patient to see his or her specialist at the next available appointment.

Level of care expectations need to be adjusted by patients as well. There are many people who consider their care to be below average or poor if they are not physically touched. While certain physicians have no problem being physical and touching their patients, certain physicians who emigrated to the U.S. may have cultural beliefs that dictate certain inappropriate contact. The ER physician will always, at *some* point, discuss your case with you, your disposition, and the medication and discharge instructions. If you like, he or she can discuss this information with the family as well.

All in all, the ER is a lifesaver, but patients need to take their patience with them. Often times a trip through a drive-in window at the bank can seem endless. You're convinced that the person in front of you has just purchased a $450,000 home with pennies that they have been accumulating since childhood. Well, understand that the difference between the bank and the hospital is usually simple…life or death.

CHAPTER 3

Registration
How do I get into the place?

One of the most important things you need to do when you get to the hospital is to let them know who you are and why you are there. This process is referred to as patient registration and can occur in the emergency room or in specifically designated areas known as Central Registration or Outpatient/Ambulatory Patient Registration. Not everyone is admitted to the hospital, but registration is the first step to anything in the hospital setting (as an in-patient, or as an out-patient).

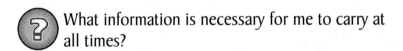

What information is necessary for me to carry at all times?

It is recommended that you carry a list of current medications, allergies, past medical history, doctor(s) names and telephone numbers, and two emergency contacts with the telephone number of each. It is also a good idea to carry your spouse's/partner's information.

So, what do you need in order to get into the hospital? Required registration information includes:

☑ Full name
☑ Date of Birth

☑ Marital Status
☑ Social Security Number
☑ Full address
☑ Place of birth
☑ Religion (optional)
☑ Spouse's/Partner's name or close relative
☑ Emergency contact
☑ Insurance Information

It is always much easier if health insurance cards are brought on the first visit.

Out-patient registration also requires a prescription from a doctor that is dated, signed, has the patient's name, and diagnosis or tests required on it.

Obviously, the patient can simplify this process by having all of the information above handy including insurance cards and, if needed, the script from the doctor.

Most registrations are for tests, lab work, and therapies. Even at a small facility, less than 100 beds, it is not unusual to have nearly 100,000 registrations of this type each year. So, it's good to know, for example, that lab work can be ordered from the registration station. This means that by the time the patient arrives at the lab, the paperwork is already there.

Once again, in patient-oriented facilities, all other procedures are prepared at the registration area, and the patient is sent or escorted to the proper place with all the paperwork in hand.

Central registration is where all patients enter the system. In some hospitals this service can be done via Internet or by phone, but it is still the point at which the hospital journey begins.

Other exceptions to this rule would, in many hospitals, be for specific ambulatory or short stay surgeries and, of course, for emergency room visits. In most hospitals, the emergency room has its own separate registration area.

 I'm elderly and have a hard time walking, how will I get to where I need to be in the hospital?

Once again, in many facilities, in-patients are escorted. A wheelchair is offered and, unless refused by the patient, an escort takes that patient in the wheelchair to their room.

Depending on the patient and the situation, less complex tests like x-rays and such are done before the patient is taken to their room. This can make the entire process smoother and quicker.

With permission from the patient, some facilities use registration cards for family and loved-ones that provide the patient name, room number, and direct phone number to that room. This helps the family and loved ones find the patient much more easily and eliminates the hassle for them.

Beyond the obvious administrative and insurance needs, the entire registration process should let the patient understand that they are in good hands, and that he or she will be well cared for. Consequently, it is important that the employees in registration have great people skills. In fact, many facilities now require their registration clerks to go through Disney or Planetree type training. It is their job to make the patient and family feel not only comfortable, but also feel valued as guests and as human beings. If the patient feels important and cared for at this first juncture, it will help them ease the tension that is often present at this difficult time.

The attitude in registration will carry over everywhere else. If the patient leaves registration feeling good and sharing a connection with the workers, then he or she will reflect on their experience as a positive one. Conversely, a bad experience in registration can set the tone for the entire hospital experience.

CASES I HAVE SEEN

Actually, one of my personal experiences qualifies to appear in this section. When our first-born son was an infant, he experienced a very high, dangerous fever. We were encouraged to rush him directly to the emergency room of our local hospital. Upon arrival, we were triaged to registration. With the baby crying in an inconsolable manner, the registration clerk began a very nasty, threatening series of relentless questions. She showed neither regard for our baby or our family. She was rude, cold, and uncaring. By the time we were finished with registration, we wanted to run out the door screaming.

> When my father was admitted to the hospital for the very last time, the registration clerk was short tempered, cold, and direct regarding the number of previous admissions and the ability of the hospital to collect from the insurance. My father worked for Blue Cross which made this point almost a non issue, but it was an extremely unpleasant experience.
>
> These two experiences, along with at least a dozen more since then, taught me that the registration area is critical. A poor experience in that area could indicate the beginning of numerous other problems.

 ## WHAT CAN YOU DO?

Not unlike our chapter on the emergency department, the secret here is preparation. It's one of those common sense issues that, in fact, are uncommon. A small, business-card-sized piece of paper listing drugs and dosages can help cut short a dozen annoying questions. Simply hand the information to the registration clerk. Another tip would be to keep everything in a business-card-sized plastic holder; i.e., insurance cards, prescriptions, vital statistics, etc. That way, if the patient is too ill to deal with this perfunctory ordeal, a loved one can simply provide the information needed. Once again, if your hospital offers the online version of this intake, it is smart to pre-register.

Not unlike making arrangements for a rental car, when you enter the facility, you will be escorted to your room. By all means, however, be prepared. Even when it's an emergency, someone has to take care of these details. Have your cards ready. The entire process will be much simpler for both the hospital and the patient.

CHAPTER 4

Laboratory Services
Sorry, I can't tell you

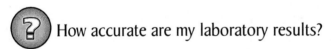 How accurate are my laboratory results?

It's common knowledge that, next to your brilliant physician, lab tests are the most efficient and clearly one of the quickest diagnostic tools available to modern medicine. Minimally, 90 percent of all patients have something analyzed through the lab at some point during a hospital stay. Even in a small hospital, hundreds of thousands of tests are performed each year. The most common and frequently performed tests include: lipid profiles, disease states, thyroid testing, and blood counts.

The equipment has been perfected to near six-sigma accuracy (very good) so that far less than one percent of errors in lab work are the results of technological blunders. Quality assurance is further ensured by constant monitoring and testing of the actual procedures with control samples.

The equipment is set up to do massive quantities of testing with little or no additional labor costs to the hospital; most simple tests cost pennies to perform. On the other hand, the more complex tests are done in very work intense, individualized, analytical settings with highly trained physicians and technologists involved in the interpretation of the results.

Common hospital glitches that result in delays in reporting to you, the patient, include such problems as couriers who spend too much time on the road with your samples, the process of actually registering the samples into the billing systems in a timely manner, pathologists who sometimes play too much golf thus causing delays in processing, and patients who don't conform to test requirements. There are probably a dozen or so other more obscure situations that disrupt the systems in place, but by now you should be getting the picture.

There are numerous precautions that you, as a patient, can take to ensure good results when being tested on a regular out-patient basis. In order to make the visit as easy as possible, it is important to understand that the lab needs easy access to you. Consequently, wearing long turtlenecks or very tight shirts or blouses that won't allow access to your arms is obviously not recommended. It's also important to follow the directions given to you by your physician prior to your test; i.e., fast for 14 hours or do not take certain medications prior to the test.

One of the most distressing and disruptive things that patients routinely attempt to do is to change their lab slips. Many patients look at the lab slip and think, "What the heck, I'd like to have my whatever checked, too," and then proceed to check off other tests not requested by the physician. Patients cannot add additional tests to their scripts without the doctor's permission. It's illegal. Your physician has to provide a diagnosis code for the test. It's the same as forging a prescription for medications.

As a patient, if you have any doubts or questions about the test results, asking can easily result in a redo of that test. If you are concerned and talk it over with your physician, the test can be retaken with the doctor's order, at no additional charge; but, the physician must order it.

As a patient you also are permitted to see records of the tests, but most hospitals will have you go through the medical records department or directly through your physician. This is primarily due to staffing availability.

So, the physicians will get the results, make the diagnosis, and discuss it with you. The lab only has the results and lab staff is not permitted to make any diagnosis. Patients should only ask lab technicians for their results, not what the results mean. Only the doctor is authorized to interpret those results for you.

Even though most hospitals are non-profit organizations, they are typically large employers in their area, and must provide funds to support their employees. Consequently, because most of us are insured by either the government or our business, it is also important for patients to be aware that the lab requires you to be registered at some point during the visit and that there will be checks for insurance no matter the circumstances.

CASES I HAVE SEEN

If you can dream it, we have seen it. Some of the most disturbing situations that occur in laboratories are those where the patient is clearly in deep trouble. In one case, an individual who was infamous for his poor diet came to the lab for a cholesterol test. When his blood was being drawn, it actually came out of his arm almost cream colored. His total cholesterol count was not in the normal range of less than 200. It was 700. The entire lab was stunned. No one had ever seen a patient with cholesterol at that level. His blood looked like white globs of fat. This test occurred a few months before he had a major heart attack.

One of the most difficult areas to address is that of phlebotomy. Although the individuals hired to perform this service typically require the least amount of education and training, they are absolutely the front line of the laboratory service. They are face to face with the patients, and their skill level often determines whether individuals consider returning to that laboratory. In fact, we had a major client, a very large nursing home, that wanted to cancel our contract due to the phlebotomy service. The term *rolling veins* is one that you do not want to hear when it's time for your blood sample to be drawn. It is so much more difficult for the phlebotomist.

Another, more humorous, case involved the 18-year-old son of an extremely prominent, national figure. He was admitted for a routine simple surgical procedure. The lab personnel asked him to step into the rest room and provide them with a sample. He was presented with a small container for urine. When he returned, he had filled the bottle with feces. He clearly misunderstood the sample need, and no one could figure exactly how he was able to so carefully fill this very small container, but the tech simply handed him another bottle and said, "From the other end, please."

WHAT CAN YOU DO?

This is clearly a situation where you carefully follow instructions. The amount of times that you fast, the food that you eat, and the diet that you follow can and will impact your results. So, get the tests done. If the results seem outrageous it may be because taking a blood sample is not unlike taking a cup of water out of a river. Every cup will be as individual as a snowflake. Consequently, it's good to follow your results from one test to the next to ensure that your readings have some degree of explainable similarities.

CHAPTER 5

Radiology

They can see right through you

The nuances of the various modalities in x-ray

Do I need a doctor's order to have a test done? How early should I arrive? Do I go straight to the department?

A physician's order is required to get a radiology test completed. As mentioned early on in this book, there are certain steps that must be followed in the hospital and there is no exception in this instance. Registering for your test may take some time, depending upon how busy the registration clerks are at the time of your arrival, so it's a good practice to arrive at least a half hour or so before your procedure is scheduled. In order to have an x-ray taken, you must first register at the patient registration desk. You will be given papers to take with you to the radiology department. Without these papers and proof of registration, they can't help you.

Why can't I eat before some procedures?

Sometimes it is necessary that the patient not eat for a certain amount of time prior to the test. Why? This is due to the fact that food in the digestive tract may interfere with the test results or even obstruct the views.

 How accurate is mammography?

Mammography has an 80-85% accuracy rating. It is currently considered the gold standard for detecting breast abnormalities, but MRI is being pursued as not only an alternative, but as the new benchmark. Mammography should be considered as one part of a three-part breast health program. The other two parts are monthly self breast examinations and regular clinical examinations by your physician.

 What is an EEG?

EEG is an acronym for electroencephalogram. This test takes a picture of your brain and how it works. The test is used to determine normal or abnormal brain activity and is only performed under a physician's order. The patient's hair must be clean with no styling products in it such as hair spray, mousse, gel, or braids.

 Why am I having all these tests done? What's wrong with me?

You go for your physical examination and your physician informs you that you will need to have several radiological tests to assure that everything is fine. He does not infer that everything is not okay. Nor does he indicate that there is a problem. If, for example, included on the list is a chest x-ray, an ultra sound of the heart and a thallium or cardiolite stress test, you may be concerned about needing all of these exams. You become concerned that he has heard or seen something that has alarmed him or that has caused him to believe that something is amiss. But, when you ask him, he simply replies that, based upon your history, it is a routine precaution to move forward with these tests.

By the time you make your appearance for your first test, you are a wreck. What did he hear? What did my EKG reveal? What does he think is going on inside me? Is my heart okay? Do I have sounds in my lungs that made him want to get a chest x-ray? What if the thallium doesn't turn out well? Will I need a heart catherization? Does he think my heart valve is leaking? These are all good questions for the physician but, unfortunately, you didn't think to ask them. They are, however, NOT good questions for the radiology technicians.

 ## Why won't those techs tell you what they see?

Technicians are the worker bees. They are very limited, by law, in their ability to communicate to you, the patient, what they see, think they see, or understand. Don't get me wrong. They are not limited regarding their understanding of these findings. They are limited by their licensing organizations as to what they can or cannot say about what they are seeing or hearing. They are not permitted to practice medicine. Even if they see, or believe that they see, exactly what is going on it is up to their physician and your physician to inform you as to these findings.

CASES I HAVE SEEN

When you go for your chest x-ray, they may ask you to come back because they have seen a shadow. That shadow may, in fact, have been as in my case, my nipple. So, they asked me to come back so that they could put markers over my nipples to ensure that they were seeing nothing else. (Or maybe they just wanted to give me grief because I was the President of the hospital? I'll never know!)

What are the physicians trying to see? They are looking to see if your heart is enlarged, a sign of congestive heart failure. Why would the physician look for that? If you have high blood pressure that is not being controlled, your heart could be working too hard.

Just a few weeks ago, a radiologist told a friend of mine that her cancer had returned. When she went to her personal physician, he confirmed that finding. She then spoke with her surgeon, and he too reported that her cancer had returned and that she was facing a new, more challenging, battle. Approximately one day later, after she requested a second opinion from radiology, she was informed that the reading sent to the physicians was incorrect. She was informed that she did not have a reoccurrence of her cancer. She was told that what had been read in the first test was scar tissue and that she was going to be fine. A miracle? No, just a more thorough reading, but the roller coaster ride to which my friend was subjected was not only unpleasant, it was terrifying.

WHAT CAN YOU DO?

What are some of the things that you can do that could ease your tension, ease your apprehension, and ease your fears? You can tell your technician that you are afraid. You can tell him or her that you are very apprehensive. What are your rights? You have the right to ask to speak directly to your radiologist.

This may be an interesting challenge. In a very busy hospital, these physicians are often overwhelmed by cases and not readily available to interrupt their readings to be at your side immediately. The latest cost-saving or profit-making opportunity for both hospitals and physician groups is to employ physicians from other continents. That's right; other continents. From approximately 11 p.m. until 8 a.m., radiologists in Australia are reading our x-rays. There are other such groups in Israel and India. The x-rays are digitized and sent via the Internet for the reading.

So, what can be done? The technicians do have the right to mark STAT on your test so as to prompt the physician to not only read the test quickly, but also to send it to your personal physician quickly. This is to ensure that you are not in limbo for hours, days or longer waiting to hear the results of your exams.

Your rights and privileges do go beyond being a number in a line waiting for your turn in the radiology suite. Employees can and should be expected to be courteous, attentive, polite, thorough, and sympathetic to your wishes, expectations, and needs. They do have the authority to ask the physician to speak with you as soon as possible and, at least at our facility, they have the power to mark STAT on your test in order to get it read quickly.

What can they not do? They can't tell you if that lump is cancerous or if your stress test is positive or that you could be on the verge of having a heart attack. It is always preferable to have your serious medical discussions with your radiologist and/or you personal physician. The buck stops there.

Don't give up. Don't panic, and don't believe everything you hear.

CHAPTER 6

Respiratory
Take a deep breath

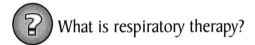 What is respiratory therapy?

Ever hear the statement, "He's got a great set of lungs?" Well, as a former professional trumpet player, I've heard it many times, but many of us would love to hear it more often. There is a very common misconception regarding respiratory therapy. The therapy itself is not just for breathing problems. The goal of respiratory therapy is to help the patient improve their lung function.

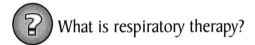 What is a Pulmonary Function Test?

A Pulmonary Function Test, or PFT, is a test used to diagnose lung disease. A PFT test measures different lung volumes and capacities. The test lasts approximately 45 minutes. Respiratory medications can not be taken at least 4 hours prior to the test.

What is a Methacholine Challenge Test?

A Methacholine Challenge Test is a breathing test wherein a pharmacological agent is inhaled. A physician orders the Methacholine Challenge Test to assist in the diagnosis of asthma.

 ## What is COPD?

Chronic Obstructive Pulmonary Disease (COPD) is an obstructive lung disease causing two or more of the following lung diseases: asthma, chronic bronchitis and/or emphysema. In this disease process, patients have difficulty exhaling and air becomes trapped in the lungs. This causes a shortness of breath. The #1 cause of this disease is smoking.

 ## Are there any important things to know when using a nebulizer?

A nebulizer is used to help a patient breathe more easily. A nebulizer should be cleaned on a regular basis using soap and water. A nebulizer should also be disinfected once a day with a vinegar and water solution.

When using a nebulizer, be it for the delivery of a child, treatment of asthma patients, pulmonary rehabilitation, or a bronchoscopy (a cancer check of the lungs), pulmonary specialists and respiratory therapists are always nearby.

Black lung, red lung, and white lung are some of the work-related diseases that have become common over the years. Working in coal mines, steel mills, or textile factories cause these occupational diseases. Employees of stone quarries and farmers are also exposed to particulates that eventually lead to lung complications or diseases and to the need for treatment directed by pulmonologists and RTs (respiratory therapists).

One of the symptoms of a lung disorder is mood swings. Unbalanced blood levels often lead to mood problems, and this affects not only the patient, but also anyone with whom that individual comes in contact.

In the trade, the RT carries out the physician's orders. In fact, that is the limit to their practice. This includes the distribution of medication and the direction and facilitation of treatments. Everything up to and including the management of ventilators comes under the direction of the physician, but is typically managed by the RT. For this reason, RTs need to be very people oriented.

One of the challenges facing the patient is that of managing personal patient and familial expectations. Typically, pulmonary therapy and rehabilitation can never fully reverse the problem, but lifestyle and attitude changes will certainly go a long way in easing some of the tension and discomfort created by the medical problem. Not unlike many of the other sections of this book, with lung ailments, as with many other life threatening or life quality diminishing diseases, lifestyle changes can make a very big difference.

CASES I HAVE SEEN

Being at a hospital in a former coal mining town where steel was manufactured a few short miles away, where agriculture is the largest industry and silos are filled with brown lung-producing dusts, where Vanity Fair underwear was manufactured, and where stone quarries are abundant, created too much familiarity with brown, black, red and white lung disorders.

On top of this rainbow of lung ailments, add a moist climate feeding hundreds of temperate species of plant life. Including ragweed, molds and plenty of spores, asthma becomes prevalent as well.

The area also had its share of tobacco, both smokeless and smoked. The result is not only industrial lung disorders, but also lung cancers and emphysema.

My father died of lung cancer, and the type of cancer detected was very rare. It could have come from smoking cigarettes famous for their effective, but later determined deadly, asbestos filters. It could have come from wrapping our basement heating pipes in asbestos paper each year, or from cutting and replacing the asbestos siding on our house or the asbestos tiles in our family room. It could have come from working on diesel and steam locomotives or working the gas pumps at a garage. Or, it could have come from living crosswind to the nuclear testing grounds. The better question is, how could he have avoided lung cancer? We lived in a small town where half a dozen of my father's peers died of lung cancer within a year of his death.

Environmentally induced illnesses may typically represent 75 to 80% of most of our diseases.

WHAT CAN YOU DO?

Call and request information regarding pulmonary rehabilitation. Ask questions about condition, treatment, outcomes, and needs. It doesn't hurt to get multiple opinions. Asking questions will always eliminate any sense of betrayal and will help manage your expectations. Knowledge will give you more control and power.

It's also important to note that therapies can be refused. If a therapist does not believe you will benefit from a requested therapy, he or she will typically be totally upfront about the recommended treatments and the reasoning behind them.

It helps for the patient to understand the disease, the disease process, and possible progressions. It is also extremely beneficial for the patient to have access to a support group for the problems being faced, so that the patient understands that he or she is not alone.

Remember, the therapist never acts alone. It is always under the supervision of a physician. Therapists can give suggestions, updates and opinions if wanted, but the physician is always in charge and will have the final say. As I've reiterated—ask, ask, and ask.

CHAPTER 7

Anesthesia

It's not about putting you to sleep; it's about waking you UP!

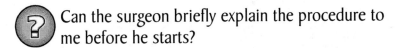 Can the surgeon briefly explain the procedure to me before he starts?

Undergoing surgery can be quite confusing and unnerving. If you would feel more comfortable speaking with the surgeon prior to the start of the operation, let your nurse know as soon as possible. Often patients are given medications that may make them sleepy or make them hazy. Hence, it's important to make your feelings known before blast-off!

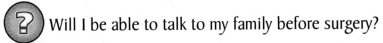 Will I be able to talk to my family before surgery?

Unless it is an emergency situation and the family is not present in the hospital, most hospitals permit family members to accompany the patient to the surgery waiting area. The family can wait comfortably in this designated area and will be informed when the patient's procedure is completed. Many times the physician will speak to the family in that same waiting area following completion of the surgery.

Will I be covered during surgery? I don't want everyone to see me exposed.

The patient's dignity is always maintained during surgery. The staff goes to great lengths to expose only the areas of the body that are necessary for the procedure. The patient's body is covered as completely as possible.

 What if my heart stops during surgery?

It is a rare occurrence that a patient's heart stops beating during surgery. There are medications immediately available that can be used during this type of emergency. CPR is utilized in surgery just like anywhere else in the hospital setting. The staff, including the physician, anesthesiologist, nurse anesthetist, registered nurses, and surgical technologists receive CPR training on a regular basis. The entire team is poised to utilize all life saving-measures during a circumstance like this.

 Why can't I wear make-up or nail polish during surgery?

We all may want to look our best at all times, but eye make-up should not be worn because it can get into the eyes during surgery and irritate them. Fingernails are used to assist in monitoring the patient's oxygen level during surgery utilizing the Pulse Oximeter. (The little clothes pin-like clip clipped to your pointer finger.) Wearing nail polish may interfere with this vital monitoring tool.

 Hospital stays after surgery used to be a lot longer. Why have they been shortened? Who determines how long you stay in the hospital after an operation?

Years ago it was common practice for patients to remain in the hospital for a month or more after having a hip or knee replaced. This is unheard of today. Research has found that the sooner a patient gets up and moving, the less the risk of possible complications. Your insurance company usually determines the length of stay permitted. It wants to get you home where you can fully recover and actually get some rest.

 ## Will I wake up after surgery?

There are risks with everything and nothing is 100% guaranteed, but the chances of you not waking up after surgery are very slim. If you are extremely ill, anesthesia could be administered, but the anesthesiologist will explain this to you. Depending upon the type of surgery to be performed, there are options other than being put to sleep.

There is an extremely rare anomaly that exists that won't allow a patient to wake up after surgery. This genetic condition doesn't permit the body to fight off the effects of certain anesthetic drugs such as Anectine (Succinylcholine). If you have a family history of Pseudocholinesterase Deficiency, it is vital that you inform your physician and your anesthesiologist. Alternative medications can be administered to counteract the effects of this genetic anomaly.

 ## I've had bad experiences with coming out of anesthesia, what are my options?

Some patients may become nauseated and vomit after their surgery; others may feel like a truck hit them. If this has happened to you in the past, you need to speak with the anesthesiologist and relate the details of your negative experiences. During your pre-operative interview, tell the anesthesiologist or Certified Registered Nurse Anesthetist (CRNA) if you have a history of nausea after surgery. There are medications and alternative types of anesthesia that can be given to help prevent nausea.

 ## How much pain can I expect and how long will it last?

Pain levels depend upon the type of surgery you undergo as well as your individual pain tolerance. No pain medication can take away all of the pain, but the goal is to give you enough of the correct type of medication so you can tolerate it. If your pain is intolerable while in the hospital or when you return home, there are things you can do to make the pain more bearable. Do not be afraid to take pain medication and remember to take it before the discomfort escalates to intolerable. Try to relax. Relaxation exercises, music, and breathing exercises can help you reduce the pain. Unless instructed by your physician, do not lie in bed all of the time. As you move around, the pain can become more tolerable. Therapeutic massage may also reduce pain.

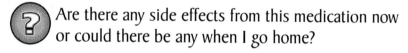 Are there any side effects from this medication now or could there be any when I go home?

All medications can have side effects. When you receive a medication prescription, the pharmacist includes printed information regarding potential side effects. The anesthesiologist will also provide printed instructions regarding possible side effects of medications administered during anesthesia. If you're experiencing extremely unpleasant symptoms, consult your physician.

How long will I be in surgery?

If you want to know how long your surgery will take, ask the surgeon and nurse. They have done the operation many times and can give you a general estimate. Remember though that surgeons don't always take into consideration the prep time and recovery time. While the surgery may be 1 hour long, it takes about 20 minutes to put the patient to sleep and position the body properly. It takes an additional 20 minutes to wake the patient up after surgery, move them to a bed, and transport them to the recovery room. And then there is the recovery time. It could take anywhere from half an hour to an hour or even longer.

What if the surgery seems to be taking extra long? Can I find out about my loved one?

If it seems that your loved one's surgery is taking a lot longer than anticipated or were told it should take, you can find out about the status of the procedure. There are usually volunteers available in the surgery waiting room ready to assist family members in obtaining such information. Don't be afraid to ask and find out what is happening.

What is the difference between the anesthesiologist and the CRNA?

The anesthesiologist is a doctor that specializes in anesthesia. They determine the type of anesthesia best suited for you based on your medical history and supervise the CRNA (certified registered nurse anesthetist). The CRNA gives and maintains the anesthetic during surgery and monitors your status.

Anesthesia services are typically required to be available in a hospital 24 hours a day, seven days a week, 52 weeks a year. The training required for both the physicians and the specialized nurses involved in this profession is expensive and takes years, but the primary cost associated with this service is the need for total, continuous availability of the practitioners.

Car accidents don't happen only during banking hours. Babies are born when they want to be. So, anesthesia must be available.

In recent years, surgery centers, both cosmetic and general, have become more and more popular. These new facilities have proven to be a godsend to the profession. All activities taking place in these specialty centers are pre-scheduled, typically during daylight hours, and they are non-emergent.

What does this mean to a CRNA or an anesthesiologist? It means that they can have a life. It means that they work normal hours, go home at night, and generally do not have to worry about taking emergency calls.

What has that meant to hospitals? It has created a shortage of skilled professionals. If you take all of the anesthesiologists in the United States and divide them by I.Q., skill level, love of challenge, love of stable family life, love of money, etc., you will begin to see certain trends. Some will be attracted to the most complex care centers, others to very busy centers offering more financial rewards. Others will be attracted to stable, less challenging centers, and the rest to centers that are not particularly high paying, not high acuity, but busy enough to allow them to earn a top income.

 ## How do I know if I'm going to the right place for my surgery?

How do you know if you found an appropriate place for your surgery? Well, the truth of the matter is that there are dozens of points that must be addressed. If your chosen hospital has a teaching program, you may or may not receive special care. You may receive teaching care. This implies that students will poke and prod and give you extra tests as they learn the necessary skills to become a doctor. On the other hand, regardless of the skill level, there should always be someone around and students aren't so bad.

At a certain point in their training, it is the norm for a top surgeon to allow his students to do a portion of the work. It is also the norm to have anesthesiologists oversee more than one room. Typically, this isn't an issue because, like the craftsmen who build the works of great architects, the apprentices are always able to ask the master for help and assistance. The questions that arise, however, are many and complex. For example, do you want to have your surgery in a major urban hospital with an infection rate of 12 percent? Or, do you want to have it in a smaller urban hospital with access to the same sub-specialists and an infection rate of less than one percent?

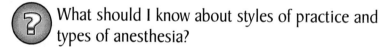

What should I know about styles of practice and types of anesthesia?

There are various types of anesthesia. You can do extensive research or you can trust your surgeon's and anesthesiologist's judgment.

Can spinal anesthesia paralyze me? If so, how long will I be numb?

The chances of a spinal anesthetic permanently paralyzing you are very, very slim. The length of time your legs stay numb from a spinal depends upon the medication injected. Some spinal medications last one hour, some last up to six hours.

What are the differences in anesthesia? Will they numb a spot or knock me out?

There are many different types of anesthetics available. Knocked out, or general, anesthesia is pretty cut and dry. Local anesthesia types vary and can include regional blocks (spinal), or local anesthesia with IV sedation (twilight sleep). Your physician and anesthesiologist will determine the most appropriate type for your procedure.

I'm afraid of IV sedation because I've heard that I'll see and hear everything during my surgery. Is that true?

If you are seeing and hearing everything during your surgery, let your doctor know immediately! If this occurs, it means that your anesthesia is not working and your anesthesiologist is probably not focused. IV sedation can have an amnesic effect and you will not hear, see, or remember anything that occurred in surgery.

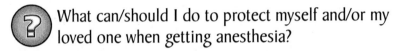 What can/should I do to protect myself and/or my loved one when getting anesthesia?

There are many things you can do to become fully informed about the type of anesthesia you will receive and why that type of anesthesia was chosen. Ask questions! Openly discuss past anesthetic experiences with your anesthesiologist or nurse anesthetist. Inform them of all medications you are taking and be sure to inform them about herbal supplements you are taking. Some herbal supplements may affect response to medications administered during anesthesia or affect how you feel when you wake up.

The real skill necessary for the anesthesiologist to be considered a "good doc" is that of bringing the patient out of difficult surgery, relatively pain free. Make sure you and/or your loved ones discuss your surgery and your options with your anesthesiologist. Find out the difference between medicines and what your options are. Some *old school* anesthesiologists are only comfortable with *old drugs*. They need to be confronted as well. Ask. Ask. Ask.

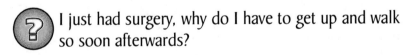 I just had surgery, why do I have to get up and walk so soon afterwards?

It is important to get moving after surgery to prevent complications such as infection, pneumonia and blood clots. Walking facilitates healing by increasing blood circulation in the body.

Will I be able to walk after my hip replacement?

The whole purpose of getting a hip replacement is so you can walk well again. After hip replacement surgery you will need to do physical therapy for strength training and walking. It can be a slow process, but it is worthwhile. So be patient and listen to the instructions.

 If I haven't fully recovered after my operation and the normal stay is up, will I be forced to leave the hospital?

Your physician determines when you are ready to be discharged from the hospital. Patients may not always be fully recovered from their operation before discharge, but they can get needed rest and heal at home. If a patient needs assistance at their home with treatments such as dressing changes or medication administration, home health services can be ordered by the physician.

 I have stairs in my house; will I be able to go up and down them after my hip surgery?

Patients who have undergone hip surgery will eventually be able to go up and down stairs, but not right away. Most patients receive physical therapy or go to a rehabilitation facility before going home.

 What should I do if my stitches fall out?

If your stitches fall out and your surgical incision opens up after you've been discharged, call your doctor's office and ask for instructions. You may need a follow-up visit to your physician's office or you may be instructed to apply a dressing to the incision site. Follow your physician's instructions closely to avoid injuring the site or putting yourself at risk for infection.

I live alone and need surgery, who will care for me when I get home?

Patients receive instructions from their nurse before being discharged from the hospital. If your physician orders it, home health nursing services will be made available to you and the home health nurse will provide care as instructed by your physician. A family member, friend, or designated caregiver may also provide care for you when you go home. They too will receive appropriate instructions on patient care. Additional support services are available through such organizations as the Area Agency on the Aging. Do research into your local resources before your surgery.

CASES I HAVE SEEN

Several years ago, my closest friends brought their only child to a facility where I was a senior administrator for a minor orthopedic procedure. This procedure typically would have begun at 7 a.m. and the patient should have been sent home by 1 p.m. that afternoon with little or no pain or problems. This young man, 19 years of age at the time, was taken to the pre-surgery area where he was to be prepped for the procedure.

Because of our relationship, I fully expected to hear from my friends by about 10 a.m. I had expected to hear that Chris was fine and heading home. Instead, at 10:30 a.m. a panic call came to my office from Carol, his mother, telling me that something was terribly wrong. Chris had not yet had the surgery, but they were not letting her see him.

When I called over to the surgery area, the nurse manager appropriately put me off. Understand that this was pre-HIPAA (Health Insurance Portabilit and Accountability Act) when administrators, physicians et. al., had relatively open access to any patient. It was clear to me that Chris was having a problem.

I quickly called the Vice President of Nursing and we headed over. We saw Chris, completely paralyzed, on a ventilator.

Apparently, one in 100,000 cases resulted in this type of reaction to the anesthesia. They had traveled 30 miles from their home to avoid their local, rural hospital only to have their only son paralyzed by the anesthesia.

What could have been done? Testing? Well, in this case it was unlikely that a test would have even been available for this type of anesthesia. He did recover fully by about 6 p.m. that evening, was removed from the ventilator and was fine, but the anguish, fear, pain and suffering took their toll.

In another instance of anesthesia gone awry, my friend had a minor surgery. When she came out of the surgery, she was sick and threw up. She became ill again in the car, and again at home. She was sick for several hours after the surgery. Her impression of the surgery was interesting: the surgery was fine, but the anesthesia was horrible.

The next day I asked the nurse what had happened. She replied that the particular anesthesiologist on duty liked to use an older type of less expensive anesthesia that made people sick. Now, as a hospital administrator with bottom line concerns, this could possibly have made me happy, but as the spouse of the patient who was having his car shampooed that day, it was not an answer that gave me any deep feeling of confidence or satisfaction.

 WHAT CAN YOU DO?

Talk and talk and talk. Talk to your physician. Talk to your anesthesiologist. Talk to your CRNA. Talk to the nursing supervisor. Talk to your nurse. Ask every question that occurs to you. Demystify your life! You have not only the right to know, but also the responsibility to find out. It should not be a secret. Your health, safety and comfort should not be mysteries.

CHAPTER 8

Integrative Medicine and Physical Therapy

Crack it, pop it, rub it, stick it ...

An objective look at Physical Therapy, Acupuncture, Osteopathic Manipulation, Chiropractic, Massage

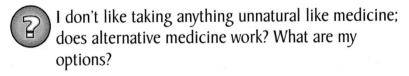

I don't like taking anything unnatural like medicine; does alternative medicine work? What are my options?

Acupuncture and acupressure are ancient systems of natural healing that originated in the Orient. These two therapies have for many years now been gaining in popularity in the United States. The basic belief behind these therapies, which coincides with a naturopathic philosophy, is that the body must be in balance to function at its peak. That philosophy offers a healthcare approach that is much more than alternative or complementary medicine. It embraces a healthier, simpler lifestyle; it promotes living in harmony with oneself in nature.

When looking at the body from the traditional Oriental medicine point of view, qi or chi (emotional and physical energy) flows through the body along specific bioelectric, biochemical pathways called meridians. You can think of these as energy highways. These pathways help maintain individual well-being by distributing energy throughout the body. The meridians correspond to specific organs and body functions. When energy is flowing smoothly, the body is in perfect balance. When it is blocked or slowed, then the belief is that physical or emotional illnesses can occur.

Both acupuncture and acupressure are painless, non-toxic therapies for redirecting and restoring the flow of energy or chi. Hair-thin needles or electrodes are used to direct and rechannel body energy. Allopathic medicine believes that the placement of acupuncture needles stimulates certain nerve cells to release chemicals in the spine, muscles, and brain. These bio-chemicals allay pain by releasing endorphins, the body's pain-relieving substances.

In the United States, acupuncture is used mainly for pain relief. It's extremely effective in treating rheumatoid conditions and has been shown to bring relief to an extremely high percentage of those who suffer from arthritis. One recent study demonstrated that patients experienced relief even when the acupuncturist did not place the needles properly.

Oriental medicine views acupuncture as a way to release blocked energy, thus allowing flow throughout the body and enabling healing. The meridian lines connect with internal organs, which allow the practitioners to treat everything from immune disorders, like chronic fatigue syndrome, to migraines, to asthma. Many of you might have seen the dramatic videos on public television showing patients going through major surgeries without anesthesiology, using only acupuncture to protect them from pain and discomfort.

The physicians that work with these therapies treat the people, not their symptoms. They evaluate lifestyle patterns that affect health and encourage the patient to restore balance and harmony with the patient's environment. They look for obstructions to the flow of energy or chi such as daily stress, emotional upsets and even the weather. They look for ways to correct these roadblocks and return the patient to wellness. These corrections may include changes in diet, use of herbal supplements, vitamins, exercise, and lifestyle changes. Again, the focus is on the balance of health rather than the treatment of symptoms. Treatment can last a few months or for more extended periods for those with a chronic disease.

CASES I HAVE SEEN

One of the most valued members of my leadership group suffered for years from arthritis of the knees and feet. After undergoing acupuncture, she relayed her experience to me. She described her concerns and feelings toward acupuncture as, at first, tentative. She suffered for so many years that she was, at best, skeptical that anything would help her, and her history was, unfortunately, that of dealing with a hereditary condition.

A year ago, as her pain increased and, as the disease progressed, she had resigned herself to not being able to participate in many of the activities she had once enjoyed. However, during an Integrative Health mini-seminar, she had eagerly volunteered to be the test dummy for an acupuncture session.

Would she experience a decrease in pain? She was about to have those questions answered. It wasn't a case of come in, lie on the table, stick in a few needles, take them out, and you're done. She described it as a total experience that helped change her attitude toward this disease.

Upon arriving at the department she was greeted by the receptionist and shown to comfortable seating. She was able to enjoy a cup of herbal tea while the RN case manager went over her paperwork. She had to answer a few of the RN's questions and fill out a few more forms.

As they talked, she described beginning to feel comfortable enough to take an honest look at her lifestyle and daily life stresses. Just being able to look at herself from within a caring environment allowed her to let go. She began to cry. According to her, it was a release that was long overdue. It let her realize that there was help. She began to understand that by taking better care of herself, she could take better care of those who needed her. Not a new medical concept, but it took being nurtured in the right setting to have those words make an impact on her.

After composing herself, she was taken to the treatment room.

The room had soft lighting, muted colors, tasteful furniture, and carpeted floors. A privacy screen for changing, comfortable terry robes and clean white socks were provided, and she was ready for treatment.

First, she was treated to a foot massage, aromatherapy, body massage, and kinesiology to prepare her body for acceptance of the acupuncture needles. In this calm and relaxed state, she could honestly say that she didn't remember much about the insertion of the needles. She told me that she experienced a twinge or pinch once or twice, but nothing that made her want to run screaming from the room.

Following the insertion of the thin-as-hair needles, Reiki was performed. This treatment too is intended to help move energy to where it would be most beneficial. She described the experience as being in a warm, safe cocoon, floating on a cloud of relaxation. Again, she described this as an awesome, wonderful experience. At the end of the session, she told me that she was gently stirred and helped from the table. How did she say she felt? Great!

The most important piece for her was that acupuncture helped her regain a part of her life that she thought was lost. Pain, which had been her constant friend, now took a back seat to a much better friend, movement. That summer, she rode a bike with her family for the first time in seven years. Yes, according to her, she still had discomfort but it was not the intense pain that had clouded her life so very recently.

Similar feelings have been reported and experienced by those who have visited massage therapists, chiropractors, and osteopathic specialists.

WHAT CAN YOU DO?

Research. Don't settle for quackery. There are very legitimate programs for American Certification for Acupuncture at places like UCLA in California. Get lists of their graduates. Find out which schools of chiropractic medicine are legitimate, certified, and producing true professionals. The vast majority of physical therapy schools are certified and producing legitimate practitioners, but physical therapy is NOT the same as chiropractic medicine. DOs, doctors of osteopathic medicine, are taught manipulation, and, in fact, chiropractic medicine evolved from these same teachings and concepts. MDs will often malign these practices, but it has been my experience that most of them have done no research, have not experienced them, are pure scientists in the American tradition, and do not approach these forms of manipulation or balance with an open mind. Be your own judge.

CHAPTER 9

Medication Errors
That's not the way I wanted to die

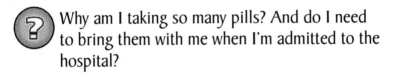

Why am I taking so many pills? And do I need to bring them with me when I'm admitted to the hospital?

Your physician prescribes medication based upon your symptoms. If you do not understand why you are taking a certain medication, do not hesitate to ask your doctor to explain the reason to you. You have a voice in your care and that includes your medications.

You should not bring your medications with you when you go to the hospital. When you are admitted to the hospital, your physician will write orders for which medications are to be dispensed to you at the appropriate time and in the proper dosage by nursing personnel.

The devil is in the details. Take, for example, the hospital administrator who was formerly a pharmacist. The man had a very complex brain that was filled with information and solutions. The problem was that his training was so methodical, and his life style was so anal retentive, that he even wore rubber overshoes in the summer so as not to scuff his shine on the gravel in the parking lot on his way into the building in the morning.

This man had housekeeping employees rake his carpet every night so as to ensure that there were no footprints. He and his lovely wife would stay up until the wee hours of the morning prior to vacations making sure that their childrens' outfits were coordinated perfectly. It was rumored, however, that after he left for a position in the Midwest the family who purchased his house actually found a dust bunny in the bedroom where the dresser had been.

The previous paragraphs weren't about a poor, tortured hospital administrator who made everyone's life hell. They were about the degree to which pharmacists are trained to protect you, the patient. No, they don't all wear overshoes in summer or have their rugs raked, but they know that every drug they dispense, every pill that they count, every complex IV that they mix could, either through its own awesome power or through mixing and interacting with other drugs, have the power to cause death or a debilitating reaction. So they worry and count and recount, and count again. They read and re-read and look at each pill, each bottle, and each drug as if it were a potential killer.

So, why then do national statistics show that thousands of people are killed each year due to medication errors? Because, they are.

If pharmacists are this careful, you might ask, how does this possibly happen? Well, there are pharmacy techs and pharmacy aids, and there are poorly written prescription orders, and there are busy RNs, and busier LPNs. There are inappropriately registered patients with similar names. There are emergency room techs or nurses or physicians that sometimes miss or misunderstand what the patient is saying about the drugs they take at home. There are patients who don't tell us the entire story; i.e., like the recreational drugs that they take just for fun.

The story doesn't end here. There are exhausted employees who misread or misinterpret the prescriptions. And there are the intellectually challenged employees who don't bother to read carefully, don't pick up what was ordered from the drug cart, and don't check to see if they are giving the correct drug to the correct patient.

Don't forget the hassled administrator who has to find a way to keep the hospital open and running. This guy or lady has a committee that adopts a formulary of permitted drugs for his or her facility based on their price. Are they always the same drugs that the patient has taken in the past? No. Are they sometimes similar yet different drugs? Yes. Do they interact differently with the patients other drugs? Sometimes. Do the patients sneak in their herbal medicines and laxatives and antacids? Yes.

You get the picture?

CASES I HAVE SEEN

During the past 17 years, I have seen hundreds of near misses and a dozen close calls but, fortunately, only a few made it to the patients, and even fewer had a severely negative impact on the patients' health.

The most awesome near miss that I've seen in the past few years was a case where the patient in room 467 had been discharged at 2 p.m. The shift had changed at 3 p.m., but a new patient had been placed in that room at 2:58 p.m. The new patient was a teenager who had had some minor surgery. The nurse responsible for room 467 came bouncing into the room with the previous patient's prescriptions and handed the pills over to the teenager. Thankfully, this kid's mom had the presence of mind to ask about the medication, and the nurse was forced to double check her work.

She went to her chart and saw that the medicine that was to have gone to the former patient was a blood thinner; in fact, a significant dose of that blood thinner. Had the mother not stopped her, the newly post-operative teenager would have consumed this drug and it might have had serious consequences. Would he have died? No, but why did this happen?

Could it have been that, instead of the four or five patients per RN that is the current ratio recommended in California, this nurse had about a dozen patients? Could it have been because she was working a double or triple shift due to the nursing shortage? Could it have been because she had a double digit I.Q. and didn't bother to even look at the patient's wristband to match it up with the orders from the pharmacy? Or could it have just been because this kid looked like a 78-year-old woman?

Any of these could haves may have been part of this particular equation, but the take away point here is that there is always going to be room for human error. I read once that the number of mistakes made in a hospital every day leads to the equivalent of a

747 dropping from the sky and killing everyone on board every 24 hours. God, I hope that's not true, but these very human mistakes certainly could play into these dangerous medication errors.

 ## WHAT CAN YOU DO?

For goodness sake, don't be afraid to ask. Don't be afraid to challenge. Don't be afraid to question. In fact, ask, challenge, and question. You need more people caring for your personal health than your doctor. You must be a player. Your family members must be players. Your loved ones and even your enemies can help. Don't just accept everything you hear or see. Sometimes top notch, seasoned veterans make mistakes too. In fact, they all do.

I remember a lawsuit that ended up in a settlement after a procedure failed. The failure rate for this procedure was one in one thousand. This happened to have been the 997th procedure of its kind performed by this physician. It happens. Ask questions. Ask for verification. Ask to speak to a pharmacist. Ask for an explanation. Explain that the drug being given to you didn't work the time you tried it at home, or that it made you sick, or that it was the one that interacted with your fish oil and made you break out in hives. Don't be afraid to challenge anything that doesn't seem right.

CHAPTER 10

Infection Control
But did they wash their hands?
The inside story on hospital infection rates

Each year, thousands of patients are infected by the people caring for them. Many of them never fully recover and some die.

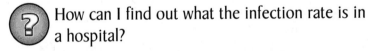 How can I find out what the infection rate is in a hospital?

The hospital's infection control department monitors all laboratory cultures from the hospital. Statistics are generally reported through bi-monthly or monthly Infection Control Committee meetings. Certain infectious and communicable diseases are mandated to be reported. Infection reports are forwarded to the State Healthcare Cost Containment Council (HC4) and the National Electronic Surveillance System (NEDSS).

What are nosocomial infections and staph infections?

Nosocomial infections and staph infections are the infection culprits. They come from nursing homes. They come from hospitals and I've been told that in old hospitals, buildings have actually had to be destroyed because there was no other way to eradicate these continuously adapting infections.

We've all seen the reports on the news about certain morphed versions of these dreaded staph infections that are completely resistant to antibiotics. They've become so virulent, that in some cases they eat away at skin and continue to ravage the patient's body until death.

 ## What are the national averages for patient-acquired nosocomial infections? How many people get sick or infected in the hospital?

The national average for patient-acquired nosocomial infections is typically around nine percent. This means that when you present as a patient at your local hospital you have nearly a ten percent chance of acquiring one of these sometimes extremely serious infections, an infection which could actually take your life. Therefore, even if your hospital stay was for a rather innocuous reason, there is a risk of your contracting a staph infection.

Many high-volume, inner-city teaching hospitals are particularly challenged by these ominous infections. Just the sheer number of indigent patients seen at these facilities makes it very, very difficult to provide care without spreading infection.

 ## What should I watch out for during my stay?

Remember Momma. Hand washing is a very important. In fact, it is the key factor. Antibacterial foams are currently considered the most effective means of stopping the spread of hospital-based infections. Don't let the nurses, aids, or techs do anything to you involving needles or catheters or invasive procedures without washing their hands. If you have more than one area that needs care, make sure he or she changes gloves, washes hands, and dons new gloves before moving from one site to the next.

What is the most important thing that a hospital can do to encourage a lower infection rate?

The most important thing a hospital can do to lower the infection rate is to require hand washing. Hospitals should regularly hold workshops; they should encourage physicians in the medical staff meetings. They must internally publicize and document their infection rates, and constantly discuss them in management meetings. Hospital employees are trained to take universal precautions. They are trained to use rubber gloves. BUT the most important question is: Did they wash their hands?

 How do I know I won't catch anything from my healthcare worker?

The percentage of healthcare workers that wash their hands or use the alcohol-based foams is 98%. Each new employee, upon hire, is required to attend a mandatory infection control in-service. The infection control/employee health nurse reminds each new employee of the importance of hand washing. Employees receive yearly updates and reminders on the effectiveness of proper hand washing.

CASES I HAVE SEEN

Once again, the numbers of cases seen in a small hospital in a semi-rural area are few and far between compared to a large urban hospital, but we still see them. When the severe cases are identified, steps are immediately taken to notify visitors and staff of the infection present by placing a sign on the door to warn staff and visitors. In addition, the rooms are specially equipped with continuous circulation capabilities to keep airborne bacteria from settling anywhere.

WHAT CAN YOU DO?

Pay close attention. Inform your loved ones. Don't let the nurse enter your room with gloves. Make sure she puts them on in front of you. Check to see that your caregivers are taking time to wash their hands. If you're in a semi-private room, make extra sure that the caregiver is not moving between you and your roommate without washing his or her hands. Watch the cleaning people. Ask them if the water is for your room. Make sure they disinfect everything. Keep them on their toes at all times. AND if you're too sick to do this, make sure that your loved one or care partner watches.

CHAPTER 11

Obstetrics

How do I know I'm in labor?

Labor can be best described as timeable, consistent contractions for one hour. Contractions will get closer together and may be felt in your back or lower abdomen. You may also experience steady cramping. Your water may break. True labor will not allow you to sleep or rest during the contractions or episodes of cramping. You may expel a mucous plug and have a bloody show at the onset of labor. For further information, consult a gynecologist. The following section will be devoted to decisions you will have to make before and when labor starts.

Obstetrics primarily deals with the delivery of babies and late-term pregnancy issues that may come up near the end (28 weeks or later) of the pregnancy. This department deals with labor, delivery, recovery, and post partum.

There are several indicators that patients should look for when deciding where they should go for their delivery. They include physician relationships, staff training, the ambience and atmosphere of the facility, anesthesia, integrative health modalities, support personnel, access to neonatal intensive care, 24-hour anesthesia, midwifery, and location of the facility.

Anesthesia or natural birth? The modern dilemma. The delivery process can be a very painful one and human beings have different thresholds of pain. Most women considering childbirth assume that they must get an epidural or an IV. This is simply not true. There are different types of medications from which to choose, and they all meet different needs. A patient should be aware beforehand of these different types before labor so as to be able to properly choose what she wants beforehand.

It is also important to realize that the differences in these pain killers can also temporarily limit your options after the baby is born. For instance, it should be thoroughly explained that if you need anesthesia, you will be restricted from getting up and moving around. You may not have access to alternative therapies (if offered) or to a labor ball (if offered). Some patients may want to take a shower or rest in the jacuzzi and taking the epidural or IV may restrict that patient from all of these modalities. It is also important to discover all that this department/hospital can offer.

 ## Can my husband be there when I deliver?

Check with the department/hospital to see who is permitted in the delivery room. You'll want a hospital that is flexible and does not restrict (within reason) your ability to have the important people in your life present during this important moment.

In addition to who is allowed to be present during the delivery, it is also important to check whether the loved one can stay and how they will be treated. Unless the patient doesn't mind being alone, make sure to check visiting hours.

Check for decentralized monitoring. Decentralized monitoring forces nurses to check each room and leads to a much more hands-on type interaction that really helps the patient feel more at ease. The patient usually feels more confident that they have received a higher level of care. Otherwise, the central nurses' station will be the brains of the OB floor, and you'll only get help when you look for it or request it via your call bells.

Staffing ratios are key to a quality delivery and hospital stay as well. You want to make sure that your hospital has a good ratio of nurses and staff to patients so that you will receive the best attention and level of care.

Check for emergency services for infants. Obviously, deliveries can have problems and it will be good to know beforehand that they have service available nearby or within the hospital to care for the infant in the event of any complications.

In order to get all of the information a new mother should have, check with your hospital to find out what types of prenatal classes they offer.

Another challenge can be the number of times the patient will be moved. Some places have separate rooms for labor, delivery, and recovery. If this is important to you, check into this first and find out how many times you will be moved. Make sure you know what to expect when you are in the hospital.

Before you leave, it is important to make sure that you receive thorough discharge instructions in order to protect both yourself and the newborn. If a patient is ever confused or does not feel she has all the answers, it is important to make sure she talks to the doctor or nurse and get more information.

CASES I HAVE SEEN

The very nature of delivering a child in a hospital can be the most beautiful or the most cumbersome of situations. Obviously, childbirth, like child making, is a natural part of life. And, thankfully, most times it does not require sophisticated equipment, comprehensive medical care, and the availability of complex anesthesia. Having said that, the American way of birth, not unlike the American way of illness, has evolved into a medical procedure.

Many sensitive, patient-centered facilities have taken steps to try and combine the natural with the procedural so that the experience is less invasive to the family. My facility moved heavily into creating a more pleasant experience. Imagine a facility where the families have single labor, delivery, recovery and post partum rooms, where the husband or significant other is invited and encouraged to stay with the delivering mom, where double beds are provided so that, after the birth, the family can become a family. Birthing balls, jacuzzis, aroma therapists, massage therapists, music therapists, doulas, spiritual counselors, and 24-hour visiting are all permitted in my hospital.

There are neonatal teams, operating rooms for emergency C-sections, 24-hour anesthesia availability, and all of the more traditional security blankets available, but the human spirit and the human touch are key elements in the birthing experience.

The birth of my own children, decades ago, demonstrated to me that removing the father from the process is unnatural and cruel. It made clear to me that inducing labor so that the physician can golf is unnatural. It showed to me that lack of access to the baby by either the mother or the father, was not normal, and finally, it proved to me that loving, caring, nurturing competent staff is the key to all patient care.

 WHAT CAN YOU DO?

Do your homework. Decide on your OB doc based on your personal needs and wants. Realize your desire to have a comfortable surrounding, competent care, and complex amenities by doing your homework. It is important to understand that this is your child, your family, your life, and your future. It is NOT up to the physician, nurse or midwife to control YOUR destiny. Take control and keep control.

CHAPTER 12

Specialty Care Units
The CCU and Y-O-U

The Critical Care Unit (CCU) offers continuous monitoring, care, and diagnostics for patients in life-threatening situations. The difference between regular and critical or intensive care is that the concentration of both physician and RN nursing coverage is significantly more intense. In this unit, the monitoring is often invasive and includes hemodynamic monitoring (Swanganz catheters) as well as the ability to provide temporary pacemakers and ventilators.

The CCU often receives patients from the operating room or the emergency room, and it is rarely a restful center. The intensity of the equipment present alone is enough to create a disruptive environment. There are alarms that are constantly beeping and pumps and ventilators that make numerous distracting noises.

In many modern CCUs, diagnostics are all done bedside. In fact, the beds themselves offer a wide range of functionality for patients. At a cost of tens of thousands of dollars each, they can include built-in scales for easy weighing of the patients, upper-torso radiology capabilities, and most of these beds will even convert to chairs.

The CCU staff will not only attempt to care for the patient to the best of their ability, but also to care for the family and loved ones of the patient. In some patient-centered facilities, this goes beyond simple physical care to include the patient and family's psychological and spiritual needs.

Many CCUs have very restricted visiting times but, once again, those with a patient-centered environment allow 24-hour visiting. If nurses need to care for the patient, they may ask the family to leave for a moment while they do their work.

Patients and families should expect superior quality care, a controlled environment, a knowledgeable and kind nursing staff, and direct access to the facility's finest and most skilled physicians in every specialty.

That being said, before this chapter becomes another rant about the misunderstanding of the purposes of healthcare, let me frame my position by saying that the CCU, in its perfect form, is a wonderful place where life-saving techniques save the most dire situations, where people who seemed beyond help are regularly brought back from the brink of death, and where people who had said their last farewells are saved by the skills, knowledge, and abilities of the dedicated individuals who run these departments.

Intensive care is the proper term for these units because the care is intense. It is the best of the best. Pulmonologists, critical care intensivists, internists, and wonderfully skilled technologists team up with RNs, LPNs and Aids to pull individuals through seemingly hopeless situations.

The CCU is part of the confluence of all the skills present in the facility. All of the best work of the laboratory, pharmacy and radiology, combined with incredible physician diagnostics and treatment come together in the CCU to extend life. In a world of unmatched technical innovation, the CCU embraces all of these technologies to sustain life. Day after day, night after night, we often take this department and these individuals for granted. They routinely deliver the impossible on a platinum platter. They routinely serve their patients above and beyond the call of duty, and the results are many times miraculous.

This is a department where dedicated leadership often does not sleep, where the physicians routinely are standing bedside at 3:30 a.m. or during holiday meals, and where shifts and hours are often ignored or forgotten so that continuity of care is available to the patient.

Having pointed out its positive aspects, if this were the end of the CCU story it would be a beautiful tale of the power and strength of American medicine. It would represent the pinnacle of perfection in a system of unparalleled care.

Unfortunately, as in all stories revolving around high finance and high costs, the CCU has devolved into the near perfect example of what's wrong with healthcare in the United States. Often, this is the arena in which the abuse of love, ego and control dominates.

My aunt said that when she was in the hospital they asked her to sign some papers about what she wanted to do if she was terminal. What was that and do I have to sign?

What she may have been talking about is an Advanced Directive. This is a form that directs healthcare providers as to what you want done in the event that you are unable to speak for yourself and would require extra care during a life-threatening event or a progression of a serious illness or problem.

The family decisions made in the CCU are often based upon several emotional or unsubstantiated elements. This often leads to excesses and abuses in the system.

In other chapters within this book we have often asked the question how much is too much care? Where are the lines? Or at least, where should the parameters be relative to the amount of care rendered for the severity of the condition? In the CCU, that question is answered on a daily basis, sometimes many times a day. The question is not answered by unscrupulous physicians, but many times by virtually unprotected physicians who are being pressured incessantly by a litigious society that questions every decision made by healthcare professionals in the US.

A model of extreme care did not become popular in this country until the 60's, but abuses of the system did not take long to follow. When every decision made by the professionals who run both the administrative and the medical care of a facility are subject to continuous, retrospective second-guessing, the manner in which people are treated quickly becomes *over the top*.

One of the realities faced by the typical US hospital administrator is finding a way to subsidize the losses created by the CCU. It is in this unit that medical treatment to the clinically dead or end-of-life patient takes on new meaning. It is in the CCU where families mistakenly replace love with anger, and power struggles and with threats and bullying, to "prove" their love for a parent or family member.

Death and dying take on new meaning as siblings gather together. Often, they are trying to establish their power within the family, and many times the CCU is the battleground upon which these rivalries are played out.

Remember, in a culture where death is considered failure, and where the common belief is that there is always a way to sustain life, the CCU is often a grim reminder of our mortality.

CASES I HAVE SEEN

When the only son of a patriarchal family comes back to town to deal with dad's terminal illness, especially if he has been the favored child in a family of females who were not given the same advantages (re: education), he usually becomes the prince.

Time and time again we have seen this son (or a strong, successful daughter) return to a dying dad or mom's bedside to take control of the family in their time of weakness and need.

It is at this sensitive time that we repeatedly see the ridiculous misuse of power and resources, both human and material. Often, these patients should have been placed in a hospice or palliative care setting. Demands and threats are made to everyone involved in the care and treatment of dad or mom, and the result is two or three more days of unconscious, unsustainable life.

This type of treatment happens on the regular nursing floors as well, but it reaches its dysfunctional pinnacle in the CCU. On average, our small facility loses approximately $52,000 per patient in the CCU in reimbursements. This is because the insurance companies will only reimburse useful treatment, but the physicians and RNs are under pressure from individuals, such as the example cited above, to continue to provide a level of care that is not appropriate.

We have spent hundreds of thousands of dollars in equipment, exotic medicines, and unusual technology when the brain function had ceased hours earlier. We have witnessed individuals ignore their family members' unwritten wishes and instruct our staff to do the opposite of verbally expressed instructions. In the case of my own mother, she had carefully instructed all of us that she wanted no extraordinary measures taken. When she collapsed at our dinner table, unconscious, it was not clear to us what had occurred. We called 9-1-1, and the paramedics intubated her and rushed her to the emergency department where she was given a CAT scan and placed on a ventilator until the nature and extent of the damage that she suffered could be ascertained.

My mom lay in the CCU on a ventilator for three days while various treatments were undertaken to determine if she would respond medically. Finally, when her regular physician returned from a weekend trip, we discussed her wishes and she was disconnected from the ventilator. It probably that should have happened two days earlier.

 WHAT CAN YOU DO?

Clearly and concisely put your wishes and thoughts in writing. Then you will have a chance that they will be honored as you instructed. This is not due to any malicious intent on the part of the medical center; it is, in fact, due to several issues, not the least of which are miracles. We have seen individuals rally to go on to live several more productive years.

Of course, we can never really tell when and if an individual is going to die. Even in cases where there are physical signs that death is present, we've seen patients rally. But if the stroke has destroyed the brain stem, or the heart is gone, or it is physically surviving without cognition, it's time to allow the transition to occur. None of the medical equipment, the medicines, or the phenomenal skills of either the physicians or their teams will bring that person back.

What can you do? Become more comfortable knowing that none of us will get out of this life alive. But, we are entitled to have input into how our transition can occur with dignity.

CHAPTER 13

Housekeeping
Can you tell by the smell?

As a first-time hospital president, it was clear to me that I could not tolerate a *business-as-usual* environment. My background included visits to plenty of hospitals that allowed me to see blood on the walls in the patient's rooms, filthy corners, stairwells, and waiting areas with waste baskets running over, cigarette butts at the entrance ways and infection rates raging at around 10%. For the most part, it was not because of a lack of pride. It was because of accepted standards, history, and tradition. It was about mediocrity. It was about doing it the way it had always been done before.

When you enter many hospitals, feel fortunate if you are overwhelmed by the smell of disinfectants. At least it smells as if someone is trying to clean the place. Feel lucky if you don't see fluids on the curtains or walls. If you don't get an infection, it is cause for a thank you prayer.

How do you know if a hospital is clean? What questions can you ask? Well, here's the drill. At a hospital with an infection rate below 1% there are several very important extra steps that take place. The public bathrooms are thoroughly cleaned first thing in the morning. This gives the patients time to eat breakfast before the housekeeping staff begins to clean their rooms. However, since patients are the focus of the entire hospital, the patient rooms and operating rooms are the priority for the housekeeping staff.

Is my room cleaned daily?

The patient rooms are cleaned every single day; the window, window-sills, floors, tables, telephones, telephone cords, restrooms, end tables, and bed trays are sanitized. The staff uses disposable wipes for each room so that the tools used to wipe up and clean up a patient room are used only once. This ensures that each room is getting its own cleaning equipment. It's more expensive, but much safer for the patients this way.

The water in the staff's cleaning bucket is changed for every room. To ensure cleanliness, and to protect from infection, any blood or bathroom accidents are handled as soon as the staff is made aware of them. If a room needs any type of maintenance or work performed, the housekeeping staff will contact the maintenance department immediately to get the problem fixed.

Staff are always on the lookout for exposed needles in patient areas to ensure everyone's safety. They also check the floors for paperclips because these little organizational tools can cause slips and falls. Furthermore, they are very careful to dispose properly of any hazardous waste material to ensure safety from infection.

Most importantly, when possible, they also have an important role in taking care of the patients themselves. If they are doing their cleaning and the patient needs a pillow, wants to be propped up in bed, needs a drink, or whatever non-medical request they might have, the housekeeping staff will do all that they can to help.

If it's a medical task, they will find the person who can help the patient. Some of these requests may seem beyond the realm of a typical job duty, but if the request is valid, they will go far beyond the norm. For example, if the patient has spilled some food or drink on their personal items, the house-keepers will even wash those items for the patient. Going a step further, they will then return the items to the patient pressed and clean. (Obviously, to avoid the spread of infection, any blood-borne pathogens are not included in this extra service.)

When the patient count is low, patient rooms are completely refinished. The floors are stripped, cleaned, and resealed with a fresh coat of wax to ensure the highest level of cleanliness possible. This happens to all of the rooms several times a year.

Other areas of the hospital are typically cleaned in the very early hours of the morning (3-4 a.m.). At this time the physical therapy rooms and showers are cleaned. This is to ensure that when the patients and visitors begin to arrive at about 6 a.m., they will find newly disinfected areas for their morning sessions.

The critical care unit is always a priority area in the hospital. There is never any waiting there. When the CCU calls, the staff immediately goes into action. All equipment is cleaned, disinfected, and cared for after each patient. Special care is taken in this unit due to the nature of the types of services performed. Blood-borne pathogens, special emergency procedures, and critical cases sometimes lead to extra maintenance issues for staff, but there are no shortcuts taken there.

The palliative care unit also presents special challenges. It is used for pain control, respite for the families, and end-of-life situations. This unit often times might have its own washer and dryer and housekeeping takes care of the patient's personal items in it. This includes special types of care; i.e., Afghans are cleaned, folded, and made available for patients.

Some hospitals use walkie talkies for housekeeping staff to keep in constant contact with nursing stations. Whoever is closest helps on the call.

The operating room floor is scrubbed and buffed every week. Each surgical suite is disinfected after each case, and special mops are designated for the OR.

Generally, the public areas and public restrooms are continuously monitored to be sure that everything is available and clean. The same holds true for patient lounges. Because patient lounges have refreshments for families, they are monitored very closely.

Infectious areas are also very carefully addressed. Depending on the type of infection, various precautions can be taken. All unnecessary equipment is removed. That limits the need for infection control to just the area immediately around the patient.

Specific chemicals can be used to kill respiratory infections. The housekeeping staff will wear masks, use gloves, and separate cleaning cloths for each room. Special hand sanitizers are also used.

Finally, chemicals can be added to disinfectants to improve the aroma. They create a nicer, non-antiseptic odor. Air fresheners are also used in bathrooms and all throughout the hospital.

CASES I HAVE SEEN

This section would probably have been better titled, 'cases we have all smelled.' Many hospitals moved to carpeting to improve acoustics overall and to generally cut down on unnecessary noise. Carpets take very special care, and the upkeep is sometimes impossible. If the art of carpet cleaning is not mastered, the odor can be deadly.

As noted above, there are chemicals that can be added to help change the hospital smells into something much more pleasant, but as also mentioned, general responsiveness is the key.

In one facility, the near toxic smells were obvious from the moment of entry. They were relentless, overpowering, and noxious. Part of the reason that they existed was poor management. In this situation, the disgruntled employees were the sources of the smell. Sometimes mismanagement permeates an entire organization, but mostly it is isolated and directly related to individual departments and services.

If the person that heads up housekeeping is not dedicated to absolutely immaculate cleanliness, it will not happen. This individual must also be a cheerleader, a parent, a superhero, and a taskmaster but, most importantly, he or she must be an advocate for the employees for which they have responsibility.

In order to correct the smells and infection rates, the manager, the carpeting and several of the employees had to be replaced.

 WHAT CAN YOU DO?

Complain. You can complain to the housekeeping staff, to the nursing staff, to administration and to the board of directors. You can write letters. You can make phone calls. You can use the local paper as a forum for your concerns. You have the power to call an inordinate amount of attention to any *cleanliness* issue. It's just wrong.

McDonald's made its reputation with good French fries and clean bathrooms. When either is publicly criticized, it brings down the wrath of administration on the offending organization. No hospital CEO and no manager can escape an accusation of a lack of cleanliness or an environment that could breed infections. It doesn't matter if the organization is a union or a non-union shop.

Complain. Start at the bottom and work your way to the top, and if that doesn't work, go public. Cleanliness is the very least you should expect from a hospital. It is not acceptable to see blood on the walls or the curtains. It is not acceptable to see dirt in the corners. It is not acceptable to see filth on trays or in stairwells. Regardless of how busy a hospital happens to be, there is simply no excuse—none.

CHAPTER 14

Cardiac Rehab

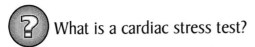 What is a cardiac stress test?

A cardiac exercise test is a test that involves monitoring by a physician while the patient walks on a treadmill or is injected with a pharmacological agent in order to increase the heart's muscle demand for oxygen. This test is done to help determine the presence and/or extent of coronary artery disease.

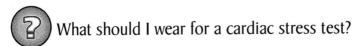 What should I wear for a cardiac stress test?

Wear comfortable clothes and sneakers for a cardiac stress test. Your physician's office will remind you to dress in this manner.

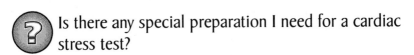 Is there any special preparation I need for a cardiac stress test?

A patient should not ingest any caffeine within 24 hours of the test. If you're taking blood pressure medication, take it on the morning of the test. However, be sure to confirm this with your physician first.

What is a cardiac halter monitor?

A cardiac halter is a 24-hour recording of your heart rhythm. This monitor is worn for 24 hours with a marked button to be pressed only when there is chest pain, palpitations, or any discomfort.

What is cardiac rehab?

Usually, the patients will need cardiac rehab (CR) for four to eight weeks following surgery depending on what was done and many other variables including age and recovery. The details of the program are laid out in the beginning and expectations are set.

Anybody of any age, weight, body type, height, and condition can do cardiac rehab, there are NO standards for participants. It is very individualized.

Medical history and orientation is reviewed. From pre-surgery to post-surgery, in as much detail as possible, the patient's history will help gauge the process. This status check also helps the patient know where he or she stands, has been, or needs to go.

Is it really safe for me to be exercising?

While exercising, all patients are on an ECG telemetry monitor to look for any heart rate or rhythm irregularities to ensure their safety.

It is important that the patient has established a functional capacity level. This is usually accomplished by performing a stress test under physician supervision. Most hospitals will complete this test without supervision, if necessary, but the test is much more scaled back. This test is only meant to give a general picture as opposed to the very specific physician-monitored test. Also, this program focuses on cardiovascular fitness and involves little to no weight lifting.

How long does this program last?

Cardiac rehabilitation is typically a six to twelve week program with thrice weekly one-hour sessions. All of these sessions are monitored and supervised to ensure patient safety. Progress is measured on a weekly basis and compared as the weeks pass by.

Early in the process, a dietician is consulted for weight and diet help. Much of the recovery process involves helping the patient change their entire lifestyle, not just cardiovascular fitness.

Insurance companies often determine the end of the program for financial reasons. Because of this, it is important to understand that the process never ends at the end of these sessions. Rehab is something that needs to go beyond the rehab and become a part of life. Dieting changes, exercise adjustments, knowing your limits and improving to the best of your ability is the most important take away lesson.

Do I really need cardiac rehab?

People tend to believe that they are not physically ready or they won't be able to handle the exercise or that they are too weak from surgery or that they will be surrounded by people in much better shape. This causes unnecessary fear and apprehension and can severely hamper the recovery. It is important to realize that people of any size, shape, and ability are able to do rehab and it will benefit them. There is no need to worry about being "able" to do it, it's designed so that you can.

Every step of the cardiac rehab program has someone monitoring or helping a patient at every step of every level.

Sometimes, patients really have no idea what they actually went through or why they need this. It is important to have asked your physician and discussed exactly what process was performed and get answers to any and all questions. Patients need to fully understand what happened and how their lives will be different now.

This is also much more than a simple exercise regimen to strengthen the heart, but an emotional and mental healing as well. People often are traumatized by their experience and need to rebuild emotionally as well.

Realize that the process goes beyond the six to twelve weeks and it's something that must be added to LIFE.

CHAPTER 15

Occupational Therapy
To do or not to do

What is occupational therapy?

Time and time again we question the purpose of services provided by hospitals. What is occupational therapy? As a vice president of administrative services in the late 80s, one of my departmental visits was to an occupational therapy center that came under the direction of our hospital. As I entered the department in an offsite location, I saw a kitchen. It made sense to me that we would help people who had suffered some type of debilitating experience by helping them redevelop skills. It made sense to me that, if possible, the patient should be assisted in maintaining their daily lifestyle and that skills in a kitchen would certainly be a welcome link to self-maintenance.

The joke was that my own skills in that area were so limited that I considered signing up for the program. It was only when they took me to our man-made coal mine shaft that I realized the interesting scope of capabilities developed by these skilled, patient instructors.

Why and when would I need occupational therapy?

Occupational therapy (OT) revolves around a series of therapy sessions that focus on an entire person and everything he or she does. The analysis of their particular needs is broken down into tasks performed on a day-to-day basis. They can be personal tasks like tying a shoe or cooking yourself a meal, combing your hair or writing a letter or job-based like bending or lifting.

If an individual has any problem performing any of these tasks, an OT will step up to the plate and attempt to help them. OT rehab involves repairing or developing new ways for the patient to enhance his or her skills to a level of ability.

Occupational therapists do not always utilize the physical rehab methodology to reestablish or reconnect the patient's abilities. OT often involves mental rehabilitation; in fact, mental rehabilitation represents the primary means of rebuilding or building the bridges necessary to reestablish connectivity.

A primary goal of OT is to restore the patient's ability to be independent again. Many times, once a patient loses the ability to perform basic tasks, he or she also loses confidence and can become very depressed. With the help of OT, patients can regain their ability to perform these tasks and regain independence.

 ## What's the difference between physical therapy and occupational therapy?

In the world of medicine, just like interventional radiologists oftentimes compete with invasive cardiologists for certain stent placements or podiatrists compete with orthopedists for foot surgery, OTs compete with PTs, physical therapists. In fact, physical therapists compete with OTs in some areas and chiropractors in different areas. This is because there are overlaps in treatments. It is a wonderful, functional hospital, out-patient department, or stand-alone therapy center where these rivalries are not apparent or have been methodically controlled by leadership. Watch out for this undertow. It can ruin your day (or your treatment)!

This lack of cooperation between departments, like many other hospital rivalries, can result in inferior care for the patient. If a physical therapist is the dominating member or head of the department, the patient may not even be recommended for OT consultation, and thus may be cheated out of the special training that separates these two professions.

Regardless of the methodology, patients are monitored throughout their progress, from start to finish. The OT process is completely individualized and treatments achieved can vary tremendously from therapist to therapist. What one therapist likes to do and finds to be effective with patients may be completely different from another. Hence, the art of medicine.

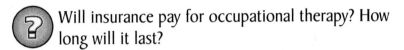 Will insurance pay for occupational therapy? How long will it last?

Insurance companies often vary their coverage for both the length and breadth of the occupational therapy program as applicable to your particular case. They do the same with other types of rehab such as cardiac rehabilitation. Usually, the variation is not in the patient's best interest. So, should you as the patient, or the potential patient, have a choice in the types of insurance available to you, it is important to determine what your rehabilitation coverage will be. That difference could literally mean the difference between success and failure to many patients. If ability to pay is a factor, this must be taken into consideration.

The term "occupational therapy" causes many misunderstandings. OT does NOT just deal with work-related tasks. This is a common misconception among patients. Occupations are everywhere and involve everything. The tasks addressed by the therapists can be as mundane as tying one's shoe to as complex as coal mining.

One of OT's challenges is that many times patients don't really understand their problems or illness. Top notch OTs will make sure that their patient disconnects are clarified or corrected in as short an amount of time as possible. If a patient is unaware of the reason for an OT recommendation, then he or she needs to become aware by asking questions and being involved in the process.

CASES I HAVE SEEN

My exposure to actual cases in this arena has been limited to my own personal family and friends. But, in my world they have been significant. In at least one case, the patient suffered permanent disability because of a lack of functional therapy made available to her. This case involved a nursing home, an insurance company, and a hospital but, as it turned out, can be a common occurrence in the healthcare delivery system.

The patient, my mother-in-law, had suffered a stroke. This stroke was significant, but the damage from the stroke ended up being almost completely reversible. The reversal occurred at a time when services by hospitals and therapists were cost reimbursed. In other words, the providers did what they needed to do, and then were reimbursed accordingly.

A few years later, she suffered another stroke, but the services were restricted and capped. As non-clinical caregivers responsible for her receipt of care, we carefully selected a specialty unit where she could be rehabilitated. This unit offered the most comprehensive care possible in this particular situation but, by this time, there were limitations placed upon the amount and number of sessions available. Our mom did not have a full recovery this time, and months after this was obvious to all of us, we were told the deep, troublesome truth. Had she had a similar regiment of care as that rendered during her first experience, there would have been an excellent chance for full recovery.

Had we known that her lack of specialized treatment would result in such a devastating lack of recovery, we would have done whatever was needed to provide for her care but, because it had become "old hat" with the providers, they knew that mentioning it to the patient's family would only cause distress.

Hospitals have seen the services provided for alcohol rehabilitation, cardiac rehabilitation, psychiatric care, physical therapy, occupational therapy and many other modalities be decreased precipitously as it became obvious to the insurance companies that the average individual would not understand this nuance of change in an average insurance policy, but that it would result in billions of dollars in savings to the company.

Sadly, this attitude toward healthcare reminded me of the time that our homeowners policy, although we had a rider for drain backup, would not pay to repair our basement after a storm sewer did not function. When we had a chance to question an insurance adjuster, we were told that insurance companies had discovered that, if they didn't pay claims, they would have more money for either their funded reserves or for their stock holders at the end of the year. In the case of rehab, if the insurance companies just didn't provide the services, they would have more money at the end of the year.

Now, to be fair, with the inventions of new types of drugs that cost $8,000 a dose and only work on one third of the patients treated with them, with the addition of new PET/CT scanners that cost millions of dollars, and with the cost of new procedures ever pushing the limits on insurance companies, cuts in rehabilitation were bound to happen. As we stated in one of our earlier chapters, there is no way that we can have the best healthcare, the fastest healthcare, and the cheapest healthcare in the world. Something has got to give. Unfortunately, in our case, what had to give was mom's ability to take care of herself. She became debilitated years before it was necessary or likely.

 WHAT CAN YOU DO?

Don't get into an accident. Don't get hurt at work. Don't allow your blood pressure to remain uncontrolled.

But if you find yourself or your loved one in any of the above situations, make sure that you are clear on what your insurance policy covers and be prepared to supplement your policy if need be. In other words, ask if you will receive enough treatments to correct your condition. Find out if you have enough coverage to accomplish what needs to be accomplished. Push the provider. If they answer with a candid "no," you will understand what your options are.

As alluded to earlier, if you are in physical therapy only, ask clearly what benefit you would receive from occupational therapy. If the PT doesn't encourage you to seek that help, and comes off in a disrespectful manner, keep pushing to get the real answer because OT really helps people.

Because many patients don't understand the activities they are performing or why, it is important to ask simply, "why am I doing this and what will it help me accomplish?"

Finally, your attitude can really make or break the outcome of occupational therapy. There is a motivational factor that the patient must WANT to get better and, if it is not present, the rehab process may otherwise fail. If you do not feel the desire to improve, you may not get there. It is okay to ask for psychological help in this process as well. Sometimes recovery time is unpredictable, and they may challenge you with the question, "How hard are you willing to work?" In that case, the ball will be in your court.

Make it a priority to follow through with home exercises and other activities.

Physical Therapy

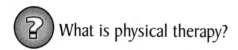 What is physical therapy?

Physical therapy (PT) deals with all types of joint, muscle and skeletal problems. The goal of physical therapy is to decrease pain, improve range of motion, and improve the patient's ability to perform activities of daily living.

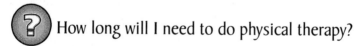 How long will I need to do physical therapy?

Physical therapy is typically a four-to-six week program that takes place about three times per week for out-patients (insurance once again will typically limit the number of visits; for financial reasons, the average number of visits to PT is 12).

I know I need physical therapy; can't I schedule the treatments myself?

PT requires a physician referral. A patient cannot come off the streets and say, my joints hurt, I could go for some physical therapy. The order must come from a doctor. It typically involves therapeutic exercise of all types along with heat, ice, ultrasound and aquatic therapies.

 ## Is it supposed to hurt?

PTs are not 'physical terrorists.' Working through the pain is not a necessarily true credo for PT, but you will be worked to the tolerance point and that is different with every patient. Understand this going in. If you do not understand why you are doing something, then ask. You have the right to ask questions and understand what you are doing and why you are doing it. It also helps if the patient gives the therapist a rundown of their capabilities right away. That way the therapist can be aware of potential issues and work them to their advantage during therapy. Patients do have the right to refuse PT, but it will be their loss.

 ## What can I do to speed up my treatment?

Motivation is the key factor; you must have the attitude that you want to get better and will do what it takes. Do the recommended exercises to the best of your ability. Otherwise the process is very difficult.

Most/all patients in cardiac rehab have gone through a traumatic heart procedure. Most things involving the heart are traumatic to the average patient but this can causes a very high level of fear and apprehension when entering a cardiac rehab program. This often leads to a high level of denial. Don't stay in denial. Your physician has recommended it for a reason.

CHAPTER 16

Food Service

I'm on a special diet; will I be able to get the right foods here?

The food service department interacts with patients and staff on multiple levels. They are typically responsible for the production of sometimes complex diets and preparation of sophisticated trays for very difficult dietary challenges; i.e., diabetics with extremely high blood pressure being treated with blood thinners. Each of these illnesses has different dietary requirements and, for the most part, unless the staff is very well trained, the food without sugar, salt, or leafy greens can be just awful. Add in the nuances of a serving system that allows the food to cool down after preparation, a glitch or two in the delivery of the hot meal, and medications that make your taste buds respond like concrete blocks in a mud pit, and you get hospital food.

To me, green jello is representative of the lowest level of hospital food. It's where the term institutional cooking comes to life. Green, watery, lime jello on a white hospital plate, jiggling in the wind is enough to make anyone sick.

So, what's the trick? What's the key? How do you survive the food? We've tried chefs (untrained in catering to the various disease states of the patients). We've tried fast food cooks (food too unhealthy to serve). We've tried home cooking from cooks trained in places like the Elks or the VFW.

Let's take a look at food service. It is an interesting, and often times frustrating, area and has represented the majority of the complaints with which a hospital with a 99% patient satisfaction rating has had to deal.

What does the staff do? Their duties include the assembly, delivery, and pickup of trays to the patients and guests. How does it come together? A clerk screens all new admissions and asks each patient a series of general questions to obtain an outline of their likes, dislikes, preferences, and allergies. Most questions and available dietary information is explained to the patient at this time.

After every screening, if they so choose, the patient is offered a chance to speak with a dietician. This is highly encouraged and recommended since the dietician can properly explain what the patient can and cannot eat and the reasons behind these dietary restrictions.

 I'm a patient and I'm hungry, can I ask them to bring me food?

Throughout their stay at our facility, patients can request anything they want from the department as long as it follows the dietary guidelines or restrictions specific to that patient. This open rule correctly challenges our dietary department to be flexible and responsive.

 Do I have a choice when it comes to the food they serve me?

The setup is *restaurant style*, because there is a selective menu. This means food services offers a few choices but, as stated above, if a patient wants something else and it falls within their guidelines, then the staff will make every effort to get it. Patients should expect to have their needs met while in the hospital.

 Where can my family eat when they come to see me?

Again, specific to our facility, the same rule applies to visitors. If they are visiting a family member and want to eat, they could simply tell a nurse or call the kitchen and request another tray. I would recommend getting the first choice option of that meal unless something else is required. The staff tries to ensure that guests aren't inconvenienced while visiting at the hospital.

There are quality assurance testing and inspections ongoing throughout the year, every year. There are three to four main regulators that watch over the food service department: the Joint Commission on Hospital Accreditation, the Department of Health (both federal and state) and the Department of Agriculture. They inspect for safety and sanitation standards, and these inspections are taken with extreme seriousness. Any violation could lead to the closing of the entire department.

Trays are also double checked before they leave the kitchen to ensure that the patients are getting what they want, what they ordered, and are within the guidelines of the dietary restrictions placed upon them. This helps reduce mistakes.

Finally, as mentioned previously, food service is tied into the complaint system at the hospital. Anything that is unsatisfactory with the food will be addressed and taken very seriously. In fact, many states require a constant flow of information regarding these complaints.

The bottom line: If unsure about anything, the patients should ask to speak to a dietician about any food-related questions while in the hospital. The patients (and in our facility) their guests should expect to be catered to as much as possible within the guidelines of their dietary restrictions.

CASES I HAVE SEEN

Unfortunately, life tends to deal cards in this category only from the bottom of the deck. Rarely, if ever, does the senior administrator hear about the unbelievable food, the great service, or the lovely presentation. Most of the cases seen have been complaints about the green jello or the tepid meal, or the lack of salt.

The most interesting case, however, was that of a 91-year-old grandmother who hated our food. Her 65-year-old daughter insisted on bringing her KFC meals every day. Typically she got fried chicken, mashed potatoes, gravy and slaw. Her room was always cluttered with empty containers of Kentucky Fried something. Well, near the end of her stay, we were approached by her senior citizen daughter who began to attack us for disposing of her mother's teeth. When we checked the inventory of her mother's possessions upon rival, it was duly noted that her mother had brought no teeth. In fact, the meals had been prepared in our kitchen to accommodate her mother's lack of dental hardware.

Well, young Cora, the daughter, told us that she had brought mom's teeth in so that she could eat the fried chicken, and now they were missing. After a thorough search of mom's room, her waste cans and, with her permission, her possessions, we found no upper or lower plates. At this point, we asked her daughter once again to calm down and give us more information about the teeth. Well, as fate would have it, the teeth were delivered in a KFC Styrofoam cup. This solved our mystery. The teeth, the empty containers, and all of those chicken bones, or maybe not the bones, were long gone to our local landfill. Sorry, mom.

 WHAT CAN YOU DO?

Make sure your teeth are not in a throwaway cup. Seriously, it behooves you to communicate openly and thoroughly with the dietitian. Don't let them off the hook. You or your company, or your insurance is paying good money for your stay. In our little hospital, the average in-patient charge is $4,000 for a three-day stay. Talk to your dietitian. Quiz him or her. Be clear about your requests and/or demands. Make sure that you explain what spices you like or don't like. If you feel like eating, make it as good as you can get. Then, if all else fails, call KFC!

CHAPTER 17

Psych
Stop the world – I need to get off

Unfortunately, in many parts of the country, an admission to a psychiatric unit is considered a personal failure, a taboo last resort. Yet, in most urban areas, life without a personal psychiatrist or psychologist would be unthinkable.

If psychiatric care is necessary, it is imperative that the journey be initiated without a stigma attached. You must begin to de-stigmatize mental healthcare in your own mind. Because so many people still look upon this care as a form of disgrace, they delay seeking in-patient psychiatric care for themselves or their loved ones.

Family members can make a psychiatric admission a negative experience by stigmatizing it. This often leads to situations that are very difficult for everyone. It creates a situation in which an emergency visit becomes the only way in which the patient/family member can be assisted.

One way of easing the tension and reducing the fear of an admission is by advance reconnaissance. Because in the case of an emergency or involuntary admission this will not be an option, it is imperative to take advantage of this opportunity while it is still an option. Do some advance work.

How do I know I'm seeing the right psychiatrist for me?

Too often, the psychiatric patient's first encounter with the psychiatrist is after being admitted. Talk with the psychiatrist to determine if he/she is someone in whom you would have confidence.

Ask about an estimated length of stay.

The same is true for exploring the unit. When it is an option, take advantage of that opportunity. Work with the administration to get permission to walk through the unit before deciding if it is an appropriate environment for your loved one. Evaluate the environment to determine whether or not it presents a healing atmosphere.

Ask what disciplines and services are available. Ask to determine if they have psychologists, social workers, recreational therapists, aids and volunteers. Or, a worst case type scenario, find out if the only therapeutic contact the patient will have is a five-minute medication check from the psychiatrist each morning.

Another very important point is knowing if the unit is locked or open. When a person is being treated as an in-patient, there is really very little reason for them to leave the unit. Nonetheless, some people might be more comfortable in a unit that allows them that option, and some would not even consider an admission unless that was the case.

It is also imperative to find out exactly what type of population is being served. Sometimes a child might be put in an adult or geriatric unit temporarily because all of the childbeds are filled. If this were the case, based upon our experts, it would be better to seek admission to another facility. Specific problems require specific care. For example, an eating disorder would best be treated in a special program directed toward those with eating disorders rather than in a general psychiatric unit or in an acute-care hospital without any psychiatric component.

As you move more closely toward admission, be sure to read and understand any statement of patient rights. Be particularly aware of policies regarding leaving the unit Against Medical Advice. Ramifications and potential ramifications attached to this AMA discharge can have a negative financial impact. Insurance can be cancelled or declared inapplicable once the decision is made to leave without consent. Check—is there a requirement for advance notice? If so, how much notice is required? If the admission is involuntary, understand the terms of the admission and the requirements for discharge.

Another important element is giving the patient information about their diagnosis. This is very important for peace of mind of the patient. The patient and or their loved one or advocate needs to be sure that this is explained thoroughly. For what is the patient being treated? Is it for depression, anxiety, or a myriad of other psychological factors? Many people leave the hospital without ever knowing what or why they were being treated.

Similarly, insist on knowing about any medications being prescribed. What are they for and what effects might be expected? How might they interact with already prescribed medications? What are the potential side affects of these medications, and how can they be managed?

Finally, upon discharge, arrange for some follow-up. In most cases, there is still work to be done, either in counseling or with medication, or both. Hospital psychiatric units provide very short-term care. A psychiatric admission is usually intended to deal only with a crisis, not to fully resolve the problem.

CASES I HAVE SEEN

As a non-clinical administrator, my experiences have been limited to drug and alcohol abuse, child psych, eating disorders, dementia, clinical depression, and suicide attempts.

The one moment that has stuck with me was a rather intimate observation within a child psych unit. It was a closed unit in a very nurturing hospital and psych unit. The children came in with some very serious problems and, during the course of their stay, improvement was exponential. By the end of their hospitalization, the patients had usually improved dramatically.

This was also the case with those children and young adults suffering from eating disorders. The unfortunate reality was that once the children were returned to their homes, the symptoms did as well. The primary reason for the evolution of these complex maladies due to a dysfunctional situation in the home. As long as the care was uninterrupted and the source of the problem was removed, there was an opportunity for healing.

Philosophically, this is no different from many illnesses heretofore thought to be incurable. If the continuous environmental insult is removed, then there is an opportunity for healing.

When this is not the case, appropriate counseling medication and nurturing can work wonders.

 WHAT CAN YOU DO?

Understand your rights as a patient, a family member, or a friend. Pay close attention to the individuals, the environment, the aides, assistants, and physicians who will be providing the care.

Carefully examine the philosophy of the institution. Is it representative of an environment that encourages healing, that embraces nurturing, and that has a commitment to patient care above all else?

CHAPTER 18

Credentials

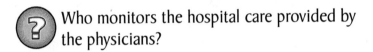

Who monitors the hospital care provided by
the physicians?

In order for physicians to be able to practice in hospitals, they must
go through a two-step process that includes credentialing and privileging.
The credentialing process involves first a background check during which
time all information is gathered about an individual physician's past. This
background check includes verification of education, training and work
experience. This information is gathered and verified against what the physician has stated to make sure that all of the resume claims are legitimate.

This information is then verified to see if the applicant has an active
license, liability insurance to cover their malpractice costs, and Drug
Enforcement Agency certification allowing them to prescribe narcotics.
Verification is also required to prove that the doctor holds board certifications. Board certification is not required, but highly recommended. Finally,
peer references from physicians of similar backgrounds are checked and
double checked.

All of the information gathered in the credentialing process goes to a
credentials committee where it is reviewed and then accepted or rejected.
The other alternative that the committee has is to put in a request to be
shown more information about some specific certification, degree, or skill

before making a decision. It is a further possibility to have the physician's credentials accepted, but to make the new physician agree to be monitored by a peer or department chairperson for a certain period of time.

If the committee approves the candidate, the physician becomes privileged. After a provisional period of service, he/she becomes a complete and full member of the medical staff. This process must be replicated every two years to ensure patient safety and quality care. Of course, every medical facility has its own rules and regulations regarding credentials and privileges, but most are similar.

In addition to the ongoing process described above, the physician must have 120 credits of continuing medical education and have a quality performance evaluation on an annual or, in some instances, a semi-annual basis.

An important point to note about the credentialing process is that, for a doctor to be rejected, there must be hard evidence for this rejection. Strong suspicion that a physician is lying or hiding his or her background is not enough for a credentials rejection. There must be proof. Several hospitals and medical staffs have been sued over the years due to unlawful or unnecessary restriction of privileges. Unless or until the institution's medical staff is closed to outsiders, it is illegal to turn away qualified professionals who apply to work on staff at the facility.

CASES I HAVE SEEN

Fortunately, I have never seen a case of forged or inaccurate credentials. There have been many times, however, when physicians have attempted to get additional certifications for types of procedures in which they claimed to have training but, in fact, had done only a small number of procedures.

We have also had cases where a physician wanted to practice beyond the scope of his or her licensure privileges. In some cases, these physicians were permitted to perform certain procedures under the supervision of experts in that field. In other instances, the physician was not permitted to perform any procedures of the type requested but, by and large, this type of gray manipulative effort has been very limited.

WHAT CAN YOU DO?

There are websites where you can check on the license and status of doctors to ensure their certification, such as:

www.docboard.org (free)
www.docinfo.org (fee)

If you suspect your doctor isn't up to your standards, then talk to the hospital administrator, chief medical officer, or head of credentials about it. If necessary, discuss your concerns with local, county and/or state medical board officials.

While the credentials department will not give up their records unless ordered by the court, with a little research, most physician information is public information. The Physician's Data Bank is also a public source of information.

So, if you don't feel right, do your research and talk to the proper people about it until you do.

CHAPTER 19

Social Services

Wheelchairs, nursing homes, oxygen and other fun

Working with a social worker to ensure the best outcome

Okay, I'm admitted, who will feed my cats?

If you do not have a family member, friend, or neighbor that can assist in taking care of your pets, the hospital social worker can be contacted regarding information on who can help provide this assistance.

I have bills that need to be paid if I'm going to be a patient for a long time. Should I make arrangements for someone to do that?

If you have a major illness or injury and think you will be in the hospital for an extended period of time, it would be best to ask a family member, friend, or neighbor to assist you in taking care of personal matters. The hospital social worker can be contacted regarding information on who can help provide this assistance.

In a hospital environment where stress levels can run high, most of the time it is helpful to know about the medical social worker. They are people available to patients and families to assist them with problem solving and discharge planning.

 ## Will someone help me after I go home? Will I have to pay anything?

Social Services will assist you in obtaining home care by contacting the appropriate support resources and setting up the services. Your social worker will review your insurance coverage to determine if the costs of home care services are covered by your insurance.

The goal and the role of the social worker is to provide appropriate education and counseling to enable patients and families to make a smooth and positive transition from hospital to home, to help them maximize utilization of support services, to help them arrange for their home equipment needs, and about rehabilitation services or extended care options.

Social workers have the knowledge and expertise to help the patient and their family find the most beneficial option for each individual. There is potentially no more understanding, helpful assistant to move the patient and their family through the hospital stay.

It is the role of the nursing supervisor, nursing manager, or other member of your care delivery team to assign you to your social worker. This service should be available to any in-patient, and is not only available to financially challenged patients or families.

Unlike the social worker who is typically called upon to deal with home issues, sometimes domestic disturbances or challenges, medical social workers are in place to specifically deal with those issues delineated above; i.e., nursing home placement, durable medical equipment needs, rehab or other challenges.

Each and every patient case is different. It is clear, however, that most families have not had experiences with these individuals, and all social workers are not created equally. Consequently, it is important to note that your rights allow you to place certain expectations clearly on the shoulders of your assigned social worker, and pressure for a medical social worker should be created if he or she has been unsuccessful at *meeting your personal needs.*

Social workers are to present to you the very best options for your care based exclusively upon your personal, financial, and intellectual desires. They should be totally objective and should not attempt to influence the patient toward utilization of their favorite option instead of the most appropriate organization, institution or equipment company. Objective options should be provided to the patient and loved ones for use in their selection process.

CASES I HAVE SEEN

A friend was admitted with end-stage lung disease. Unfortunately, he was his wife's primary caregiver. He was very concerned about his wife's ability to care for herself during his hospital stay. He was especially concerned about her staying alone at home while he was hospitalized. With a quiet intensity, the social worker on this case began to work out the details needed to bring the man's spouse into the hospital as a guest. She was placed in his room where they both stayed until his release from the hospital. Amazingly, this was just the beginning of the commitment made by this social worker.

Because he was a very independent man used to being in control, and because it was clear that they could not return to their two-story home, the social worker actively involved him in the selection and decision-making process. It led to his and his wife's placement in an independent living apartment. They were also referred to home support services upon discharge.

In another case, an aged, single woman who resided with her elderly sister was admitted to the hospital. She and her sister had lived together their entire lives, and rarely sought medical help. Both required a higher level of care. By working with their designated power of attorney, the social worker was able to place the sisters together in the same nursing home. Following the patients' recovery, they were both able to return home together. Exactly where they wanted to be.

 WHAT CAN YOU DO?

You need to be proactive; ask to meet your social worker. Explore questions with him/her that could put your mind at ease. Understand that a social worker's entire world is built around you, being your advocate, your assistant, your supporter. Do not allow them to be anything but respectful, helpful, and caring toward you. He or she should be dedicated to your well-being and to assisting you during your challenges.

CHAPTER 20

This is a Bill

How to survive without health insurance

Is it possible to survive financially without insurance?

The very thought of living in the United States without health insurance brings fear to the hearts of millions of people. How could you even consider living in this country without coverage? Most of us are willing to do whatever it takes to get that coverage. Many senior citizens are living either in poverty, or on the edge of poverty, due to their health insurance bills each month.

We've all heard the stories about families being torn from their homes, literally evicted, so that the house could be sold in order to cover the medical bills. We've all seen *60 Minutes* or *48 Hours* episodes where a family member is stricken with some type of dreadful disease or is in an automobile accident and their injuries or illness depletes the entire family savings, and the family is now living in an old Chevrolet on the streets of Miami, or New York, or L.A.

There have been several steps taken by state and federal government to protect these individuals. Some laws were passed to protect uninsured or underinsured patients from being transferred or, worse yet, rejected, from being admitted to emergency rooms. Again, there were actually cases where a traffic or gun shot victim was being flown to trauma center after trauma center, and they were being denied care because of their insurance status or lack thereof.

As for-profit hospitals began flourishing in this country in the early nineties, several did all that they could to immediately remove those services that attracted uninsured and under-insured patients. Neonatal intensive care units, trauma care, psych units, substance abuse centers, et. al. were quickly dropped from the menu of services available to incoming patients. These services were considered magnets for low or non-paying patients.

One of my favorite ironies was the investigation of a famous surgeon's wife for conflict of interest because she ran a non-profit corporation devoted to assisting families in their efforts to raise enough funds to allow their loved one to receive an organ transplant. Her husband was a transplant specialist. Now, of course her work was important, but the IRS position inferred a conflicting position. This particular situation always made me wonder about the concept of pro bono work in surgery.

 ## How many people live without any health insurance here in the United States and who are they?

Sadly, in the richest, most industrialized nation in the world, we have more than 44 million individuals living on a daily basis without insurance coverage. Some estimates are that as many as 47 million people get out of bed each day with the fear that a medical necessity will virtually wipe out their savings and possessions.

Many of those individuals without insurance are young, underemployed, single moms with small children. Because they are also typically not highly educated, they are usually living in a vicious trap, a circle of poverty. Many of them work more than one job, make minimum wage, and have no benefits.

The other shocking reality that many of these individuals face is that they make too much money to be covered by Medicaid. Even if they do have Medicaid, many physicians prefer not to accept Medicaid patients into their practices. So without a primary care physician, the uninsured or under-insured individual typically waits until there is an emergency situation before seeking treatment.

Will physicians see patients without insurance in their offices?

The physicians who would not accept these patients created an ethical conflict in the early years of my career in administration. My first position was with a Christian faith-based hospital that prided itself on its availability to provide care to the poor. This was a clear part of their mission, and those mission statements appeared everywhere in their hospitals. Yet with 188 physicians on staff, none of the primary care physicians at that time were accepting Medicaid patients in their practices. The sisters referred to these patients as *marginated*. Those of us in administration referred to them as *screwed*.

Because the good physicians refused to see or treat them, they were seen in the hospital emergency room, and their $45 sore throats became a $1,200 emergency room visit. That hospital, by the way, went out of business. As the sisters used to say, "No money. No mission."

SOME OF THE MOST TRAGIC CASES I HAVE SEEN

To begin to identify all of the tragic cases that I have seen or heard about during my tenure would fill several pages, but there have been several instances that will stay with me forever.

Most of these cases resulted in the death of the patient. Sadly, many of the most horrific cases involved either young children whose parents underestimated the severity of their illness before finally bringing them to the hospital or else they involved relatively healthy individuals who could have easily been cured had they just been treated in a timely manner.

The most tragic case that I can remember was that of an infant whose mother had a limited medical education. The baby was not able to hold down either breast milk or formula. Although this was not a first child, the family did not recognize the seriousness of the situation. When the child was finally brought to the emergency room, it lasted only a few minutes before all systems shut down and the baby died.

Had this family been insured, would they have responded sooner? Would the physician queried in this situation prior to the emergency room visit have been more responsive to the family if they had had insurance? Only God knows.

One of my closest friends, a great saxophone player, developed a cough. Unfortunately, due to the challenges of the local economy at the time, he had not worked steadily in some time. His cough became worse and worse, and nothing that was available over-the-counter helped him. Because he still had teenage children, and money was tight, he did not seek medical attention. On the day that he finally decided to go to the emergency room, he was admitted and died within hours.

Now, understand that my experience is in a low crime, very stable area that is representative of middle America. It is not an urban slum. Many of us have heard about the county-run hospital for the poor with the elevator that stopped short of the basement. Upon investigation, it was discovered that for years and years blood tubes and other tests had been thrown into the elevator shaft until the passageway had been blocked.

 ## WHAT CAN YOU DO?

If you find yourself in a situation where your health insurance has expired, been taken away or is not available to you, and you need hospitalization, understand that, by and large, the person in charge of billing and collections for that facility is empowered to negotiate with you.

Each and every contract that is negotiated with the various insurers who pay the hospital for your care is negotiated at a discount rate. That rate typically can run as high as a 50% discount and sometimes even higher.

If you are having or have had care at a hospital and have no insurance, you should call the individual manager in charge of the billing department and begin negotiations. Typically, if you can come up with a lump sum that is equal to 40-50% of your total, it is likely that the individual in charge of this activity within the hospital will embrace your offer immediately, if not sooner.

If payments are required, what should I expect?

If, however, payments are necessary in order to fulfill your obligation, your chances of an extreme discount diminish. So, negotiate, negotiate, and negotiate. To a hospital, some payment is better than no payment. A lump payment is better than ongoing payments and, most importantly, they're not doing anything for you that they haven't already done for every insurance company with whom they deal on a daily basis.

One of the most distressing realities ever imparted to me by one of my most learned and gifted professors was that only the very poor and the very rich have freedom in the United States. The poor have nothing to lose; they have nothing to be taken away. The very rich are capable of purchasing almost total protection from all forms of assault upon their wealth. Be it through legal channels, insurances, investments or just great accountants, they have protection. It's the middle class that has the most to lose.

In the healthcare delivery system, there's a lot of truth to a popular quip: If you've got money, we cannot only take care of you, we can do it in a room with Persian carpets. If you don't, we try to take away your savings, your investments, your home and your car, unless of course, you live in a box under a bridge. Then, we can try to turn you away. At least the not-for-profit hospitals have an obligation to provide you with care.

Just Stuff…
(Things you may need to know)
Certificates to prove that you're either here or you're gone

So, you were born in a hospital. That hospital still exists. You are now applying for a passport, or trying to get your child into school, or you want to vote. It seems simple enough. The hospital gave you a birth certificate when your child was born, or you've seen one in your baby book. Why not call the hospital?

The truth is that the hospital can't give you a birth or a death certificate. These very important documents come from the Bureau of Vital Statistics in your state. Well, what about those pieces of formal paper signed by the physician and the hospital administrator? They're just for show. *They are just to make you feel good.* They have absolutely no real value in the legal world.

Why then, you ask, are they given to patients? I guess it just seemed like a good idea to someone 50 or 60 years ago. I remember trying to use my fake birth certificate to register to vote. That was nearly 100 years ago. (Well, some days it seems like it was.) Hospitals can provide you with neither birth nor death certificates.

CHAPTER 21

Research

Giving it back

Donations: blood or tissue – it all matters

As we grow older, we think more and more about time. Can we ever put a price on time? Can we give back something of ourselves to allow someone else to have a little more time? The reality is that there is plenty of time, just not enough life for many of us. When we donate organs, tissue, blood, or other bodily fluids for medical research, we, as a society, gain valuable information. As the scientists study tissue and develop vaccines and treatments to slow or prevent progression of disease, we can give them the tools to create more time for the terminally ill.

 What does a donation mean to ill patients?

It means hope that they will live a few months or years or decades longer than they may have without the discoveries made in research.

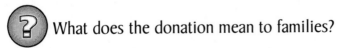 What does the donation mean to families?

It means more precious moments with their loved ones.

What does tissue donation mean to scientists?

With tissue and blood donation to science, the resources or tools needed to perform important work on clinical studies become available. The data collected from these studies may help in the development of vaccines and treatment alternatives for many terminal illnesses. Whether working on healthy or diseased tissue, the knowledge scientists acquire from the DNA, RNA and protein studies is priceless. The ultimate goal is to find cures and donation enables this mission.

 What happens to samples if they are not donated?

When a specimen or sample is removed in any clinical setting, it is sent off to a clinical laboratory for analysis. A pathologist (physician specializing in laboratory science) then examines it. He makes a diagnosis and when he is completely done the remainder of the sample is discarded as biohazardous waste. It is then incinerated at a cost of $32 a pound.

"One man's garbage is another man's treasure."

CASES I HAVE SEEN

When a young woman I know was 15 years old, her father began to experience back pain. He was 49 years old. The year was 1970, and he was diagnosed with a ruptured disk in his back. He was told he needed back surgery. Of course he immediately told the doctors to schedule him and, within several days, he was in the operating room. The young woman and her mother waited patiently in the waiting area for the doctor to notify them that her dad was out of surgery and doing fine. When they saw the surgeon walking down the long hallway, they were relieved. He called them into the hallway, looked the mother in the eyes and said, "Your husband has a large tumor on his spine. It is cancer and he will be gone in three months." Four months later, this father and husband passed away.

He never had any type of treatment, radiation, or chemo-therapy. It took many donations of tissue and blood for research, but years later scientists have now developed many ways to extend life for those with critical illnesses. Many diseases which were once fatal are now totally curable.

What would five more years have meant to that young woman? Five more years with her dad would have meant his seeing her graduate from high school, graduate from laboratory school, and start her first job. He would have walked her down the aisle on her wedding day. How can you ever put a price on those experiences?

We never have the people we love the most long enough, but with donations we can give a little of ourselves to help others.

 ## WHAT CAN YOU DO?

Anytime you are having a surgical procedure done, it is your right to have the remainder of your specimen donated to medical and scientific research. You need to notify your surgeon and remind him that you want this done. You are in charge of making this happen.

Can I withdraw from the studies? You have the right to withdraw from any study, at any time, and to request that any of your remaining specimens be destroyed.

 ## Bottom line…why should I donate?

Because you just never know. You never know what the scientists will find. You never know who they will find it in. You never know how many people will be helped by their findings. You never know how much time will be added to the life of loved ones. You never know what cures will be found for particular diseases. All of this can happen with specimens that would have been otherwise "one man's garbage."

Today's research is tomorrow's miracle.

CHAPTER 22

End of Life
When dying is finally enough

On Thursday evenings from 1970 until 1975 I had a standing invitation to play pool at my buddy Jim's dad's house. As young school teachers, most of us barely owned houses, let alone a pool table, so one of my colleagues generously opened his parents' home, refrigerator, and supply of beer. It was a miracle of safe, affordable recreation. During those innocent days in my mid-twenties, many of the world's problems were seemingly being solved. Jim's father was a wise old philosopher. He was in his early sixties, had been a coal miner all of his life, and loved to be around "the kids."

One night, during a particularly difficult game of pool, we began discussing religion, faith, and death as we mechanically yelled out lines like "the 8 ball in the side pocket." The discussion became particularly heated when it came to the hypocrisy of our healthcare system. We "kids," or at least this kid, listened in amazement as old Carl explained how life was "*in the old days.*" His relatives from the old country had salves and ointments, herbs and mustard plasters, that took care of virtually every ailment known to man. When they failed and death was inevitable, death was accepted. He used to laugh and say, "But now, everyone wants to go to heaven, but nobody wants to die."

It was then that the subject progressed to modern day care where there was truly a cure for everything, or so it seemed at 23. Get sick? Take a pill.

Get a shot. But then, during one week hours before our boys' night out, my father was diagnosed with lung cancer and given less than a three percent chance of survival. As Carl and I discussed this, he put his arm on my shoulder, and wished me luck. At 58, my dad was still a kid, and neither my education, nor my prayers, nor my love could save him.

The American attitude toward death is that death is not acceptable at any age, at any time, for any reason. Death is never seen as the inevitable future that we all face, as the transition from human to spiritual existence, or whatever belief systems decree occurs post-life. Our American system of death demands that death should not ever happen. It is no longer accepted as part of life. It is not accepted as our passage to a better place. Oh, yes, we hear those words, but when it becomes personal, we reject the transition.

Our medical schools, our nursing schools, our technology schools train students to believe that death is failure. This is why we have a system of healthcare crumbling under our very eyes. Through drugs, machines, and other miracles, we have the ability to enable individuals to live longer than ever before in the history of mankind. More people than ever before will live more than 100 years, but at what cost, and with what degree of quality?

 ## What is hospice and palliative care?

When an individual's illness progresses to the point that medical treatment/services become palliative, i.e., painkilling, analgesic, calming and soothing, the individual and his or her family face numerous difficult decisions. On the one hand, until the eleventh hour, it is usually difficult to find a physician who is willing to admit to the family that this is the case. Why? Because they are trained to regard death as failure. There are also sometimes economic factors involved in some decisions being made by both oncologists and surgeons. These factors require another book exposing the current health system. This is neither the book nor the topic of this chapter. (I'll need to write that chapter/book from somewhere in the Greek Islands.)

It is difficult for both the patient and loved ones to "give up." This is the current mindset not only because we all believe in miracles, cures, and the Lazarus Effect, but also because we are raised to be optimists and view death negatively.

Consequently, we fight death until we are shocked by it. The result is that we, as families, miss the wonderful opportunity to allow our loved one a peaceful, beautiful, comforting transition to the next phase of life.

Palliative care, a.k.a., hospice care, provides that transition. In a hospice program, we experience love in all forms until death. As a new hospital president, my introduction to hospice literally rocked my world. It was like Disneyland for a kid. Physicians allowed pets to visit, loved ones to stay 24 hours a day, music, massage, and anything else because *the patient was going to die anyway*. Actually, hospice and palliative care were my inspiration for transitioning all care in our facility to the hospice model because *we're all going to die someday anyway*.

There are still some very difficult choices to be made during palliative care that revolve around such topics as resuscitation, feeding tubes, chemotherapy, radiation, and hydration. Such decisions are seldom easy and can cause turmoil among well-meaning family members. It is the staff's role in supporting the individual's right to choose, regardless of the families' preferences, that makes the palliative care experience real and meaningful. It's about control, control of self.

The staff must to be sensitive to the challenges being faced by the patient as they begin to face their transition. When the patient must begin to give up freedoms such as driving, ambulation without assistance, independent personal care, he or she deals with every human emotion. Patients need support. However, the worst scenario is one of *over care* because their independence is taken away prematurely.

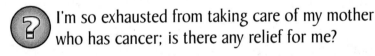 I'm so exhausted from taking care of my mother who has cancer; is there any relief for me?

A patient with end-stage Alzheimer's disease, cancer, heart disease, or COPD, that meets the criteria set by Medicare, can be admitted to a hospice program. The patient is entitled to five days of respite within the palliative care unit every 90 days. These are non-medical stays. The family or primary caregiver can use this opportunity to get much needed rest and relaxation.

Hospice provides a womb-like environment where love can replace fear, where family can be the center of that love, and where the transition can be a beautiful, healing journey for everyone involved. With clergy, 80 volunteers, two golden retrievers, music therapists, aroma therapists, massage therapists, and a loving, nurturing staff, death becomes what it should be, a peaceful transition and a part of life.

Philosophically, there are millions of reasons, actually trillions of reasons, why we need to embrace palliative and hospice care now and in the future. We cannot afford to treat every patient, every case, and every death as a failure. We are spending more in this country on the last 30 days of life than we spend on prenatal care. We are wasting our resources and not changing any aspect of the quality of life for the dying.

CASES I HAVE SEEN

Too often we see a guilt-ridden, absent child return to a parent's deathbed and try to bully the care-giving siblings returning at the last minute from far away. He or she demands that we "do everything you can to keep my parent alive."

These overall ineffective interventions might cost $100,000, extend a painful or completed life for an additional day or two, and achieve nothing. The patient has lost consciousness, has zero quality of life, and is barely lingering. The individual who causes this prolonged pain will often attempt to override their loved one's own wishes and desires, and will force his or her opinions on all of the caregivers. This is a classic case of an abuse of the system that happens in every hospital every day of the week, every week of the year.

There are also physicians who take similar stands until the family or the patient simply says, "Enough is enough. Just stop it." The "Greatest Generation" oftentimes feels that to stand up to your physician is not unlike blasphemy. It is at those special moments when the family detects that the physician has taken over, that they need to intercede. The physician will be checked due to fear of litigation, but it often takes that full family effort to stop the madness.

WHAT CAN YOU DO?

Your homework. Begin to talk to your loved ones early on about their wishes. Make those wishes as clear as you can. Do not be fearful that anyone will let you die before your time due to some stupid mistake. Trust that your family can support you in your intentions, and be sure that you put everything in writing that you possibly can. Visit or volunteer for hospice work. Find out how loving, wonderful and gratifying it can be. Learn to be at peace with yourself.

CHAPTER 23

They Really Hate Those Kids
What's really going on in this system?

At a national meeting lunch, there was a discussion, with a very intelligent and gifted group of healthcare professionals, about a prominent children's hospital where children where facing bone marrow and organ transplants, all forms of terminal cancer, and every other pediatric illness. We spoke about the realities of dealing with those kids and of the even harsher reality of the kids dealing with adults in such a setting.

Rocked by the gut wrenching, emotional realities of the suffering, pain and hopelessness faced by these delicate little people each and every day of their hospital stay, everyone was moved. In the hospital, the docs often walk into a child's room and say, "Well, today we're going to give you a bone marrow transplant. It's going to hurt, but I'm sure you'll be strong." That's it. Sometimes, a kids cries from fear. Many of them drop into total silence as their minds begin to sift through their memories or their visions of just how bad this newest challenge will be for them.

The really moving part of the description was, however, when the discourse turned to just how often the children were hospitalized and for how long. One of the physicians said, "Yes, these kids are in for weeks, sometimes months at a time." It was then that the nurse sitting across from me replied, "And then they return for several more weeks, and they sometimes do this several times a year." It was a very daunting thought. It was an arresting, sobering and daunting thought. These kids spent several months a year in their rooms in these children's hospitals.

Then, the nurse said, almost as a throw away, "Yes, the staff grows to hate those kids." "What?" I said. She looked at me in a very matter of fact way and said, "Yes, of course, the staff grows to hate those kids." My idealistic mind went blank and raced to the fact that some of the nurses, physicians, and school teachers whom I have known in my life have simply become tired of the daily challenge of dealing with other people's otherwise normal kids, who have been forced into this abnormal situation. They grow to hate those kids. They see them visit after visit. They sometimes see them month after month.

Be it kids, regular patients, or the terminally ill of any age, employees grow tired of their needs, their fears, their presence, their demands. When you hear the critical care nurses laughing and carrying on while your mother is dying, or you hear the radiology techs yelling diagnoses to each other as if the patient was not even present, you know that you're around calloused employees. Your first loss of a parent is their thousandth, and your first tumor is their 546th tumor. The difference is that it is happening to you and not to them.

As mentioned earlier, the number of seriously overweight healthcare employees mystified me and, even more so, the smokers. I could dedicate a chapter to the impaired physicians. It became clear that, not unlike the church or the military, hospitals are dealing with humans. It also became clear, however, that we, as professionals, have choices. We can decide who works for us. The question haunting me after the luncheon was why this patient-hating attitude was accepted.

My answer goes back to Descartes, and the agreement between the church and the scientific community to separate mind and spirit from the body. Hospitals became "body shops." Patients were not allowed or encouraged to have a connection between their minds/spirits and their bodies. They became body parts. They became ailments that a drug treated or a removed organ fixed, or not. They became the heart attack in room 433, the stroke in 12, or the miscarriage in 566.

Although the terms of the agreement were set years ago, that the church would nurture the mind and soul and the scientists would do their science, many many years later this agreement is still embraced as fact by at least the healthcare profession. Yet, if you asked every healthcare professional in the world why this culture existed, it would be my guess that less than one percent have ever heard of this or any treaty that separated body from soul and mind.

Consequently, and sadly, the kids became objects. Attachment and connection is never completely embraced by all healthcare professionals because detachment and disengagement becomes even more difficult. That's right, detachment becomes even more difficult. Protection from pain for the caregiver is priority in this system. Protection from pain for the patient is sometimes, however, stashed away, and <u>that</u> is the topic of this book.

When did it become acceptable? When did cruelty, callousness, and inhumanity become acceptable? Why is it that for the $160 weekend special, the Ritz Carlton will shine your shoes when placed outside your door, will give you down pillows and 700-thread-count sheets while tripping all over themselves to take care of you? Why is it that for $1,300 a night, a hospital employee will believe that it is acceptable to ignore call bells, to turn away from requests, to refuse to embrace the needs of that same person? Descartes?

The very first rules that we examined in our human resources policy manuals were rules regarding patient courtesy, patient care, patient attention, patient nurturing. We looked at those rules and reinforced them. We put teeth into them. We took action based upon them and that meant that we helped more than three-dozen people find their dreams. We helped more than three dozen people find work at a different hospital or physician's office. Reforms like this are the only way healthcare can improve. They are the only way to begin to turn the tide of callousness.

How can this change happen? One very important way to change the environment is to find ways for the employees to regain contact with their souls, their inner selves. How does one do that? Currently, our medical center has a very low turnover rate. It is not a coincidence that that can be attributed to the wonderful atmosphere, but it is also not a coincidence that we have removed that bottom 10% of employees who never have and never will be service-or-emotion-friendly.

CASES I HAVE SEEN

All too often, I have made rounds and overheard staff talking too loudly, too callously, too coldly about "that brain dead guy in room 3," or heard "number 22 is going sour and will be gone by 6 p.m." We know that the last one of the senses to stop working is hearing. If the patient is, in fact, not brain damaged, will cold statements like this drop them even further into their illness or demise?

 ## WHAT CAN YOU DO?

Call employees on their rudeness. If you don't like confrontation, write a letter to the president of the hospital or the head of nursing. Ask to see the supervisor. If the supervisor is the offending party, ask to see their supervisor. Well written letters to the editor are like missiles into the heart of the center.

CHAPTER 24

Questions and More...

Patients, families, and visitors to hospitals have many questions related to the best way to navigate the white waters of healthcare. This chapter addresses many of the questions that almost each and every one of us has asked at one time or another.

Unless you're admitted to a specialty-care unit such as critical care or obstetrics, you will most likely be admitted to what is referred to as the med-surg unit. The staff on this unit is trained to treat a diverse listing of diseases and illnesses. Every sort of illness, from the patient who just had their gallbladder removed, to the gentlemen with COPD (Chronic Obstructive Pulmonary Disease), to the lady with diabetes, will be admitted to this type of patient care unit.

 Why do I have to answer the same questions, over and over each time I visit?

The information related to your current medical treatments must be verified on each admission to the hospital because the rules change daily. Usually, your medical information has not changed but, in order to assure accuracy, the nurse will ask about your current treatments and medications. A lot of elderly patients, in particular, see their physicians regularly and their physicians may tweak medications and treatments. It is those major (or minor) changes in medications and treatment regimes that could greatly affect your current illness and the type of treatment you will receive on this admission to the hospital.

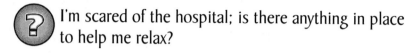 **I'm scared of the hospital; is there anything in place to help me relax?**

Ideally, hospitals try to be open to their patients' questions and expression of fears. The family should be encouraged to stay with their loved ones or significant others. Patients should be allowed to bring personal items with them to the hospital. Many times patients feel more at ease when they have familiar items with them such as a photograph, or perhaps their own pajamas. Something as simple as a clock or a calendar in the room can help patients relax and keep them oriented in an unfamiliar hospital room. Some hospitals provide CD players so patients can listen to soothing music. Massage therapy and aromatherapy are great relaxation tools that may be available in your hospital as well.

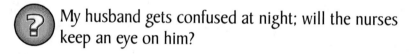 **My husband gets confused at night; will the nurses keep an eye on him?**

The nursing staff will do all they can to keep patients safe and minimize their confusion during the night. Patients may be assigned rooms closer to the nurses' station so they can be more easily and frequently observed and will be close enough to be heard if anything should happen. Many times just hearing the voices of the nurses or saying hello to a passing visitor helps many elderly patients stay oriented and less confused, especially at night.

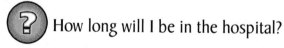 **How long will I be in the hospital?**

One of the first questions a patient asks his physician or nurse is, "how long will I be in here?" The answer to this question varies and is determined by a number of things. Your physician diagnoses your ailment and develops a treatment plan. Your treatment plan may involve tests such as blood work or x-rays to assist the physician in determining the exact reason for your health problem. Your doctor may put you on new medications or change the dosage of medications you are already taking. He may order special breathing tests, physical therapy, intravenous therapy, insertion of a catheter, or countless other treatments that will assist in improving your health. Every patient is different so their response to their individualized treatment plan will also be a determining factor in the length of their hospital stay.

Of course, the insurance companies play a role in the length of a stay in the hospital. They have a list of illnesses or diseases and a predetermined time allocation when, according to their estimates, you should be well enough to go home. This predetermined time allocation can be challenged by your physician, but he will need to provide medical evidence in order to get the insurance company to approve, and pay for, any additional time.

 ## Do I have a choice in my treatments?

Patients may not know this, but they have a definite say in their choice of treatment. After discussing your proposed treatment plan with your physician, you can decide what you will, or will not, have done. Remember, your physician has your best interest in mind, but there are times when the patient feels he or she knows what is really best. Sometimes patients just get tired of all the poking and prodding, or following the difficult diet or cannot take the side effects of medications and choose not to follow their doctor's recommendations. A word of caution: make sure you tell your physician about your choices. Your physician needs to remain fully informed about your decisions regarding your care and will want to document this information so it can be referred to, if need be, in the future.

 ## Where can I get additional information about treatment options?

To obtain additional information about available treatment options ask your physician or other healthcare providers such as your nurses. The Internet has a lot of valuable information available regarding outside sources and contact information that would actually enable you to discuss new therapies that are available. It is best to be fully informed on all of the available treatments. Researchers and health specialists are continually working on new and improved methods of treating diseases and illnesses and creating new treatment modalities that result in lesser side effects to the patient. Don't settle for archaic, twentieth century medical care.

What should I do if I have a concern about the quality of my care?

If you are concerned about the quality of care you are receiving in the hospital, you should express your concerns to your physician. If you can not discuss your problem with your doctor or the staff nurses, you can address your problem with the department manager, the clinical coordinator, patient advocate, the Vice-President of Nursing, the Chief Medical Officer, or the president of the hospital. If you feel you have a legitimate concern that you don't want handled by the hospital, you can report the problem to a regulatory agency. If your concern is more of a personal problem, you could also discuss it with the hospital chaplain or the social worker.

 ## I have bad arthritis; will someone be there to help me do things?

The nursing staff assesses your individual needs when you are admitted. Be sure to tell your nurse about your limitations or concerns regarding any restrictions that you may have, and they will provide assistance as needed. Sometimes volunteers are trained to provide assistance to patients such as helping them to feed or dress themselves. The hospital's physical and occupational therapy departments may have adaptive equipment available for you to use. They may also provide direction as to the best way to achieve personal independence or improved mobility.

Visitors

 ## Can children visit me in the hospital?

In years past it was common practice not to allow children to visit patients in the hospital, but times have changed and, in general, children are now permitted to do so. Research has proven that family ties are strengthened if the entire family shares in the birthing experience or stays with their mother and their new brother or sister after delivery.

Depending upon the time of the year, visitation may be limited, especially when it comes to younger children. This is not only for the benefit of the patient, but for that of the young visitor. You should ask your hospital about their visiting policy to be sure.

 ## Can I stay with my loved one?

In general, loved ones may be permitted to stay with a patient during a hospitalization.

In patient centered care hospitals, sleeping arrangements can be made by your nurse. Just inform the nurse that you would like to stay overnight. Comfortable sleeping arrangements can be made for you or your loved one.

 ## Can my pet visit me?

Some hospitals have realized the health benefits of pet visitations for their patients and permit family pets to come in to the hospital. For those hospitals that permit pet visitations, they generally require that the pet has current vaccinations, be bathed within 24 hours of the visit, and be well behaved.

Research has proven that pet visitations decrease stress and actually help patients heal faster. If your hospital does not offer pet visitation, let them know that you value this type of therapy and would like to see it started at your hospital of choice.

Roommates from Hell

 ## Why are there two sick people in a room? I know the hospital isn't full, why can't they put me in a room by myself?

Most insurance coverage only provides payment for a semi-private room. If a patient requests a private room, and one is available, the price difference between the semi-private room and the private room will be billed to the patient. In general, patients are placed in rooms according to their type of illness and medical requirements.

If you find that you are uncomfortable, for any reason, with the other patient in your room, you may ask to be transferred to another room (if one is available). If you are encountering problems with your roommate, ask your nurse for assistance.

Rooming-In

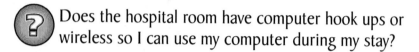 **Does the hospital room have computer hook ups or wireless so I can use my computer during my stay?**

Many hospital rooms are getting Internet accessibility. If you feel you are well enough, you can use your personal computer. Check with your hospital of choice to inquire about the availability of Internet access. You just may be surprised as to who provides this service to their patients.

Can I use my cell phone in my room?

Ah, staying connected. That's very important for most of us, and being in the hospital should not hamper our ability to stay in touch. Cell phones may be used in the patient room and throughout most of the hospital. If you are concerned that your cellular phone will interfere with certain equipment, just ask your nurse. Remember that there are certain areas in the hospital that may require cell phones to be turned off. These areas will have a sign prominently displayed alerting the public to this restriction.

Can I smoke in my room?

The rise in non-smoking public facilities is increasing almost daily. What better place than the premier promoter of healthcare, the hospital, should a non-smoking policy be in place? If you are a smoker you will find the majority, if not all, hospitals are non-smoking facilities and do not permit smoking in the rooms or the hospital. If you must smoke you should inform your physician immediately. There may be a designated outdoor smoking area that, if you are well enough and your physician permits it, you may be allowed to smoke during your hospital stay.

Can I request softer lighting in my room?

The patient room should be conducive to healing and many times hospitals have bedside lighting as well as free-standing floor lamps available. This can eliminate the need for overhead, bright lighting when there is no need or desire for it. Softer lighting in patient rooms may help patients relax and get better faster.

 ## What reading materials are available during my stay?

Hospitals receive free and subscription magazines on varying subjects. There may be magazines and books available in the patient lounges. Volunteer Services may also have magazines, books, and an art cart available for pastime activities.

 ## Can I request additional blankets and pillows?

The hospital staff is concerned with keeping the patient comfortable and providing the best atmosphere to promote rest and healing. If you need additional blankets or pillows, just ask the nurse and they will be provided to you.

 ## Why are the rooms cold?

Hospitals do not have to be cold. The temperature of the patient rooms can be controlled for your comfort. Seasonal changes between air-conditioning and heat may be problematic in establishing a comfortable temperature, but will be adjusted to suit the patient's request. Just ask hospital personnel to adjust the thermostat.

I shower every day at home, will I be able to do that in the hospital?

Just because you are in the hospital doesn't give you the green light to skip your regular hygiene practices. Every effort will be made for you to continue your usual self-care. Your condition, however, may require some alteration in your normal routine. Ask your physician or your nurse if you are permitted to shower. If you require some assistance with your personal hygiene care the nursing staff will gladly assist you.

Nursing Staff

 How do I know who is in charge?

With the flurry of staff you see going in and out of your room you may be asking yourself, "Who is in charge here?" You can ask any staff member in the department who is in charge of that particular nursing unit. You are entitled to know who is in charge and if you have any questions about the care you are receiving, you have the right to speak with that individual.

 Which ones are the nurses?

In years past, nurses were identified by their white uniforms and nursing caps. Now, most nurses wear colorful, more comfortable uniforms and almost all have eliminated their nurses' caps. Each employee that you come in contact with should have an identification badge on and should introduce themselves as one of your caregivers. Many hospitals will post a note in your room listing the names of the nurses assigned to personally care for you during your stay. Become familiar with your nurses and don't be afraid to ask them their names or speak with them regarding your care.

Can I request a different nurse if I don't like the one assigned to me?

Life is not perfect and sometimes patients and nurses just don't seem to hit it off. In this instance, remember that the nursing staff has received special training and is licensed by the State Board of Nursing to take care of your individual patient care needs. If you have a conflict with a nurse assigned to care for you, it is best to ask for a supervisor to alter the staffing assignment.

 ## What is the difference between a Registered Nurse and a Licensed Practical Nurse?

A Registered Nurse (RN) and a Licensed Practical Nurse (LPN) receive similar education in many areas of patient care; however, an RN has a minimum of a 2-year nursing degree. RNs administer all types of patient care and direct the patient care administered by LPNs. An LPN may only administer medications after receiving special training and under the direction of a n RN.

 ## How do I find out the staffing ratio?

Sometimes it may appear to the patient that the nursing staff is running full speed and overwhelmed by their patient load. Much care is given to assure that the staffing is suitable for patient needs. Staffing plans are based upon a pre-determined number of patients and their acuity (which means how sick the patients are and how much care and attention they need). Staffing ratio information can be obtained from the department manager or any clinical coordinator. If you feel that your nurse is too busy to address your needs, you must voice your concerns as soon as possible to the charge nurse.

So, what should I watch out for during my stay at the hospital?

You must take an active role in your care while in the hospital. You or your care partner should be sure that the staff is correctly identifying you prior to any treatments, medication administration, or any procedure. Not only should the nurse be checking your identification band, they should ask you what your name is before administering any type of medication or treatment. The Joint Commission and State Departments of Health have mandated that hospitals establish concrete guidelines regarding patient identification. This is in order to ensure that accidents or missidentifications do not occur. Be sure to ask your nurse questions about what is being done to and for you.

 ## What should I do if the nurse does not respond to my call bell?

If the nurse does not respond to your call bell in a timely manner, ask to speak with the person in charge and voice your concerns about the amount of time that it is taking to have your call bell answered. Maybe the call bell isn't working properly, or maybe the nurse is too busy. You won't know unless you voice your concerns.

 ## Why are there so many health professionals either overweight or smokers?

There are many reasons why a lot of health professionals are overweight and/or smoke. The main reason is that it is their personal choice. We all make choices about what we put in our mouths and in our bodies. You may wonder why educated professionals who observe, on a daily basis, the health risks of being overweight and smoking do both. Often, people smoke to reduce stress, and there is no doubt that being in the medical field can be very stressful.

Working odd and irregular schedules may also lead to healthcare professionals becoming overweight. This can be due to a lack of regular exercise and eating the wrong foods. Many times they do not have time to eat a well-balanced meal so they consume conveniently packaged junk food. Junk food has a lot of empty calories, fat, and sugar, and it really doesn't satisfy their appetite. All of these factors can lead to weight problems. Just like for the general population, sometimes it takes a scare such as chest pain or labored breathing caused by the slightest exertion to motivate a change. For them and us, it's important to take control and realize that we can take simple steps to improve health.

My personal belief is that healthcare professionals are exposed to the sometimes randomness of life and realize that we are all mortal. Consequently, it is oftentimes more an attitude of "We're going to die anyway" that leads them to abuse food, cigarettes or alcohol.

Physicians

 Why do they wake you up at all hours of the early morning to see your doctor? Can't they wait until a decent hour?

Physicians often see their hospitalized patients prior to their regular office hours. This enables any studies required to be completed in a timely manner, thus detrmining further plans for your care. We encourage our physicians to come in as late in the morning as possible so as to have time to interact with the patients and their families. Since most physicians start regular office hours around 8 a.m.; you can understand how early they must start in the morning in order to see their patients prior to the start of their busy, often long, days in the office. It is not unreasonable for many physicians to see their patients in the hospital at 5 o'clock in the morning. Others, even earlier than that!

 Why can't the doctors let you know in advance what time they will visit so that family members can be present?

Most physicians have a routine as to what time they see their patients in the hospital. If you want to have a family member present when the doctor visits you in the hospital, ask the nurse what time the doctor is expected to visit. The nurse can usually give you an approximate time so that you can plan accordingly to have family present. Be prepared to speak with the physician. It helps to write your questions down so as not to forget to ask them.

 ## What if I don't have a primary care physician?

Having a primary care physician (PCP) is a requirement of some health insurance plans. If you are required to name a PCP, you must do so in order to receive medical care reimbursement from your health insurance. Contact your insurance company (usually there is a telephone number on the back of your insurance card) for details on how to name a particular physician as your PCP. If your insurance company does not require you to name a PCP, then you can most likely use the physician of your choice.

 ## Does the doctor have enough time to answer all my questions and address all my concerns patiently?

While your physician may be extremely busy, he/she should permit enough time for you to ask questions and to fully inform their patients about their health status. You should be prepared to provide a clear explanation of your complaints and symptoms. Have a list of the questions you need answered at the ready. Listen carefully to what the physician tells you and then ask any additional questions you may have. Even if the physician has his hand on the door knob to leave the room, continue to ask your questions until you are satisfied that you understand your condition and any medical instructions you've been given.

For older patients, hearing what the doctor says may become a real issue. If you are not able to hear your physician, tell him, and ask him to speak more slowly and perhaps a little louder. You are the most important partner in your care. Ensure that you hear and understand all discussions and instructions.

 ## What is the difference between an MD and a DO?

A medical doctor (MD) has successfully completed four years at a college or university and earned a BS or BA degree, usually with a strong emphasis on basic sciences such as biology, chemistry and physics. MDs must also successfully complete four years of undergraduate medical education at a medical school accredited by the Liaison Committee on Medical Education, with training in pre-clinical and clinical areas. MDs must also complete additional training before practicing on their own as a physician. Newly graduated medical doctors enter a residency program that is three to seven years or more of professional training under the supervision of senior physician educators. The length of residency training varies depending on the specialty chosen and can take up to five additional years of training.

A doctor of osteopathy (DO) is trained to look at the person as a whole. This holistic approach to patient care means that osteopathic doctors integrate the patient into the healthcare process as a partner. A doctor of osteopathy has successfully completed four years at a college or university earning a BS or BA degree, and 200 additional hours of training in osteopathic manipulative medicine (equal to four or more years of additional training). They too may specialize and continue their education. Many DOs conduct clinical research to help advance the frontiers of medicine and to demonstrate the effectiveness of the osteopathic approach to patient care.

 ## What are physician assistants and nurse practitioners and can I demand to be seen by a real doctor?

Physician assistants (PAs) and nurse practitioners (NPs), also called physician extenders, are trained to carry out certain patient care activities that were once only performed by a licensed doctor. PAs and NPs function under the supervision of a licensed physician who reviews the care given by the PAs and NPs. In essence, a patient is seen by a physician when treated by a PA or a NP. Physician assistants and nurse practitioners save time for both the patient and the physician. Tasks such as casting, removal of stitches, the taking of histories, and physicals can be successfully handled by the PA or NP, which permits the patient to get in to and out of the office faster. Waiting to schedule minor care with the physician takes precious time from both the patient and the physician. However, as the patient, you always have the right to request to be seen by a physician.

If for any reason you feel your care by a PA or NP has not been quality care, you should discuss the circumstances with the supervising physician.

How do I know if this doctor is any good? I don't know anything about him.

If you are being referred by your family physician to a specialist, ask your family physician about the new physician: the extent of his training, work experience, and reputation. To some degree, you can depend on the experiences of family and friends with that particular physician. If someone has been treated by the physician, he/she can give details on his/her experiences. However if serious research needs to be done, it can be carried out through your state licensing board and local or state medical society. There is a national practitioner databank that tracks problematic medical practitioners, but this database is not available to the general public.

 What does it mean if a doctor is board certified?

To hold Board Certification means a physician has successfully passed a national examination in his/her field of medicine. The experts from that particular branch of medicine have developed the exam, which measures the extent of the physician's knowledge. However, knowledge needs to be coupled with experience, especially when addressing complex medical problems or surgery.

 How do I know the doctors are educated and have the ability to provide services to me?

This can be a concern on the first visit to a new doctor. Ask him or her from which school they graduated and if they have undergone any additional training. Look for school diplomas or certificates hanging on the walls of the office. Ask about continuing medical education. Doctors must continue to learn as the field of healthcare changes very quickly. If you want to research a particular physician, you can contact a county or state medical society or your state licensing board.

What should I do if I don't agree with my doctor?

There will be times when you may not agree with your doctor and his or her recommended treatment plan. Talk through the differences and give him/ her chance to address your concerns. If this does not satisfy you, seek additional information on the subject via other medical professionals, library research, or the Internet. Provide a copy of what you find to your doctor. Schedule an appointment with a different physician and get a second opinion. If you can not work through the differences, consider selecting a new physician.

When should I get a second opinion?

You should get a second opinion when you feel your physician has not clearly heard your concerns and addressed them to your satisfaction. You should seek a second opinion when your gut feeling tells you something is wrong; i.e., the return of old symptoms or feeling" just not right." You know your body better than anyone else and you should always follow up on any changes in any patterns, reactions, feelings, sensations, etc.

Sometimes patients worry that their physician will be offended if they seek a second opinion. The truth is that if your physician is concerned with you and your health, he or she will understand and support your decision to seek another medical opinion.

Why does it take so long to get discharged or released from the hospital?

So the doctor has finally agreed to discharge you from the hospital, but it seems to be taking forever to get out of the place! What is going on? Often, the physician makes rounds very early in the morning and writes the order for you to be discharged. He may instruct the nurse to obtain the results of lab studies or x-rays before allowing you to leave the hospital. Additionally, your physician may consult another physician to see you before letting you go home. Depending on the consulting physician's schedule, this may result in a delay in your discharge. The nurse also wants to ensure that morning medications are administered before discharging you from the hospital.

And, of course, there's always that little delay in reaching the family member to come and give you a lift home. All of this can be very time con-suming so relax, sit back, eat your breakfast (and lunch), watch your favorite television program, or read those ever-popular discharge instructions.

Back To Basics

 Does the hospital gown tie in the front or the back?

Everyone is familiar with the image of a patient's derrière hanging out of an ill-fitting hospital gown. They generally tie in the back, but some hospitals use front ties. Some hospitals provide robes or pajama bottoms which can make the patient, and visitors, feel more comfortable. Some hospitals permit their patients to wear their own sleep gear if it permits easy access to treatment or IV areas.

 What's the hat in the toilet for?

You walk into the restroom and see something resembling a hat in the toilet. Is it a spy camera strategically placed to see who's using up all of the toilet paper? No, the "hat" in the toilet is a device used to measure the amount of urine one excretes during voiding or urination. The physician may order these measurements be taken to assist him in determining your treatment plan.

 Will the tiny bubble in my IV line kill me? Should I pull out the IV myself?

Your breathing becomes labored and more intense as you observe a tiny bubble slowly creeping in your IV line. Is this the end? Should you pull out the IV? A resounding NO! It normally takes a large volume of air (about 20cc's or more) to cause an air embolism significant enough to cause con-cern. The tubing itself is designed to prevent large air bubbles from entering your blood stream. Pulling out your own IV could put you at risk for bleed-ing, infection or, even worse, an embolism, should a fragment of the catheter break free and travel into your circulation. In addition, you may be receiving potent medication through your IV line that may cause extreme side effects if stopped abruptly by pulling our your IV catheter.

Spiritual Care

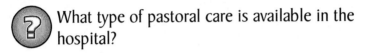 ## What type of pastoral care is available in the hospital?

The goal of chaplain services is to meet the spiritual needs of the patient, family, and staff. The spiritual care team is available to meet such needs or contact individuals who can fulfill the specific spiritual need that arises.

Can I take communion in the hospital?

Communion can be provided by the chaplain's office contacting the patient's church or pastor to make this available. The chaplain can provide the sacraments of communion if the patient/family so desire.

Are there any Bibles available in my room?

Many hospitals have Bibles available in the patient rooms. If one is not present in your room, you can ask your nurse to request one from the chaplain's office.

Will my priest know I'm in the hospital?

Similar to the regulations pertaining to patient privacy, there are also regulations pertaining to when your spiritual care person can be informed of your admission into the hospital. Certain procedures have been established to enable a patient to have their spiritual care provider notified of their admission. Upon admission to the hospital, a patient may be asked to complete a spiritual care form. This form asks two specific questions:

- Does the patient "opt-out" of the clergy directory? This means that the patient does not wish to have any specific religious/spiritual care person notified of their admission to the hospital.
- Does the patient "opt-in" to the clergy directory? This means that the patient wishes to have their spiritual care person notified of their admission to the hospital. The patient provides the church name and contact information. The chaplain's office will contact the church or pastor to inform them of the admission.

The hospital will adhere to the personal decision of the patient in this regard.

CHAPTER 25

Epilogue
What went wrong?

Several years ago while on the campus of her university our daughter had a severe attack of excruciating pain. She was 20 years old and her pain was debilitating. As a hospital administrator, I rushed to get her to the facility where I was employed so as to watch over her and to be sure that she was receiving the very best possible care.

She went to the emergency room, had x-rays taken, and was told that she had probably passed a kidney stone. They released her from the emergency room and suggested that she be given an ultrasound. The two of us went up the three stories to the ultrasound area where we were greeted by at least 35 people, both men and women, in the waiting area.

We dropped off our paper work and several minutes later an ultrasound tech came out of the exam room, walked over to my daughter handed her an open-back hospital gown, and said, "Okay, sweetheart, go into the dressing room, take off all of your clothing including your panties, and come back out here and sit down." This attractive, 20-year-old college student turned to me and said, "Dad, let's get out of here. I never want to come back to this hospital again."

A few years later I was diagnosed with heart disease, went through the angioplasty, had stents inserted, and was taken back to my room. A few hours later my breakfast was served—bacon and eggs.

Two years later, I began feeling discomfort in my chest. When I checked myself into the hospital a day later, another 90% blockage was detected. As I lay in my hospital bed, depressed from the thought of having grown another lesion in only 24 months, my friend, Dr. Dean Ornish, called to speak with me. He insisted that I confront my cardiologist with information regarding my new blockage. He had me ask my cardiologist if, in fact, the second blockage might have been caused from an injury to the right descending coronary artery caused by the first heart cauterization. In fact, it is a blind procedure and, yes, it turned out that the second blockage originated from the first procedure. Welcome to the human factor.

At around the same time, my mother was diagnosed with an occluded carotid artery. The ultrasound exam revealed a blockage of 70%. We took my mom to a vascular surgeon. He asked her numerous questions. They admitted her the next day, performed the surgery and found a 90+% occlusion. The surgery was relatively routine except for the slight stroke that my mom suffered, and the fact that her heart went into arrhythmia. When I asked why she was staying in the hospital for several additional days, I was asked why the surgeon hadn't been told the results of her stress test. She had not had a stress test. She had not been asked to have a stress test. She had not been told to have a stress test.

My favorite memory of that particular healthcare experience involved a quick trip to the volunteer snack shop. My brother and I took a moment to have a quick cup of chicken soup. Exactly eight hours later, we both became violently ill with a horrible case of food poisoning. It turned out that the volunteers had been placing the garbage on the same cutting block as the chicken.

Then there was the little boy who swallowed a jacks ball. Just weeks before that little boy had presented himself to the emergency room, the CEO had *fired* all of the emergency room physicians without instituting a Plan B. The day the little boy's parents came rushing into the emergency department with the love of their life dying in their arms, there was a non-board-certified pathologist working as a locum tenum, a.k.a., substitute emergency room physician. The little boy died.

There are thousands of stories like this about the human elements of a hospital. For every sad or discouraging story, there are dozens of wonderful stories about life-saving events where just the right talent was present.

The general public is totally dependent upon people in my position to stand up and take responsibility for running a competently staffed hospital.

Each and every one of us is dependent upon those individuals trusted with our lives to be kind, competent, capable and sure of their skills.

This book was never intended to be an expose of the bad things that happen. It was not intended to point fingers at the 10% of people who do not take life seriously or who are miserable in their jobs. This book is about what you need to do as an individual to take control of your situation.

There is no reason for people to treat you poorly. Don't be afraid to stand up and be counted. There is no reason for you to receive poor treatment. There is no excuse for poor treatment. There is absolutely no rationale for anyone to ignore, talk down to, or mistreat either you or a loved one. This book is about demystifying healthcare. It is about empowerment. It is about allowing you, the reader, to take advantage of an insider's knowledge so that you can have more control over your destiny.

You should not be exposed to unnecessary infections. You should not be subjected to incompetent physicians. You should not be kept in the dark about your treatment. Your loved ones should not be kept away from you. Your loved ones should not be controlling your destiny. You should do or have done what you want.

So, empowerment, patient centered care, respect, love, second and third opinions, hope and control are all concepts that should be embraced. What went wrong is that the most comprehensive, miraculous, complex, expensive healthcare system in the world is being run without a national health policy. It is running out of control with anywhere from 44 to 47 million Americans living without health insurance. It is stealing from our future to overmedicate our past. There is an intergenerational theft going on that does not make sense. Babies are not getting prenatal care while octogenarians are being treated with open heart and brain surgeries that will not extend or improve the quality of their life. All of this is because one generation votes and the other doesn't.

Hospitals are providing emergency care for individuals who might have been treated in a physician's office for thousands of dollars less. Why? Because businesses are being squeezed more and more and more to subsidize the costs of multimillion-dollar pieces of technical equipment and billions of dollars in drug development. The result? Victoria's Secret products, which were formerly made in Windber, Pennsylvania, are now being made in El Salvador where health insurance is generally not a part of any employment package. The reason? Businesses can't compete on a global basis due to the high costs of health insurance.

Health coverage is vital, but so is managing expectations, and so is the global economy, and so is the ability of drug companies to do research. None of this is easy, but your role can be clearly defined. Make it work for you. People are paid to listen to you. Speak out. Vote and, most importantly, don't be a victim.

If you have any hospital experiences you would like to share, please send them to **www.askahospitalpresident.com**

APPENDIX

Your Rights as a Patient and a Person from A-Z

The hospital setting can be a daunting one, but it can be less disconcerting with knowledge. Knowing the hospital, the type and quality of services provided, and knowing your rights as a patient are vital to the success of your care and treatment.

What rights should you expect while in the hospital? You can expect to be treated with respect by skilled healthcare personnel, regardless of age, race, color, religion, sex, ethnic background, or means of payment. You have the right to confidentiality and privacy, but more importantly, you have the right to be safe. You have the right to be involved in your own care and decision making and refuse any drugs, treatments or procedures.

I demand a copy of my chart!

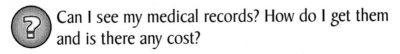

Can I see my medical records? How do I get them and is there any cost?

Well, in many states, the hospital chart is the property of the hospital. As the patient are you entitled to a copy of that chart? Absolutely. But try to imagine living in a world where attorneys are advertising that they will sue your physicians or hospital at no cost to you. They will only collect if they get money for you. The three lawsuits that we had pending last year were all frivolous. With no retribution requirement for frivolous lawsuits, everyone can try to cash out.

Consequently, if you want a copy of your medical record which, incidentally, due to the dozens of regulatory agencies that control hospitals, may be as much as six or more inches thick, you should expect to pay a fee. At our facility the fee is $15 and a per page per copy fee is added. While CEO of an 82-bed hospital, I realized that we could dedicate a full-time employee to making chart copies.

My best friend is in the hospital, I think?

 I don't want my ex-husband to know I'm in the hospital. You won't tell him if he calls, will you?

Lone hospitals in small towns are especially vulnerable to patient confidentiality breaches. If Susan Patel gets admitted to the hospital, her neighbor might be the nurse, and her preacher's wife could be the radiology technician, and the security guard may be her cousin's husband's wife's best friend (but that's another chapter), and everyone knows not only that she is in the hospital, but which vertebrae is bothering her and which exam she is scheduled to have after lunch.

Even when people try to keep things a secret, patient confidentiality has always been a problem in hospitals. So, a law that is lovingly referred to as HIPAA was passed a few years ago that makes breaches of confidentiality a punishable crime. Don't get me wrong, all hospitals would dismiss employees if they were caught releasing information, but now the federal government is involved. So, when you hear a rumor that your best friend was in a car accident and taken to the community hospital, don't be upset when the response that you get from the hospital operator is "I don't know if Mr. Iacoboni is a patient here." Even if you've had a telephone conversation with your friend and forgot to write the number down to call him back, unless the patient signs away his or her rights to confidentiality, you will not receive any information about the patient. So, call the family or *forget about it.*

CASES I HAVE SEEN

Last year, three lawsuits were filed against the hospital. One was over a fall that was initiated by a visitor's decision to attempt to retrieve a discarded piece of trash from a steep hill. The visitor lost their balance and fell. Another was from a physician who voluntarily resigned from the medical staff and then decided to sue every hospital where he had previously worked. The final one was over a former employee who accused the hospital of allowing negative comments by employees to become public knowledge. So far these lawsuits have cost about $45,000 in non-retrievable legal fees.

The new HIPAA, a.k.a., Kennedy/Katsenbaum Legislation, has caused numerous confrontations within the walls of our modest facility. I am humbled when I try to imagine what has happened in the 1600-bed hospitals.

Patients' families, clergy, and neighbors become outraged when they are informed that the hospital does not know if their friend or loved one is present. That, unfortunately, is the law. The most difficult case as yet has been one of a severely retarded 20 something year old who was dying and, due to the fact that the patient was not a minor, we were not even legally able to inform her parents that she was a patient.

We do believe that patients have the right to know and make their own choices, not family members. Many of us come from families where one member is the alpha member, and it is normal that that strong personality attempts to make all of the decisions for everyone involved. HIPAA at least ensures that the patient should have some control over other's access to him or her.

 WHAT CAN YOU DO?

Read this book. You can get copies of your needed documents from the Bureau of Vital Statistics. You can keep people from knowing you're in the hospital by simply saying that you do not want to release information regarding your stay or your condition. You can ensure that your child's guardian or teacher has a release certificate that allows that child to be treated at an emergency room if you cannot be reached. You can be sure that you will be charged for an observation and finally, you may always, have a copy of your chart. Just understand that it costs the hospital tens of thousands of dollars each year in equipment, employees and products to make copies for everyone who wants them.

 What is JC?

JC stands for the Joint Commission. It is an agency that governs the practices of hospital procedures and policies. They conduct intensive surveys on site. The following is a summary of the various patient rights that are outlined by The Joint's standards. They state that "patients have a fundamental right to considerate care that safeguards their personal dignity and respects their cultural, psychosocial, and spiritual values." A hospital's attitude toward its patients affects a patient's response to care.

Joint Commission

(some of these are also mandated by The Code of Federal Regulations Medicare Conditions of Participation and the State Department of Health)

- Patient Rights should be prominently displayed at appropriate locations within the hospital and will be given to all patients when admitted.
- Patients have the right to reasonable access to care.
- Patients have the right to care that is considerate and respectful of their personal values and beliefs.
- Patients have the right to be informed about, and to participate in, decisions regarding their care.

Patients have the right to be involved in at least the following aspects of their care:

- Giving informed consent and making care decisions. Staff members should clearly explain any proposed treatments or procedures to the patient which include potential benefits and drawbacks, potential problems related to recuperation, the likelihood of success, the possible results of non-treatment, and any significant alternatives.

- Patients have a right to participate in ethical questions that arise in the course of their care, including issues of conflict resolution, withholding resuscitative services, forgoing or withdrawal of life-sustaining treatment, and participation in investigational studies or clinical trials.

  Patients asked to participate in a research project must be given:

    - a description of the expected benefits
    - a description of the potential discomforts and risks
    - a description of alternative services that might also prove advantageous to them
    - a full explanation of the procedures to be followed
    - information indicating that they may refuse to participate and that any refusal will not compromise their access to healthcare services.

- Patients have a right to security and personal privacy and confidentiality of information.

- Patients have the right to designate a decision maker in the case that the patient is incapable of understanding a proposed treatment or procedure or of formulating advanced directives.

- Patients have a right to access protective services such as child protective services, elder protective services, etc.

- If a hospital is not willing to provide the type of care a patient requests due to its stated mission and philosophy, staff will fully inform the patient of his/her needs and the alternatives for care and, if medically advisable, the hospital will transfer the patient to another facility.

- Patients have the right to be informed of the name of the physician or other practitioner who has primary responsibility for their care, the identity and professional status of individuals responsible for authorizing and performing procedures or treatments, any professional relationship to another healthcare provider or institution that might suggest a conflict of interest, their relationship to educational institutions involved in the patient's care, and any business relationships between individuals' treatment the patient, or between the organization and any other healthcare, service, or educational institutions involved in the patient's care.
- Patients (and their families, when appropriate) have a right to be informed about outcomes of care, including unanticipated outcomes of care.
- Dying patients have unique needs requiring utmost concern for the patient's comfort and dignity:
    - Patients have the right to appropriate treatment for symptom control, according to their wishes (or those of their legal representative).
    - Patients have the right to have pain managed effectively.
    - Patients have the right to have issues such as autopsy and organ donation discussed with them in a caring, sensitive manner.
    - Patients have the right to have their values, religion, and philosophy respected.
    - Patients have the right to involve their family in every aspect of their care, if they so desire.
    - Patients have the right to have their psychological, social, emotional, spiritual, and cultural concerns met.
- Patients have the right to appropriate assessment and management of pain, including initial assessment and regular re-assessment of pain, and education of patients (and families, when appropriate).
- Patients have a right to pastoral care and other spiritual services upon request.

How dangerous is your healthcare?

Hospitals are governed by state and federal guidelines on safety and compliance with policies and procedures to insure quality care for all patients. These measures help prevent dangerous situations and errors while you are hospitalized. The following federal regulations were established to make healthcare safer.

Code of Federal Regulations
(Medicare Conditions of Participation)

- The hospital must establish a process for prompt resolution of patient grievances and must inform each patient whom to contact to file a grievance. The hospital must provide the patient with written notice of its decision that contains the name of the hospital, contact person, the steps taken on behalf of the patient to investigate the grievance, the results of the grievance process, and the date of completion.
- Patients have a right to personal privacy.
- Patients have a right to receive care in a safe setting.
- Patients have a right to be free from all forms of abuse or harassment.
- Patients have a right to be free from restraints of any form that are not medically necessary. (The term restraint includes either a physical restraint or a drug which is being used as a restraint.) A restraint can only be used if needed to improve the patient's well being and less restrictive interventions have been determined to be ineffective. Restraints must be specifically ordered by a physician, implemented in the least restrictive manner possible, in accordance with safe and appropriate restraining techniques, and ended at the earliest possible time. The condition of the restrained person must be continually assessed, monitored, and re-evaluated. Staff who have direct patient contact must have ongoing education and training in the proper and safe use of restraints.
- Hospitals must provide or make available social work, psychological, and educational services to meet the medically related needs of patients.

What if I don't speak English? Will they still be able to help me?

Many hospitals participate in an interpreter service called Language Line which provides translation in more than 150 languages. The telephone-based service can translate documents as well. The services are available 24/7 and many hospitals offer special services for the deaf. This is one of the defined regulations of the Pennsylvania Department of Health.

PA Department of Health
NOTE: Other states may have different regulations

- A patient has the right to have all records pertaining to his medical care treated as confidential except as otherwise provided by law or third-party contractual arrangements.
- A patient (or their duly empowered legal representative) shall be given access to or a copy of their medical records. Hospitals may charge a reproduction fee, set in accordance with PA state law, for these records. *NOTE: Records governed by the PA Mental Health Act may be subject to additional requirements in certain instances.*
- A patient has the right to expect emergency procedures to be implemented without unnecessary delay.
- The patient has the right to good quality care and high professional standards that are continually maintained and reviewed.
- The patient has the right to full information <u>in layman's terms</u> concerning his diagnosis, treatment, and prognosis, including information about alternative treatments and possible complications. When it is not medically advisable to give such information to the patient, the information shall be given on his behalf to the patient's next of kin or other appropriate person.
- Except for emergencies, the physician must obtain the necessary informed consent prior to the start of any procedure or treatment, or both.
- A patient has the right to refuse any drugs, treatment, or procedure offered by the hospital to the extent permitted by law. A physician shall inform the patient of the medical consequences of his or her refusal of any drugs, treatment, or procedure.

- A patient has the right to assistance in obtaining consultation with another physician at the patient's request and own expense.
- A patient has the right to medical and nursing services without discrimination based upon race, color, religion, sex, sexual preference, national origin, or source of payment.
- A patient who does not speak English should have access to an interpreter.
- A patient has the right to examine and receive a detailed explanation of his bill.
- A patient has a right to full information and counseling on the availability of known financial resources for his or her healthcare.
- A patient has the right to expect that the healthcare facility will provide a mechanism whereby he/she is informed upon discharge of his/her continuing healthcare requirements following discharge and the means for meeting them.

HIPAA

(Health Information Portability and Accountability Act)

- A copy of the hospital's "Notice of Privacy Practices" must be given to any individual who receives a service after April 14th, 2003. (The hospital is also required to post this notice.) This notice must:
    - describe how the hospital uses and discloses protected health information
    - contain a statement of the individual's rights with respect to protected health information and a brief description of how the individual may exercise these rights
    - provide the individual with a complaint process for resolving perceived breaches in privacy practices. It should allow reporting of perceived breaches to the Department of Health and Human Services if the patient is unsatisfied with the outcome of the hospital's actions and responses.
- A patient has the right to request that their name, location in the facility, general condition; e.g., good, fair, poor, etc.) be omitted from the hospital's facility directory for anyone not involved in their care (or administrative functions surrounding their visit).

- A patient has the right to request that their name and religious affiliation not be disclosed to clergy.
- Hospitals are required to make all reasonable efforts not to use or disclose more than the minimum amount of protected health information necessary to accomplish the intended purpose.
- A patient has the right to expect that any individuals not involved in their care, or administrative functions surrounding their visit, are denied access to confidential healthcare information unless such information is de-identified.
- A patient has the right to have reasonable safeguards taken by the hospital to protect individual information from view or access by unauthorized staff or to prevent incidental disclosures to individuals and their families without hindering clinical operations of the staff.
- A patient has the right to request to receive alternate communications by alternate means or at alternate locations.
- A patient has the right to request restrictions to their protected health information (with certain limitations, including public health authority mandated reporting, when required by law, etc.). Hospitals have the right to determine if the individual's request for privacy restriction is reasonable and will not interfere with the individual's care needs or claim adjudication process.
- A patient (or his legal representative) has the right to inspect and obtain a copy of protected health information about that individual contained in a designated record set for as long as the personal health information is maintained. The hospital may deny access under certain circumstances; however, individuals have the right to appeal those denials.
- A patient has the right to request an amendment of their personal health information contained in a designated record set for as long as the record is maintained. The hospital may deny the request for amendment under certain circumstances; however, individuals have the right to submit a written statement of disagreement with the denial.
- A patient has the right to request an accounting of all instances where protected health information about them is used or disclosed (after April 14, 2003) for reasons other than the following:

- to carry out treatment, payment, and healthcare operation
- to the individual of protected health information about them
- for the facility directory, as directed by the individual
- to persons involved in the individual's care or other notification purposes
- for national security or intelligence purposes
- to correctional institutions or law enforcement custodial situations.

CASES I HAVE SEEN

Probably the single most disconcerting case that I have ever witnessed in my nearly two decades of administrative responsibilities was of a patient who was brought into our emergency room with a ruptured aneurysm. His religion did not permit him to have a blood transfusion. He was prepared to face his death. When he passed out, his wife insisted that we give him blood and begin the surgery. He made it and made a full recovery, but we, as a hospital, had gone against his wishes and his beliefs. He felt disgraced by the experience, and believed that he would never reach paradise due to his wife's decision. His spiritual life felt destroyed. We had numerous meetings with representatives of his religious sect to ensure that we would never allow a family member to interfere in this manner again, but for him the damage was done. We had saved his life but, according to his beliefs, jeopardized his soul.

 ## WHAT CAN YOU DO?

As a patient, it's important for you and/or your advocate to know your rights within this very complex and regulated system. The previous summary covers only a small portion of the actual volumes of printed patient rights, but it's a very serious beginning. Read them, discuss them, and decide which of these rights would help you meet your needs.

To order additional copies of the book:

Name _____

Mailing Address_____

City, State, Zip_____

Optional:

Phone _____   Fax _____

Business or Occupation_____

Mail to:

Nick Jacobs
120 Glory Drive
Windber, PA 15963

Interested in contributing to the next edition?

If you or your loved ones have had a health care experience that you would like to share in our next edition, please send it to us at **askahospitalpresident.com**.